The Sugarbush

A Novel

By

Jerry S Jones

© 2000, 2002 by Jerry S Jones. All rights reserved.

No part of this book may be reproduced, stored in a retrieval system, or transmitted by any means, electronic, mechanical, photocopying, recording, or otherwise, without written permission from the author.

ISBN: 1-4033-55207 (e-book)
ISBN: 1-4033-5521-5 (Paperback)
ISBN: 1-4033-5522-3 (Hardcover)

Library of Congress Control Number: 2002093425

This book is printed on acid free paper.

Printed in the United States of America
Bloomington, IN

1stBooks – rev. 03/25/03

"ACKNOWLEDGEMENTS"

To my wife, Leora Garcia-Jones, a genuine cowgirl from Dolores, Colorado, for her patience and support.

To John Russell "Russ" Smith and his wife, Alice, formally from Ashland, Ohio, now retired in Tucson, Arizona, for their expert knowledge in the art of making maple syrup.

To Sidney Halma, Director of the Catawba County Historical Association in Newton, North Carolina, for his time and valuable research assistance.

To Richard Charnov, Esq., (one of the two best lawyers in the world) of Montgomery Center, Vermont and Brooklyn, New York, for his assistance, friendship, and encouragement.

To Leonard G. "Lenny" Learner, Esq., (the other best lawyer in the world) of Wellesley, Massachusetts, for his editorial comments, friendship, and encouragement.

To Josephine Carpenter, retired public school Principal in Tucson, Arizona, for editing.

To June Volner Utley, a fellow Christian, formerly of Jackson, Tennesee, now retired with her husband, John, in Tucson, Arizona, for providing the key phrase in the author's, "Note To The Readers."

To my neighbors, Richard and Mary Darling, for many hours of computer instructions.

"DEDICATION"

In memory of

Lucy Irene Hefner Jones
'Koki'

She was born on, December 10, 1928, in a two room shanty on Island Ford Road near Lookout Dam, in the rural community of, Catfish, North Carolina.

The only child of Suma Lee Little Hefner and Fred Obed Hefner, she died during open heart surgery in Phoenix, Arizona, on March 20, 1987, and is buried in the public cemetery in Buckeye, Arizona.

As a young woman, through determination and persistence she broke free from a legacy of ignorance, violence and complacency to leave behind her own remarkable legacy of achievements, endurance and courage now evident in the inner-strength and accomplishments of her children. Before her death she composed her own epitaph which is engraved on her tombstone.

"As the sun shines through the trees on her energetic soul, we know the sun shines on her still, in another dawn."

and to our children

Sharyn Lorraine Rector Jones

Tana Leigh Jones Wrublik

Jerry Stephen Jones, II

Julie Anna Jones Van Orden

"PROLOGUE"

Through the repeal of the Nineteenth Amendment to the Constitution of the United States prohibiting the manufacturing and distribution of alcoholic beverages, the Era of Prohibition was nearing its end.

Gathering in the Blue Ridge Mountains of Western North Carolina, the Catawba River flows easterly into the Piedmont Region to form the northern border of Catawba County, then meanders abruptly south to form the eastern border.

In the spring of 1932, the high sheriff of the county led a raid on a moonshine liquor distillery hidden deep in the woods along the Catawba River, in the rural community of "Catfish", an area notorious for a lingering history of lawlessness, vendettas and vigilante justice.

Through ignorance, a determined resistance to changing times placed the majority of the residents outside even the fringes of society.

Friendships were shallow and fragile. Humor was raw and vulgar. Retaliation for the slightest of provocations, whether real or imagined, was barbaric.

The overconfident sheriff recklessly underestimated his clever quarry. As a consequence of his carelessness, sixteen arrest warrants known only to the sheriff and concealed in the pockets of his jacket, were foolishly left unattended and fell into the hands of the culprits he sought to apprehend.

Even more mysterious and baffling, in the aftermath of the ill-fated raid the stolen warrants, none of which charged serious crimes, were never reissued for execution and arrests of those accused.

The reasoning behind this unusual and puzzling turn of events is a question that has never been answered and can only be left to speculation.

As though guided by a dark foreboding influence, the warrants covertly rose from the ashes of a mock kangaroo court trial to take on a sinister life of their own. Defying inconceivable odds of chance, a strangely prophetic reign of terror, violence and death was set in motion.

In the midst of the chaos and terror, two lonely young people collided and found new meaning for the future in a refreshing, warm, and passionate romance.

On the authority of trustworthy persons, all now deceased, who were there, directly involved and deeply affected, this novel is based on true events.

Central to this story, the legendary community of, Catfish, now exists only as a state of mind, having long ago perished in the mire of a reputation so foul, that only eradication could subdue.

The Piedmont Region, Catawba County, the Catawba River, the cities, towns, and communities named, are real places.

Many of the characters are purely fictional, while others whose lives were touched by events involving the missing warrants and on whom the action of the novel depends, have been changed to protect the innocent.

Those, to whom this book is dedicated, are closely related to five of the story characters who meet violent deaths.

"NOTE TO THE READERS"

The vernacular spoken by the rural characters during the time period in which the story takes place, has been toned down so that the readers might better understand what is being said. Being poorly educated with limited vocabularies, the use of profanity, which has also been toned down, was the only way they knew to express, in the most profound sense of the word, their humor, happiness, excitement, sadness, pain, inner turmoil, anger and rage. This is not to say that well educated people did not use profanity because they did, but in a different context for which there was no excuse. I ask the readers to bear in mind that it is the characters who are speaking, not the author.

The author cordially invites readers to visit his website at www.thesugarbush.net.

x

The Sugarbush

The Sugarbush

I

It was early Saturday morning, May 21, 1932. Rural driving conditions on the red clay dirt roads during bad weather were ruts, mud holes and tire puncturing rocks that left many a traveler stranded for lack of an extra spare tire. Just as bad, good weather promised bone rattling washboards that sent clouds of stifling dust swirling inside the cars, permeating the occupant's clothes and leaving clammy sweating faces streaked with miniature termite like tunnels of mud.

The Model 'A' Fordor sedan was jarring up and down, as well as pitching side to side, as it lurched its way through the deep ruts of the back woods road. Snow-melt and spring showers had left the road slippery, treacherous and in places almost impassable. The county did grade the back roads on occasion, but had not done so for several months, a neglect that was causing considerable discomfort for the five lawmen crowded inside the car: Catawba County Sheriff, Burton Coley; Chief Deputy, Travis Gant; Deputies', Pace Tanner, and, Chick Yount; and Federal Prohibition Enforcement Agent, Sonny Lavin. The five occupants were a character study in diversity, guardians of the law appearing to be the only thing they had in common.

Sheriff Coley, boisterous, brazen and profane, was nevertheless a heralded champion of the Christian majority whose praise and support echoed from the pulpits of protestant churches regardless of denomination. Expert use of radio and newspaper publicity continually bolstered the sheriff's popular image which was anchored firmly in his success in stamping out the evils that most often tempted the sisters and brethren to backslide; gambling, alcohol and the more lustful sins of the flesh.

If it weren't for Prohibition and its enduring companion vices, the sheriff's department wouldn't have that much to do.

One thing for sure, the sheriff didn't conjure up any notions of the tall ruggedly handsome individualist lawmen of the old west often dramatized in books and movies. Five eleven, weighing in at one hundred and seventy pounds, his long narrow face made his small ears look out of place. Folds of weathered skin loosely wrapped around large bones, concealed rock hard muscles and sinew that supported the sizable paunch drooping over a worn polished belt buckle. His expressionless steel gray eyes could survey a situation taking in every detail without anyone present realizing he was doing so, a talent that also complimented his favorite pastime; playing poker. Thick prematurely gray hair neatly trimmed high above the jacket collar revealed deep circular scars left behind from a severe case of adult chicken pocks. Unimposing as he might appear, there was no doubt about who was in command.

In the South, before Prohibition, the role of a sheriff in maintaining law and order was more symbolic than anything else. The mere presence of a uniformed officer with a pistol hung on his belt and wearing a badge of authority, was the principle deterrent relied on to discourage crime. The traditional role of a sheriff was one of servitude, primarily responsible for defending the establishment, protecting wealthy families and simply keeping the peace. On occasions of murder and other heinous violent crimes where maximum punishment was deemed the appropriate measure of punishment for the accused, the sheriff's role as a mere figurehead was made unmistakably clear. Quietly, he would be relegated to the position of a powerless bystander while a quasi-secret vigilante committee made up of community leaders took charge of the situation. After inciting the good citizens to rage, the vigilantes would melt into the shadows leaving the mob to see justice done. In the event later evidence proved that the person lynched was innocent, the committee would decry the injustice, vehemently denying complicity and declaring that the tragedy would have been prevented had the courageous sheriff only been there to protect his prisoner.

An example of this suspected practice was dramatically demonstrated near the turn of the century by one of Sheriff Coley's predecessors. In that incident, a Catawba County resident by the last name of, Church, ventured across the Catawba River into, Alexander County, where he robbed and murdered an old man and his daughter. The sheriff was nowhere to be found when the murderer, who had been captured and jailed, was dragged from the jail in the middle of the night by a lynch mob of fifty men. Taken to a farm two miles northeast of town, Church was blindfolded with a red handkerchief and promptly hanged by the neck from a post oak tree until he was dead. A note left by the lynching party in the shirt pocket of the corpse, vowing quick and decisive justice for wrong doers, was unnecessary. The gastly sight of a hanging corpse was warning enough.

On January 1, 1920, Prohibition ushered in a new era of lawlessness that required a new breed of lawman. Sheriff Coley was up to the task. Quick to recognize the potential, he exploited it vigorously throughout a gradual rise to a position of political prominence. The transition was subtle but sure. Servitude yielded to prestige, power and influence. Not to be underestimated, Sheriff Coley became a force to be reckoned with and he made no bones about it. It was in those early years that he earned the respect of both friend and foe for his physical and mental toughness.

The sheriff's plans for early retirement suffered a devastating blow in October of 1929 with the crash the stock market. Investment savings lost, he was left with only his salary, a dilemma he shared with no one.

Chief Deputy Travis Gant, the tallest of the group at six two, weighted one hundred and eighty pounds. Clean cut with broad shoulders, his trim muscular build was symmetrically well balanced. He was personable, a handsome man with dark brown hair, bright blue eyes, erect posture and graceful stride. Unpretentious and approachable, he could also be a frightfully intimidating presence during confrontational situations.

At eighteen, under the guidance of Sheriff Coley, he became the Southern Regional Golden Gloves middle weight boxing champion and a local celebrity. Admired and popular with the public, his name and face became well known. After graduating from high school, Deputy Gant worked part time for the sheriff while attending college.

At twenty one, he graduated from Wake Forest College in Winston Salem, North Carolina. Since Criminology was not in the curriculum, his chosen field of psychology and philosophy were the courses he felt would be of most benefit to a career in law enforcement.

A college professor who befriended Travis, confided the preliminary results of research he was conducting in an ongoing study that focused on the problems of children who suffered parental abuse.

The study showed that regardless of heritage, environment, rich or poor, these children exhibited almost identical patterns of behavior. Intrigued, Travis' goal was to apply those findings to his own study to determine if criminals who committed the same type crimes displayed similar patterns of behavior that could be predicted in advance within a reasonable degree of accuracy.

Excited about beginning his career in earnest, Travis went to work full time as administrative assistant to the sheriff. Two years later, Sheriff Coley created the rank of chief deputy. The only one surprised when he promoted Travis to the job was Travis.

Regardless of the popularity Chief Deputy Gant enjoyed as a champion boxer and the only college graduate in the sheriff's department, promoting an inexperienced young deputy to a position of succession to the reigning high sheriff created dissension among the senior staff and drew sharp criticism from the ruling democratic party and county government leaders. After a closed meeting called by Sheriff Coley, his critics emerged eager to welcome Travis into the political grooming process. Secretly, they still harbored the same old resentments.

Deputy Pace Tanner, the son of a successful corporate lawyer in the nearby City of Hickory, was intrigued with law enforcement. His parents, socially prominent civic leaders, demanded that their son follow in his father's footsteps. Pace gracefully declined, but as a consequence of his insubordination was forced to drop out of college before graduating because his parents withdrew their financial support in a futile effort to force him into submission. On the recommendation of then, Deputy Gant, Sheriff Coley hired Pace in deference to political pressure not to do so, indignantly chastising the angry parents for implying that their son's choice of a career in law enforcement was a less than honorable calling.

Calm, deliberate and articulate, Pace was fascinated with criminal investigations, but got very little practice at detective work simply because there was very little crime in the county. Although the fear of public disgrace did act strongly as a deterrent, the low crime rate was not necessarily bound by the fear of being publicly humiliated or ostracized. More so, it was a state of mind firmly instilled and nurtured from childhood through consistent and sometimes relentless

The Sugarbush

Biblical teachings that confirmed Christian virtues as constant reminders that being labeled a thief and rogue was the worst thing that could happen to a person.

However, there had always been a smattering of vice in Catawba County which was not viewed as less sinful by Christians, but was viewed as distinctly separate from crime. The vices attracted all walks of life whether men, women, rich, poor, educated, uneducated, good, bad, believers and non-believers. The indulgent participants passed off the attraction and enjoyment of their favorite sins to a temporary backslid condition attributed to the fall of Adam and Eve in the Garden of Eden. Since the sinful nature of man was not their fault, they also expected to be absolutely forgiven on a regular basis without fear of placing their heavenly rewards in jeopardy.

The variety and choices of favorite sins saw a significant increase after the introduction of Prohibition, then again during the early years of the Great Depression. In Catawba County, surprisingly enough, neither Prohibition nor the Great Depression contributed to any significant increase in the local crime rate, including petty theft. The daily challenges facing the sheriff's department were concentrated on attempts to control a burgeoning traffic problem, enforcing Prohibition, and most importantly, rooting out vice. Pace was assigned that task and was good at it. His consistent successes kept Sheriff Coley in the limelight.

Pace was also handsome and athletic. Just under six feet, weighing two hundred pounds and constantly fighting a weight problem, he was the heaviest of the three deputies. Engaged to marry his high school sweetheart, he was also the most settled of the three.

Chick Yount, a good ole boy from, Sherrill's Ford, spent most of his free time hunting and fishing. He was the shortest and stockiest of the five men. Crowned with a wiry mop of carrot red hair, his fair complexion was abundantly sprinkled with freckles that ran together in bunches, appearing from a distance to be splatters of mud pasted to his sensitive white skin. Light brown eyes tinged with different shades of yellowish orange specks, blended in perfectly with his complexion.

As a teenager, Chick was a rowdy, street brawling rabble rouser. Easily offended and quick to anger, his face would turn fire red, the pupils of his eyes dilating to three times their normal size. In a flash, he was out of control. Otherwise he was outgoing, witty and popular with the country girls.

When Sheriff Coley hired Chick, he turned him over to Travis commenting; "that little bulldog will make you a good hand, but you'll have to keep an eye on'im. He's excitable, kind of a loose cannon. I owe his folks a favor and besides that, I like the rascal."

A few months after completing basic training and being assigned a patrol, Chick had written up more collars for resisting arrest than all the other deputies put together. This prompted his supervisor to put him back on probation working with an experienced officer for continued training.

Sonny Lavin was an Irish Yankee from Baltimore, Maryland. At five eleven and weighing one hundred ninety pounds, his physique was thick, sturdy and solid. Dark complexion with expressive brown eyes, the veteran crime fighter was intense only when he had to be. He enjoyed a good laugh even if it was on him. Biding time until the end of Prohibition when he would take over as Agent in Chief for the southern regional office of the Bureau of Investigation, Sonny wasn't making any waves, although for his own amusement, he didn't miss a chance to pull Sheriff Coley's chain.

Traffic in this remote farming hamlet during daylight hours was not uncommon, but never went unnoticed. Even more so, the sound of a car entering the community at three o'clock in the morning would be a topic of conversation and concern at the breakfast tables of those awakened by the intrusion. Already noted for the watchful caution of its residents, hard times had fostered an even greater awareness and suspicion of any occurrence that seemed out of the ordinary. The Great Depression was devastating. Each day was a daunting struggle for survival that challenged the reality of civilized behavior, Christian virtues and accepted moral standards.

Two hours earlier back in the Catawba County seat of Newton, North Carolina, Sheriff Coley had slipped out of bed leaving his lover sleeping soundly. In late1918, at age thirty eight and preparing to run for sheriff, Burton wisely joined a church. It was there where he first met Edith Burch, a thirty five year old spinster.

The Sugarbush

In keeping with a strict religious up bringing, Edith dressed in high necked, ankle length, loosely fitting cotton frocks and wore no make up or jewelry, a trait that over emphasized the plainness of her appearance. A tightly coiled bun on the back of her head disguised a mass of soft, chocolate brown hair. Quite, private and reserved, Edith was patient, but neither timid nor shy. When underestimated, her confident assertiveness often shocked the unwary.

Burton was attracted to Edith and assumed correctly that she was attracted to him. At church each Sunday, where ever Edith was, Burton was nearby. Subtly he made his attraction known to her, but remained unsure whether or not she was deciphering his signals. Indeed she was and thrilled at the prospects, however, coyness was a female ploy that the sheriff could not relate to.

After winning the election, Burton hired Edith as his private secretary. Dependable, efficient and unquestioning, her loyalty and sense of duty to confidentiality would become legendary.

The staff liked Edith, but could not understand how she could so idolize a boss who treated her with such indifference.

Several months after taking office, Burton sat at home alone drinking, brooding and talking to himself. "That woman's got me crazy!" He mumbled. "I can't tell if she wants me the way I want her or not. All I do is think about makin' a pass at her to find out. Well by damn, if I'm gonna be thinkin' about it all the time I might as well do it!"

Edith lived in a secluded cottage on the edge of town. She was sitting up in bed reading in preparation for the Sunday morning Bible study at church. An unexpected heavy knock on the front door startled her! Now and then visitors would stop by, but rarely at night and never this late. From the heavy knock, she sensed who it was. Standing nude with her hair undone, she draped a house coat over her shoulders, pulled her hair to the front and went to the door.

"Who is it?" she asked softly.

"It's Sheriff Coley."

Edith cracked the door. "Give me a few minutes, Sherif…"

Burton forced his way in and slammed the door. His eyes suggested more than a need for conversation.

"You've been drinking liquor. I can smell it. Please leave,"she whispered unconvincingly."

In the dim light Burton stared unbelieving at the shapely figure that until this moment had been hidden from sight by swathes of loosely fitting garments, but now stood before him seductively draped to the hips in a shawl of silken hair.

Edith had been expecting him. Now that he had finally come, her fantasies seemed somehow less sensual. She saw Burton's eyes deepen with desire. Trembling, she let the house coat slide off her shoulders, falling with a soft rustle into a heap around her feet. She backed slowly into her bedroom. Burton followed, throwing off his clothes as he came. Not a word was spoken. Staring curiously at the naked man before her, Edith suddenly stepped forward and began pummeling his chest with her small fists.

Stumbling, the two naked bodies fell across the bed. Edith crossed her legs tightly, clawing and fighting with all her strength. Again and again Burton would pry her legs apart and each time she would grab him by the hair with both hands and pull him back down on top of her, crossing her legs once again. During the furious struggle, the eroticism of Edith's fantasies came dramatically to life. Engulfed in ecstasy that far surpassed any fantasy imagined, she burst into tears of pleasure. Her body arched in rapid contortions in response to the continuous muscle contractions releasing the flow that wet her thighs. Reeling, she fell back in trance-like state while Burton moved clumsily between her legs and lifted them to rest on his shoulders. Oblivious to Edith's cries of pain, he soon collapsed heavily on top of her. Moaning and sobbing, they began consoling one another.

From that night forward the bond between them grew stronger and stronger. Edith became his confidant and confessor. She hung on his every word, never questioning, only offering tepid agreement and encouragement.

The frequent late night visits always began with an accounting of the solutions the sheriff had found to resolve the problems he had told her about on the last rendezvous. After stewing about the new problems he faced, the encounter invariably culminated in a grappling, tumultuous entanglement of bodies groaning and crying out in fits of pain and pleasure.

The Sugarbush

Sheriff Coley had arrived at his office to find the other members of the raiding party waiting.

"Good mornin' men, looks like everybody's here and rarin' to go," he shouted. "Now if we ain't a lucky bunch of part poopers, I don't know who is. This mornin' we're gonna be bustin' up a still and chasin' down some moonshiners in the meanest snake infested den of iniquity south of the Mason Dixon line. I'm talkin' about, 'Catfish', and before this day's over some of Catawba County's most prominent citizens just might end up buildin' time in the county jail. I had Chick pick up some sandwiches and drinks. I hope you came prepared for a long day, Agent Lavin!"

"I'm ready for anything, Sheriff," Lavin replied. "From what I've been hearing, if you want to arrest some of Catawba County's most prominent citizens for prohibition violations, they aren't so far away that we need to pack lunches. If we start now, we can probably bust them all and be back in time to eat breakfast at the City Diner."

For a moment the sheriff was startled and clearly irritated. Regaining his composure and without hesitation, he barked. "The part about the prominent citizens was supposed to be a funny, but since you seem to know something I don't, we'll do it your way! What's the plan, Lavin?"

Sonny smiled, raising both hands to a stop position. "Easy there Burton," he replied. "I was joking too. Your plan is my plan. I thank you for inviting me and I'm ready to go when you are."

"Well I'm not jokin' now! If you have information about somethin' goin' on right under my nose that I don't know about, Catfish can wait!"

Grinning in amusement, Sonny repeated, "Like I said, I was joking."

"Well men," Burton continued, a victorious ring to his voice, "now that I got that shit straight, let's get goin'. Travis! You drive. Don't take the Rock Barn Road; it's in bad shape. Let's go through Claremont. A couple miles past Setzer's Depot, take a left on Island Ford Road. It'll take us over the Bunker Hill covered bridge at Lyle's Creek and then veers right past Thyatira Lutheran Church. It comes out just below Huitt's Store. From there, drive on toward the river. I'll show you where we turn off.

Catfish did not earn a bad name and sinister reputation, it merely maintained the one it was born with. It all began around 1775 when a band of cutthroat bandits evading retribution by hiding behind the guise of American Revolutionary War Patriots, discovered mud holes teaming with catfish trapped in pools of water left behind by a receding spring flood.

Led by the ruthless, Sam Brown, and his sister, Charity, the savage band of thieves were attracted to the area by a series of caves in the nearby sheer rock bluffs along the river where they could hide out and stash their booty. The terrain consisted of rugged, steep, rocky hills and hollows covered with dense undergrowth, evergreen and hardwood forests. When cleared for cultivation, the soil was so poor and void of nutrients it was hardly worth the effort, providing at best, only subsistence farming. Mostly dirt poor, the impoverished Pennsylvania Dutch and German settler's existence necessarily depended on other creative sources of income. Since they grew their own grain, the quickest, easiest, and cheapest way of raising cash money was making and selling moonshine whiskey, an art and established way of life long before Federal Government intervention. Frequent outbreaks of violence among families, neighbors or intruders, embellished with the telling, were well publicized, serving to keep the community's frightful reputation of over a hundred and fifty years securely in tact.

Catfish was also noted for a stern attitude of autonomy that prevailed among the residents. The uninformed were surprised to discover that several of the families were big land owners, timber men, dairymen and successful country businessmen who disapproved of any vice or unlawfulness, but remained closed-mouthed, fiercely protective of the community's privacy. Besides that, it would have been extremely unhealthy to do otherwise.

As the raiding party drove toward the river, Sonny listened with interest to the youthful banter and laughter of the three deputies swapping war stories about their adventures in law enforcement. Puzzled, he noticed the conversation had come to an abrupt halt when Travis turned onto Island Ford Road. In the darkness, an unseen smile crept across his face. "Hey Burton," Sonny asked with a chuckle. "Why is it your deputies got so quiet all at once?"

The Sugarbush

"Noticed that myself," came the replied. "I reckon they know when we cross over the Bunker Hill covered bridge, we'll be enterin' rebel territory and worse yet, when we pass Huitt's Store we'll be behind enemy lines. They probably figured if they stopped bullshitin' and makin' such a racket, we could get to where we're going without anybody knowin' we're here."

Everybody burst out laughing, relieving the mounting tension.

Upon crossing Lyle's Creek the road improved allowing the party to roll down the car windows without fear of being splashed with mud and water. The cool early morning air was filled with the fragrance of blossoming trees and newly plowed fields. The full moon settling down to raise the sun enhanced a misty scene so tranquil it obscured the reality of the lawmen's presence there.

Sheriff Coley broke the silence. "When you hit the flat on top of the ridge you'll see a lane to the right. Turn in there and follow it down about a quarter mile and we'll find a place to park."

"We're gonna leave tire tracks," Travis remarked. "Anybody passing by will see somebody's turned in here. Maybe we should brush'em out."

"No, I don't think so," Burton answered. "With all this mud, trying to conceal'em will raise more suspicion than just leavin'em be. We've arrested a few bootleggers around here, but we've never captured a single man at a still place. These characters always manage to stay one jump ahead of us no matter what we do! We bust up what they leave behind which is no more than a nuisance to'em. Within a day or two they set up again in the same place. We're bound to get lucky one of these days and this could be it.

We'll be parked about a mile upriver from the still place so maybe we can slip up on'em. We'll see."

"What's the rest of the story, Burton?" Agent Lavin asked.

"Here's what I was told, Sonny. There's supposed to be four men working this operation. Two of the Hagan boys, Cal and Bobby, and the Grimes' brothers, Jess and Jarred. Cal will fight if he's pushed, but as a rule he's easy going. His younger brother Bobby is an arrogant hot tempered son-of-a-bitch just like his old man, Cush Hagan. Anybody lookin' for a racket with either one of those two can get one damn quick. Other than making moonshine the Hagans generally steer clear of trouble unless somebody brings it to'em and that somebody don't have to get very close for the shit to hit the fan. Hell's fire, Cush's sister, Candace Shuman, is just as bad when her feathers get ruffled. A while back, she was walkin' through the alley in, Conover, and come up on some ole boys sittin' back there drinkin'. They offered her a drink and bein' how Candace is, she didn't turn it down. I reckon they thought that cleared the way for a little grab ass, so one of'em latched on to her tit. They mustta been awful drunk or plumb crazy to do somethin' like that. Candace jerked a picket off a backyard fence rail next to the alley, nails and all, and pert near beat those fellers to death with it. A rusty nail punctured one of'ems left eyeball and yanked it clean outta the socket. Those Hagans' go plumb crazy when they get mad. They don't care who they're fightin' with and they don't care who wins. They just wanna get in their licks and see the blood fly.

On the other hand, the Grimes' brothers are just plain mean and they take pleasure in being mean. They like hurtin' people. They're not so tough they can't be whipped, but nothing is ever over with'em. I've seen'em in action. They're clumsy as hell, but they've got stayin' power and can take a punch. The more they get hit, the madder they get and harder they fight. The only way you can win with them is to kill'em."

"Sheriff Coley," Chick interrupted. "What do these men look like? I don't think I've ever seen either one of'em."

"Cal and Bobby have deep set beady brown eyes, brown hair, long narrow noses, and wide mouths with thin lips. Cal is a six footer, big boned and lanky. Bobby is a couple inches shorter with a medium build. Dressed up, they're pretty good lookin' hillbillies.

Jess and Jarred have bushy eyebrows and great big black brown eyes that set tight against their noses. If there's such a thing as being almost cross-eyed, they are. Their faces are wide with flared flat noses and thick lips. Both of'em are missin' a couple front teeth and the ones that ain't missin' are growing a crop of green moss. They have short thick necks that make 'em look like their heads were squashed down between the shoulders with a cider press. They both have curly black hair and are over six feet tall. They look like a couple of English bulldogs and that translates ugly! Jess will go two hundred and twenty five pounds and Jarred's not much lighter, if any. Like I said, they're mean for the sake of bein' mean and as big and

The Sugarbush

strong as they are, they can afford to be. They've been accused of assault and rape several times, but the charges were either dropped or never brought against'em. Besides bein' threatened, the victims had such bad personal reputations they figured they'd lose anyway. I guess they figured it was safer to do nothin'."

"They're probably right too, Sheriff," broke in Travis. "Remember what happened when the mill hill girl took that barber from Marion to court for rape? By the time the defense attorney and the newspapers got done with her, the barber ended up being the victim. Just because the girl ran with a rough crowd, the jury decided she brought it on herself."

"Yeah, Travis," I remember. "Rough crowd or not and no matter how bad the reputation, no woman deserves to be raped. Jess and Jarred's day's gonna come. It's just a matter of time. They're gonna end up killin' somebody.

"This is the old Cline place." Travis commented as he turned in.

"That's right!" the Sheriff answered. "As I understand the barn and out buildin's are still standin', but the main house was apparently struck by lightnin' and burned down some time back.

Before that happened, it had been vacant for a long time. The Clines' had three children, a boy and two girls. The boy was killed in the war and the two girls married and moved away. After the old folks died, the daughters sold the farm. Taylor Upton and that snotty kid of his own it now."

The car dropped off the hill past the north end of an orchard that blocked the view of the barn from the old home place.

"You wanna park down by the barn?" Travis asked.

"No. I believe if you turn right and head up the hill, you'll end up in the front yard."

The sheriff was right. The home site sat on a flat area of about two acres. Several large white oak trees shaded the front yard facing the river. Just beyond the back corner of the house by the edge of the orchard, stood a towering hickory tree. The debris from the fire that destroyed the house had been removed, leaving only the outline of the foundation and two massive rock chimneys.

Travis parked facing the river and shut off the engine. From the distance he could faintly hear dogs barking. "Sound sure carries out here," Travis muttered. "If we woke up the hounds we probably woke up the whole countryside."

"No doubt about that," Burton remarked. "I'm hopin' by the time we move out to find the still, folks will have forgotten about hearin' us comin' in."

The Sheriff would have been right had he stayed under the hill and parked below the orchard by the barn instead of choosing the front yard. That was his first mistake.

II

The sheriff was right on both counts. The moonshiners were the Hagan and Grimes brothers alright, and they did hear the lawmen's car coming in. Bobby Hagan followed the sound to see where it was going. As the noise began to fade toward Lookout Dam, he decided whoever it was did not pose a threat. About to return to the still, Bobby's heart began to pound with apprehension when across the valley he saw the headlights of the sheriff's car as the raiding party pulled in to park.

Relieved to finally be out of the car, the group marveled at the many variations of silver moonlight streamers pouring through the trees creating rhythmic shadows dancing all around them as the moon slipped in and out of the fleeting clouds above.

Strained through filters of drifting fog, silver reflections tinted with gold glided gracefully over the surface of the river below. The murmur of water curling along the banks and around the sandbars completed a magical moonlit scene.

Sonny turned to Burton. "If a person wanted privacy, they couldn't do any better than this. Notice how quiet it is?"

"Yeah Sonny, but I'm a city boy," Burton replied. "This is the loudest quiet I've ever heard. With all the noise in town I sleep like a baby, but this country quiet is like cannon fire to me. Hear those crickets and toads chirpin'? To country folks, that's pure music that puts'em to sleep at night and wakes'em up in the morning. But for me, hell, I wouldn't sleep a wink with all that racket goin' on. The longer I hear it the louder it gets. I won't be sleepin' on the job today, that's for damn sure.

"Now let's talk about what we're gonna do," Sheriff Coley continued. "Right now it's three thirty and won't be light enough to see for another hour or so. About that time we'll start making our way down river along the bank. When we get to Gunpowder Creek, we should be close enough to the still to hear'em workin' and talkin. Then we'll spread out as best we can and move in on'em. If we're lucky, you youngsters might have a chance to run'em down. Me and Sonny don't plan to do any chasin', but if you happen to run'em to us, we'll catch'em for you. That's about it. While I'm makin' a nature call, somebody break out the coffee."

Familiar with the terrain, Bobby quickly made his way back to the still. "It's the law all right!" he exclaimed in excitement. "They parked at the old Cline place. I got close enough to see'em perty good. Best I can make out, they's five of'em."

"I figured as much!" Jess growled in disgust. "Who else would be a comin' down Island Ford Road this time a mornin? For damn sure, one of'em's that pus-gutted son-of-a-bitch hypocrite, Burton Coley. He's the rogue that oughtta be in prison. The liquor he ketches, what he don't drink up hisself, he sells with his own bunch a bootleggers. Worst yit, he gits by with it."

"That's easy enough to figure out," replied Cal. "I ain't never heared a no sheriff arrestin' hisself."

"Talkin' 'bout the sheriff ain't gittin' us away from here," cried Jarred. "They'll be a comin' on in here and it ain't a fer piece. We gonna finish runnin' this last charge or not?"

"They won't start out 'fore light enough to see," Cal answered. "I figure that gives us a couple hours head start, but Jarred's right. Let's not take no chances boys. Outtin' the fire and pour water on the still to cool it down. Pull the dick spout plug and let her empty out. Take the still, blow pipe, 'E' connection and condenser worm across the creek. Hide'em amongst the honeysuckle thicket down in that big gully. We done hid the liquor 'cept fer what we jist run. We kin hide what's left on our way outta here. Roll the doublin' keg down in the creek. Let it fill with water and sink. Maybe they won't notice it. Jess, whatta ye say we fill that Black Draught bottle ye been proofing with and leave it here fer our visitors. By the time they git here they jist might 'preciate a taste a good whiskey fer all the trouble they goin' to. We might not make the most liquor in these parts, but we do make the best. Anyhow, we ain't leavin'em much else to bust up and brag about."

Working quickly, the four men were soon ready to leave.

"What the hell!" Jarred shouted, slapping his brother on the shoulder. "We needin' a vacation 'bout now anyways, ain't that right Jess? We been talkin' 'bout it, ain't we Jess?"

"That's right, baby brother, that's right. Let's git to the house and git slicked up. We oughtta be a pluggin' a couple a whores 'fore dark. Cal, you'uns wanna come along with us?"

The Sugarbush

"No thanks." replied Cal. "Me and Bobby got thangs to do. We gonna stay 'round to see what else the sheriff's up to. Once he's away from here, we'll rest a lots easier."

With this, they parted company and set off in different directions.

"Cal!" said Bobby. "Let's git to yer place, wash up and change clothes. Then we can drive down to the old Cline place to look thangs over."

"That's a good idea, but we better not take the Model T. Let's saddle up the horses. It'll be quieter and less suspicious thatta way."

Travis and his two deputies were first to reach the still.

"Sheriff," Travis, shouted. "Come on up. They knew we were coming and hightailed it outta here."

"How do you know that?" Chick asked.

"It's simple!" Travis answered. "Can't you smell it? They knew we were comin', so they dumped the mash.

When Burton and Sonny arrived, Travis continued. "They pulled the still out of the furnace, and a big one at that; at least a two hundred gallon cooker. This is a big operation for the woods and from the looks of things, they've been workin' here a long time."

"Before we dynamite the mash boxes and hogsetts," Burton ordered, "let's make a sweep around the woods to see if we can find where they stashed the still and liquor. If we don't have any luck in an hour or so, we'll get on back to the car and make a couple house calls. Travis, be sure to get some pictures."

"Hey, Burton," Sonny asked, "What is Black Draught?"

"What you got there, Sonny?"

"A Black Draught bottle full of moonshine whiskey. What is Black Draught anyway?"

Everybody began to laugh. "Well Sonny," answered Burton. "Black Draught is a harsh acting snake oil remedy the country folks prefer for the relief of constipation. Those clod-hoppin' hillbilly sons-a-bitches are makin' fun of us. Let'em have their laugh now because my fun is just gettin' started. They're about to see how bad things can get."

The sheriff did not realize the significance of his prophecy which would indeed come to pass, but in a way he never imagined.

Jerry S Jones

The woods echoed with Sonny's laughter as he walked up the hill and handed the pint bottle of liquor to Burton. "Well gentlemen, the message is clear. Our painfully shy and reluctant hosts think everyone of you guys are full of shit. They can't be talking about me because I'm not from here."

Cal and Bobby reined up their horses at the entrance to the old Cline farm and observed the tire tracks leading off down the lane.

"I think it best we ride through the woods along the ridge to where we can look down on the place jist in case they left somebody guardin' the car," said Cal.

From the edge of the wooded ridge, Cal and Bobby carefully surveyed the scene below.

"Don't look like nobody's 'round, 'less they asleep in the car," Bobby whispered. "Let's leave the horses here and walk down."

Making their way down the hill to the large hickory tree at the corner of the orchard, they cautiously approached the car.

"Ain't another soul here besides us," exclaimed Cal. "They ain't locked the car."

"Ner the cooter shell neither," replied Bobby. "Looky here how nice the law is. They done left us a five gallon lard can fulla cokes and store bought sandwiches all iced down. They knowed we'd be tired and hungry after workin' all night. Let's eat!"

Sitting down on the hearth of the nearest chimney, they devoured the sandwiches and cold drinks.

"That City Diner shore makes good sandwiches," Bobby chortled. "I'd love to see old Burton's face when he opens that lard can to git his lunch."

"So would I," replied Cal. "Folks hates to lose somethin' they really lookin' forwards to."

Laughing as he walked back toward the car, Cal asked, "Anythang else in the trunk?"

"Yeah," replied Bobby. "A couple boxes a twelve-gauge shotgun shells, double aught buckshot at that. Anythang in the car?"

"No, not a thang. I figure they didn't lock it 'cause they ain't left nothin' worth stealin'."

"Hold on, Bobby! Look down yonder in the orchard. Ain't that a jacket hangin' on one a them fruit trees?"

The Sugarbush

"Shore looks like it, Cal. Hang on a minute. I'll go git it."
"Hey Cal, this is the sheriff's coat. His name's wrote inside the collar. He took it off to take a dump and mustta fergot it. Looky here! Looky here! He brung a bunch a warrants with'im, sixteen of'em!"
"Who they fer?" Cal asked.
"Some folks we know and some we don't. By damned here's one fer me!"
"What fer?" Cal exclaimed in surprise as he peered over Bobby's shoulder.
"It says fer assault and battery. Hell, that wuz months ago and's already been settled," cried Bobby. "Why in hell he's got it in fer me, I'll never know?"
"Whatever he's up to it'll have to wait," said Cal. "They ain't nobody gonna be servin' these here warrants on nobody, least not today."
"Ye mighty right 'bout that," replied Bobby. "I been wantin' me one a these here jackets with all them fancy patches on it. I reckon the sheriff left it jist fer me and I aim to thank him proper by a washin' all a that red mud off'n his car."
Bobby climbed into the driver's seat of the car. "Give me a push down the hill!"
"Whatta ye aimin' to do?" Cal asked.
"I'm gonna wash his car! In the river! Now ole big shot sheriff's gotta reason for writin' up a warrant if'n he kin find out whose name to put on it. Old Burton likes to fish. Let him fish his car outta the river or else walk back to town. Now give me a shove!"
Bobby's descent started out slow, but began picking up speed when the mechanical brakes heated up and failed. Above his own laughter, Cal could still hear Bobby yelling obscenities when the car hit the rivers edge, momentarily vanishing under a cascade of water. Laughing while secretly thankful to be in one piece, Bobby opened all four doors, allowing the floorboard deep water to flow through the car and continue downstream. Then he sloshed to shore and back up the hill where Cal lay on the ground laughing. The distant roar of a blast of dynamite reminded them it was time to go.

On the return hike from the moonshine still, Sonny was the first to reach the parking place. Looking puzzled, he turned and shouted back down the hill to the sheriff.

"Hey Burton, this is where we parked, right?"

"That's it. Did you think I got you lost?"

"You still got that pint of moonshine?" Sonny asked.

"Sure do. Why?"

"You better hope we're lost. If we aren't, you're going to need a double shot of that whiskey because I don't think you're going to like what you see, or that is what you don't see, when you get up here."

It took Burton a few seconds before he realized something was missing. "Travis," he yelled. The car's gone! Some son-of-a-bitch stole our car."

"No they didn't," Sonny shouted. "I see it. They dumped it into the river. It's going to be a long walk back to town. Maybe they'll be kind enough to come back and give us a lift."

"I'm gonna give them a lift with a boot up the ass," Burton shouted. "They're the ones gonna do the walkin', barefooted, all the way to the Federal Penitentiary in Atlanta, Georgia.

Travis, about a half mile down the road there's a farmer who owns a yoke of oxen. Send Pace and Chick to ask him if he'll give us a hand. Tell'im we'll pay him cash money for his trouble, but we need him right now.

If it takes every man on duty to find'em, I want those four slugs in jail before dark today and that's an order! Before I'm through with'em, they'll wish they'd drowned in the process."

The team of oxen easily pulled the car out of the river and back up the hill to the front yard with the farmer laughing all the way. He had a pretty good idea how it got there in the first place.

"Sheriff Coley," he said. "I don't recollect ever seein' nobody wash a car thatta way. I don't see no fishing' poles neither. So's how come it to be in the river?"

Sonny burst into laughter, shouting. "I think somebody forgot to put on the emergency brake."

"Yeah, that's what happened," said Burton. "Will two dollars' do for your trouble?"

"That's a plenty Sheriff," replied the farmer. "Thank ye now. I'll be gittin' on back to the house."

Pace and Chick had already begun drying out the distributor and coil so they could start the car.

"Somebody break out the lunches," Burton said curtly. "We'll eat first, then we'll start makin' house calls."

Flushed cherry red and furious, Chick shouted, "Our lunches and drinks are gone! There's nothin' left in this lard can but empty bottles and meltin' ice."

Sonny began laughing again. "One thing you can say for these good ole' boys, Sheriff. They have a sense of humor. They must love to see you guys coming."

Ignoring Sonny's good natured ribbing, Burton growled. "Travis, I left my jacket hangin' on a tree in the orchard. Ya'll get the car runnin' and pick me up on the way out. I'll be waitin' at the county road."

Having a federal agent see him being made a fool of was hard on the ego, especially at the hands of Catfish moonshiners who Sonny already knew had notorious reputations for taunting the law, quite often sending them back to where they came from, always empty handed, and sometimes like today, with even less than they came with. Burton chuckled to himself at the audacity of his ornery adversaries and only hoped that, at least today, they would forego sitting by the roadside to wave goodbye as he and his raiding party headed back towards Newton.

Glancing from tree to tree, Burton realized his jacket was not where he thought he had left it. "Surely as hell those hillbillies didn't find my jacket with all those warrants in it," he mumbled in frustration.

Leaving the jacket and its contents hanging in the orchard was his second mistake.

III

"Hey Chick," shouted Travis. "I left the shotgun leaning against that hazelnut tree over by the blackberry briar patch. Pick it up for me, will you?"

"I'd like to stick it up somebody's ass," Chick answered, fumbling to fill a coke bottle with melted ice water from the lard can. He sauntered over, picked up the shotgun and cradled it under his arm. Guzzling down the water, he tossed the empty bottle into the briar patch. The falling bottle startled a cottontail rabbit from its bed. The rabbit sped across the backyard toward the hickory tree on the brink of the hill.

Still angry and humiliated over the events of the day, Chick shouted. "It's dinner time." Leveling the shotgun on the speeding ball of fur, he pulled both triggers. The rabbit disintegrated into a red mist. The roar of the blast echoed through the countryside, then all was silent except for the sound of the car motor chugging in the background.

"What in hell's the matter with you Chick?" yelled Travis. "Huntin' season on rabbits doesn't open 'till next Thanksgivin'. Get over here. If I was a game warden I'd write you a ticket!"

"Was the sheriff gonna come back here?" came the quivering choked reply as the ashen faced deputy walked briskly toward the car.

"He wasn't going to," Travis answered. "After hearin' that shot he probably will and all the excuses you can come up with won't keep him from taking a big bite outta your ass."

The instant Chick pulled the triggers, the violent recoil allowed him only a fleeting glimpse of another object beyond the intended target that suddenly appeared out of nowhere, quickly vanishing in the shower of blood and fur. Gripped with dread as the vision of that split second image revolved in his mind, he handed the shotgun to Travis and collapsed into a sitting position on the running board of the car.

Seeing the apparent anguish on Chick's face, Travis, in a low stern voice asked, "What's wrong with you? It was just a rabbit."

"I don't feel good," Chick mumbled. Voice cracking, he blurted out. "I think I mightta shot somebody!"

With Pace and Sonny close behind, Travis sprinted toward the spot where the rabbit had exploded. The hickory tree had obscured

The Sugarbush

their vision of the sheriff as he walked diagonally up the steep slope toward the waiting car. They found him lying on his back, feet pointing uphill. Blood, bits of flesh, bone fragments attached to bloody shanks of hair and brain matter were scattered everywhere, pasted to foliage, and hanging from twigs and limbs. Both barrels of double aught buckshot passed through the hapless rabbit striking Burton squarely in the right side of his head, leaving the mangled remains embedded with fur and body parts from the rabbit that died with him.

"For god's sake," Travis moaned. "Is that Burton? It can't be! It is Burton! For god's sake, Chick! You shot the sheriff! He's dead! Pace! That is Burton, right?"

"It's Burton alright," Sonny answered softly. "He never knew what hit hit'im."

"It's gotta be the sheriff, Travis," Pace answered. "How did he get over here? He was gonna wait for us at the road. I keep wanting to go see if he's sitting up there waiting on us."

"I know what you mean, Pace," Travis replied. "Let's all take a couple deep breaths. I need to gather my thoughts."

Chick was still sitting on the running board of the car, his face buried in his hands.

"Get that blanket out of the trunk and bring it here and hurry," Travis shouted.

Chick staggered to his feet. Approaching unsteadily, he handed the blanket to Travis, then looking down at the carnage, emitted a groan and began to vomit.

"He's not gonna be any help," said Travis. "The three of us will have to handle this."

Standing beside the body, Travis continued. "Here's what we're gonna do. I'll spread the blanket right over here on the ground beside him where there's no blood. Pace, you lift his feet. Sonny, you and I will lift him by his belt and arms. We'll lay him on the blanket so it comes to his waist and put his arms against his sides. Then we'll fold the blanket down from the top over the torso and wrap it as tight as we can. I'll take off his belt and use it to hold the blanket in place. After that's done, we'll carry him to the car and sit him up on the passenger side of the back seat. We can empty the five gallon lard can we brought the lunches in and use it for a prop. One of you will need to sit beside him on the way into town to keep him from falling over sideways. If nobody wants to do that, I'll sit beside him and somebody else can drive."

"I'll sit beside him," Chick shouted from above. "Hold on Travis. I'm coming down to help."

"Thanks Chick, we can sure use you. Okay, let's do it!"

As the car sped toward town, Travis explained what he wanted to do when they got there.

"I've been thinking about the best way to handle this. After you've heard me out I'm open to suggestions. We're going straight to the county morgue. It's closed today, so nobody will be around. I have a set of keys to let us in. After we have the body inside, I'll call the coroner, the judge, and the Chairman of the County Supervisors and asked'em to meet us there. While the coroner is performing his examination and filling out the paperwork, I'll call the newspaper offices and tell'em to send their reporters to get the story. Last and most important, none of us is to say anything about this to anybody until after we talk to the press. No one is to leave or make any telephone calls until all that's done. Of course, Sonny, that doesn't include you."

"I know," Sonny replied. "I want to stay out of this completely. Besides the four of us, does anyone else know I was goin' along on the raid?"

"No!" Travis answered. "Pace and Chick weren't told what the operation was or who was involved until they got to the office this morning."

"Good, that's real good. I want to keep it that way. I'm not asking any of you to lie, I'm asking you to forget I was here. Catawba County, the Sheriff's Department, and you as individuals won't lose or gain anything by leaving me out of it. What do you say?"

"You're right Sonny," Travis answered. "I think I can speak for us all. Your name won't come up. What do you wanna do?"

"When we get to the morgue I'll help you unload Burton's body. From there I'll walk to my car and head back to Charlotte. I'll be back for the funeral."

The Sugarbush

From the coroners private office Travis made his telephone calls, including a call to his secretary, Melinda, asking her to personally break the news to Sheriff Coley's secretary, Edith Burch. Then he motioned for Chick and Pace to join him.

"Pace, our statements will be simple," he said." We saw Chick shoot the rabbit. None of us had any idea that Burton was anywhere near. He said he'd be waitin' for us out by the county road, and that's where we expected him to be. When Chick told us he thought he'd shot someone, we ran to investigate and found the body."

"That's what I thought too," said Chick. "When the sheriff's head come into my sights, the hammers was on the way down. He wasn't supposed to be there and I tried to tell myself I was seein' things, but in my heart I knew I'd shot somebody. I knew who it was and I knew he was dead."

Astounded, Travis asked. "You said hammers. You fired both barrels at the same time?"

"That's right, Travis. That little ole cottontail and the sheriff never stood a chance. All I was thinkin' about was gettin' even for all the embarassin' shit we was goin' through and I didn't even know who I was supposed to get even with. Who ever it was dumped the car in the river and ate our lunches was havin' a lotta fun and didn't mean us no harm, they was just tryin' to devil us.

I let it get under my skin so bad I started huntin' somethin' to take it out on. I been doin' that as long as I can remember and for as long as I can remember, every time it happens, I swear I'll never do it again. I keep makin' the same old mistakes over and over agin'. It never hurts me, it always ends with somebody else gettin' hurt. Today it killed the one person that was willin' to give me the chance to make somethin' of my life. Now he's dead and I still ain't hurt.

I quit, Travis. I ain't stayin' in this morgue another minute. If you need me, you know where to find me. I ain't goin' nowhere."

"I understand," said Travis. Thanks Chick. Now get on outta here, but remember. There's a place for you with the sheriff's department. Give it some time. When you're ready, come on back to work."

As Chick walked out he passed the judge and coroner coming in.

"I've got it, Travis, I've got it," Pace cried, pounding the table with his fist. "There was somethin' missin' that I couldn't put my finger on. I've been rackin' my brain 'till right now tryin' to think what it was. The jacket, the sheriff's jacket! Where is it? Remember! He said he left it hanging on a tree in the orchard and was goin' to get it. He never found it! That's why he was comin' back."

That was the sheriff's third and final mistake.

IV

When the coroner and judge walked in, Travis explained what happened and answered their questions. When the coroner left to examine the body, Travis closed the office door.

"Judge," he said. "Instead of dumping all of the alcoholic beverages that were confiscated, Burton was sellin' them through his own ring of bootleggers and several speakeasies that were payin' him for protection. His nephew, Deputy Carlton Barnes, was in charge of the bulk evidence warehouse. Besides the sheriff, Barnes is the only one who had a key, which makes sense because he was the distributer and collector. Whether on his own time or the county's, that's been his full time job for three years.

I showed the sheriff several anonymous letters I received accusing him of that kind of stuff. He denied the accusations as frivolous attempts to undermine his credibility and I believed him. Last night I found out the truth and have been sick ever since. I met with a couple women whose husbands were bootlegging for Burton. Like all the rest of the ring, the men had been involved in some shady dealings in the past, dodgin' outstandin' warrants and such. Barnes recruited them by promising that the sheriff would fix everything plus give'em a cut of the profits.

The wives claimed that after a month of dealin' with Barnes, their husbands realized what they had gotten themselves into and tried to quit. Barnes threatened to trump up new charges that would send'em back to jail. This had been goin' on for over two years before the women decided to do somethin' about it. That's when they started writin' letters. When that didn't work, they caught me alone and ask for help. After a little investigatin' on my own, things looked bad for Barnes, but I still thought Burton was clean. I was wrong. Last night I followed Barnes on his route. His first stop was the bulk evidence storage warehouse where he loaded the liquor. I saw the deliveries, the collections and heard the threats being made. His last stop was Burton's house. I watched them divide up the money.

I knew what I had to do. For good reasons I put off talking to Burton until after the raid and I'm glad I did. That doesn't mean that I think he's better off layin' in there on that slab of granite, it means I don't have to expose him. I still have Barnes to deal with and I hope he's the only one.

Last night I heard Barnes implicate you and our County Attorney, Gordon Jackson. Should I be concerned about that?"

From the expression on the judge's face, Travis wasn't sure whether it spelled surprise, guilt or relief.

"No you shouldn't," the Judge replied solemnly. "I received the same letters you did and I didn't believe them either until I talked to Gordon. He said he had known about it for a long time and hoped nobody else would find out until after Prohibition ended. That's when he intended to take care of the problem and nobody would have been the wiser. Understandably, it was a sensitive situation that neither of us was prepared to deal with in an open battle because Burton had us over a barrel. We didn't know if you or other officers were involved so who could we trust? We didn't want the Federal Agent, Sonny Lavin, to get wind of it and start an investigation that could hurt a lot of innocent people. I better explain what I mean by that.

It began a couple, maybe three years ago. At the time, nobody, not even you, had any idea that Burton was dirty. He was our friend and we trusted him. Anytime he confiscated bonded brands of good imported booze he would send Barnes around making deliveries to all the magistrates, judges and I don't know who else. He made a big joke out of it by saying that he had so much booze to dump down the sewer that he needed our help and he didn't care where we dumped it. Technically, nobody was breaking the law because no money was changing hands. It's against the law to make the stuff and sell it. It's not against the law to drink it. I thought it best to go along with Gordon and do nothing until next January. I don't know what Gordon was going to do about it, I'm just glad you found out because somebody that can't be blackmailed has to deal with Barnes.

I'm also relieved to know that you're clean and that the malfeasance is not widespread. I'm assuming this conversation is a prelude to your revealing a plan for dealing with the problem without implicating anyone else."

"It's my job to deal with the situation one way or the other," said Travis. "I'm prepared to do that today.

The Sugarbush

First I want to say that with or without Sheriff Coley's knowledge, Carlton Barnes, nor anyone, anytime, ever once offered me any booze, money or anything else.

I'm not a lawyer or a judge, but I know the law and keep abreast of any changes to old laws and the signin' in of new ones.

You may get by with saying it's not against the law to drink alcoholic beverages, but in the way you came by it, I wouldn't hang my hat on it. Far be it for me to lecture the superior court judge, but you started it by trying to justify what you've been doin'. You broke a lot of laws and if it ever came to light, your position is indefensible.

Burton's motives for getting' you into a compromising position are plain to see. It was easy for him to do because you trusted him. I can see how that happened because I trusted him too, implicitly. I'm sayin' all of this because you told me that you were relieved to find that the malfeasance is not widespread and to know that I'm clean of any involvement in the corruption.

I will take that remark as one of genuine concern havin' been made sincerely and in good faith. On the other hand, your comment, however well intended, could also be interpreted as an attempt to wash your hands of the matter by misdirectin' the emphasis from your office to mine. This is not my problem or your problem, it's our problem."

"You've made you're point," said the Judge. "How do you think we should deal with our problem?"

"As you said Judge, quietly," answered Travis. "Burton's corruption and betrayal of public trust cannot be justified by makin' allowances for his good years and I'm not going to. Dealin' with this quietly is the right thing to do and I don't need to justify why it is, other than to say that under the circumstances, riskin' the loss of public trust in the whole of county leadership, especially our judicial system, is the wrong thing to do.

Essentially, this whole mess ended with Burton's death. Barnes doesn't know that yet, but he will if you are in agreement with what I wanna do. Barnes will keep his mouth shut, but his silence will come with a price. I'll be bendin' the law because I've gotta let him walk scot free. That means I'll be stickin' my neck out to protect you and whoever else is involved. I expect you to do the same for me."

"I'm sure you do," said the Judge. "How should we go about sticking our necks out for you?"

"By seeing to it I'm appointed to fill out the rest of Burton's term as sheriff and also his replacement on the democratic party ticket as candidate for sheriff in the November general election. I need your support because I know the party has one of their fair haired boys waitin' in the wings. I like my job and I wanna keep it."

"And I think you should," the Judge replied. "Provided that you can make this problem vanish without a trace, you'll have our support along with our gratitude. You've always voted our party ticket, right?"

"No. I'll sign on with whoever guarantees I'll win! My thing is upholdin' the law and that means everybody's party."

"A guarantee doesn't come with our support. You better understand that, and by the way, the democratic party expects your loyalty, win, lose or draw. Burton was running unopposed. You won't be. I've always liked you, Travis, and I don't know anyone who doesn't. But I must tell you that when Burton's influence and power blossomed, he began flexing his muscles and did so in defiance of the ruling party. That left a bad taste in everybody's mouth. Insubordination shows a lack of party loyalty. For that reason, some of the party heavy weights have been biding their time until they could get their own candidate for sheriff on the ticket. They're not going to be too happy with being told they have to support you. I'll try to clear the way for you. I have confidence in you; given time so will they. Gordon is the party's pretty boy. If you have a problem, that's who it will be with. He doesn't really care who's sheriff, so long as it's a democrat, but he will try to intimidate you."

"Thank you, Judge. You might remind those party heavy weights that what I'm doing for them shows my party loyalty in a way that goes far above and beyond the call of duty. That should make'em happy again damn quick."

"I intend to do exactly that," the Judge replied with genuine amusement. "Give me a call when you've resolved our dilemma. As soon as I can get out of here and get home, I'm going to ask my wife to pinch me and tell me I'm not asleep. It's a hell of a sad day when you're told that an old friend got his head blown off and along with sorrow, you breathe a sigh of relief."

The Sugarbush

After being sworn in, Travis left the morgue and drove to headquarters to break the news to his staff. He was brief and to the point, which was good. They could hardly wait for him to stop talking so they could get to the telephones and start spreading the news.

Pouring a cup of coffee, Travis motioned for Pace to come into his office. "You look perplexed. What's on your mind, Deputy Tanner?"

"You noticed," answered Pace. "I can't tell you how bad I feel about everything that's happened today, especially after watching the reactions of the press and staff to the bad news. None of'em seemed as shocked and saddened as I thought they'd be. If anything, they were excited and didn't try to hide it. I'm not excited. I feel a terrible loss for the sheriff who's dead and Chick Yount who wishes he was dead."

"Don't let people's first reactions to the news get under your skin," Travis replied. "Look how different their circumstances are. They didn't hear the shot, they didn't see the carnage, they didn't ride ten miles with a corpse reeking with the stench of blood, mutilated flesh, rabbit guts and gunpowder. To the press, it's a big story. Right now our staff doesn't know exactly what it is they're feelin'. That's why they could hardly wait to get to the telephones. They need to talk about it with someone close to'em. For anybody who wasn't there or close to the sheriff personally, the first emotion they'll experience will be excitement because they're not thinking about, Burton Coley, the person, they're thinking about, Burton Coley, the Sheriff. It's morbid, exciting news, something to talk and speculate about. Being excited doesn't mean they aren't caring and sympathetic because I'm sure they are. When his loss as a person sinks in, they'll show it. We're not over it either, not by a long shot. Why don't you take a break for lunch and be back here as soon as you can. We have a lot to do."

A short time after Pace left, there was a knock on the office door and Melinda entered. Trying not to cry, she exclaimed. "This is awful! I just came from Edith's!"

"How did she take it," Travis asked?

"At first I wasn't sure," Melinda answered. "She turned pale and her body became ridged, just standing there clenching her fists. After what seemed like forever she sat down, bowed her head and started rocking back and forth. When I told her you said she could take off a couple of days if she wanted to, she said to tell you she wasn't ever coming back and for nobody to try talking her out of it. She asked how it happened and I told her. I offered to pray with her, but she ignored me. We sat a long time talking about the most mundane things, then finally she said she would like to be alone, so I left. As I was about to drive away I noticed I'd forgotten my scarf. I got back out of the car and as I walked toward the house, I heard her begin screaming. No, wailing! I froze in my tracks. A chill went all over my body. I have never in all of my born days heard such a mournful sound. I'm sorry Travis, I couldn't get away from there fast enough."

"That's okay Melinda. I really appreciate what you did for me. I'll go see Edith as soon as I can get away. Right now, thanks for comin' in to work. I really need you until midnight tonight and I want you to work tomorrow. There's so much to contend with I can't get anything done if I'm talkin' on the telephone. I want you to run interference for me. You're gonna be flooded with calls from all over the county and state. You know how public officials are. They won't be content unless they talk to the top. Tell the switchboard operator to keep my private line open. Keep tryin' to reach Gordon Jackson. If you find'im, I need to talk to'im right away."

"Oh, I forgot. He just called, Sheriff. He's on his way over."

"Good! I've got some calls to make. When he gets here tell'im I'll only be a few minutes."

At thirty two, Gordon had been the county attorney for four years. Still a bachelor, he was the youngest son of one of the states wealthiest and most influential men. Early on, his parents had seen the tenacity of their precocious son and decided he could better serve and protect the family business interest by pursuing a career in law. It was the father who encouraged, planned and guided his son's future.

Charismatic and intensely competitive, Gordon was accustomed to having his own way, sparing no effort to insure he got it. He could be ruthless and vindictive.

Tall and slender, impeccably dressed in the latest men's fashions, what he lacked in good looks he made up in charm. Blond and blue eyed, his nearly invisible eyebrows tapered to a sharp nose, full lips and a prominent dimpled chin. A protruding Adams apple seemed to totter precariously atop the Windsor knot of a stylish silk necktie. Diligent in his duties as a public servant, he was no stranger to hard work.

The family business consisted of cotton, knitting and fabric mills that produced yarn, socks, hosiery, gloves and various weaves of cloth.   It was traditional for the male offspring to enter an apprenticeship that would take them from the initial manufacturing process through to the finished product in each facility. By the time they graduated from college they would know the business from a bale of cotton to marketing and sales.

At age fifteen, Gordon's indoctrination began with the annual spring inspection tour of low rent homes furnished by the company for their employees. These isolated, confined communities of wood frame houses were appropriately called, mill hills.

The narrow dirt roads in the cramped villages were either muddy and treacherous or dry and dusty. A coating of red dust streaked by rain and dappled with morning dew, clung to the hundreds of shacks creating an even more dismal portrayal of the poverty that existed among the hardworking residents. Some cheerfully accepted their lot in life, happy to have jobs, while others chose to wallow in self pity which they blamed on anyone but themselves rather than risk seeking new opportunities that would gradually lead them to a better life. When one of their own did break the barrier and achieve even modest success and lifestyle gains, they were scorned as hypocrites trying to live above their raising. Values of genuine kindness and goodness were viewed with suspicion and disdain. Good table manners and the use of proper english were the object of ridicule and guffaws of sarcastic laughter. This mentality shielded them from having to admit or face their ignorance and complacency. Such endearing values dared to challenge the validity of long established barriers that stood as a bastion between them and the thing they feared most; a morbid dread of venturing beyond the safety of their comfort zone to risk almost certain social rejection and failure. With few exceptions they much preferred to remain safe, surrounded by their 'own kind', sharing self satisfying complaints about their misfortunes and endless speculation on how much worse it would be to live like the uppity rich folks.

Jerry S Jones

    This was an existence and way of life that Gordon had heard his elders and the plant supervisors talk about, but had never seen. Many times, unaware or uncaring of his presence, the men talked about their sexual trysts with young female employees during working hours. Their lewd descriptions of the encounters excited him.
    As the inspection tour progressed, Gordon was not the only one staring at the barefooted young girls in slip-less, snug fitting cotton dresses that they had out grown, flattening their breasts and outling their panties around triangle shadows of pubic hair.
    The girls gazed back with flirting eyes and teasing gestures that aroused his sexual impulses in ways he had not felt before.
    His first job at the mill was stoking the steam boilers with coal and loading bales of cotton onto steel wheeled carts that he hand pulled into the spinning room to be spun into yarn.
    One morning, caught up with his work he rested, hidden among the bales of cotton. With all the noise from the production machinery, he did not hear the approach of an eleven year old girl who had stolen a bucket of coal and stopped directly in front of his hideaway to catch her breath before proceeding to a hole in the fence to make a getaway. Seeing him, she dropped the heavy bucket and turned to run. Gordon caught her. As she struggled in his arms, her fear and warm squirming body, helpless to escape, gave him a feeling of power and sensual pleasure. "I won't tell on you. You can keep the coal," he whispered in excitement while pulling her into his hiding place. "Do you know how to fuck?" he asked. She nodded her head yes.

    The next week, Gordon slipped back to sneak a cigarette. He looked toward the hole in the fence and saw two girls carrying empty coal buckets. The girl was back. She brought along a friend who had larger breasts and pubic hair. She knew about different things and they did them to each other. Sometimes they took turns watching each other do things.
    By the time he went off to college the sexual encounters in the cotton bin had become less exciting, almost boring. Something was missing. Gordon knew what he craved to do, but didn't know where to start. His room mate at college, a six, four two hundred and twenty pound athlete, three years his senior and the pride of a wealthy Statesville family, provided the solution. At their first meeting they

sensed the dark secret between them. After days of cautious hedging, it was out in the open.

Travis had just hung up the telephone when Gordon burst into his office. "Why in the hell am I hearing about the sheriff's death from the press?" he shouted. "Why wasn't I notified, Gant?"

"Sheriff Gant, to you," Travis replied. "We couldn't find you, that's why!"

"Bullshit," Gordon yelled. "My secretary knows where I am and can reach me at all times."

"If that's the case, why did she tell the press where you were but wouldn't tell Melinda. If you're ready to listen I'll tell you what happened."

"You must be punch-drunk, Gant! I just finished telling you, I know what happened.

You raided a liquor still in Catfish, but ended up getting raided!

You didn't find the still, only where it had been!

You didn't find any liquor or moonshiners!

The moonshiners did the finding, ate your lunches and dumped a taxpayer owned car into the Catawba River!

Your redneck deputy sworn to up hold the law, shoots a rabbit out of season and in the process kills the sheriff who was in the line of fire!

That's what the press is going to print on the front pages!

I gave them the caption myself: 'County Sheriff, Burton Coley, killed during Catfish cluster fuck!' How do you like it?"

"If you don't calm down," said Travis, "I'm going to do something and you're not gonna like it at all."

"I'm not worried about that, Gant," Gordon shot back. "You won't be here that long! You're pretty damn smug sitting there thinking you're going to fill out the rest of Burton's term. Well don't get comfortable. Have you given any thought to what you're going to do for a living when we kick your ass out of this office? Your ass is gone pal and so is Chick Yount. I'm charging that ignorant bastard with negligent homicide. He belongs in the penitentiary. I'm going to hang both of you!"

"You're not gonna hang anybody but yourself if you don't shut up," said Travis. "Let's see if you're still in a hanging mood after I've finished talking."

Shortly thereafter, Gordon emerged from the sheriff's office, red faced and sweating profusely, but smiling. He apologized to Melinda for his earlier rudeness, then hurried out of the building.

"Mr. Jackson sure left here with a different attitude," Melinda commented.

"He suffered a big blow to his ego," Travis replied. "Besides having to endure hearing about Sheriff Coley's death from the press, I out maneuvered him. He's okay now."

"Do you think you'll have trouble with him in the future?" Melinda queried.

"I don't think so," Travis answered. "Time will tell. He's looking towards the Governor's mansion and has a lot of support to make it happen. Politically, I'm small potatoes to'im. When he walked out of this office, I'm sure he had already forgotten about me."

"Sheriff," Melinda said quietly, "Pace Tanner and Seth Stephens are waiting to see you. I haven't been able to find Barnes."

"Keep trying," replied Travis. "Seth, Pace! Come on in and have a seat. This won't take long. We want the public to know we were prepared for an emergency like this. In the interest of administrative expediency I want to have my new organization in place before the day's over and announced on the front page of the Sunday morning newspapers. That means I have to dispense with formalities. The following promotions are effective as I speak. Seth, you're now my Chief Deputy and Pace, you're now my Administrative Assistant and Operations Coordinator. Promotions to fill the vacancies you leave will be made on the basis of your recommendations. Until this crisis is over, there will be extra duty and assignments for everybody. I want you to work until midnight tonight and be back at eight o'clock in the mornin'."

"Sheriff," Pace asked. "With our organization in place, what's the crisis?"

"I was getting to that, but it's still a good question," Travis replied. "Although it doesn't happen that often, when the top law enforcement official in a basically rural county like ours gets killed in the line of duty, the Bureau of Investigation's 'Unified Crime Report' shows that as soon as the word gets around, the local crime rate takes off like a bullet because the would be crooks assume nobody's watchin' the store.

Your work is cut out for you Seth. I suggest you call in all of your field supervisors, on and off duty. Get'em lined out for tonight and next week. Be sure they understand this is a bad time and we're depending on them."

Melinda opened the door.

"Sheriff," she said. "Deputy Barnes is on his way in."

"Fine," Travis replied. "Pace, get with Melinda and put together a press release for the promotions. Include photographs. Better do one for me too. See to it they come out in tomorrow mornin's newspapers. Melinda, as soon as Barnes gets here, send'im in!"

Carlton Barnes had performed well in his role as distributor and collector for his uncle. Conniving and clever, he selected bootleggers he could intimidate and easily control. When they had an exceptionally good week in sales, Carlton cut their take. They despised him.

Deputy Barnes entered. Flushed and unable to conceal his excitement, he launched into an obsequious display of regret and remorse so obvious, Travis thought to himself. "Carlton's already countin' the profits he inherited."

"I already know how sorry you are Barnes," the Sheriff said sternly. "Shut the door, but don't sit down. This won't take long. I don't wanna stink up my office any more than I have to! I"m gonna give you the best break you'll ever get in your life and it sickens me to do it. You can do one of two things. You can go to jail right now on charges of misappropriation and sell of confiscated liquor belonging to the county and the United States government, or you can resign and walk out of here a free man. What's it gonna be."

As the sheriff was speaking, Carlton's face went pale.

Stammering in surprise, he yelled. "Whoever told you that is a lying son-of-a-bitch!"

"What's it gonna be?" growled Travis. "You're gone either way."

"I'll resign, but I don't want nobody else to know why," Carlton answered.

"Nobody will know that doesn't already know," Travis growled. "If you ever show up at any of our stations again, it better be because you're under arrest. One other thing Barnes, all those bootleggers you had workin' for you already know that you're outta business. Now get the hell outta here before I change my mind."

Travis opened his office door.

"Melinda! Barnes just resigned for personal reasons. Help him word his letter of resignation and type it up for his signature."

"Seth," the sheriff continued. "See to it that Barnes turns in all of his county issue. Have one of your men escort him to the bulk evidence lock-up to pick up his personal belongings. Starting now, I want that building manned twenty four hours a day, seven days a week. Get a complete inventory tonight for my review tomorrow."

"That ought to be easy," Travis mumbled under his breath. "There's probably nothin' left to inventory!"

V

While Sheriff Coley was conducting the raid in Catfish, a well known roadhouse was preparing for another busy weekend.

Kirby Suggs' fifteen foot bullwhip flashed through the smoke filled room, cracking like a pistol shot as the startled crowd saw a cigarette snatched cleanly from the lips of his nervous attendant, Bernice Boles.

Even knowing Kirby's ability with the bullwhip, invariably, after a few drinks the customers would pool a wager they seldom won.

"All right, y'all losers!" Bernice shouted. "You'uns owe us five bucks. Now ante up."

Collecting the winnings she turned handing Kirby the money.

"That's mighty sweet of ye," he said, to which a customer in the small crowed replied. "She's sweet all right 'cause that's what she gits paid fer bein'!"

"I don't work if I don't get paid and I'm always sweet. All us girls are sweet. That's why Shelly calls this place, The Sugarbush."

The owner, Shelly Summers, was a large but shapely woman. Nice looking and always well groomed, her presence commanded respect. The employees liked her and so did the customers who frequented the popular roadhouse located in the remote and isolated northwest corner of the county.

Eight miles from the nearest town and accessible from the north or south by a single dirt road, popularity of the nightspot stemmed from its suggestive name, the variety of entertainment, a western style bar, inside restrooms and most importantly, it's safety. It hadn't been raided in years.

The exterior of the large rectangular shaped wood frame building was covered with unpainted cypress ship lap siding that with age had weathered to an aesthetically pleasing silver gray sheen. The coffee shop, serving sandwiches and breakfast had a separate entrance from the bar and dance hall.

Shelly was fortunate. She had luxuries that were rare in rural settlements. Running water, inside plumbing and electricity.

Several dams scattered strategically along the river supplied the surrounding towns with water and power. By providing right-of-way for water and electric transmission lines going to the more densely populated areas, the utility companies ran supply services to Shelly's business and residence.

The Sugarbush had the well deserved reputation for being a rough house dive frequented by ruffians, two bit gamblers, transients and fugitives. Nevertheless, on Friday and Saturday nights it attracted people from far and wide and all walks of life.

For the city crowd, spending a weekend evening at The Sugarbush carried with it the status symbol of a dedicated reveler.

Shelly kept six to eight women for pleasuring men. Occasionally she had the good fortune to hire girls from the northern states who were working their way to all points south. Even though they didn't tarry long, they were in great demand. The good ole' boys' in particular stood in line, money in hand, anxious to hear the distinctive accents and earn bragging rights for having literally screwed a damn yankee.

Shelly's western style bar was her most creative and profitable exhibit. Until their first visit to The Sugarbush, few of the customers had ever seen a bar of any kind, much less a western bar. The appeal seemed to come from being able to belly up to the bar as depicted in western movies, slap down two bits and order the bartender to pour you a shot of whisky. It was a real man thang!

Kirby coiled the whip, hung it on his belt clip and returned to the table where Bernice and several of the regular customers were talking and drinking coffee.

"Ye looked a little shaky standin' up there, Bernice," Kirby remarked.

"Yer mighty right I was shaky and rightly so," she whispered. "Ye damn near hit me 'cause ye been a drinkin'. We ain't doing this no more 'til ye sober up and that's final. Look at ye! It's jist now noon and ye been a drinkin' since ten o'clock this mornin'."

Bernice was the most recent addition to The Sugarbush brothel. She was five feet, three inches tall, slightly plump, large breasted and attractive. She didn't consider herself a whore, just a survivor trying to scratch out a living through the hard times doing what comes naturally. Other than paying customers, Kirby was the only one she slept with which garnered her privileged status, special treatment and much needed protection. Haughty and confrontational, Bernice ingratiated herself with the tough regulars by slipping them free drinks. In turn they protected her when Kirby wasn't around.

Kirby was five, ten, medium build with broad shoulders. He had a round face, high forehead and thin brown hair that was combed straight back without a part. Whether poker faced, smiling or laughing, his narrow almond-shaped eyes showed little change in expression. His appearance was made even more disarming and threatening due to a quirk of nature, a condition unceremoniously referred to as snake eyed, one brown eye and the other one blue. His wide mouth and thin lips appeared to be molded into a permanent defiant smirk which became more prominent when he was on a binge. Like most binge drunks, the longer he drank the more sullen and unpredictable he became.

Kirby lived in a small log cabin on the edge of his parents' nearby farm, taking time off each year to assist in the spring harvest gathering maple sap for making pure maple syrup and the fall harvest, picking apples. Other than that, he worked full time as manager of The Sugarbush dance hall and bar.

Shelly's favorite story was how The Sugarbush dance hall became a reality. According to her the name came first. In the spring of 1918, she bought the land with intentions of planting an apple orchard. At that time, the Suggs family was making maple syrup and invited her to watch the process. When she heard the expression, sugarbush, a new idea was born. A year later, Shelly opened the doors for business.

"Kirby," Bernice said curiously, "I been meanin' to ask ye somethin'. When yer gatherin' maple sap, how do ye git it outta them trees and make it into syrup?"

"With a lotta hard work," Kirby answered. "Ye use a brace and bit to drill a little hole in a whole helluva lot a maple trees, drive spiles in the holes and hang buckets on'em. The sap drips out a the tree through the spiles into the buckets. When a bucket gits full, ye pour the sap into a holdin' tank 'til it's full, then ye fill up the first pan a the sugarbush and put the heat to it. What we call, the sugarbush, is the whole setup ye use to cook the sap down 'til it thicken's into syrup. Now don't ask me to explain how we do all a that. Ye come watch next sprang and ye'll know."

"What's a spile look like?" she asked.

"It's a little old tube 'bout three inches long with a stop on top to hold the bail of the catch bucket."

"Yeah, Bernice," interrupted one of the men sitting at the table. "I'd like to drive my spile into yer sugarbush right now."

Joining the raucous laughter, she retorted. "I bet ye would and that's 'bout the size of your spile, too! Yer jist like all the rest of them clodhoppers that come in here with little ole cigarette peckers, complainin,' big pussy, big pussy!"

"Ye kin say what ye want woman, but I ain't got the first complaint. I please myself ever' time I use it."

Speaking to Bernice as she approached the table, another of the girls confided, "I jist came from the grill. Those doofus Hensley twins that ye like to pick at are back agin'. The cook is fixin'em up some hamburgers."

The same man Bernice was joking with a few minutes earlier spoke up again.

"You'uns talk 'bout the size a spiles, them two Hensley boys is hung like ponies."

"How do ye know that?" asked Kirby.

"Yeah," chimed in Bernice. "This oughtta be good!"

"I'll tell ye how I know," he replied. "A while back I wuz seinin' minnows fer fish bait under the bridge over Willow Creek when a car stopped right on the bridge. I heared talkin' and somebody gittin' outta the car. Next thing I knowed they was two streams of piss a hittin' the water downstream from me. I clum outta the creek and eased along one side so's I could see who it wuz. It wuz them twins all right. They got some awful tools on'em and I ain't a lyin'."

"Compared to ye, anything looks big," chided Bernice.

"I'm tellin' ye," he continued. "They unhuman! Ye'd have to see it to believe it. They ain't no women could take them prods; livestock maybe, but not no women. Anyways, 'bout that time I yelled, what the hell ye thank yer doin' up there? Ye oughtta seen'em jump, pissin' all over theirselfs. They piled in the car and took off. Funniest damn thang I ever seen."

The Sugarbush

Scoffing to hide her excitement, Bernice waved her hand in disbelief, remarking, "they might be freaks, but they still men and I've seen'em all."

"I tell ye what," he retorted. "Ye think I'm a lyin' and jist to prove I ain't, we'll take up a collection and pay fer ye to take them boys on, but ye gotta do'em both live so's we can all watch. Whatta ye say boys. You'uns wanna see a live double fuck!" The raucous crowd were already digging into their pockets.

"Put yer money where yer mouth is!" Bernice shouted.

"We got twenty five dollars, Bernice. Take it or leave it!"

"I'll take it. Where they at now?" Bernice asked the girl.

"Where they always at," the waitress answered. "By now they got their sandwiches and RC Colas. They don't never eat in the grill. They go up where they parked under that big poplar tree and eat. It's the same routine ever time they come. First they park under the poplar tree. Then they git outta the car and spit out their chaw a 'baccer. Then they scoop up a couple hands full a nasty old water from the drain ditch or a mud hole to wash out their mouths. Then they come in the grill and order RC Colas and hamburgers ever'time. If the cook sees'em drive in she starts workin' on their order before they ever git inside. It's plumb funny, no matter how many times I see'em do it."

"Is Shelly takin' her nap?" Bernice asked.

"No, she left fer town 'bout twenty minutes ago."

"Here, hold the money fer us. "Alright fellers, come on outside with me. If I kin persuade them boys to show off their plumbin', we'll see if it's workin' proper right yonder in the middle a the dance floor."

The Hensley brothers, Dooly and Dorsy, were not identical twins though they shared a distinct likeness. In their early twenties, they were over six feet tall with big boned angular frames. Exceptionally long thick arms were corded with bulging muscles that rippled at the slightest movement of their large calloused hands. Their protruding eyes, dark and distant, matched their unkempt black hair.

It was immediately obvious the two men were mentally slow. Most people who knew them attributed their condition to incest which was a common occurrence in the deep Blue Ridge Mountains from where the Hensley family had migrated following the Civil War.

As Bernice approached, the twins had just finished eating and were leaning against their car.

"Howdy, boys!" she said jovially.

"Howdy!" they replied.

"What're y'all boys doin' in this neck a the woods? Yer a fer piece from home."

"It ain't so fer," answered Dooly. "We lookin' fer farm work. Ain't found none yit."

"Well now if that ain't the shits, fellers. Jist so happens I got a middle that needs plowin' out right now and it won't take you'uns but a skosh to git done. Do ye wanna plow it fer me?"

"Yes'um," Dooly answered. "Me and Dorsy kin do it fer ye right now. How much ye payin'?"

Giggling, Bernice answered. "Damned if this ain't a switch! When yer finished and ye done a good job, I'll give you'uns a dollar a piece. How's that?

"Alright," said Dooly. "Where's the middle at and…

"Hold on a minute, fellers, I'm fixin' to show ye the middle, but then ye gotta show me how deep ye kin plow. If'n yer plow don't go deep enough, the deals off. If'n I let ye see the middle, you'uns gotta show me what yer gonna plow it with, okay?

"Yes'um. Where is yer mule and plow?" Dooly asked.

"Right under yer noses, dummy. Let's see if I kin perk 'em up!" With this, Bernice dropped the straps off her shoulders and pulled her blouse down, exposing her breasts.

She now had their full attention as penetrating gazes riveted on her bosom rising and falling with each heavy breath.

"That ain't all. This here's the middle that needs plowin'," she said, teasingly raising the front of her skirt to expose the triangle of pubic hair.

Bernice, flushed with her own excitement got the result she was looking for. Her eyes widened as she observed the large bulges appearing in the pants legs of the twins' blue bib overalls.

Shyly grinning and clearly aroused, the twins gently reached for her crotch.

The Sugarbush

"Hold on a minute," she said, dropping her skirt. "I showed ye the middle, now show me the plows."

Dorsy and Dooly just stood there grinning, chuckling and looking at each other.

"Haul'em out boys, times a wastin'. I gotta see'em 'fore ye git yer dollar. Here, I'll help ye," Bernice said excitedly, reaching to grab Dooly's bulge with one hand and unbutton his fly with the other.

Surprised, Dooly took a step backwards and pushed her hands away.

Up until this moment, the twins, in their excitement, had ignored everything else around them including Kirby and the others who had drawn closer and began roaring with laughter. Unaware of their growing erections, the frustrated brothers looked down at the bulging pants legs. Embarrassed and confused, the intensity of the spell was broken.

"Let's go, Dooly! They a laughing at us!"

"Oh, no," said Bernice. "I offered to pay you'uns, I done showed you'uns everythang and ye ain't showed me nothin'. You'uns ain't making no fool outta me! I'll not be outdone."

The soft, sexy voice gone, Bernice continued, shouting angrily. "Wait a minute, ye stupid morons. Unbutton them pants!"

"We're goin' away from here."

"Not yit, ye ain't!" she screamed, grabbing for the receding bulges.

Spontaneously, two powerful hands sent Bernice stumbling backwards to the ground.

"Kirby!" she shouted.

"Ye lummoxes," Kirby growled in a low menacing voice. "Git outta the way, Bernice," who moved to the side shouting, "Whupp'em Kirby, whupp'em!"

Kirby's whip moved in uninterrupted motion as the punishing lashes cut ugly wounds on the faces, necks and arms of the twins as they attempted to ward off the onslaught of blows.

The cook, who had watched through the window as the situation developed, came to the aid of the twins, spinning Kirby around, shouting. "Stop it, damn you!"

Then standing as a shield between Kirby and the stunned targets, she screamed in anger. "See what ye caused, Bernice Boles? These boys are harmless. They ain't done nothin' to none of ye. Ye ain't nothin' but a damn drunk bully, Kirby Suggs. Now leave'em be!"

Looking intently past the cook toward the brothers, Kirby began moving slowly backwards.

"Okay everybody!" Kirby shouted. "Show's over! Let's git back inside."

The cook turned to the twins. "Boys, I'm sorry 'bout this. Come in the grill and I'll treat ye to anything ye want."

Ignoring the invitation, Dooly and Dorsy stared at the retreating crowd. Still confused, after examining each other's wounds they got into the car and drove away.

Back inside the crowd was laughing at the spectacle they had just witnessed. Bernice and Kirby returned to their table.

"Here's yer money boys," Bernice shouted, secretly disappointed at having to give it back. "I'm keepin' five dollars fer my trouble. It don't look like we'll ever know the truth, but we had some fun anyways."

"The fun wuz jist gittin' started if'n the cook hadn't a got between us," Kirby replied. "I was fixin' to cut the overalls right off'n them goofy bastards. They wuz skirred shitless and a lookin' at me like a couple a mad dogs that ain't got sense enough to know they gittin' hurt."

As the Hensley twins drove away, they passed the Grimes brothers turning into the parking lot.

"We almost there, Jess," Jarred shouted, laughing and slapping his knee. "Jist thinkin' 'bout them naked whores layin' spread eagled on a bed is got my dick so hard I ain't got enough skin left to blink my eyes."

"Me too!" said Jess, joining the laughter. "By the time we git done workin' our way through'em, we won't be comin' nothin' but dust. There she is little brother, The Sugarbush. I'll park so's nobody can block us in. Seems like every time we come over here we end up leavin' in a hurry!"

"We parked a'plenty good, Jess. I cain't wait to git in there. Let's go!"

VI

Back out in Catfish, the situation remained tense at Cal Hagan's farm. Cal and his wife, Dessie, sat on the front porch watching the road. "Here they come," Cal said calmly. "I jist hope they don't turn in here to pester me. I don't believe I kin keep a straight face."

"Are ye shore that's the sheriff," Dessie asked.

"That's them alright, honey," he answered laughing. "Ye caint hardly tell 'cause Bobby ain't done a very good job a washin' their car."

"They ain't a slowin' down none," she commented. "I reckon they done had enough a Catfish and the Hagan boys fer one day. I pray ever'night you'uns'll quit the liquor bizness. Why don't you'uns go back to work at Dellinger's Mill or maybe work in town at one a them furniture factories."

"Dessie," Cal answered, "when we wuz workin' at Dellinger's Mill, we never stopped a makin' liquor. Now, makin' liquor's the onliest job we got outside a farmin'. We don't owe nobody a dime and we got a couple a snuff cans fulla cash money. Anyways, Dellinger's don't need no help. His mill ain't runnin' but two days a week and it's the same way ever'wheres else. Thangs is so bad that startin' next week, the Catawba River ain't gonna be runnin' but two days a week neither."

Dessie jumped on Cal's lap laughing, playfully pulling his hair. "You rascal. You wuz a talkin' so serious and I wuz a listenin' so serious, I pert near said, 'ye don't mean to tell me no sech a thang.'"

Dessie, short, petite and cute, had a sweet disposition and matching personality that made her a pleasure to be around. She wore bright colored, long billed handmade bonnets over her light brown hair to shade a peaches and cream complexion from the sun. When amused, her smile turned up doll-like in the corners, terminating in small dimples. When laughing, her telling blue eyes narrowed to elongated slits literally sparkling with pure delight.

At the age of six, Cal and Dessie met for the first time on their first day at White's Church School. Miniature in size, Dessie at once became the target of cruel teasing, but not for long. Cal came to her defense with such a fury, that for punishment, the teacher sat him on the dunce stool, hat and all. At recess, embarrassed and humiliated, Cal sulked in the far corner of the playground. Dessie walked over to where he was, looked up at him with those telling blue eyes and without so much as a word, smiled ever so sweetly and took his hand in hers. Cal quickly pulled away and stuck both hands into his pockets hoping no one had seen her obvious display of affection. It was love at first sight.

"Dessie, I'm goin' over to pick up Bobby," said Cal. "He baited up a fish basket and I wanna go with'im to check it. I should be home 'round dark."

"That's fine. I'll wait 'til ye git back to cook supper. We'll have catfish head soup and cornbread. By the way, how's that good lookin' rascal doin'?"

"He's okay. He wuz here this mornin', but ye wuz gone somewheres. I worry 'bout Bobby. Ye seen one of them warrants wuz fer him. I never even knowed 'bout the fight he had in town. He's jist like Pop, ain't got sense enough to walk away from trouble and ye never know how he's gonna take something. One time he'll stay calm and easy and the next time he'll fly crazy mad jist like Pop."

"Well now, Cal, don't worry. Bobby ain't but eighteen. One of these days he'll marry and settle down. He'll be all right!"

"I don't know 'bout that!" Cal replied. "Pop got married and he ain't never changed. Ye asked Mom, she'll tell ye."

"Ye go on now Cal," Dessie said. "We seen the sheriff's car headed back to Newton. The excitement's over 'till he comes back lookin' fer his jacket and them warrants."

"Not yit it ain't," Dessie. "I got the carbon copies of them warrants in my pocket. Me and Bobby's gonna have us a kangaroo court while we fishin'. I left the top copies in the sheriff's jacket. Maybe one a these days we'll mail it back to'im. That'll be shore to git his goat."

Cal and Bobby arrived at the lake and built a campfire. Then they hauled in the fish basket by a hemp rope tied to a sapling on the bank and attached to the basket at the bottom of the lake.

The Sugarbush

"Man, look at that!" Cal exclaimed as they pulled the basket out of the water. "They must be thirty catfish in there. What ye usin' fer bait?"

"Old bread," Bobby replied. "I been meanin' to try it and it shore works good. Corn gits too heavy and makes a mess when it sprouts. Chicken guts makes a worse mess and besides that, they nasty. Ye cain't hardly git the stink off'n yer skin and clothes."

"Where'd ye git the bread?"

"In town! I stopped by the Waldension Bakery. They'll give ye all the old bread ye want. They throws it away if nobody takes it. A lot a folks feed it to hogs and chickens. Some poor folks eats it."

"Let's git them fish cleaned right quick," said Cal. "Then we'll open court."

They put the basket back into the lake and cleaned the fish, placing them in a five gallon bucket of spring water.

"Okay Bobby. I got the warrants right here in my pocket," said Cal. "I'm the Judge. Yer the court crier and prosecuting solicitor."

They sat down beside the campfire.

"Mr. Court Crier," said Cal. "Will ye please bring this here kangaroo court into session!"

"All please rise," Bobby shouted. "The Catfish Kangaroo Superior Court of Catawba County is now in session, the Honorable Judge Calvin Hagan presidin'. Please be seated."

Cal began. "They's sixteen cases to be tried here today so y'all defendants raise yer right hand and swear on the Bible to tell the truth, the whole truth and nothin' but the truth so help ye God and if yer willin', answer I do so swear.

Mr. Solicitor, will ye please show some of them folks which is their right hand. Thank ye! I'm tryin' these cases like the ABC's. The first warrant here is fer Fentress Akers and the charge is petty larceny. Mr. Akers, the charge says that yer the mailman on rural route number three and in the course of deliverin' mail ye been stealin' roastin' ears outta Sorghum Hawley's corn field. How do ye plead, guilty or not guilty?"

"Yer Honor," said Bobby, "Mr. Akers pleads not guilty. I've questioned him and he says it ain't no sech a thang 'cause Sorghum

Hawley ain't got no corn field, least not yit. He jist planted his corn last week and it ain't even sprouted. Mr. Akers says he ain't been a stealin' corn, but he has been borrowin' hay to feed his saddle horse. Only problem is, the horse done et up all the evidence."

"I see," said Cal. "I'm throwin' this here case outta court on a technicality. Not knowin' what's bein' stole."

"The next warrant here is fer Bernice Boles and the charge is solicitin' prostitution. Now Miss Boles, the charge says ye wuz in town a walkin' the streets when ye come up on the recordin' clerk a city court and propositioned him right on Main Street. How do ye plead, guilty or not guilty?"

"Yer Honor," said Bobby. "Miss Boles pleads not guilty. I've questioned her and she says it's the other way 'round. Miss Boles says she was a mindin' her own business when this skin crawled, shriveled up, bug-eyed grub worm come up to her a leerin' and snirrin' and says: "Ye been in court enough times I know who ye are and ye know who I am and the trouble I kin cause ye." Then he hands her a door key and says, "meet me in room 204 at the Main Street Hotel. I'll be there in fifteen minutes. Ye better be ready 'cause I already am."

"Well sir, 'bout that time, a big corn fed redheaded woman come out a Kate's Bakery Shop a crammin' her mouth fulla donuts and hollered. Filbert Dingle, what ye up to with that woman?"

"Now Miss Boles figured that redheaded woman wuz Filbert's wife, so she says. "I'll tell ye what the two timin' varmint's up to. He give me this here door key and ordered me to meet him in a room at the Main Street Hotel. Here it is! Go meet'im yerself!"

"While that corn fed red headed woman wuz a beatin' Filbert over the head with a long handled parasol, Miss Boles snuck off down the street."

"Mr. Solicitor," cried Cal. "The facts shows that Miss Boles passed on the solicitin' key to Filbert's wife fer consummation, makin' her a whore by proxy. I'm throwin' this case out 'cause Fibert and his wife cain't tell on each other in court. Besides that, it ain't agin' the law to consort with a whore if'n she happens to be yer wife. Ye tell Filbert Dingle he's lucky his wife wudden carryin' a ax."

The Sugarbush

"The third warrant we got here is fer, Shelton Brooks, and the charge is runnin' a poker game and sellin' ten cent shots a whiskey on the side. How do ye plead, guilty or not guilty?"

"Yer Honor," said Bobby; "Mr. Brooks pleads not guilty. I've questioned Mr. Brooks and he claims the plaintiff did stop by his house where some friends and neighbors wuz having a friendly game a hearts, but he was already drunk when he got there. As he wuz a leavin', his wife caught up to him and he commenced to tell her that Mr. Brooks sold him the whiskey to git him drunk so's them friends and neighbors could cheat him outta two dollars playin' poker. Mr. Brooks claims the whole story is a bald face lie that's come outta the plaintiff's drunken mouth. Howsomever, Mr. Brooks says he wants to be fair, so's if'n the plaintiff'll come on over fer another game, he'll give'im a chance to win his two dollars back."

"Mr. Solicitor," Cal shouted. "Case closed. I'm askin' ye to thank Mr. Brooks fer bein' willin' to settle this charge outta court."

"Next case on the docket is a warrant fer Ross Elders and the charge is fraud. Mr. Elders, accordin' to this warrant, ye cruised a parcel of timber fer Coley Burton, the county sheriff, and he claims yer estimate a the board fee he got paid fer by the furniture factory wuz a whole lots less than what wuz cut off'n the stump. How do ye plead, guilty or not guilty?"

"Yer Honor," said Solicitor Hagan. "Mr. Elders pleads not guilty. I've questioned Mr. Elders and he says his estimate wuz inside a two percent a the timber cut. Mr. Elders says that after the cuttin' wuz finished, the sheriff sent Carlton Barnes, who jist happens to be the sheriff's nephew, out to cruise a second estimate by looking at the stumps the timber wuz cut from, and 'dadgum' if his tally didn't come out higher. Well now, Yer Honor, Mr. Elders swears that the onliest way Barnes could cruise timber by lookin' at stumps would be if he had a vision from God Hisself. Mr. Elders says he don't have no recollection of the Bible prophets cruisin' or prophesyin' timber estimates, but he does recollect that when Joseph was in Egypt workin' fer the Pharaoh, he did prophesy 'bout seven years a overflowin' grain harvests and reported his tally to the Pharaoh. Now a keepin' that in mind, Mr. Elders allows that Barnes taken his vision wrong and instead a lookin' at stumps to cruise timber, he's 'posed to be a lookin' at grain stubble that's left in the fields after this year's harvest so's he can prophesy how many bushels a acre the yield wuz 'posed to be and report what's been stole to President Hoover."

"Case dismissed," shouted Cal. "Mr. Solicitor, I'm orderin' ye to swear out a bench warrant for the arrest of this here feller, whatever his name is, and charge him with the crime of cruisin' when he's 'posed to be a prophesyin'."

"It'll be done, yer Honor," Bobby replied.

"Yer Honor, "I'm ponderin' whether or not ye'd be willin' to try two cases at the same time. The next warrant on the docket is fer Landis DeHart. The charge is fer violating his parole and his cousin, Garrett Simms, is charged with the same crime. But they's a big problem. DeHart's name starts with 'D' and Simm's name starts with 'S'. Now at the outset, ye declared ye wuz gonna try these cases like the ABC's. I don't intend to make a liar out a His Honor, the Judge."

"I thank ye fer that, Mr. Solicitor," Cal answered. "Bein' as how I'm the Judge, I kin do any damn thing I take a notion to, and bein' as how yer my brother, I'll allow it.

"Mr. DeHart and Mr. Simms, these two warrants read the same and the charges say ye violated yer parole from county jail. How do you'uns plead, guilty or not guilty?"

"Yer Honor," said Bobby. "Mr. DeHart and Mr. Simms plead not guilty. I've questioned these two polecats and they's tellin' a half a dozen different stories. They say that's 'cause every time they git their stories straight between'em, when it comes time to tell, they fergit which lie they decided to stick with."

So's the court and yer Honor don't git confused, I solved that problem. I had'em draw straws and Mr. DeHart won. He done all the talkin' and Mr. Simms kept his mouth shet so's they won't git caught a lyin'.

Mr. DeHart says Sheriff Burton let'em outta jail on parole so's they could work fer'im sellin' the whiskey he captures from them low down dirty moonshiners and bootleggers that won't give up breakin' the law no matter how nice he asks'em not to.

Mr. DeHart says the sheriff told 'em the only condition of their parole wuz that they don't cheat'im out of none of his hard earned liquor money.

The sheriff told'em he had to go to a heap a dangerous trouble to capture that liquor, but he didn't mind the danger 'cause he was doin'

The Sugarbush

the Lord's work and tithin' half the money he took in to the church. If yer stealin' from the sheriff, yer stealin' from God Hisself.

Mr. DeHart says it jist so happens that when him and Mr. Simms wuz in jail, they accepted the Lord Jesus Christ as their savior and ordained their selves Pentecostal preachers, witnessing and ministering to the convicts.

Mr. DeHart and Mr. Simms, bein' ordained preachers of the Gospel, claim they righteously done Sheriff Burton's biddin' to tithe half the liquor money to the church. Mr. DeHart kept half the money and Mr. Simms kept the other half. Mr. DeHart says the sheriff come plumb undone and revoked their parole, which accordin' to Mr. DeHart proves past a doubt that the sheriff's a lowdown hypocrite and of all his other bad habits, now he's took up a lyin' too. That's the truth of it."

"Mr. Solicitor," Cal said. "I wanna thank ye fer all yer hard work a sortin' out all the lies them two rogues been a tellin'. It appears ye finally come up with the god's honest truth."

"Thank ye, yer Honor," Bobby answered.

"Case dismissed," shouted Cal.

Next case is a warrant fer Bobby Hagan and the charge is assault and battery. The warrant claims that Mr. Hagan did inflict bodily injury 'round an 'bout the head and shoulders of the plaintiff while doin' a tap dance on his eyelids. How do ye plead, guilty or not guilty?"

"Yer Honor," Mr. Hagan pleads not guilty. I've questioned him and he says this case was settled the time it happened. Mr. Hagan says the plaintiff come askin' fer trouble, so Mr. Hagan obliged him. The town policeman wuz a pullin' out his handcuffs when Mr. Hagan told'im, if'n he wuz goin to jail, so wuz his horse, and a feedin' that horse would cost more than the fine wuz worth." Well sir, the police scratched his head and allowed that made good common horse sense and turned Mr. Hagan aloose."

"We'll nol pros this case," said Cal. "Mr. Solicitor, Ye tell that officer that we 'preciate him a usin' good horse sense to save our taxpayer's money.

The next two warrants is fer Dooly and Dorsy Hensely. Bein' as how these boys are twins, it's proper they be tried together. The charge is failin' to control a vehicle. It says here that the accused failed to negotiate a curve on Shady Grove Church Road, endin' up in Neil Hanson's hog lot pert near runnin' over Neil's blue ribbon Poland China brood sow. The investigatin' deputy says since the twins couldn't remember which one wuz a drivin' at the time, he wrote'em both a ticket. How do ye plead, guilty or not guilty?"

"Yer Honor," replied Bobby. "Dooly and Dorsy Hensley plead not guilty. I've questioned them two simpletons and they both tell the same story. Well, not z'actly, but pert near. They claim the charge wrote down on them tickets is not what happened 'cause they was the ones a drivin' the car and oughtta know better'n anybody. Howsomever, no matter how many times they told the deputy, he wouldn't pay'em no mind.

They do own up to the fact they got behind on their steerin', but deny they failed to negotiate' the curve a sayin', the fact wuz, they wuz jist a goin' too damn fast to make it."

"I see, Mr. Solicitor," said Cal. "That does make a tolerable difference. We a throwin' these cases out on a technicality. Thangs not bein' wrote down right."

"The next warrant's fer Jodeen Keller. He's accused a stealin' a whole carton of socks from the knittin' mill. It says here, Mr. Keller is the janitor at the knittin' mill. The knittin' room floor boss says on Friday evening after Mr. Keller mopped up and left fer the weekend, he noticed a carton of blue cotton socks a missin' from the store room. Readin' on, it says the floor boss swears that Jodeen Keller don't wear shoes 'cept on Saturday when he goes into town to play billiards and Sunday when he goes to church. The only time his stinkin' feet gits washed is when he walks through a mud puddle after it rains and it ain't rained in quite a spell.

On Monday evenin' when the accused showed up fer work, the floor boss noticed Mr. Keller's bare feet was plumb blue, the very same blue them missin' socks wuz dyed with. He knowed right then who stole that carton of blue cotton socks and fired Mr. Keller on the spot. How do ye plead, guilty or not guilty?"

"Yer Honor," said Bobby; "Mr. Keller pleads nolo contendere. I've questioned Mr. Keller and he says he come by that carton of blue cotton socks fair and square. The accused says he wuz in the store room a moppin' up when the floor boss come in a pesterin' him a sayin' if'n Mr. Keller would start a wearin' shoes to work, he'd

The Sugarbush

sell'im a pair a them blue cotton socks at the employee discount price. Well sir, Mr. Keller told the floor boss he wouldn't have a pair of them blue cotton socks 'cause they had holes in'em. At that, the floor boss flew mad, a callin' Mr. Keller some dirty names and allowed if'n Mr. Keller could find airy a hole in airy one a them socks, he'd give'em the whole carton full. So when Mr. Keller left work, he took that carton a blue cotton socks with'im 'cause every one of'em had a big hole in it where ye put in yer foot. There ye have it, yer Honor."

"Thank ye, Mr. Solicitor!" Cal replied. "This here's a clear cut case a welchin' on a bet. Mr. Keller kin keep the carton of blue cotton socks and I order ye to order the floor boss to put Mr. Keller back to work and pay him fer wages he's lost from bein' fired."

"Mr. Solicitor," said Cal. "This next warrant is swore out agin', Linus Lamar, and the charge is disorderly conduct not becomin' a gentleman. Howsomever, it don't give no details. How do ye plead, guilty or not guilty?"

"Yer Honor," said Bobby. "Mr. Lamar pleads not guilty. I've questioned the defendant and he declares he wuz standin' on First Street in front a the picture show house when he wuz hit with a terrible pain from somethin' he et. Naturally, he raised up his leg and let go a considerable fart which give'im instant relief. Well sir, a feller and a woman wuz a passin' by and this feller took a holt a Mr. Lamar's shoulder, spun'im 'round and hollered. "How dare ye pass gas 'fore my wife!" Now Mr. Lamar says he was embarrassed fer shore and never meant to be ungentlemanly, but he swears up and down he didn't know it wuz her turn."

"Mr. Solicitor," said Cal. "In front a the picture show with sech a crowd, I 'magine it would be easy to fart outta turn. Let's drop the charges agin' the defendant, but do caution'im to try and keep better count next time and if he fergits his turn, raise his hand and ask permission.

The next warrant brings up Pursy McCall and the charge is destruction a private property. It says here the plaintiff had a jenny mule that wuz bad 'bout gittin' outta the pasture and wound up in Mr. McCall's soybean field not doin' no harm. Mr. McCall, bein' unneighborly as he is, threatened to shoot the jenny mule if'n he ketched her there agin'. Seems the plaintiff's jenny come up missin', so suspectin' foul play, the plaintiff walked along the fence line between the two farms and found his jenny layin' in a red clay gully shot in her right side, dead and bloated. The plaintiff claims that Pursy McCall pulled the trigger that laid his jenny low. How do ye plead, guilty or not guilty?"

"Yer Honor!" Bobby replied, "Mr. McCall pleads not guilty. I've questioned the accused and he says that jenny mule got outta the plaintiff's pasture onto his property ever day 'cause the plaintiff don't keep his fences mended. He claims he's chased her out from tromplin' and eatin' up his crops so many times, she runs back onto her side a the fence soon as she sees Pursey a comin' outta the house of a mornin'. Mr. McCall claims he's left handed from birth and rests his defense on one statement a fact. How could a left handed man shoot a jenny mule in the right side?"

"Not guilty," cried Cal. "Even I know that ain't possible."

"The next warrant is fer, Chadwich Odom, and the charge is assault with a deadly weapon. It says here that the defendant has pulled his hawk bill knife on folks more'n wunzt. A couple months ago out in the parkin' lot at The Sugarbush, he cut up a feller real bad, but in the case 'fore us today, he never cut nobody, howsomever, he wuz talkin' on it. The town policeman heared'im tell the plaintiff, first I'm gonna cut the hide off'n ye. Then I'm gonna gut you out like a root hog. Then off comes yer peaked head!

How do ye plead, guilty or not guilty?"

"Yer Honor," said Bobby; "Mr. Odom pleads not guilty. I've questioned the accused and he says it's true he cut up a feller in The Sugarbush parkin' lot, but allows he figured to cut that feller jist barely enough to git a loose from him. Turns out it took a lotta slicin' to git his attention. In the charge Mr. Odom's facing today, he claims it started when him and the plaintiff, Polebean Sebastian, wuz a frog giggin' on Crooked Creek and wuz takin' turns with the giggin'. Chad wuz up on the bank a leanin' agin' a sourwood tree and Polebean wuz in the water fixin' to gig a bullfrog on the other side a the creek. Mr. Odom happened to look down and seen a big old harmless water snake a layin' under a log. So's he grabs up the snake and throwed it down 'round Polebean's neck, hollerin'. Look out, Polebean! Cotton Mouth moccasin! Well sir, after Polebean recovered from a near 'bout fatal heart palpitation, he come a wadin' 'cross the creek makin' plain how he wuz fixin' to beat Chad's eyes out. So

The Sugarbush

Chad, fearin fer his life, pulls out his hawk bill knife, opens it up and commences tappin' the blade on the bark of that sourwood tree, a sayin' in a threatenin' voice: 'Polebean, ain't it strange the way a woodpecker's bill is sharp enough to penetrate this here bark?' Well sir, Polebean stopped dead in the water, turned 'round, climbed outta the creek and left, takin' the sack of bull frogs with'im.

Next day, Mr. Odom was a walkin' down Main Street in town when he got hit behind the head with a balloon fulla stinkin' yeller water. At the same time, somebody hollered: 'Look out, Chad! Horse piss!' Well sir, passers' by wuz a laughin fit to die and when Mr. Odom turned to see who done sech a dirty trick, there stood, Polebean Sebastian, grinnin' like a 'possum. Now Mr. Odom does admit that hell flew into'im, so's he takes holt a Polebean and sure 'nuff did say he wuz gonna cut the hide off'im, then he wuz gonna gut him out like a root hog, then off wuz a comin' his peaked head. Only thang is, that there policeman never told the last thang Mr. Odom said to Polebean. The last thang he said he wuz gonna do, wuz kiss Polebean's ass and turn'm aloose!"

"Yes!" cried Cal. "And that's what the policeman should a done to Chadwich Odom! Another case throwed outta court on a technicality. Not a tellin' ever'thang."

"Now," Cal continued. "This next warrant wuz swore out by the game warden agin' Kirby Suggs and the charge is poachin' deer outta season. Seems the game warden come up on Kirby a skinnin' out a deer at his home place up yonder on the river. How do ye plead, guilty or not guilty?"

"Yer Honor," said Bobby. "Mr. Suggs pleads not guilty. I've questioned him and he claims that since it's his folk's property he's got a right to set gill nets in the river ever' sprang so's he kin catch fish to salt down fer next winter's stores. Well sir, it seems Mr. Suggs went down to the river to fish his gill nets and found a white tailed deer hung up in one of'em. Not knowin' what to do with this critter, he pulls out his huntin' knife, cuts its throat, untangled it outta the gill net and carried it home to butcher. Well sir, wouldn't ye know, along comes Griff Hance, the game warden. Not knowin' when the poachin' season starts, he writes up Mr. Suggs anyways. Now then, Mr. Suggs says it ain't fair 'cause if'n Griff Hance'll keep his deer

Jerry S Jones

outta Kirby's gill nets, Kirby'll keep his fish outta Griff Hance's corn fields."

"Case dismissed," shouted Cal. "Ye tell Griff he oughtta take Kirby up on the offer."

"Mr. Solicitor," said Cal. "This next case is a little on the touchy side. It's swore out fer Taylor Upton, Jr. who's been charged with cruelty to dumb animals. Now we knows that Junior's daddy's a well thought of dairy farmer and a big land owner out in Catfish. So we want to help Junior if'n we kin. It declares here that one a the hired hands seen Junior standin' on a stump a pokin' one of his daddy's milk cows. Now Mr. Solicitor, I hope ye understand what I mean by pokin'? I jist can't bring myself to say it no plainer. Fer twenty two years old, ye'd think Junior would a knowed better. How do ye plead, guilty or not guilty?"

"Yer Honor," replied Bobby. "I do know what ye mean by pokin' and thank ye fer not embarrassin' this court with plainer talk. Junior Upton pleads not guilty, yer Honor. He claims he feels sorry fer them milk cows 'cause they git their tits played with twice a day, but don't get bred but wuntz a year. He declares if'n he'd a knowed folks wuz gonna make such a fuss over it, he'd a married that durn cow."

"I'll tell ye what," said Cal. "We gonna drop the charges agin' Junior 'cause ignorant as he is, he showed he wuz willin' to do the honorable thang. Howsomever, the court cain't allow Junior to live on in ignorance 'bout sech thangs. Jist so happens, we got two self-ordained Pentecostal preachers a sittin' back there and the court hereby orders Reverend DeHart and Reverend Simms to take Junior Upton under their wings a Bible learnin' so's they can learn him 'bout what, how, when, and who ye do thangs to. That a way, this won't come up no more."

"Amen to that, Judge," replied Bobby.

"Looky here, looky here," said Cal. "We done come up on the last case to be tried in this here court today, Mr. Solicitor. This last warrant is agin' Casey Workman and the charge is assault with intent to inflict bodily harm, but it don't give no details. How do ye plead, guilty or not guilty?"

"Yer Honor," replied Bobby. "Mr. Workman pleads not guilty. I don't know a nobody in this here county that ain't acquainted with Casey Workman. 'Long as I been a livin', Mr. Workman and his wife

The Sugarbush

Sue's been a tendin' a booth at the Farmers Market over in Newton sellin' herbs and home remedies they raise on their farm. This trouble started when the plaintiff, Snort Johnson, come over to their farm complainin' that he wuz a goin' deaf. Well sir, Mr. Workman asked him jist how bad his hearin wuz?

Snort asked "What'd ye say there good buddy?"

So's Casey hollared louder and asked him agin'. Snort heared'im that time and answered that his hearin' wuz so bad, he couldin' hear his own self fart, and inquired if Mr. Workman could help'im.

Mr. Workman told Snort that he come to the right place 'cause he did indeed have a remedy he knowed would help. At that, Mr. Workman broke out a gallon jug of stock from boiled skunk cabbage, directin' Snort to drink a cupful right then and a half cup three times a day thereafter.

Well sir, Snort drunk down a cupful on the spot and as he was a walkin' off, he hollered back to Mr. Workman and asked'im if'n he was shore the remedy would help his hearin'? Mr. Workman hollered back sayin' he didn't know if'n it'd help his hearin' or not, but it wuz guaranteed to make'im fart a whole lots louder!

Snort went on maddern' a hornet mindless a the fact that fifteen minutes later he could hear hisself a fartin' loud as a horse mule draggin' logs to the sawmill. He swore he'd git even and git back ever' cent a his money somehow another.

Mr. Workman and his wife always keep a fresh ten gallon batch of home brew they work off in the tater cellar in a ten gallon crock. When they come in from the Farmers Market ever' day they have a sip or two. Well sir, they noticed the crock was emptyin' mighty fast. Well now they said, somebody's a stealin' our beer when we at work, but we know how to find out who it is."

In the sprang when farmers' plants corn they dip the kernels in crotin oil so's the crows won't scratch it out and eat it. At first the crows will dig out a kernel or two and eat it, but after they git a bad belly ache and the shits, they pass the word on to the rest a the crows so's they won't make the same mistake. Casey figured if'n it worked fer crows, it sure oughtta work fer a home brew thief. Jist so happened they was a quart of crotin oil left over, so, Mr. Workman mixed it in with what wuz left of the home brew.

Jerry S Jones

When they come in from work the next evenin', ole Snort was a layin' agin' a shade tree in their front yard a prayin' to die and shittin' all over hisself. "I'm a surely gonna die," he was a moanin', askin' if Mr. Workman could git him out of his misery.

"Yes sir, I can," Mr. Workman told him. "Ye git on home and drink lots a water."

"Is that all I have to do to git cured?" Snort asked.

Mr. Workman told Snort it would cure him fer shore, but if he wanted to stay cured, he better quit a drinkin' home brew, 'specially other peoples."

"Not guilty," shouted Cal. "Justice was rightly served, bellyache and all."

Mr. Solicitor, as ye knows, me and yerself gits paid our wages outta the fines we collect and today we ain't collected nothin'. I don't care who it wuz filed all them there charges, ye send ever' one of'em a bill fer twenty five dollars to cover court costs. We aim to git paid. This here court's adjourned 'til I tell you different."

As Cal and Bobby watched the last warrant go up in flames and turn to ashes, they laid back on the ground laughing.

"If'n we wuz runnin' court they wouldn't be nobody in jail," said Bobby. "Them folks we jist turned aloose would be mighty surprised to know what the sheriff wuz chargin'em with, but if'n they knew what we tried'em fer, our lives wouldn't be worth a plug nickel."

"Yes sir," replied Cal. "Now ever' time we run across one of them folks, it's gonna be hard to keep a straight face. I heared a some a them people, but the onliest ones we know personal besides yerself, is Fentress, Casey, Pursey, Junior and the Hensley twins."

"Yeah!" said Bobby. "Do ye reckon we oughtta warn'em?"

"No, we better not!" laughed Cal. "Dessie asked me the same thang and I told her it wouldn't do no good 'cause I'll betcha right now them warrants is bein' done over fer servin' next week. I ain't worried 'bout'em, but if'n talk gits back to the sheriff, he'll be after us like stink on shit, if'n he ain't already. Word's bound to git around 'bout all we done to'em. We the onliest ones knows 'bout them warrants and we better keep it thatta way. Let's git on to the house. Dessie wants ye to eat supper with us. I told her we'd be home 'round dark. By the time we git there, it will be."

VII

At The Sugarbush, it was 6:30 PM. A heavy overcast made it seem more like night time. Kirby Suggs pushed his chair away from the table. "I'm goin' out back to the toilet. I'll be back in a few minutes."

Bernice nodded her head.

The country band that had been playing continuously announced they were taking a break. Jess, Jarred and several ruffians were sitting at a table talking to one of the girls who was giving a detailed description of the incident that Bernice had instigated earlier in the day which culminated with Kirby flogging the Hensley twins with his bullwhip.

"We know Kirby Suggs," said Jarred. "Who's Bernice Boles?"

"She ain't been workin' here very long. You'uns probably ain't never seen her before."

"If she's in here now, point her out to us," said Jess.

"Her and Kirby jist come in a while ago. She's a sittin' by herself over at that table near the back door."

"Well now, like she told them Hensley idiots this mornin', ye wanna do some plowin? Come on, Jarred. Let's see if'n we kin git that good lookin' hussy to show off her plumbin'."

Jess' and Jarred's smiles turned to insolent, tight lipped sneers as they sauntered towards Bernice who was unaware of the menace approaching from behind her.

The brothers, one on each side of the chair, leaned forward over the table and looked down into her startled face.

"Well now perty thang, who might ye be?" Jess said in a coarse whisper.

Bernice knew trouble when she saw it. Glancing nervously at one glaring face and then the other, she tried to fake composure. "I'm Bernice," she answered. "Who are you'uns?"

"I'm Jess Grimes and this here's my baby brother, Jarred, all two hundred and twenty pounds of'im. We hankerin' to do some real personal business with ye. We wantin' to see if yer plumbin's a workin proper."

"Sorry boys! Ye don't gotta see nothin' 'cause I kin tell ye right off, my plumbin' ain't a workin' proper fer what you'uns is a lookin' fer. That's why I ain't a workin' today. Come on back next week and I'll be glad to accommodate ye."

"That ain't what we heared," Jarred replied.

"I don't care what ye heared. I done told ye I ain't a workin' today."

"That's gotta be a lie comin' outta yer mouth woman!" interrupted Jess. "Why jist this mornin' ye wuz out front offerin' to show Dorsy and Dooly Hensley a good time; even showed'em yer tits and ass. It ain't nice! Matter a fact, it's down right insultin' to me and my brother that ye'd favor them two above us. They wuz two a them and they's two a us. If'n ye wuz willin' to take them on double and ain't done it, me and Jarred done made up our minds to take their place. Now, git off'n yer ass and let's git to it!"

With this, they jerked Bernice to her feet, sending the chair she was sitting in tumbling backwards.

The crowd in the dance hall grew hushed. Just then, Kirby, who had come back inside, barked, "Git yer hands off'n her! She ain't a workin' tonight!"

They glanced at Kirby disdainfully. Ignoring his half-hearted command, Jess yanked the blouse off Bernice's shoulders down to her waist, exposing her heaving breasts.

"Looky there, Jarred! In a few minutes ye'll be suckin' on one a them big tits and me on the other'n. Now women, lift up that skirt like ye done this mornin' so's we kin see what we a payin'fer."

"Kirby," Bernice cried, trembling in anger.

Kirby yanked the whip from his belt clip and slapped it against his leg. "I said let her go. Let her go now!"

"Ye see that, big brother?" Jarred growled. "Suggs is threatenin' to give us a floggin'."

Kirby's bouncers started to move in closer.

"Stay right where yer at fellers!" said one of the ruffians standing nearby. "Jess and Jarred ain't by theirselfs neither."

"Ye done done it now, Suggs," said Jess. "Ye want this whore, come and git her."

Shelly burst on the scene.

"Stop right there!" she cried. "Y'all boys always been welcome here, but yer trouble ain't."

The Sugarbush

"Jist hold it boys! Ever' body calm down. Ya'll letta go a Bernice and leave here," Shelly said in a soft conciliatory tone.

"We're a leavin' all right," Jess snarled, backing slowly toward the front door. "We'll turn aloose a yer whore on the way out. Kirby Suggs, the reason ye stay holed up in here is 'cause ye ain't nothin' but a snake eyed, yeller bellied, pigshit kyard. Me and little brother'll be back. Ye gotta git outta here sometime and when ye do, we'll be waitin' on ye. We gonna hang ye with that bullwhip and watch ye quiver like a dyin' chicken with yer tongue lollin' out a lickin' yer Adam's apple.

"Goddamn it Jess," Shelly shouted. "You'uns shorely as hell won't threaten to kill a man fer doin' his job."

"That weren't no threat," Jarred shouted. "It's a nat'ral born fact! We'll be back and don't ye fergit it.

And perty thang here, we gonna corn hole yer fat ass. When we git done a reamin' out yer asshole, ye'll be a shittin' in a bushel basket."

Jess and Jarred began to snicker and laugh.

"Ye think we don't see that shot gun ye holdin' behind ye, Shelly Summers!"

"Ye goddamn right I got a shotgun and ye know I'll use it. You'uns know I don't allow nobody tearin' up my place and runnin' off my customers. What the hell's got into y'all? You'uns started this. Nobody done a damn thang to you'uns! Now turn Bernice aloose!"

With a powerful heave, they sent Bernice tumbling across the dance floor and during the distraction, faded into the darkness of a gathering storm.

"Quick, lock that door!" Shelly shouted. "Whoever's on the back door, slip out 'round front and be shore ye see'em leave. If'n they don't leave, let me know. Kirby, come with me up on the stage. Trouble like this is contagious as hell. We gotta talk to this crowd and git'em settled down damn fast. I don't want no more trouble tonight. Bernice, go wash up and change yer clothes. Ever'thang's alright now. Come on back out quick as ye kin and act like nothin's happened; it'll help calm the customers."

Jerry S Jones

The bouncer guarding the back door came back in. "They wuz already drivin' off when I got 'round to the front," he whispered to Shelly. "I watched'em 'til they wuz outta sight."

"I ain't takin' no chances, Kirby," said Shelly. "Send one a the boys out front to watch. He kin sit in my car and check ever'body comin' in, and tell him to stay awake! I don't think they'll be back, at least not tonight. If'n they do, we'll be ready fer'em."

Fights were common place at The Sugarbush, especially on weekends. It wasn't long before the altercation was forgotten and things were back to normal. Kirby and Bernice returned to their chairs at the table close to the back exit door and continued talking, watching the crowd with amusement.

"If'n people don't git mean or too drunk, they shore kin do some funny thangs," Bernice remarked. "They keep ye a laughin' all the time. Speakin' a drinkin', yer gittin' perty high yerself, Kirby!"

"I might be a little unsteady on my feet, but I'll be fine by the time we git to the cabin."

"I'll let ye know in the mornin'," Bernice replied with a sarcastic snicker.

"Kirby," she continued, "I need to go to the bathroom really bad. The parlors are all full, they's a line a waitin' at the others and I ain't 'bout to bother Shelly in her private quarters. Will ye break in the line and let me go ahead a them women?"

"Ye know better'n that," he replied. "Ye can use the outside toilet jist like we always do when we gotta packed house. Ye ain't no better'n the rest of us."

"I ain't a goin' out back," she whispered. "Ye heared what them Grimes' said and besides, it's a rainin'!"

"They is a helluva thunder storm movin'in, but it ain't here yit. And them loud mouth Grimes' is jist that, all talk."

"If'n they all talk, how come I got jerked around, my clothes ripped off and my ass bounced all over the dance floor in front a all them customers? I didn't see nobody jumpin' in to save me."

"I'm sorry it happened that a way and I'm sorry it wuz you," he replied sympathetically, "but it wuz best handled like we done it. They's a guard on the front a sittin' in Shelly's car. If they come back, which they won't, he'll let us know. I'll go out with ye and stay

The Sugarbush

'til yer ready to come back in. We a wastin' time Bernice! Come on; let's git it over with."

The guard on the back door had asked one of the girls to watch the door while he took a lunch break.

"Unlock that door and let me outta here quick!" Bernice whispered to the girl.

"That storm's a comin' in fast!" Bernice shouted above the thunder as she ran to the outhouse. Already fearful and apprehensive, she entered the small dark enclosure cautiously.

Kirby allowed enough time for Bernice to get seated to go about her business, then he picked up a rock and threw it striking the side of the small building. The uneasy quiet inside the confined space resounded with the impact.

Bernice screamed, "damn ye, Kirby Suggs. That wudden funny! Ye ain't worth killin'."

Kirby laughed, shouting. "I jist figured to git ye off to a good start so's we could git back inside 'fore it pours rain!"

Several minutes later, Bernice yelled again. "Damn it, Kirby, quit carryin' on at me. It's bad enough havin' ye standin' out there while I'm doin' somethin' personal, much less agervatin' me and makin' it worse!"

Kirby's response was drowned out by the rising wind, thunder, and sporadic raindrops splattering on the tin roof.

Glad to be back in the fresh air, Bernice yelled. "Where ye at ye ornery devil? Oh there ye are. Yer mighty right 'bout one thang," she said. "Ye ain't too steady on yer feet. Come on, damn it! I don't want my hair gittin' wet.

Bernice walked quickly to where Kirby was standing and pulled him by the hand. Come on!"

Shelly, sitting at her private table in the grill, was approached by Marcella Macon, the girl who helped her manage the brothel.

"We need to talk," Marcella said anxiously. "Ever since ye took in Bernice, trouble 'round here's got worse ever' day. It ain't jist the hold she's got on Kirby which is bad enough, it's the other girls too. They got it good here same as me. Now for the first time ever, they a gripin' and grumblin' all the time 'bout nothin' and Bernice is back of it all. If somebody don't straighten her out or send her a packin', she's gonna mess thangs up fer all of us!"

"I think yer right," Shelly replied. "Right now I'm plenty riled 'bout the trouble her and Kirby brought on today and that ain't all! When Kirby took Bernice to town awhile back, somehow another she stirred up a fuss with Burton Coley, the Sheriff, and dragged Kirby into the fracas. Now the sheriff's got it in for both of'em. I've knowed Burton all my life. We got an arrangement that's good for me and him both and well worth the money. I can't stand back and let nobody mess that up. After the way this day's gone, they ain't no time like the present to set thangs right. If'n it means either one or both of'em's gotta go, it's gonna be done before anything else gits haywire."

"Go git Bernice," Shelly ordered. "We'll talk to her first. I'll talk to Kirby later."

Finding no one sitting at the table Kirby and Bernice occupied earlier, Marcella approached the doorman on the rear exit.

"Are Bernice and Kirby out back?" she asked.

"If'n they are," he answered, "they're gittin' wet 'cause it's pourin' rain. I been sittin' here for over a hour and ain't nobody gone out or come in. Maybe Bonnie knows where they at. She watched the door for a half hour while I went to eat supper."

Marcella found Bonnie standing by the jukebox playing records while the band was on break.

"Bonnie," Marcella asked. "When ye wuz on the back door, did Kirby and Bernice go out?"

"They shore did," she said, laughing. "Bernice said if she didn't git to the toilet fast she was gonna mess her drawers."

"Did they come back in while ye wuz still on the door?"

"Not while I wuz there they never. They prob'ly come back in after I left. Ask whoever's on the door now."

Marcella returned to the rear doorman.

"Kirby and Bernice went out when Bonnie wuz relievin' ye but they never come back.

"It's plain enough to see what's goin' on here, the doorman replied. It's Bernice's night off and Kirby don't come back to work 'til Monday. They mustta went to his cabin fer the night."

The Sugarbush

"I fergot 'bout that," she replied. "That's prob'ly where they at, but none of us girls is 'posed to leave without tellin' Shelly and that goes fer Bernice too?"

Marcella unlocked the door, pushed it open and stepped out under the stoop that covered the doorway. The small overhead light lit the area dimly as she peered out into the torrent of rain. Just as she started to step back inside, lightning momentarily lit up the edge of the woods where her gaze was fixed.

She turned pale and felt faint, quickly stepping back inside and locking the door.

"Pourin' down out there ain't it Marcy," the doorman remarked.

"Yes it is," she answered, then hurried back to the grill to find Shelly.

Marcella sat down at Shelly's table.

"What's wrong with ye Marcy?" Shelly whispered. "Yer pale as a ghost!"

"Over a hour ago, Bernice went out back to use the toilet and Kirby went with her. They ain't never come back in. A few minutes ago I went out on the stoop to see if I could see anythang. I don't know why I done it, I jist did. Lightnin' lit up the edge of the woods behind the outhouse and I seen a feller standin' under a tree watchin' the back door. It made my blood run cold 'cause I know it's them Grimes' brothers come back to make trouble. I'm scared to death a them two."

"Where's Kirby and Bernice," Shelly asked, angrily.

"They over at Kirby's I guess. Bernice took off with'im and didn't tell nobody."

"I figered as much," Shelly replied. They over there shackin' up and a'leavin' me to clean up the damn trouble they started. When they git back I'll straighten out both of'em. Ye wait right here. I'm goin' out back to see if this shotgun and a load a birdshot in ass won't convince Jess and Jarred Grimes that I mean bizness!"

Shelly hid the shotgun under her coat, covered her head and ran out the grill entrance to the car. She jerked opened the door and jumped into the front passenger seat.

"Start the car!" she shouted to the guard. "Drive 'round back and shine yer lights towards the edge a the woods behind the outhouse."

As the car lights lit up the edge of the woods, Shelly and her driver grasped their faces in horror. Kirby was hanging by his whip from the branch of a tree, his bulging eyes wide open, his tongue protruding grotesquely from his mouth.

Bernice was lying face down near his feet, her white skin shining wet in the headlights.

"Let's go git Kirby!" the guard yelled. "Oh hell, that is Kirby! Let's go git some help!"

"No!" said Shelly. "Sit still! Jist sit still 'til I tell you different. I've got to git out and see if'n they're alive."

"I ain't gittin' outta this car! They dead Shelly! They dead! Bernice ain't movin'! I ain't touchin no dead people."

"Damn it, ye don't have to git out. Set still!" she ordered.

Shelly didn't care about getting wet. She walked slowly toward Bernice. Kneeling down she checked the small white wrist for a pulse. There was none! Rising, Shelley walked slowly to Kirby's body twisting and swinging in the wind. He was cold and stiff."

Two hours earlier, impatient, irritated and partially blinded by the rain, Bernice tugged at Kirby's hand, looking up just as his face was lit up by a shimmering flash of lightning. The puzzled expression that leaped from her eyes quickly changed to one of terror. She stumbled backward trying to scream and fighting for breath, but only choking gasps and guttural garble leaked from her paralyzed vocal cords.

Suddenly, a large callused hand grabbed her by the hair, followed by a stunning blow to the left side of her face. Forced down on her knees, two legs clamped around her neck, squeezing so tightly she could hardly breathe. An arm reached under her waist lifting her up to a bent over position, the other hand stripping down her blouse, groping her breast savagely. From behind, her skirt was ripped down to her ankles.

Terrified and in pain, Bernice's racing thoughts revealed her worst fear. It was the Grimes' brothers.

Suddenly she was penetrated with a thrust so violent it lifted her feet off the ground. Two hands clasped under her midriff now held her up as the furious pounding in and out of her suspended body began. The audible heavy breathing, grunts and groans grew louder

The Sugarbush

as the pounding thrusts intensified, coming faster and faster then gradually coming to a halt. Finally she felt her feet touch the ground.

"It's my turn now!" Bernice heard an excited whispering voice say. "Hold her! Hurry up!" As the attacker behind withdrew from inside her, she dropped to her knees. The legs clamped around her neck released. Begging and pleading in a sobbing whimpering voice, Bernice began to crawl away in a futile attempt to escape the torment.

She heard low chuckling as she was grabbed by the hair and jerked violently backwards, reversing her direction. Once again her head was clamped between a choking vice of legs. Her eyes widened and her face distorted in agony as the perverted plunge sank into her body. Her legs suspended in mid-air began to thrash instinctively in a hopeless attempt to run. Her bleeding fingers raked the ground repeatedly.

The internal mauling from the relentless pounding was more than Bernice could bear. Unconscious, her thrashing legs came to a halt, falling limp and still like a puppet moving only to the punishing rhythm of cruel thrusts slamming into her body.

VIII

It was 10:15 PM. Travis sat in his office writing a report detailing the bizarre events of the day. "Sheriff Gant," Melinda said. Seth is on the phone. He's got an emergency."

Travis answered the phone and listened intently. "Could it be a crank call?" he asked. "Okay, I'm on my way."

"Pace," he said incredulously. "I just got a call from Seth at the Hickory Station. They're responding to a call from The Sugarbush roadhouse. The owner says two of her employees have been murdered. That's all Seth knows right now. Let's go!"

The next morning out in Catfish, everything was quiet and peaceful, but not for long. Cal and Dessie were eating breakfast when they heard the galloping hoof beats of a rapidly approaching horse.

"That'll be Bobby," said Cal. "He wuz gonna lay in where the liquor wuz hid to see if Jess and Jarred Grimes would try to steal it."

Bobby dismounted, laughing as he burst through the backdoor into the kitchen. "They wuz there at daylight," he cried. "When they left here last night I figured they'd try to steal our liquor.

It's a good thang we moved it 'fore they had the chance. They kin have the still, the bottom's damn near out of it anyways."

"I'm mighty proud y'all ain't workin' with them two no more," Dessie said. "Sit down here Bobby and drink yer coffee while I fix ye some sausage and eggs."

"I see yer riding Pop's sorrel this mornin'," said Cal.

"Yeah!" answered Bobby, "Here lately he's been behaving' like he's got good sense. Pop wanted me to ride some a the corn out of'im 'fore Fentress Akers comes to git'im today."

"Pop sold him to Fentress?" Cal asked.

"Yep! Fentress loves that horse. He's been after Pop to buy'im ever since he first laid eyes on'im. Pop bought'im 'cause he was a calvary horse and the Army don't buy nothin' but the best. He wondered why they put sech a good lookin' horse up fer auction and it weren't long 'fore he found out why. It's funny now that ye look back on it, but it weren't funny then."

"What happened?" Dessie asked.

The Sugarbush

"Oh, me and Sis was gittin ready to go to a church social. Pop harnessed ole red and hooked him up to the buggy. 'Bout then, that devil took to rarin' and kicking' like he wuz crazy. Pop grabbed'im by the ears, threw his legs 'round ole red's neck, and the fight wuz on. Ye ain't never seen nothin' like it. They wuz all over the barnyard with Pop a hangin'on the horse's neck and cussin' ever breath. We thought shorely ole red wuz gonna kill'im, but Pop hung on and wrestled'im down. Then he jumped in the buggy and down the lane they went. Pop was a beatin' ole red with the buggy whip plumb unmerciful. Down the county road they went a tearin' as fast as that horse could run. They went plumb outta sight toward Foggy Bottom Creek and in a little bit, here they come back and they ain't slowed down a bit. When they got back to the front yard they wuz both calmed down. Pop jumped outta the buggy and handed the reins to me. 'You'uns go on now. He ain't got no fight left,' Pop said. He wuz right too. Ole red pranced off perty as ye please. Ye never knowed when somethin' wuz gonna sets'im off. Mom says that horse is jist like Pop and me. Pop thinks ole red got shell shocked or somethin'. That's why the Army got rid of'im. Pop's been wantin' to git shed of'im jist as bad as Fentress wanted to buy'im, but he wuz afraid the crazy devil would hurt somebody if'n they didn't know how to handle'im. Pop done told Fentress over and over agin' how dangerous that horse kin be. Ye think Fentress cares; hell no! Pop finally give in.

Me and Mom and Sis never laughed so hard as we did when they was makin' the trade.

Ye oughtta heared it. Fentress asked Pop if the horse had a name. Pop says, "He shore does. His name is Us."

"Ole Fentress asked. What the hell kinda name is Us?"

"Well sir, Pop says. That wuz his name when I bought'im. Bobby, go to the barn and brang'im up here."

"I led ole red up to the front yard and handed the halter rope to Fentress."

"Jist looky there, Fentress," Pop hollared, "Somebody likes that name so good they done burned it right into his left front shoulder."

"When Fentress seen the U. S. brand, he had a good laugh but I got a feelin' that name ain't gonna stick. Anyways, he's comin' to git'im today. He's gonna carry the mail on'im when the roads is bad. That old bay horse Fentress is been a ridin' fer years died on'im.

While Dessie cleaned up the kitchen, Cal and Bobby moved to the front porch just in time to see a car turn into the driveway.

"Here comes Casey Workman and Sue," Cal remarked. They stay over in Newton most ever' Saturday night after the Farmers Market closes. They always come home in time to go to preachin' over at Thyatira Lutheran Church.

Git out and set a spell," shouted Cal. "Dessie's in the kitchen, Miss Sue, jist go right on in."

Sue, her expression serious and concerned, hurried up the porch steps and into the house.

"Looks like y'all ain't heared the news," said Casey. "Looky here at the Sunday paper headlines. Yisterday mornin' right here in Catfish, jist down the road a piece at the old Cline place, Sheriff Coley got killed by one of his deputies. Then of a evenin' a man and woman wuz murdered that works at that roadhouse 'way up yonder on the river near 'bouts to the old J. B. Little Ferry."

Like everyone else, Cal and Bobby were shocked at the news but for more personal reasons.

"Who wuz they?" Cal asked.

"I fergit. It'll tell ye in the paper there."

After a lengthy discussion, Casey changed the subject.

"That's not all I come by fer," he said. "Y'all cannin' anythang?"

"Yeah," Bobby answered. "How much ye want?"

"I need a five gallon demijohn. I run out yisterday evenin'. Anytime the moon's full, folks drinks lots a liquor."

"We got it. Drive yer car down to the barn and I'll load it up fer ye."

Bobby loaded the whiskey into the trunk of Casey's car and they returned to the house.

After Casey and Sue left, Bobby said to Cal. "Them two that got murdered up the river wuz named, Kirby Suggs, and Bernice Boles. That's two a them warrants that won't never git served. Thanks fer the breakfast, Dessie," Bobby shouted. "I'm gonna git on back to the house to tell Mom and Pop the news then I'm goin' seinin' fer minnows. Pop needs some bait for crappie fishin'."

The Sugarbush

It was 7:00 on Sunday morning before interviews with witnesses at The Sugarbush murder scene were completed.

Travis arrived at his office at 8:30. Melinda was already there. "It sure didn't take long to spend the night at my house," he said with a chuckle.

"You look tired," Melinda remarked. "I hope you did better than me. I didn't sleep at all."

"I was jokin'," said Travis. "None of us have had any sleep. I just got back from the murder scene. Seth and Pace are in Catfish checking on the whereabouts of two suspects. The telephones are awful quiet. Any calls?

"Only one, but that will change as soon as everybody reads the Sunday paper. Mr. Gordon called and asked for you. I told him you were tied up and left orders not to be interrupted. He wants you to call him at home."

"Thanks Melinda. Call him for me. Tell him I just got back and will be in touch as soon as I know somethin'. Field all of my calls. I need some time to review this stuff."

While he waited for Seth and Pace to return, Travis reviewed the information gathered at the murder scene. Evidence was scant. Heavy rainfall had obliterated footprints other than faint outlines that indicated the murderer had big feet. Eye witness accounts of the altercation and threats involving Jess and Jarred Grimes convinced Seth that it was an open-shut case. As promising as it looked, Travis wasn't so sure. He was reading the pathology report when Seth and Pace returned from Catfish. They didn't look too happy.

Seth collapsed into a chair in Travis' office. "Jess and Jarred have alibis, but we brought'em in for questioning anyway."

"Good,"said Travis. "What's their story?"

Seth continued. "They say they got to The Sugarbush at 1:30 yesterday afternoon and left at 7:00 that evening, which jives with eye witness statements. That's good.

They say they got home at 8:15 PM and their Dad and Mom both say the same. That's bad, because if it's true we can't place'em at the scene when the murders were committed.

They say that around 10:00 PM they left home again to go to Cal Hagan's place for a short visit, arriving there at 10:15 PM. Cal

Hagan, his wife Dessie and Bobby Hagan say that's right. That's good, because if we can prove they're lying about the time they got home, that leaves three hours they can't account for."

"Can you prove they're lyin' and their parents are lyin' about the time they got home?" Travis asked.

"Let me put it this way," Seth answered. "Those four were makin' liquor together, they're the ones that ate our lunches and dumped our car in the river and I know they're lyin' whether I can prove it or not. I'm gonna hold'em in jail until I can."

"That's bad," Travis replied with a mischievous grin. "Because until you can prove it, you can't charge'em with a crime, and if you can't charge'em with a crime you can't hold'em, and if you can't hold'em, that means you have to turn'em loose! After what we've been through in the last twenty four hours, especially without any sleep, emotions are runnin' high to hang somebody, the sooner the better. We're gonna conduct a thorough investigation and gather evidence that will support an arrest that will stick before we charge anybody with rape and a double murder.

What about the Hensely twins, Dorsey and Dooly? They had motive."

"I know," Seth replied. "They were home by 2:30 yesterday afternoon. They don't sleep in the main house, they've got a bunkhouse out back, but their Mom and Dad saw'em come in and say that's the time they got home and that's where they've been ever since. They left their car at a repair shop down the road from the house and walked home. The car was still parked there this mornin'."

"That narrows it down to the Grimes' boys for now," Travis sighed. "Our troops are waitin' for us in the muster room. Let's fill'em in on what we have."

The muster room was buzzing with excitement fed by rumors and gossip.

"We have a double murder to solve," Travis began. "To do that, we depend on facts and evidence, not rumors and gossip. What you hear here stays here. Do not discuss the investigation with anyone outside this office. Refer any queries to me. That's my job.

All of you are familiar with The Sugarbush roadhouse where the murders occurred. At 7:50 PM last night the male victim escorted the

The Sugarbush

female victim to the outside toilet because she was afraid to go by herself. That's the last time they were seen alive.

At 10:00 PM, their bodies were discovered in the edge of the woods about a hundred feet from the backdoor of the building. The male had been beaten and then hung from the limb of a tree by his neck. The female had been beaten, raped, sodomized and then stabbed in the heart.

As of now, this is where we stand on facts and evidence. Due in part to the rain, the murder scene didn't offer much in evidence such as footprints or signs of a struggle. There are no eye witnesses to the murders and no murder weapon was found, other than the male victim's own bullwhip that he was hanged with.

The pathology report on the male victim, Kirby Suggs, shows severe trauma to the left side of the face indicating he was struck hard rendering him semi-conscious. The cause of death was strangulation. Suggs weighed a hundred and eighty pounds and to have been lifted up and hung from the limb of that tree, the killer has to be tall and strong, or he had to have some help."

"You said semi-conscious, Sheriff. Could the blow have knocked him completely out?" someone asked.

"Yes. It could have knocked him out, but it didn't," Travis answered. "Several of the victim's fingernails on each hand were ripped off, attached only by the roots. There were fragments of bark under the others which indicates he was conscious of being hanged and was trying to lift himself up for air. Witnesses say he had been drinking heavily all day. Even suicide victims by hanging who are cold sober, instinctively try to save themselves and seldom succeed unless the noose breaks. Once they're committed, the diminishment of physical strength along with panic and shock begins immediately. In a matter of seconds their bowels and bladder release. It's an ugly mess.

The report on the female victim reveals severe trauma to the left side of the face, both sides of the neck and the breasts. There is also evidence that she was dragged around by the hair. The bruising to the face suggests a hard blow with an open hand. The only explanation for the neck bruises is that she was choked someway other than with hands. The breasts are completely black and filled with blood from being repeatedly crushed with hands. The fingers of both her hands are lacerated and there are dirt and leaf particles under the fingernails from clawing the ground.

In regards to internal trauma, the autopsy revealed deep bruising and severe tissue tears through the vaginal and rectal orifices. The autopsy also indicates that all sexual penetration was initiated from a position behind the victim. There is a stab wound extending from the left armpit into the heart. Although the internal injuries resulting from the rape could have been life threatening, the cause of death was the stab wound into the heart. The stab wound was inflicted with a pointed object razor sharp on both edges, one inch wide and eight to ten inches long, probably a dagger of sorts.

The times of death have been placed at between 8:00 PM and 10:00 PM. We believe that while the woman, Bernice Boles, was inside the toilet, Suggs was attacked and hanged. She didn't hear anything because of the wind, thunder and lightning' and the rain beatin' down on the tin roof of the toilet. When she came out of the toilet, the killer was waiting for her.

We believe the murderer is left handed. Both victims were struck from behind on the left side of the head and the female who was found lying face down was stabbed in the left armpit.

We believe these were grudge murders committed for revenge. We have two suspects, but we can't tie'em to the scene during the time the murders were committed. They are brothers, Jess and Jarred Grimes from Catfish. Chief Deputy Stephens will keep you informed of any progress in the investigation. If there are no questions, let's get back to work."

When Travis returned to his office, Gordon Jackson was waiting. "You've done a lot of work in a short time," he said enthusiastically. "Thanks for the report you sent by the house. It's good, real good. It's all I need to get an indictment and conviction. You've got the killer's in jail, why haven't you charged them?"

"Because I don't have enough evidence to hold'em," Travis replied. "They have alibis that were confirmed by both parents."

"They're lying and you know it," Gordon said, his voice rising. "Let's look at the facts.

We know that Jess and Jarred have histories of violence all the way back to elementary school. We know that over the past several

The Sugarbush

years they've gotten away with assault and rape, and in each case the incidence of violence and injury to the victims became increasingly more severe. They were bound to go over the edge sometime and this was it. We have eye witness statements from over fifty people who saw the altercation and heard the death threats."

"You're not listenin'," Travis said wearily. "They have confirmed alibis."

"It's the other way around, Sheriff, you're not listening. What I'm telling you is to charge those vermin and leave the rest up to me. I'll get you a conviction!"

"On emotion and circumstantial evidence. No thanks," said Travis. "Why are you in such a damned hurry to pin this on somebody? The investigation is less than twenty four hours old. If the Grimes boys are guilty, I'll get you the evidence to prove it without a shadow of a doubt."

Suddenly calm and professional, Gordon answered. "Without a shadow of a doubt in my mind, I know that you already have the killers in custody. If you turn them loose, it's going to look bad on you and without a shadow of a doubt, your decision will be criticized."

"By who, Gordon, the public? I doubt it. The churches and their congregations won't give the murder victims or the Grimes brothers a second thought. They've heard stories about The Sugarbush for years and consider it to be a den of sin that should be burned to the ground and any misfortunes that befall its patrons' are deserved. They had probably never heard of Kirby Suggs or Bernice Boles until they read the names in the newspapers. The brutality and perversion of the murders will raise some 'ooes and ahs' I'm sure, but that's about it. A blow was struck against satan and that's all they care about.

Telephone calls expressing sympathy for Sheriff Coley are still pouring in. So far, not one caller has even mentioned the murder victims, and to me that shows a calloused indifference by the public. They can't relate and don't understand how bad it was or the kind of person that could do something like that. I don't know. For the time being, maybe it's better they don't understand."

"You could be right," Gordon replied. "I'm leaving. Thanks again and keep me informed."

Travis was right. The public treated the incident as an occurrence apart from civilized society, one that affected only the wicked reaping what they had sown.

Six weeks passed and no new leads had come to light. The lull in progress presented a new challenge for Travis. Thurlo Thomas, also a democrat and former chief of police for the City of Hickory announced he would oppose the interim sheriff as an independent write in candidate in the upcoming general election.

IX

Bobby Hagan, carrying his seine and minnow bucket made his way toward, Brushy Creek, behind the Fontaine farm.

"I could sure use a nap before I start wading in the water," Bobby thought.

On a ridge that followed alongside the creek, he found a cool well concealed spot behind a large granite boulder and was soon fast asleep.

Meanwhile, Reicie Dupré, with her two Airedale dogs was approaching her secret swimming hole. The pool, formed around an old maple tree stump, was within sight of the granite boulder behind which Bobby lay sleeping.

At age fourteen, after the untimely death of her mother, Reicie had come to live with her mother's only sister, Lila Fontaine, and her husband, Beau. Riecie's father, a government hunter and trapper, still lived alone near Grandfather Mountain in the Pisgah National Forest. He was called on quite frequently to travel to other national forests throughout the country when his services were needed. Knowing that without his beloved wife to care for her, Reicie would be left alone for indefinite periods. He was relieved when Lila and Beau, who were childless, offered to provide a stable home for his daughter. Reicie's two dogs, badly injured in a ferocious fight with a bear, had been brought to her by her father with the promise that if she could nurse them back to health, she could keep them for her own. They were her constant companions.

Even at fourteen, Reicie's beauty had turned the heads of men and women young and old. Now seventeen her fully developed and well-proportioned body was a marvel to behold.

She was five six with long auburn hair that framed and elegant, refined face, then cascaded to a small waist. Expressive violet blue eyes and full lips completed a provocative and sultry portrait of loveliness.

"Mud, Sand, down! Stay!" Reicie said quietly. Noiselessly slipping out of her dress, she removed her panties and waded into the pool, shivering as the water crept up to her neck.

Bobby's eyes opened suddenly. He lay still, wondering how long he had been sleeping. Then he heard soft splashes of water from the nearby creek. Sitting up slowly he moved cautiously to his knees and peered over the granite boulder to the pool below.

His eyes widened in surprise. "Maybe I'm a dreamin'," he thought. There was a woman's bronzed naked body walking up out of the water onto the bank. As she brushed back the glistening wet hair that clung to her back, Bobby waited in excited anticipation for her to turn around. Reicie made no effort to dry her self. Slipping into her panties, she gracefully dropped the dress down over her head and for her hidden observer, the show was over.

A few moments earlier when Reicie bent over to pick up her panties, Bobby pressed forward straining his eyes for a closer look. As he relaxed, the metal clasp and button on the galluses of his blue bib overalls scraped ever so slightly against the rock surface. Abruptly the dogs came to their feet. Alert, ears perked up, they looked curiously in the direction of Bobby's concealment.

The movement of the dogs didn't go unnoticed. After dressing, Reicie turned calmly gazing across the pool, running her fingers nonchalantly through her hair.

Bobby froze, not daring to even blink his eyes. It was only when the dogs jumped to their feet that he became aware of their presence.

To his relief, Reicie and her bodyguards casually walked away, disappearing up the path into the woods.

The fright of nearly being discovered left Bobby's heart pounding, instantly relieving the intenseness in his groin. Excitedly pounding his thighs with his fists, he was ecstatic. "Damn, damn, damn," he muttered. "That wuz Reicie Dupre. She's the first naked woman I ever seen. If she had jist turned 'round, damn!

After the dogs alerted, Reicie sensed she was being observed, but wasn't sure. She took her pets a safe distance away and commanded them to stay put. Then she turned back toward the pool. Positioning herself behind a tree where she could see the area across the creek, she waited. It was a tense and scary moment. If her swimming hole had been discovered and she was being watched, she wanted to know by whom.

Soon she detected movement as Bobby, with his seining net in one hand and his minnow bucket in the other, walked out from behind the boulder and made his way down the hill toward the creek.

The Sugarbush

Reicie breathed a sigh of relief. "At least it's someone I know. My secret pool may not be a secret any longer, but neither is your observation post," she thought to her self. About to leave, Reicie was startled to see Bobby, who was barefooted and shirtless, unbuckle his galluses and drop his overalls to the ground. Completely naked, he instinctively looked around to insure he was alone.

Reicie's heart leaped and began to beat rapidly. Her face flushed brilliant pink. It was now her eyes straining for a closer look. She watched breathlessly as Bobby began to casually fondle himself. Her breasts became firm, her nipples extended, sensitive against the cotton fabric of her dress. She began to gently massage them sending tingling sensations down to her genitals. Her curiosity was at last satisfied. She had finally seen a naked man.

As Bobby entered the water, she reluctantly subdued the excitement of the moment, stealthily making her way back to the dogs. She hurried toward home, anxious to tell Aunt Lila the news of her exciting discovery.

Lila Fontaine was a striking figure of a woman. At forty, her youthfulness and beauty were equaled only by her poise and charm.

When Reicie burst through the kitchen door, Lila began to laugh merrily.

"Look at you!" she giggled. "You're lit up like a lantern! What have you been up to?"

Reicie, clearly enjoying herself, confided all the details of her encounter at the creek.

"Well now that you've seen a naked man, what do you think. Was it what you expected?" Lila asked mischievously.

"Almost!" replied Reicie. "I was a little surprised. His penis was larger than the ones you see on ancient Greek and Roman statues."

"Believe you me young lady, they come in all sizes, just like women's breasts. Are you by any chance sweet on Bobby?"

"Oh no! Not in the least! He's not bad looking and I like him all right, but that's as far as it goes. Before I started attending school in town, we were in the eighth grade together at White Church School and got along fine. Bobby doesn't have many interests outside of hunting and fishing. Like all the other boys, he quit school that year. He really wouldn't have spent the first day in a classroom if his dad hadn't made him come. He told me so! He's hot tempered and always ready for a fight. That's the way most of the boys are out here in Catfish, except Junior Upton. He's graduating from college this year.

Aunt Lila, when I saw Bobby naked I got excited, I mean like numb, sort of tingly and I liked the feeling. I've had tingly feelings before, but never like today. I asked my mother about it before she died. She said they were normal. Do you ever have them?"

"Oh yes. Everyone, women and men alike have them to some extent. They're natural and wholesome, but the benefits depend on how well you understand and use them. Giving in to your passion with someone you love and who understands that you have needs too, is a kind of pleasure that is hard to describe. You have to experience it yourself to really know what I mean."

"I can hardly wait," said Reicie, "I've heard women say their wedding night was the most wonderful event of their lives, so thrilling and passionate. Was it that way for you?"

"Yes it was," Lila answered. "Only women who truly feel that way are willing to talk about it and it's more than the sex. It's wonderful because two people in love are consummating a commitment to each other for life, joining, becoming one. The young lady is making the transformation from that very special age of innocence to womanhood. As for the sex, the husband's deflowering of his bride is a conquest, a prize so to speak, and very enjoyable to him. For a woman who's still a virgin, it can be uncomfortable and quite painful. It took a little while before I found complete pleasure. There are many women who get no pleasure at all from sex. They go through life dreading to go to bed at night with their husbands."

"Well I'm not going to be one of those," Reicie exclaimed.

"I should hope not dear," Lila replied. "But remember, when you give up your virginity, make it special. I don't know where I read this or who wrote it, I only know it's true." 'A sigh too deep, a kiss too long, a mist in a blinding rain, and things are never the same again.'

X

It was the end of the seventh week since The Sugarbush murders. Just south of the cotton mill hill, Shelton Brooks was preparing for a busy weekend at his poker parlor. "Lindy, Lindy Blue," he shouted. "Hold up a minute."

"Howdy, Mr. Shelton. How ye comin' on?"

"Jist fine, Lindy! Jist fine, thank ye. Ye headed home now?"

"Yes sir, I shore is. I wanna git pass them railroad tracks 'fore that switch engine gits here or I'll be a standin' 'til dark waitin' to cross."

"Ye better hurry on then," Shelton replied. "On yer way stop by the house; the wife has some washin' and ironin' fer ye to pick up."

"I'll do that! I need all the work I can git and I thank ye."

"Yer welcome, Lindy. Tell the wife I'll be on soon as I pick up a few thangs she wanted from the store."

Lindy, a single woman of twenty two years, lived with her parents in the nearby negro community. Shelton gave Lindy as much household work as he could afford. It took a burden off his wife and was a big help financially to Lindy and her folks who were all out of work.

Shelton's weekend poker parlor normally played to a full house of regular customers. His cut from the pot and profit from the ten cent shots of whiskey he sold made him a better than average living. Someway, somehow, even in hard times, people seemed to find enough money for drinking and gambling.

Before Sheriff Coley's death, his nephew, Deputy Barnes, had given Shelton an ultimatum to either work for his uncle or risk going to jail for running a gambling parlor. The sheriff's death eliminated that threat.

Shelton stood by the track waiting impatiently for the switch engine to either pull forward or backward just enough for him to get across the tracks and be on his way. He had been standing for about five minutes when the switchman approached.

"Shelton ole buddy!" he shouted above the noise. "How ye been?"

"Jist fine," thank ye "I'll be a tad better off if'n you'll move this train!" Shelton replied with a laugh.

"Sorry about that. We're having a little trouble with a switch down the track a ways, so it's likely to be a few more minutes 'fore we outta the way."

"Thanks fer telling me. Since yer right here and the engineer won't move the train 'til ye signal'im to, let me climb over the couplers between the cars and go on. I really need to git to the house."

"I don't like to do that, Shelton. Still yit I don't know how long it's gonna take to throw that switch. Well let's see. Climb over right quick! Jist be careful and don't drop yer bag a groceries."

Shelton climbed between the cars and down the ladder dropping to the ground on the other side. Shouting thanks, he made his way up the red clay bank along the well worn path through the patch of woods toward home.

Sheriff Gant answered his phone.

"This is Seth," the voice said hastily. "I hate to call you at home, Sheriff, but it looks like we may have another murder on our hands. The switchman at the switch yard south of the mill hill says a man's been cut in half by the boxcars they've been switchin'. He swears it's no accident either. Pace is here workin' so he's going with me to the scene."

"Tell me exactly where it is and I'll meet you there," Travis replied.

At the scene, the switchman repeated what had happened only an hour before, explaining that he saw Shelton clear the tracks and walk on towards home.

"Shelton was carryin' a sack a groceries and they ain't here," he said. "Shorely somebody didn't kill him fer that little ole sack a groceries?"

Travis walked over to the path leading up the red clay bank and saw faint drag marks that were almost unnoticeable in the packed soil. Following the path into the patch of woods, the first thing he came upon was the groceries scattered over the ground. Then he saw the body of a negro woman lying face down in a pool of blood. She was naked except for a yellow dress that was knotted around her small waist.

The Sugarbush

He hurried back to the railroad siding.

"The switchman was right, this was no accident," Travis said quietly, motioning for his men to follow. "I found another body. It's a woman, a young negro woman. It's almost exactly like the murder scene at The Sugarbush. The only differences are the cause of the man's death, it's daylight, and it's not raining."

"Sheriff, Pace asked. "Could it be that the killers at The Sugarbush weren't laying in for Kirby Suggs at all, but were huntin' a woman, any woman! Maybe Suggs got in the way just like this guy did!"

"Could be, Pace. I considered that angle from the beginning and it didn't seem to make sense under the circumstances. What are these brown splatters? They're all over the body."

"Oh yeah!" Seth answered. "It smells like chewin' tobacco or snuff."

"Ask the coroner to confirm that," said Travis. "Look! It's even in her hair! What kind of lunatic are we dealin' with! Get the bodies over to the morgue as soon as you can and get the pathology started. "Canvass the neighborhood. Somebody might have seen something. When you're finished doing that, meet me back at the office."

Back at the office, Travis paced the floor stopping occasionally to jot down notes on his thoughts. It was late when Seth and Pace joined him. "Any good news?" Travis asked.

"We struck out," replied Seth. "Lots of, 'I think I saw and I think I heard,' but that's about it. We found several different ways the murderer could have gotten in and out without being seen, provided he was careful. The flour and feed mill storage yard borders that strip of trees on the west. If we had to pick a route, that would be the most likely one. There were signs of foot traffic and lots of tire tracks, but nothing helpful. The Grimes' brothers have alibis. By the time we got to their place, they were in bed and naturally hadn't been off the farm all day."

Travis interrupted! "Do you guys realize the magnitude what has happened here? What we thought was an isolated crime of rape and murder for revenge, has now turned into rape and murder for the thrill of it. These perverts were after the woman. You don't have to be smart to figure that out. Shelton Brooks was killed because he walked in on'em.

I know you're thinkin' Jess and Jarred Grimes, which to me doesn't make sense. They're our prime suspects in The Sugarbush killings and I'm not counting them out by any means. I'm simply saying that things aren't addin' up. Think about it! They're bullies! Everytime they go out drinkin, they end up threatenin' to kill somebody. That's nothing new! The women they're supposed to have raped in the past were roughed up, but they weren't sodomized or killed. Another thing, how on god's green earth did they pick out Lindy Blue? She's a home body who seldom leaves the neighborhood! The settings do have something in common even though they're miles apart. There's another curious thing goin' on here. Both women were stabbed in the heart exactly the same way. Why not the men? It doesn't make sense. Let's call it a day. I wanna sleep on this."

When Seth and Pace arrived at the office the next morning, Travis was waiting for them to review the pathology report.

"It reads exactly as we expected," he said. "We'll start with the woman. The areas of trauma, internal and external, are identical to those found on Bernice Boles. The dark colored stains and particles found on the victim's skin and in her hair are chewing tobacco spittle, which went unnoticed on, Bernice Boles, because the rain mustta washed it off. The time of death is placed between 6:00 and 7:00 PM. The cause of death, a stab wound from the left armpit into the heart. For the male, same as Kirby Suggs, only the cause of death was dismemberment by the wheels of a train. It's pretty plain that Brooks blundered into the scene, was beaten unconscious, dragged to the track and thrown under a moving boxcar. That was the end of him!

The killer is reckless. With all the activity going on in that community, he slipped into that little patch of woods, set up the ambush, subdued the victim, committed rape and killed two people in broad daylight, then slipped back out without being seen by a single soul. Maybe the activity and noise is a key factor in the murderer's site selection for an attack, but it could also work against'im. The switch engine covered up any sounds of a struggle, maybe even screams and cries for help. It would also have drowned out the sounds of anyone approaching. With all the noise and the killer bein' so involved in the attack, Brooks almost got away. If he had, this would be over with now."

"Travis," Seth interrupted with obvious disgust. "You better go back to bed and sleep on this again or better yet, quit sleepin' on it. All that college psychology and stuff ain't worth the time you spent learnin' it. You keep sayin' killer when you oughtta be sayin' killers, Jess and Jarred Grimes to be exact. We're wastin' time sittin' here listenin' to you complicate somethin' that's as plain as mud. Just what makes you think Shelton Brooks almost got away? You weren't there."

Travis counted to ten, then patiently replied. "Little things observed at murder scenes give us insight as to what kind of person we're lookin' for. "Because of the rain, The Sugarbush murders didn't leave much to get us started. The switch yard murder scene is much more revealing, but I'm not ready to talk about that. Shelton Brooks was a big man, tough and strong yet he was no match for the killer. The fact that he made a nearly successful attempt to get away was obvious. A trampled box of corn flakes was layin' at Lindy Blue's feet. Six feet away, the ripped paper bag and the rest of the groceries were scattered in the direction Shelton had come from. That's where the drag marks started that led back to the railroad tracks where he was thrown under the train."

Seth, looking defeated, but still defiant, interrupted again. "I didn't pay any attention to the groceries or the way they were scattered so I guess you might be right there, but what damn difference does that make. We know who the killers are. From the looks of things, they ain't done yet and here we sit talkin' and not doin' anything about it."

Travis saw the wilted expression on Seth's face and replied sternly. "There is a proven structure for thorough murder investigations and we will follow it to the letter. Seth, you will not be any help to me in this investigation if you continue to maintain such a narrow focus and refuse to be thorough because you have already arrived at a verdict. I will endeavor to reach a consensus on the direction our investigation takes, however, understand this! If a consensus cannot be reached, I will decide what does or doesn't make a difference and you will proceed accordingly. I have good reasons for questioning the absolute guilt of the Grimes brothers. My references to a killer instead of killers is a figure of speech that I consider to be appropriate at this time.

He's like us, learnin' as he goes and we wanna get smarter quicker than he does. After the close call he had yesterday he'll be more cautious, but as soon as the urge hits'im, he'll forget about how close it was and come huntin' again. I can feel it in my bones. It makes the hair stand up on the back of my neck.

I'm asking the radio stations and the newspapers to make public announcements warnin' the people of the danger and asking them to report anything unusual or suspicious. I'll ask that the women travel in groups and not venture into isolated or remote areas even close to town. I want everyone to be alert, but I don't want to cause a panic.

When you appeal to the awareness of the public you have a price to pay, but sometimes it's worth it. Somewhere I read that ten percent of the people walking around on the streets today are mad as hatters so we're bound to get some crank calls. Regardless, we have to check'em all. We need a lead and you never know where it will come from."

Melinda opened the office door. "Sorry to interrupt Sheriff. Mr. Jackson's here."

"Good mornin', Gordon. Come on in," Travis shouted. "We just finished reviewing the pathology report."

"So did I," Gordon replied. "It sounds familiar, don't you think?"

"Yes it does."

"What are you going to do about it?"

"I'm gonna continue the investigation until we have enough evidence to make an arrest."

"How's that going?"

"Not good. We need a break."

"I'll say you do! I just hope you get one soon."

"Yeah. Before there's another killin'."

Out in Catfish, Cal and Dessie turned into their driveway and parked under a shade tree to wait for, Fentress Akers, who was approaching on his big red horse.

"I thought Fentress only delivered mail a horseback when the roads wuz bad muddy," Dessie remarked curiously.

The Sugarbush

"That's what I thought too," Cal replied.

"Howdy, Cal, Miss Dessie!" shouted Fentress. "I ain't got no mail fer you'uns but I got some news. Yisterday evenin' they wuz another double murder; another man and women."

"It ain't done it," Dessie cried.

"Oh yes'um, 'tis done it."

"Why don't they close that joint down? Cal exclaimed.

"It weren't at the same place, Cal. This'un wuz over yonder by the switchyard spurs south a the mill hill. A feller was throwed under the train and the wheels cut him in half. The woman was a mess, too."

"Who wuz they?"

"I don't rightly know. The feller was a white man and the woman was a young negro. I'm carryin a gun from now on and so will ever'body else if'n they smart."

"I guess yer right 'bout that. People git skittish with sech as that goin' on. Speakin' a skittish, how ye and yer horse gittin' on?"

"Me and ole Fireball is doin' mighty fine. That's what I call'im. The wife says we ain't havin' no horse named 'Us'. She says he's the color of our potbellied heater stove when it's red hot, so's she named'im thatta way. He's fine a horse as is in the county and no doubt one of the fastest. He kin hold his own with Beau Fontaine's saddle horses. I been ridin'em ever'day 'cept Saturday and Sunday. He ain't acted up 'nairy a time."

"Glad to hear it," said Cal.

"I'll be movin' on now. See y'all tomorrow," Fentress shouted as he rode away.

"Cal," said Dessie. "I meant to tell ye 'bout runnin' into, Grace Upton, while ye wuz in the store. Junior's gittin' married in October, so she's havin' a party on July 8th to announce the engagement and make everybody acquainted with the bride to be. She wants us to come."

"We don't wanna miss that!" replied Cal. "The onliest way Junior Upton could ever git a wife is to find her where nobody knows nothin' 'bout'im."

"Shame on yer mouth, Cal Hagan! Junior's a nice feller. He might be a little sissified, but lots a women chooses men like that."

"Yeah, so's they kin henpeck'em and drag'em 'round like Aunt Candace does Uncle Bud."

"Yer henpecked Cal Hagan. 'Specially when it comes bedtime."

"Yer mighty right 'bout that and I ain't complainin'," laughed Cal. "Difference is, we the onliest ones that knows it."

Taylor Upton and his wife were community and church leaders who had never met a stranger. They were well thought of by the community, wealthy by Catfish standards, well educated, talked and dressed differently, but were not pretentious.

Their son, Taylor Upton, Jr., was not so much pretentious as he was defensive against the teasing and mischief by his classmates at White Church School. Growing up, he always had the best of everything whether at school, church or play. The best pony, the finest saddle, the best clothes and as a young man, the finest automobile and had no qualms about showing them off. All the girls liked Junior and it wasn't that the boys didn't like him, they couldn't resist teasing him because of his comical reactions to their mischief.

Junior had no interest in farming of any kind. He graduated from college at the top of his class majoring in business and finance. That's where he met his fiance'. They were a good match, excited about the future and anxious to complete construction of their furniture manufacturing plant which was already well underway.

The evening of the engagement party was hot and humid, never the less, the guests were in high spirits. Drinks and food were abundant.

The future bride was attractive, outgoing and personable. When in the immediate presence of his betrothed, Junior's pompous pride was more comical than anything else. He was smitten in the most profound sense of the word and very proud of his catch.

Driving home after the party, Cal remarked to Dessie. "Ye know, I gotta hand it to Junior. He come up with a fine little woman. I guess I never have give'im enough credit. He really done good graduatin' from college and all."

The next morning, Cal and Dessie had just finished breakfast when they heard a car coming in the driveway. It was Casey

The Sugarbush

Workman and Bobby. They got out of the car looking drawn and tired.

"Cal!" Casey said sadly, "After you'uns left the party last night, Junior Upton went down to the lake and got hisself drowned. Me and Bobby jist found his body a while ago."

"Oh, dear Lord!" cried Dessie. "Come on in the kitchen, I'll fix you'uns some breakfast while ye tell us what happened."

"I thank ye fer the offer," Casey answered. "I better git on to the house. Sue's bad tore up 'bout this and she's a sittin' there by herself. I gotta go. Bobby can tell ye everthang 'bout it."

After Casey left, Bobby sat down to eat.

"How in god's name did Junior git from his party to the lake?" Cal asked.

"Well you know Junior!" said Bobby. "He had some of his city buddies there and decided to show off the new boat Munroe's Cabinet Shop built fer'im. Six of'em wuz in the boat, but Junior's the onliest one that drowned. It was black dark, so they had a kerosene lantern in the boat with'em. Somebody knocked it over, spillin' the kerosene and settin' the boat afire. Besides bein' perty high from a drinkin', they mustta panicked and somehow 'nother turned the boat over. They weren't more'n fifteen foot from the bank, so's they swum over to where they could tetch bottom and walk on outta the water, all 'cept Junior. He mustta got turned 'round and swum the other way. It's a long ways 'cross that lake; he never made it! His buddies heared'im a screamin' fer help and finally ever'thang got quiet. They knowed he wuz a goner. They come back to the party with the bad news and ever'body went plumb crazy. Me and Casey told Taylor to take care a the women folk while we went a lookin' fer the body. We took Sue home and went back down to the lake. It was too dark to see, so's we slept on the bank 'til daylight. When it was light enough to see, we got in the boat and paddled straight across from where they turned over. That's where he wuz, hung up on a water log, one arm stickin' up outta the water like if'n he was a wavin' to let us know where he wuz at. I got'im aloose and hung on to his collar while Casey paddled back to the other side. All the dead folks I've saw looked like they wuz sleepin', not Junior. His eyes wuz open wide, real sad, like he wuz skirred and fixin' to cry. It wuz plumb spooky!

"It shorely mustta been," Dessie exclaimed. "Theys somethin' worse'n spooky goin' on here and it all started the very same day the sheriff got killed and you'uns found his jacket with them warrants in it. I never thought on it no more 'till last night when Sue told me that Brooks feller who wuz cut in two by the train wuz Casey's first cousin. I knowed I'd heared that name before. Now here I sit worried plumb sick. Four people named on them warrants is dead! Don't ye fergit, Bobby, they's one fer ye, Casey, Fentress, Pursey and them Hensley twins and we the onliest ones knows it. Ye gotta be careful yerself and warn all of'em ye kin find 'bout what's been a goin' on so's they kin too."

"Now listen here Dessie," Bobby interruped. "People gits killed or dies ever'day. It ain't nothin' but a accident some of'em wuz named on them warrants and it don't got nothin' to do with Junior gittin' hisself drowned while he wuz a showin' off. I ain't one bit worried 'bout that kinda stuff and don't ye neither. Whatever happens is a gonna happen and we can't stop it nohow.

One thing we can stop from happenin' is me and Cal goin' to the penitentiary or worse yit, the crazy house over in Morganton. That's 'zactly where we'll wind up if'n we start goin' 'round tellin' people they a fixin' to die 'cause the day the sheriff got his head blowed off he had a pocket full a death warrants with their names on'em. Anyways, when me and Cal kangarooed them folks, 'nairy a one of'em wuz found guilty. Besides that I'd druther be dead than in jail or the crazy house."

XI

Travis sat in his office contemplating his chances of winning the election. Considering his personal popularity and the support of the ruling democratic party, how could he lose. His opponent, Thurlo Thomas, had some support from the business community and press, but Travis wasn't worried. The incumbent always won because regardless of who was sheriff, the voters didn't expect any real change to take place anyway.

If it ever crossed a political candidate's mind that the favored status afforded only to the white upper classes was wrong, they never mentioned it. The word discrimination was nonexistent in the vocabulary of the ruling white class of the south. They provided the means that made life bearable for the underprivileged hoards regardless of skin color, and nothing should be any different. Travis racked his brain for a campaign theme that would make the poor working class people want to register and vote for him, something he believed in, a promise he could keep that would bring positive change without offending the ruling class.

It was his Aunt Bertha who came up with the idea. An inoffensive position that the opposition could not attack without exposing themselves as harsh, class conscious and insensitive to even the basic needs of the working poor.

She explained her idea. "Let's look at what we know. People are feeling pretty helpless and could use a moral boost to give'em something to look forward to. Not something temporary, something permanent. Not on the grand scale of Franklin Roosevelt's campaign but something they can benefit from in the short term if you win.

Plain and simple, if you're white, based on what part of town you live in and the class of society you're born into there's a big disparity in the quality of services you receive for your tax dollar, like police protection, legal representation and treatment by the judicial system. I know! I saw it everyday when I worked at the county courthouse. We know that petty misdemeanors and even felony crimes committed by the privileged classes, short of murder, are dealt with quickly, quietly and lightly. The same crimes committed by poor people of any race are widely reported and draw harsh penalties from the courts. With the Depression so terrible the poor feel like they're bearing the burden of retribution for all society and they don't like it. They're primed and ready to fight. They could be a political force in Catawba County, but they don't register or vote because they don't think it will change anything. Let's convince them otherwise."

It was mid-August. Travis was under fire from his staff, the public, the press and democrat party supporters because of his stubborn refusal to arrest and charge the Grimes brothers on what he publicly decried as the flimsiest of circumstantial evidence. He would not budge.

Now smug and confident, his opponent, Thurlo Thomas, began taking Travis lightly, treating him as a novelty rather than a threat, suggesting that the job of county jailor was a position he felt the inexperienced youngster was much better suited for.

"At political rallies," Thurlo shouted. "Our actin' sheriff claims the poor working folks are the voting majority, yet they're deprived of equal judicial process by our courts. What he doesn't tell you is that the majority of the crimes committed in this county are done so by those poor working class folks. If his majority wants equal judicial process, they better start behaving like our upstanding citizens that make what jobs they have possible.

He also claims his majority doesn't have equal representation in our courts. The answer to that is simple. If you want a good lawyer, pay him with money, not milk, eggs and fresh vegetables.

His last big claim is that the county won't provide enough money in the budget to fund equal law enforcement presence on the mill hill and rural communities to protect his majority.

I can tell you right now, those people don't know how good they've got it. If we were any more present in those communities, there would be a whole lot more of those yokels in jail."

The backlash of this insensitive rhetoric was creating strong undercurrents of resistance to the Thomas challenge, but Travis was in trouble himself. He was secretly beginning to doubt he could win unless the murders were solved.

Travis left the office to visit his Aunt Bertha who lived on a farm near Conover. Before retiring, Bertha worked for many years as a clerk in the County Register of Deeds Office. A pleasantly plump

The Sugarbush

matronly women, she was well known and liked throughout the county.

Like just about everybody else, Bertha sincerely believed that the Grimes brothers were the murderers. She knew Travis would be arriving soon and hoped to convince him that if he expected to stop the killings and win the election, he better arrest them. She incorrectly assumed that what happened to Travis' father was the reason no arrests had been made.

Travis never knew his dad; he only knew that at the time he died in a Texas oil field explosion, he was a fugitive from justice for a crime he had not committed, and died not knowing he had been vindicated. The charges had been based on circumstantial evidence. Later cleared of any involvement, apologies from the judicial system brought little comfort to the surviving family for the injustice and loss of an innocent man.

Bertha hurried towards the barn. Now widowed, the daily chores, milking, gathering eggs and feeding the livestock, was left to her. She entered the feed room at the end of the barn and began mixing the hog feed. Finishing the last bucket, she turned, screaming at the sight of a figure that suddenly filled the doorway of the small dark room. "Good Lord!" she shouted, dropping the bucket and clutching her breasts. "You scared me half to death slipping up like that! I didn't even hear you drive in. Just for that, grab a couple of those buckets. If you aren't afraid to get your hands dirty you can help me feed the hogs."

Travis pulled into the front yard and parked. Climbing up the porch steps, he called out for his Aunt through the open door. There was no answer, then he remembered that at 5:30 each afternoon she would be finishing up her chores. Approaching the barn, he heard the chickens cackling and hungry pigs squealing in anticipation of being fed.

As he rounded the corner, he saw Bertha's blood stained body, naked except for a slipper on her left foot. She was laying face down, arms stretched above her head, her hair and body splotched with chewing tobacco spit. Trembling, he knelt down beside the warm body and felt for a pulse. There was none. His eyes followed the drag marks back to the feed room in the barn where the attack had occurred. The missing shoe and clothing had been dragged for several feet through the pool of blood that had poured from her pierced heart, smearing the ground in lurid shades of red already covered with flies.

"This time something was different," he thought to himself. "The body was being moved and must have been dropped at the sound of my coming. Where were they taking it?" Already choked with grief, Travis was suddenly outraged. "They were dragging her to the hog lot to feed her corpse to the hungry pigs."

At that moment, from the woods behind the hog lot, a car engine started. Running to intercept the sound, the heavy undergrowth and briars tearing at his flesh and clothes, Travis soon broke into the narrow track of a logging road. So close yet so far, in a last futile effort, he raced down the narrow logging road following the sound until it faded. Returning to the barn, Travis covered Bertha's body with empty burlap feed sacks and ran to the house to phone for help.

Once again the pathology report read nearly identical to the ones on Bernice Boles and Lindy Blue, with one exception. The stab wound into the heart was not the cause of death. During the assault, Bertha died of heart failure! The killer had brutalized a corpse, an act too despicable to contemplate.

It was early September and autumn was in the air. South of town, Fannie Mosely, and her three sisters, sat on the back porch talking and busily peeling peaches. Annie Mosely, Fannie's twelve year old daughter pleaded with her mother. "Mom, I wanna peel peaches too. Please! I know how. I won't cut myself."

"No, no, dear!" Fannie replied. "Ye go out on the front porch swing and wait fer the mailman. We'll take care a the peaches."

Annie was a sweet child, unfortunately, born with Downs Syndrome.

"But Mom, he won't be here 'til three thirty."

"I know sweetheart! Ye lie down on the swing and take a nap 'til then. Go on now, and take yer dog with ye. After awhile ye can help us fill the fruit jars."

Later on Annie was awakened by the sound of an approaching car. She watched as the car stopped at the mailbox.

Since age nine, Annie had made it her daily routine to retrieve the mail. The mailman always gave her a piece of candy and if she wasn't there waiting for him, she knew the candy would be in the mailbox.

Happily, she and her dog, a beagle she called, "Critter," walked down the long path toward the road. Just as Annie pulled down the lid to open the mailbox, Critter began barking furiously and cowering behind her. Annie turned, a sweet innocent smile spreading across her face. A nice man was walking out of the woods beckoning to her.

"Annie!" her mother shouted! "You can come help us now. We're ready to fill the jars.

Annie, are ye asleep?"

As Fannie opened the front porch screen door, Critter dashed into the house and ran behind the sofa, whining and trembling.

"Critter, where's Annie? Annie's gone!" Fannie shouted to her sisters. "We gotta find her! Come on! The four sisters ran down the lane calling out Annie's name. Fannie reached the mailbox first.

"Annie was here!" she cried. "The lid's open, but the mail's still here, so's her candy! Annie! Annie!" she screamed.

A neighbor coming from town saw the four women emerge into the road. As he drew closer they began waving their arms and shouting for help.

He did his best to calm the women, asking them to wait while he looked around, reassuring them that Annie had only wandered off and was somewhere nearby.

Milling around in front of the mailbox had obliterated any footprints Annie might have left, but as the neighbor started across the drain ditch they reappeared heading toward the woods. Reaching a bare dusty patch of ground, his heart sank. There he saw a small footprint inside a much larger one.

A half hour later he hurried back toward the shade tree where the frightened women anxiously waited. He had discovered the child's torn body, already cold and covered with green flies. His face pale and lips quivering, he spoke quietly, "I found her and it ain't good. Please don't ask to see her!"

Fannie fainted into the arms of her sisters.

At noon the next day, Seth and Pace met with Travis to review the pathology report on Annie Mosely.

"Before we review the pathology, tell me what you have so far?" Travis asked.

"Less than we've had on the last two murders," Seth answered. "Nothing new at the murder scene, no good footprints and no new suspects because nobody saw anything. Pace and I tracked the killers to where they parked. It was a good quarter of a mile away. It's the same old story. They came in on a route that leads off of a different road than the one the victim lives on. It looks like they'd been in and out a few times before. Nothin's any different that I can see."

Pace interrupted. "I agree with Seth up to his last comment, but there's a lot that's different. In every other case the killer ambushed the victims from a hiding place as close as an arms length away, attacking from behind immediately after they walked by. For the one assault that occurred in the woods before yesterday, the killer carefully selected the ambush to include two large trees about six or eight feet a part right beside the path. You could see where he would stand behind one for awhile and then walk to the other, that is unless we have two killers working as a team. In Lindy Blue's case, the trees he was hiding behind were only two feet off of the path. The assaults at The Sugarbush and the one on your Aunt Bertha are not that different. All of the victims were attacked from behind and bear the same pattern of injuries. The Mosely girl's murder was a huge departure from the first five. This time the killer came out of ambush, exposed himself, walked two hundred feet, took the victim by the hand and led her back into the woods. Annie Mosely was not beaten, she was not choked and her breasts were only fondled roughly, not severely bruised. They played with her as though she was a doll, but in the end, injuries from the rape and sodomy were the worst yet. She was killed the same way as the others."

"All of that doesn't mean a thing, Pace." Seth replied. "The girl's dead! The only thing you said that's important, is two killers workin' as a team. Where are you comin' up with all this stuff?"

"From the pathology report and past history," Pace answered. "And it does mean something. It means the killer is getting braver. His success yesterday expanded his mode of operation and opened up a broad range of new targets. The way he toyed with Annie before he

The Sugarbush

raped her is one for Travis, and I don't like the sounds of it. That to me is the most sadistic of all; like a cat playing with a mouse for hours before he eats it alive. Another thing that's still hanging is the time of death. The mother and witnesses say Annie went for the mail at about 3:20 PM and never came back. Her body was found two hours later. The coroner says she died between 1:00 and 3:00 PM and he's stickin' to it. I haven't been able to verify what time the mail was delivered yesterday because the mailman left for a months vacation to do some deep sea fishing on the gulf coast near Brownsville, Texas. He could have done his route early. I'm still checking on it.

"You're missin' my point," said Seth. "What time they trapped the girl, how they trapped her, how they played with her, how they raped her, and what time they killed her are unimportant now. We already know all of that. The girl is dead, murdered by the same killers as the other five victims, and they have not been arrested."

"You're over simplifying things, Seth," Pace calmly replied. "The Grimes brothers have an alibi and it checks out. They were at the Farmer's Market from 3:00 PM until it closed. If the mailman delivered the mail around 1:00 PM yesterday, they don't have an alibi, but even at that we still don't have enough evidence to arrest and charge them. The new revelations in this case will help us develop new suspects. There is still a strong reasonable doubt we must overcome."

"Over simplifyin', maybe I am," Seth answered in defense. "As far as Jess and Jarred's alibis are concerned, they go in one ear and out the other. They're lying and one day we'll have the proof. There's no reasonable doubt in my mind about their guilt. You're back on the sodomy thing, Pace. Remember, not one of the girls who admitted being raped by Jess and Jarred came forward on their own. Somebody else who knew about it told Sheriff Coley. The girls only admitted it when he questioned'em. If the murdered women had not been killed, I don't think they would have come forward either. If women won't come forward and admit rape, they would die before admitting bein' sodomized."

"In most cases that's probably true," Travis replied. While we're talkin' here, just remember we're playin' the devil's advocate. It's not just the sodomy, it's the whole picture. The Grimes boys are braggarts, bullies, showoffs! They don't know how to be sneaky. I can't picture them hidin' in ambush to assault anybody. Suggs and Boles maybe, but that was a much different situation. The others; it remains to be seen. Pace is on the right track with the new implications in the Mosely murder. It's already told us a lot.

I've got to get to a meeting right now. Let's talk again in the mornin' and go through a complete review of our investigation up to now."

XII

"Travis arrived at his office the next morning to find Seth and Pace waiting for him. "Good morning," he said. "I've been thinkin' about this all night, so let's get right to it.

The bits and pieces I've put together so far that describe the killer physically, his habits, his personality, the part of society he comes from, where he lives, what kind of work he does, how he selects his victims, and the way he operates are pretty conclusive. These are the conclusions I came up with that y'all have agreed with. Let's review them carefully to see if we can find something buried in there that we've missed.

We'll begin with his physical features:

Kirby Suggs was hanged from a tree limb that was over seven feet above the ground. The killer is tall.

Suggs weighted a hundred and eighty pounds and was dead weight when he was lifted up to be hanged. The killer is strong.

Foot prints observed at the murder scenes are large and left deep impressions in the ground cover. The killer is heavy and has big feet. With the exception of Annie Mosely, all of the victims, men and women, were struck from behind on the left side of the head leaving a large area of trauma. The victims were all found face down with stab wounds in the left armpit. The killer has large hands and is left handed.

That covers the physical aspects for now. Lets' look at personality traits, habits, likes and dislikes:

The murder scenes were filthy with tobacco spittle. He chews tobacco incessantly, which means he's anxious and excitable when he's huntin'. He owns a car, probably a Model "T" ford. He knows every pig path in the county, on and off the road. He likes to drive and prowl around the country side watchin' people. He has been doin' that for a long time. He's knows the habits of his victims and how to get to them without being detected.

No attacks have occurred outside of Catawba County. He stays close to home.

The victims are of all ages. He has no preference for looks or skin color, as long as they're women.

There is no pattern that indicates where he will strike next. The assaults have been scattered from one end of the county to the other, which shows he is clever, but he's also reckless. So far he attacks only during daylight hours.

The brutality of the rapes, spitting on the victims and murder by stabbing in the heart, shows the bitter contempt he holds for women.

The murdered men were no more than intrusive inconveniences, but were killed differently from the women which indicates the killer holds some sort of perverse discriminating respect for the dominant male status symbolism.

Let's look at the level of society he represents, where he lives and what kind of work he does:

He chews tobacco to excess. He wears heavy soled work shoes. He only attacks in isolated, sparsely inhabited communities, preferable from a wooded area because that's the habitat he's most comfortable in. These traits can only be attributed to a poorly educated person who lives in a rural environment. Poorly educated doesn't mean he isn't smart. If he works at all, it's at menial chores and only part time. Otherwise, he would not have time to ride the county roads and learn his victim's habits.

Because of the way he operates, it's impossible for us to predict what he's gonna do next.

He selects his victims from a personal knowledge of their habits of comin' and goin' based on availability, vulnerability and adequate cover from which to conceal himself in ambush, observe the victims approach and attack.

That's it. Did I cover it all? Any questions or new revelations?"

"Sounds like the Grimes brothers to me," Seth answered. "That's all I can say."

"Travis," said Pace. "You just described half of the population in Catawba County. You've got'im all in the same box. How are you going to single out the killer?"

"I'm not, Pace. The killer will single himself out from the rest. We'll talk about that in a minute. I want to fill y'all in on some other stuff I've been workin' on.

Since 1930, The U.S. Bureau of Investigation in Washington, D.C. has been putting out an annual publication called, 'The Uniformed Crime Report,' which quantifies evidence of crime trends and incidents of serious crimes nationally. It contains statistics on cases similar to ours that validate some of my assumptions and that's encouraging. The Bureau did send us a historical report that is conclusive in one disturbing statistic. In recorded criminal history, this type predator-killer always works alone.

Comparing individual statistics I found that heinous rape assaults ending in murder were spread pretty evenly throughout the different class distinctions. Meaning the wealthy, professional, well educated upper class and the well to do educated middle class commit this type of crime as often, if not more so than the poor uneducated working class living on the fringes of society.

Regardless of class distinction, collectively the kinds of persons who commit multiple crimes of passion have near identical personality traits. As a consequence of this, in the early stages of an investigation, trying to determine the class of society a rapist-murderer travels in depends on the clues they leave behind. An organized or disorganized pattern of attacks will not give you the answer, but careful analysis of the clues will.

The Crime Reports confirmed we're on the right track. For example, if we had no suspects at all our analysis just showed us that our killer travels on the fringes of society, was raised in the country, but does not necessarily still live there, is poorly educated, which does not mean he's dumb and if employed at all, does menial part time work.

Just to be sure I wasn't leaving a stone unturned, I sent our crime reports and conclusions to the Bureau's new Washington, D.C. Crime Laboratory that opened this spring. They're supposed to have all the latest gadgets to identify crime suspects and their methods by using techniques that on a local or state level we can't replicate. The things they can do is impressive, but again, they were no help to us at this stage of our investigation because all of our evidence is circumstantial. I've talked to scholars, experts, sheriffs and police chiefs all over the place and none of 'em have ever run up on anything like this. One thing we all agree on is that the kind of killer we're after is driven by urges he can't resist! He will strike again and again until he's locked up or dead.

A while ago I told you that our killer will single himself out from all the others in the box. We're gonna help him do that. This plan is gonna put a smile on your face, Seth. Gordon Jackson's too.

I want Jess and Jarred in jail where they're isolated, but we can't arrest them unless they've broken the law.

Isolatin' them will accomplish two things. First, somebody out there could know more about who killed Suggs and Boles. With those guys locked up where they can't hurt anybody, someone might come forward. Second, if the rape-murders stop while they're detained, that will be a pretty good indication that we've got our killer. If the assaults continue we'll know the killer is still out there.

Start tailin' Jess and Jarred. They can't go long without breakin' a law of some kind. When they do, arrest'em and lock'em up. Gordon will think of somethin' to keep'em there a while.

One more thing. The switchboard operator received a call from a man claiming to be a member of the Ku Klux Klan, saying they're going to ferret out the murderer for us. We don't need that kind of help. If it comes up let me know.

Seth, you know Oscar Dokes, the local Klan heavy. Have a talk with'im and find out what he's up to, what he's hearing on the redneck telegraph and so on. Pace, give Seth a hand on this. Dokes' could come up with a good lead and if he does warn him not to act on it. You might remind him of what happened the last time they took the law into their own hands."

"You mean the lynching party over in Rowan County some years ago?" Seth asked.

"Right," Dokes and his bunch were in on it. He'll know exactly what you're talking about. You guys get right on this. We'll meet again later today."

Travis grimaced at the thought that in 1922 as a freshman in college he had seriously considered joining the Klan motivated by the election of Judge Henry Grady to the North Carolina State Superior Court and at the same time appointed Grand Dragon of the Invisible Knights. On the advice of his mentor, Sheriff Burton Coley, he changed his mind. In 1927, while Travis prepared to graduate from college, Judge Grady was being publicly and unceremoniously booted out of the Grand Dragon-ship because of his adamant opposition to policies of mass recruitment, secret membership and violent practices. Travis and the Judge had both earned a valuable education. It was only then that Travis took the time to check on the origin of the KKK. To his dismay and delight, he discovered that it all started in 1865 in Pulaski, Tennessee, as "a harmless prank."

While the sheriff was holding his meeting, Jess and Jarred Grimes were at the Farmer's Market clearly enjoying the wide path they were given when people saw them coming.

Typically, they paused to harass a young woman, as a gathering crowd of spectators looked on, afraid to intervene. When the girl asked for someone to summons the sheriff, the bullies threatened revenge and left.

Travis was elated when the incident was reported. Now legitimate warrants could be issued for the arrest of the brothers.

Before the deputies arrived, Jess and Jarred left town and went into hiding. With a new moonshine operation to work everyday, they couldn't afford to be sitting in jail while the mash rotted.

The next morning, Travis and Pace drove out to question the young woman at her home and have her sign two arrest warrants.

Emmy Waite crossed the road following a path through a pasture and up a slight hill into a narrow strip of woods that hid the view of her neighbor's farm house from Cedar Hill Loop Road. Along the path in about the center of the wooded area, she veered off the trail to a nearby wild muscadine vine abundantly clad with clusters of the sweet grapes. Breaking off a bunch, she returned to the path and continued her journey, eating as she went.

After working several hours on quilt frames with her neighbor, she left to return home. Happily humming a tune as she walked through the cool dark woods, she once again left the trail for the short distance to pick another cluster of muscadines from the laden vines that climbed high above the arbor of low hanging tree limbs.

Driving slowly, Travis saw a girl walking toward the road and pulled over to intercept her. "Good morning," he shouted, to which she responded with a cautious wave of the hand.

"I'm Sheriff Gant and this is Deputy Pace Tanner. Can you tell us where the Waite farm is?

"Yes sir!" she replied, pointing toward her home. "Right over yonder, that's our place."

"Are you Emmy Waite," Pace inquired?"

"Yes sir, I jist come from our neighbor's house beyond that patch a woods. We make quilts together.

"Yeah, we saw you come out of the woods, but we weren't sure who you were. We'd like to talk about the Grimes' brothers. Had you ever seen'em before they threatened you in town?

"Yes sir, more'n wuntz a drivin' our road. After the first time a hearin' their dirty mouths hollarin' stuff at me, I always run if'n I seen'em comin"

"Had they ever bothered you before at the Farmers Market?"

"No sir. That was the onliest time I ever seen'em away from out here a drivin' the roads, and I hope I don't never see'em agin'. They said the nastiest thangs to me and when I called fer the law, they said worser stuff they wuz gonna do to me to git even. I wuz really skirred then, but my daddy told me not to worry myself. He ain't skirred a them two nairy a bit. He's got his shotgun leanin' right agin' the wall by the front door."

"That's fine when you're at home," said Travis, "but what about out here? You know about the rapes and murders. You just told us the Grimes' brothers have seen you going back and forth more than once, yet you still do it. If they've seen you and we've seen you, who else knows your habits? If you're going to and from your friend's house, you need to start taking a different route each time. Maybe your daddy can drive you over and pick you up? This path you're using everyday is exactly what the killer is looking for. Now do you understand how very dangerous it is for you to keep using this route to and from your friend's house at all, much less everyday?"

Visibly shaken, she answered. "I understand. In a week or two we'll be done a quiltin' fer this year anyways."

"Hold on a minute,"said Travis. "I want you to sign these two warrants. One for Jess and one for his brother, Jarred. I'm charging them with bein' public nuisances, disturbin' the peace and assault for threatening you with bodily harm."

Emmy signed the warrants and handed back the sheriff's lead pencil. "I'll be a goin' now. I'll do like ye said, Sheriff Gant."

"That's good and thank you Emmy. Nice talking to you."

The Sugarbush

Several miles away, Ross Elders, timber cruiser for a furniture company, turned off State Highway 16 onto the other end of same county dirt road that looped five miles through the countryside past the Waite farm to emerge back on Highway 16 a mile farther north. Close to his destination, Ross flagged down a Deputy Sheriff and his partner who were patrolling the area.

"Good mornin'," Ross shouted jubilantly. "Much to fine a mornin'to be countin' timber when I could be squirrel huntin'. No rest for the weary, don't ye reckon?"

"Yes sir, Ross, I do reckon the same," the Deputy answered "Your grumbling won't get you any pity from me. I'm working rotating double shifts that have me so mixed up I don't know day from night. When I go to bed and try to sleep, I get hungry and when I sit down to eat breakfast my dick gits hard. The wife's 'bout ready to run me off!"

Laughter echoed off the surrounding hills as though a hidden audience had joined in the friendly exchange.

"Now I know how much worse off I could be," Ross remarked. "Do ye think it's safe enough fer me to git busy and earn a paycheck come Friday?"

"Hop to it," the Deputy shouted, "I'd say you're in no danger unless you're wearing a dress. Where're you gonna be working?"

"Right up that deep hollow. The company owns about four hundred acres in that parcel and they want me to cruise it agin'. About a hundred feet behind yer car, they's an old wagon track that runs a quarter mile or so and dead ends on the ridge but ye can't see where it starts 'cause it's growed over with weeds. After I drive in and mash'em down, ye won't be able to miss it. Bein' as how yer out here on patrol, I thought it best ye knowed I was the one drove off in there in case ye seen my tire tracks.

"We appreciate that, Ross. Is the company planning to start cutting timber off that parcel?"

"No! I kinda doubt if'n they will. They jist want to update the figures on their reserves. They own thousands of acres of timber all over the Piedmont and I've cruised it all one time or another. As long as I've worked fer'em, they ain't never sawed a stick of their own timber, and they won't, long as they can buy it cheaper from private

Jerry S Jones

land owners or other companies. They'll save their reserves for as long as they kin."

"I guess that makes sense!" remarked the Deputy. "Well agin', thanks for lettin' us know what you're up to. If you don't mind, when you're done workin' in here, call the office and let us know, okay?"

"I shore will, but 'less it's raining, that'll be everyday fer the next month. That's how long it'll take me to finish up."

Ross turned in across the shallow drain ditch and drove over the tall weeds that concealed the old wagon trail, leaving clear tracks where he left the county road.

Parking at the end of the wagon road, Ross attached the string holding his tally pad to the gallus button of his overalls and strapped on a belt that held a small hatchet and hunting knife used to mark each type of wood to keep track of his progress. He walked quickly toward the far property line where he would begin the tally, working his way back toward the Cedar Hill Loop road.

A "Model T" ford pickup truck with four young men, two in the cab and two standing in the bed, drove slowly past the old wagon road where Ross Elders had turned off into the woods. "Stop!" Harley Dokes yelled.

"Back up. I seen some tracks back there." After backing up, the four teenagers got out of the truck to look. "Somebody's drove off the road here!" he said excitedly. "It could be that murderin' rapist. Let's follow the tracks and see where they go."

"What about the law?" the driver asked. "Ye know what them two deputies said awhile ago when they stopped us. Besides that, yer Pop told us if we seen anythang to report it to him."

"What Pop and the law don't know won't hurt'em none," Harley answered. "Them deputies said they didn't wanna see hide ner hair of us when they come back 'round and they won't neither, if'n we git a move on."

The truck came to a stop in front of Ross' car which was headed back out the way he came in.

"Looky here, looky here," Harley whispered. "Peers like whoever owns this here car wants to leave in a hurry when he gits back. Pull up in the woods outta sight. Git our hoods so's we can take' em with us. Leave our robes behind the seat. We'll spread out a couple

The Sugarbush

hundred feet apart and work our way up through the timber. Me and Buddy'll go up this side and you'uns can cross over the holler to the other side. We'll give ye a couple minutes to git over there. If ye see anybody put on yer hoods and start yellin'. We'll come a runnin'."

Ross Elders was just making the second pass on his grid. Harley came to a barbed wire fence and was about to begin looking for his partner to plan their next move when he heard the sound of Ross' hatchet marking a tree. He moved away from the fence and crouched down peering through the woods toward the intermittent sounds which were getting louder.

He began to tremble and sweat as excitement turned to fear. Shaking and breathing heavily, he reached into his overall pocket and withdrew a 38 caliber revolver. He had seen nothing, but the intermittent chopping sounds were getting closer. He looked nervously for his partner who was nowhere in sight. The pistol slipped from his slippery palm and dropped quietly on the soft damp leaves with what Harley imagined was a deafening roar. Jerking the hood from his back pocket, he wiped off his hands and pulled the hood down over his head backwards. Close to panicking, he twisted the eye holes in the hood to the front, frantically groping in the leaves for the pistol. Just as he recovered the gun, Harley detected sporadic movement about two hundred feet away as Ross moved erratically from tree to tree.

To an uninformed observer, the stop and go, back and forth traverse would have appeared odd and threatening. Even knowing his presence was unknown to the mysterious menace, Harley was nevertheless terrified. Thoughts of one man hanged, another thrown under a train and four women raped and stabbed in the heart, his earlier bravado failed him. As he jumped to his feet and turned to flee, his hood caught on a small tree branch jerking his eye holes to the side.

In the dark and blinded, instead of jerking off the hood so he could see, he began firing the pistol wildly with no idea of direction.

Ross got one momentary glimpse of the hooded figure and with bullets whizzing around, he broke and ran along the side of the ridge in the direction of his car.

The panic stricken Harley, eye holes back in place, caught glimpses of the quarry running away. With renewed bravado he gave chase, firing until the gun was empty and yelling continuously to the top of his lungs. "There he goes, git'im boys."

Harley was gaining on the older man, who was running along a granite ledge above a creek below.

Running downhill too fast to keep his balance, once more, a branch pulled the awkward hood to the side. Blinded again, Harley plowed into a large tree. He sat up slowly, stunned and incoherent, blood pouring from a busted nose and mouth, the eye holes of his hood twisted to the back of his head and a lump the size of an egg on his forehead. The adrenaline still flowing, he regained his senses enough to relocate the eye holes just as his partner caught up with him.

"What in hell happened to ye?" his partner cried breathlessly. "Did ye git shot?"

"Hell no! I lost my eye holes and run into a tree, I think."

"Well, yer a bleeding all over. Yer hood's sopped with blood. Take that damn thing off 'fore ye kill yerself."

"I ain't takin' it off and put yourn on 'fore ye git found out!"

"Found out! We the onliest ones here, Harley. Anyways, who wuz a doin' all that shootin'?"

"I wuz! I might'a hit the murderer."

"What murderer?"

"The one I was chasin' ye dumb ass! He was a runnin' along that ledge when I seen'im last. Come on, let's git back after'im."

"The way ye wuz a shootin' at'im, he's in the next county by now."

"No, he ain't! No, he ain't! Looky down yonder by the creek! I got him! I got him! There he lays!"

Ross, running for his life and tiring, had tripped on a protruding root that sent him crashing over the ledge, head first onto the rocks twenty feet below. As he came down, his head jammed into a rock crevice, the momentum and his weight snapping his body savagely to the ground, breaking his neck. The body lay face down but the head, wedged snugly in the crevice, stared blankly skyward, blood trickling from the mouth and ears.

Scrambling down the steep precipice, the two trembling figures cautiously approaching the body were joined by a third member of the group.

The Sugarbush

"Who is that, Harley? Did you shoot'im?"

"I don't know fer shore, but I mustta. See there, he's a carryin' a huntin' knife. That's what he killed them women with. Wonder why he's got his overalls on backards?" Harley muttered, curiously.

Making a final pass around Cedar Hill loop Road, the deputies saw a second set of tire tracks leading into the woods where Ross Elders was working. "That's gotta be Oscar Doke's boy and his buddies," said the driver. "We better drive in and warn Ross that they're prowlin' around somewhere."
"There's Ross's car and over there's Harley's truck."
Stuffed behind the seat, the deputies discovered four soiled white robes, but the hoods were missing. Laughing, they remarked. "If those shitheads are wearin' those dunce hats, they sure won't be hard to spot!"
Suddenly, in the distance, gunshots and indecipherable yelling echoed through the woods.
"We got trouble. Grab our shotguns! We'll stick together and go toward the sound double time!"

The fourth member of the goblins, gasping for air, ran toward the other three gathered around the body. "Who is that feller, Harley? What happened?"
"I got him! I got the killer! We're gonna be famous, boys, 'specially me!"
"Killer! That ain't no killer!" he screamed. "That's Ross Elders! He's a deacon in my church and ye done shot'im dead!"
Deacon's ain't above rapin' and killin'," Harley shouted. "Pop told me 'bout one that done raped a girl and left her fer dead and if'n he ain't done it, why wuz he a runnin'? We all in this together, fellers! Ain't we?"
"That's right!" came a loud voice from above.
From under the pointed hoods the startled men gawked awkwardly up on the ledge into the muzzles of two double barreled shotguns.
"Get your hands above your heads just as damn high as you can reach."

While one deputy covered, the other worked his way down and disarmed the now pale and shaking youngsters. "Take off those hoods! Now!" He demanded.

"We ain't 'posed to takin'em off!" Harley said stubbornly. "If'n we do ye'll know who we are!"

"Take it off, Harley!" said one of his companions "They done know who we are."

Examining the body and routinely checking for a pulse, the deputy turned to his partner. "He's dead all right; his neck's broken! I can't tell whether or not he's been shot. Look's like Harley did all the shootin'. His pistol's empty, the other's are still loaded."

Harley, his bloodied swelling face and eyes growing blacker by the minute, began to fully realize his predicament. "Now you'uns jist hold on there! We ain't kilt nobody! That's the way he wuz when we come up on'im! Wudden he boys?"

"Lyin" now will just make things worse," quipped the deputy. "We heard everything ya'll said before you knew we were up on the ledge. You'll have plenty of time to think over what you've done here, but right now, the four of you are under arrest for murder. Just for the record Harley, how did your face get so banged up?"

"When I was a chasin' that feller, I run agin' a tree. My face ain't all that's a hurtin', I'm a hurtin' all over."

"I'll take Harley to the truck," the deputy said to his partner. We'll make a gurney out of the robes. You three take the knife and hatchet from the body and cut two three inch saplings into poles about ten feet long."

"What fer?" they asked.

"You'll see, just do it!"

When they returned with the robes, the poles were ready.

"Okay, you heroes. Slip those poles up through the bottom of the robes and out the arm holes on each side, two robes from each end of the poles, then lay it beside the body."

"Okay, Deputy! What ye want us to do now?" Harley asked.

"Get on each side of the body, pick it up, turn it over and lay it on the gurney. Oh, hell! Lay it on that thing you just made!"

As the teenagers lifted the corpse and the head came out of the confinement of the rock crevice, the taut neck muscles snapped it around to the natural position.

At this sudden movement, they stumbled backwards dropping the body.

Saying nothing, the deputies stared at the terrified boys.

Once again, they lifted up the body, turned it over and laid it on the gurney.

"Huh!" Harley muttered. "I thought he had his overalls on backards."

"What did you say?" asked the deputies' in unison.

"I said, I thought he had his overalls on backards, but it weren't that. His head is what wuz on backards."

"We're glad you figured it out, Harley. All right, two of you on each end. Pick'im up and don't stop 'til we get to your truck. Move it!"

XIII

Cousins Garrett Simms and Landis DeHart had spent time in the county jail with the Grimes' brothers and following their release continued an uneasy relationship with them.

Simms and DeHart needed a source of moonshine whiskey and the Grimes brothers needed help with their new moonshine operation.

Jess and Jarred complained that they had had problems with the liquor scorching and were looking for ways to speed up the moonshine distilling process without having that happen.

Garrett and Landis suggested they bring in Chad Odom, another of their cousins who knew how to set up a system that would get the results the Grimes' brothers were looking for.

Jess and Jarred were interested but wanted to talk to Chad first.

Garrett, Landis and Chad, all bachelors, lived together in a small house near Conover. That's where they chose to meet.

As soon as the two brothers walked in the house and saw Chad, they began to laugh. "We'd a knowed that feller was yer kin with not never bein' told. Look at them big ears, jist like you'uns!"

"That's right, fellers," Chad replied good naturedly. "Big ears hear better. That's why deers have great big ears. They can hear a twig scratch on yer overalls from a hundred yards away, so can we. Like the big bad wolf, the better to hear ye with. I'm Chad Odom. Y'all come in and set a spell."

Jess had brought along a pint of scorched moonshine whiskey to test if Chad knew the difference.

"Here, have a taste of good liquor."

Chad poured out a drink and tasted it.

"It might be good to you'uns but that liquor's scorched. It cain't be made fit to drink neither. The onliest thang ye kin do is pour it back in the mash and run it through the still agin'. That away it ain't a complete waste 'cause ye git some of the alcohol back out of it."

"Yer right 'bout it bein' scorched," Jess replied. "It'll make ye jist as drunk jist as fast as any other liquor but it tastes so nasty ye pert near have to give it away. Simms says ye kin fix thangs fer us."

Chad recognized they had a lot worse problems than scorched liquor. He would have to pull the information out of the suspicious brothers and then convince them that they needed him to fix the

The Sugarbush

problems. He and his cousins needed money to go into bootleggin' themselves and this was their best hope.

"I kin fix most anythang when it comes to makin' liquor," he said. "But remember, they ain't nothin' fool proof, 'specially when ye workin' in the woods. First off, how big's yer still and how many charges kin ye run a day?"

Jess answered. "We gotta two hundred gallon copper upright with a double bottom. We lucky to run three charges a day."

"That's a perfect size fer the woods. Them upright stills makes as good a whisky as kin be made. Using two hundred and twenty gallon stave barrel hogsetts or oak mash boxes works out jist right. A hundred and ninety gallons in the still and thirty gallons to charge the doublin' keg. How many gallons a liquor are ye gittin' outta two hundred pounds a sugar?"

"Five gallons I reckon," Jess answered.

"Somethin's bad wrong fellers," said Chad, "I ain't got no green thumb when it comes to mashin' in sugar head whiskey 'cause I never wuz no good at cookin' a no kind, not even boilin' water. I do know the recipes and the right way to mash in so's ye git the most alcohol outta the beer and into the jug. If'n you'uns fellers mash in 'zactly like I tell ye to, I can git ye up to twelve gallons from two hundred pounds a sugar. Let's talk a tad more 'bout that. I'm perty shore ye got another problem. Have ye had any trouble with yer still beer turnin' to vinegar 'cause that'll cut yer production to pert near nothin'?"

"I ain't never heared a no sech a thang," Jess answered. "What'd ye ask that fer?"

"I asked it 'cause most blockaders new to the trade is like you'uns. Their production falls off and they don't know why. Most a the time the beer's goin' to vinegar. You'uns got lots a problems and that's one of'em, but I kin straighten it all out fer you'uns."

"How come it to go to vinegar," Jarred ask.

"'Cause ye ain't cookin' yer corn meal done enough," Chad answered. "It's 'posed to be cooked the same way ye cook corn meal mush ye eat fer breakfast, done, but not over done. If'n it's green cooked, it'll go to vinegar ever'time. If'n it's over cooked, it takes longer to work off and won't make as much alcohol. It has to be jist right to git the most alcohol out of it.

Another thang is leaks. Theys two kinds and they both bad. First we'll talk 'bout steam leaks. That steam is pure alcohol that's floatin' away and condensing' in the breeze. Rye meal makes the best paste fer sealin all the joints to keep that from happenin'. The onliest place ye git steam leaks is from 'round the cape of the still when you cap it, the blowpipe connection goin' into the doublin' keg, and the E connection comin' out of the doublin' keg into the worm. If'n ye paste the joints up proper with rye paste and keep checkin fer leaks all the time, ye'll put a lot more liquor in the jug.

Of a daytime, joint leaks is easy to see, but of a nighttime ye have to paste real good and watch closer. Ye kin lose alcohol where the liquor pours outta the worm into the catch tub too. If'n the water in yer coolin' barrel gits to hot, the worm don't stay cool enough to completely condense all the steam to liquor and there agin', yer alcohol puffs out the end of the worm and goes floatin off in the breeze. That's easy to put a stop to, but you have to be careful. Ye cain't jist dump a whole bunch a cold water in to cool it down 'cause if'n ye do, the shock will knock the bead off'n yer liquor. Ye have to add it a little at a time. Ever wunzt in a while, ye stick yer finger in the coolin' barrel water. If'n it's so hot ye cain't stand it, ye keep addin' a little more cold water 'till ye kin stand it. But like I said, ye pour it in slow, say a gallon at a time."

The other kinda leak is air leaks in yer condenser worm. They kin cause the liquor to come out cloudy and customers don't like that neither. It don't taste bad, it jist looks bad. Usually, if'n the condensin' system is soldered up right and the connections comin' from the doublin' keg are sealed tight with rye paste, ye won't never have no air leaks. The heater box system I figure y'all boys need is a little different from the setup ye got now. The condensers I make don't leak. It's up to you'uns to paste up the connections right."

The knowing glances passing between the brothers told Chad he was on the right track.

"A lot of this stuff I'm tellin' ye, ye already know, but I'm gonna say it agin' fer good measure. If'n ye wanna ask a question jist butt in. Now let's talk 'bout why liquor scorches.

When ye mash is worked off, all the corn meal settles to the bottom of the barrel. As careful as ye kin be dippin' out the beer to charge the still, yer always gonna git a certain amount of cornmeal

The Sugarbush

mixed in with it. That cornmeal is what causes the nasty taste when it sticks to the bottom and scorches. Even with the heater box system I'm talkin' 'bout, the first charge a beer is gonna be cold, so ye gotta be careful and mop the still steady 'til ye cap.

What happens is that little bit a cornmeal settles to the bottom of the still and when ye put the heat to it ye have to stand there and steady stir the beer, all the time a moppin' the bottom a the still 'til it's hot enough to cap. If'n ye don't, it'll stick ever'time and scorch on ye. After ye cap ye don't have to worry 'bout that. It ain't no different than scorchin' a pot a pinto beans on a cook stove. It happens the same way.

Now here's the best part. Y'all fellers are runnin' three charges a day. With the heater box system I'm talkin' 'bout, I kin git ye six charges a day and ye'll be home 'fore night not near as wore out tired. Here's how it works.

Yer set up don't change that much. Fer the heater box, we'll set a hogsett up behind the still. That way when ye recharge, ye jist drop a spout and dump the beer right into the still.

I'll make a double coil heater worm that goes in the heater box to preheat the next charge. When ye cap the still, ye go from the cap elbow stem right to the heater box worm. When ye come outta there, ye connect on to the doublin' keg blow pipe. Yer "E" connection comes outta the top a the doublin' keg to the worm in the coolin' barrel jist like always. Besides preheatin' the next charge, the steam runnin' through the heater box worm helps cool the steam so's the water in the coolin barrel don't git to hot on ye. By the time a charge is run, the beer in the heater box is hot enough ye kin dump it in the still and cap it right then. Ye don't have to stir or mop or nothin' and the corn meal won't stick to the bottom and scorch. That's what I can do fer ye; it's up to you'uns."

"Let's talk about this," said Jess. "We cain't put no thirty gallons a beer in the doublin' keg 'cause it don't hold but twenty."

"Oh hello no fellers," Chad cried. "That won't do a'tall! Yer doublin' keg has got to be half the size a yer still. Ye got more problems than scorched liquor! No wonder ye havin' trouble sellin' it. Let me tell ye somethin'. Makin' good liquor is easier than makin' rotgut and ye keep yer customers. The doublin' keg is the most important part of yer still. Not only does it save ye a helluva lot a work and time, it takes out impurities, heps raise the alcohol content and makes the liquor fit to drink. Grain alcohol has to be doubled over. If'n you run a batch a liquor without usin' a doublin keg, ye have to run it through the still agin' or ye cain't drink it. That's what the doublin' keg does fer ye. It saves ye from havin' to run the same alcohol twice. The steam outta the still goes straight down the blow pipe and bubbles up, doublin' through the beer in the keg. That's how it works."

Jess and Jarred were listening intently as Chad continued.

"Now the best way to proof yer liquor is with clear cool spring water. Don't never use low weaks fer proofin'. Ye know yerself when the liquor first starts condensin' through the worm the stream comes out twistin' jist like a boar hog's dick. As soon as that stream stops twistin' and smooths out, it's time to pull the dick spout plug and fill the still with another charge. That smooth stream comin' outta the worm is nothin but low proof alcohol; what I called low weaks awhile ago. It's alright to pour that stuff in the doublin keg fer the next run, but don't never proof with it like a lotta folks does. It'll give the liquor a sickenin' taste that makes ye wanna throw up.

They's another thang y'all fellers is doin' wrong and I can tell ye how I know. That scorched liquor ye brung with ye is cloudy and's got tiny grains a corn meal in it. They ain't but one thang causes that. The fire under yer still's to hot. It's boilin' the beer so hard that it gits up in the cap, blows over into the doublin' keg, fillin' it up and forcin' cornmeal into the worm. That's dangerous as hell too! If'n that cornmeal clogs the worm yer still could blow all to hell maybe takin' ye with it.

Ye kin keep that from happenin' if ye'll jist punch a little hole 'bout half way up on the cap and stick a dogwood peg in it. When yer runnin', ever few minutes pull out that peg. If straight steam spurts out, yer heat's jist right, but if steam mixed with cornmeal comes out, the beer's in the cap and ye better pull some fire damned quick. Now do ye want my hep or not?"

"How much is this gonna cost?" Jess asked.

"The copper, solder and flux will be 'bout ten dollars. I'll make up what ye need fer a hundred dollars.

"A hundred dollars," shouted Jarred. "We might be teched, but we ain't that crazy!"

The Sugarbush

"Yer crazy if'n ye don't" Chad replied nonchalantly, "I jist finish tellin' y'all fellers that I kin double yer production."

"Does that include settin' it up fer us?" Jess asked.

"I don't like hangin' 'round a still place," Chad answered. "If'n you want me to set it up and work with ye the first day, that'll cost you another fifty dollars. Ye'll make that hundred and fifty dollars back in a day and ever'day after that. That's a helluva good deal and you'uns is grumblin. While I'm makin' up the double coil worm and stuff, ya'll dump two pounds a bakin' soda in each one a them barrels to boil the vinegar out a the mash. When that's done and quits frothin', dump in a little more bakin' powder. If'n it don't go to boiling' up agin', ye done got rid a all the vinegar. Then ye kin run the liquor. I don't know why it does it but that bakin' soda treatment will make ye liquor come out crystal clear. Ye don't wanna go back with the same mash. Dump out and cook up brand new mash jist 'exactly like I tell ye. By the time it works off ready to run, I'll have ever'thang else ready.

That's the deal fellers and I ain't arguing no more 'bout the damn money. If'n you'uns are ready to do business, give me a hundred and sixty dollars right now. If'n ye ain't, no hard feelings."

"All right, ye gotta deal" said Jess. "Peel'im off a hundred and sixty dollars baby brother so's we kin slip on back out to Catfish. Simms, we'll see y'all at the still bright and early in the mornin'."

"Before you'uns leave," said Chad. "I'm gonna let ye in on another money makin' secret. Nobody makes straight corn liquor or pure brandy any more 'cept fer their on use 'cause it takes to long to work off. Like pure brandy has to ferment and work off in the fruit sugar, straight corn has to ferment and work off in the corn sugar. My secret only works with sugarhead liquor. Here's what ye do.

Take a burlap sack full a corn and soak it in the creek or a barrel a water 'till it sprouts. Then ye lay that sprouted corn out on a tarp and let it dry in the sun 'till it rattles when ye shake a handful. Then ye grind it up into flour. That's what they call corn malt. When ye sugarhead mash gits to workin' good, ye put a double handful a yer malt to ever fifty pounds a sugar and I'll guarantee ye kin sell it fer straight corn liquor and nobody'll know the difference. Best part, ye double yer money agin. Once we runnin' with the new setup, I'll make some and ye kin try it fer yerself.

"Make it up now," Jarred said. "When we mash in the new batch, we'll try it in a couple a barrels. If'n it works that good, we might jist make ye a partner."

A week later the new mash was ready to run. Chad had set up the heater box and the one hundred gallon doublin keg the day before.

Everything was working like expected and the turn out was close to eleven gallons of whiskey to two hundred pounds of sugar. The whiskey with the corn malt spike tasted enough like straight corn, that it could fool anybody after the first drink.

Jess and Jarred were so dumbfounded by the overall successes, they were congratulating each other for the good job they were doing. They were good students and learned fast. All day long Chad had patiently guided them step by step, orchestrating dangerous and wasteful practices, then effecting the solutions right before their eyes.

By the time they were running the sixth and final charge for the day, Jess and Jarred had become the experts. All at once, everything was their idea. They became sullen, barking orders and complaining about the way the cousins were doing their jobs.

Garret and Landis were proofing the liquor and filling five gallon demijohns while Chad checked the alcoholic content pouring out of the worm into a five gallon copper catch tub.

The tub was full. Grasping the container by its two handles, Chad set it aside and quickly placed an empty one under the spout. He picked up the tub of potent alcohol, carefully carrying it toward the spring where Garrett was proofing.

Suddenly, the quiet was shattered by the angry voice of Jess Grimes.

"Ye crazy son-of-a-bitch! Don't walk in front of the damn furnace with that whiskey!"

Startled, Chad made a three quarter turn looking back toward Jess and as he did, stepped into the doubling keg slop hole full of scalding hot beer that had been dumped a short time before.

Crying out in surprise and pain, he stumbled and fell backwards in front of the blazing still furnace, spilling the entire container of alcohol over his body and into the fire.

Chad was immediately enveloped in white hot blue tipped flames. Screaming in agony, he bounded to his feet blindly running through

The Sugarbush

the timber, jumping, twisting, turning, falling and getting up to run again. Garrett and Landis chased the human torch, screaming for him to stop and roll on the ground. They caught up with him a hundred yards away just as he collapsed. He lay on his back, his hair an ashy stubble, his face and bare arms one huge blister, his eyes shriveled and colorless and his ears charred into the shape of miniature cauliflowers. Gently they attempted to snuff out the smoldering clothes. Shivering and emitting low groaning sounds, Chad's blistered throat swelled closed. The air flow to his lungs choked off, he went into convulsions and died.

Jess and Jarred, carrying axes approached angrily, indifferent to the tragedy.

"He's burned up dead!" said Landis, emotionally. "What we gonna do?"

"I can tell you what ya'll gonna do!" shouted Jess. "Ye gonna git that carcass away from here. They's shovels at the still place. Drag him on down yonder in the hollar where the dirt's soft and bury him. Nobody'll know the difference."

"What the hell ye talkin' 'bout! This here's our cousin and he's dead. He ain't a dog like you'uns!" shouted Garrett.

"How many times did ye tell that dumb son-of-a-bitch to stay away from the fire with that liquor tub?" Jess growled. "He got 'zactly what he had a comin'. He not only burned hisself up, he wasted five gallons of good liquor and I'm takin' it outta yer part."

"I'll kill y'all worthless bastards!" screamed Landis, awkwardly attempting to pull a pistol from his pocket.

"Pull it on out ye sorry son-of-a- bitch," Jarred shouted. "While ye at it, me and Jess'll chop off yer goddamned heads."

Sympathetically restraining Landis, Garrett backed away.

"We'll take Chad's body away from here," he said. "We'll be back to git our share a liquor and don't try shortin' us none."

"DeHart jist threatened to kill us, so's I'll tell you'uns what ye'll git. Nothin', not a damn drop. Now pick up that stinkin' pork rind and git it outta here!"

Backing up slowly, axes still poised, Jess and Jarred turned and walked back toward the still.

"Jarred," Jess said chuckling. "Did ye see how he wuz a jumpin' and twistin'? Funniest damn thang what a feller'll do when fire hits his ass."

"Yeah! He looked like one of them fireballs that comes a flyin'n down a lightning' rod rollin' 'round and bouncin'off'n ever thang. Onliest thang is, fireballs don't scream and hollar. That worthless low life bastard shore did have a set a lungs on'im. My ears are still a ringin' from all that squallin'. Jess, we best see what Pop thinks 'bout this."

"We will baby brother, soon as we finish up and carry the liquor outta here. Pop ain't gonna believe the turnout we got and its all our'n. We'll need him to help us tear down. I gotta feelin' we better find a new place."

Melinda opened Sheriff Gant's office door. "I thought I better interrupt you and Seth," she said, "the coroner's on the phone and it's urgent that he talk to you."

"Fine, Melinda, put him on."

Travis picked up the phone. "This is Sheriff Gant." Frowning, he said. "Somebody will be there in five minutes," and hung up the phone. "What in god's name is goin' on," he mumbled.

"Seth, the coroner is over at the funeral home. An hour or so ago, two men brought in a body that had burned to death accidently, asking for it to be embalmed. The mortician reported it to the coroner who examined the body then called us because he thinks the men are lying about the way the man died. You and Pace get over there right now. Bring the two men in for questioning. They're cousins on parole from the county jail. We know'em both, Garrett Simms and Landis DeHart."

Sheriff Gant leaned against the wall as Seth began questioning the distraught cousins.

"Okay guys!" said Seth. "Tell us what happened and don't start by repeatin' that cock and bull story about Chad catchin' on fire when a cigarette fell outta his mouth into the pan of gasoline he was usin' to wash the grease off of a crank shaft."

"We wanna tell ye in the worst way," Garrett answered. "We don't wanna go back to jail fer violatin' our parole. We got a score to

The Sugarbush

settle, a big score! We kin help ye more outside than we kin behind bars. Can we make a deal that'll keep us outta jail?"

"You know we can't promise anything," Seth replied. "After we hear your story, if we agree that you're more help to us out here than in the slammer, we'll see what we can do."

Garrett and Landis told in detail all the events that led up to Chad's fiery death.

"Do you think they'll move the still place right away?" Travis asked.

"No doubt in my mind 'bout that, but it'll take'em all night if'n they move ever thang," Landis answered.

"Are you willing to tell us where it is?"

"Do we have a deal?" they asked.

"You have a deal!" If they're tearing down and moving like you think they are, the chance of catching them in the act is slim, but it's the best chance we've got. Tell us where it is. We'll hit'em at daylight tomorrow morning."

"We'll do better'n that! We'll show ye where it is! Me and Landis ain't gonna take the law in our own hands when it comes to them two. Goin' to jail for murder won't bring us no proper satisfaction. We wanna wave at them two devils when yer cartin'em off. We ain't gittin' off'n their trail 'til they's done in or we're six feet under, one way another."

"Seth!" said Travis. "You know what to do. Let me know what time you want to leave in the mornin'. I'm goin' with you."

At daybreak the next morning, the raiding party moved in on the location. As they got closer, Travis asked. "Do you smell that?"

"Yeah!" Pace answered. "It smells like mash and it's strong. They've dumped it, right?

"Right, they're gone, beat us to the punch agin'."

When they reached the still place, Travis' suspicions were confirmed. The culprits had dumped the mash and removed everything.

"Seth," said Travis. "Your men can finish up the search here. You and I need to get back to the office. Bring Simms and DeHart."

From a place of concealment, the Grimes' brothers had seen Simms and Dehart leading the raid.

"Pop was right," Jess whispered. "Put them rats on top a our list of folks that needs killin'."

XIV

In Catfish, Beau and Lila Fontaine, were recovering from an unexpected visit by one of Beau's cousins from Bayou Cane, Louisiana. The cousin, Lucian Devine, and his wife, Lacy, were a warm pleasant couple, but their fourteen year old son, Cass, was another matter. He was well into a difficult stage of his life, puberty.

When the relatives arrived and the youngster got out of the car, Reicie knew by the way his eyes lit up when he looked at her that he was having a hormone attack.

After greeting the unexpected guests, Beau said. "I don't believe y'all know our niece, Reicie Dupré. She lives here with us."

Reicie chuckled in amusement as she greeted the wide eyed Cass. The chuckle quickly turned into rippling laughter when she heard his croaking voice which reminded her of a young rooster making his first attempts at crowing.

Cass was smitten by her beauty. His eyes shifting alternately from her infectious smile to the firm rounded breasts moving rhythmically in time with her laughter.

Lucian and Lacy were humbled and embarrassed. They had come north looking for work and finding none, needed to earn enough money to get them back home.

"You know," said Beau. "Y'all come along just at the right time. I'm behind on gatherin' in my corn and hay. I was gonna hire a couple hands but if you and your boy want to help, I'd as soon pay you as somebody else. We can finish bringing in what's left in the fields next week and y'all can be on your way."

All the bedrooms were upstairs except Beau and Lila's. The next morning Reicie got out of bed and poured a bowl of water to take her morning sponge bath. Just as she was about to slip out of her nightgown, she heard a board squcak outside her door. Curious, she casually opened the door to a surprised Cass, obviously peeping through the keyhole.

"Having trouble tying your shoes?" she asked curtly.

Stammering for words, the red faced peeping tom retreated down the stairs.

Blushing, she sighed deeply and leaned against the door.

"I was just as surprised as he was!" she said, to herself. "Boys at school do things like that, but I never expected it to happen at home. Well now I know what to expect for the next week. At least I won't have to worry about it while they're working in the fields."

That day after lunch, Reicie paid a visit to the outhouse. As soon as she closed the door she noticed a small hole in the side of the building that had not been there before. She looked closer and saw that a pine knot had apparently fallen out of one of the boards leaving an irregular one inch hole.

Thinking no more about it, Reicie started back toward the house then remembered she had seen Cass come out from behind the toilet just before lunch. She returned to examine the knothole from the outside and found the grass and weeds trampled down on the ground below the hole, indicating that Cass was at it again. "Maybe, I can cure him of this nuisance. I'll think of something!" Reicie said under her breath.

That evening after supper, Reicie filled a basting syringe with the sticky reddish purple juice from polk berries she had gathered earlier and walked to the toilet.

She closed the door behind her. A beam of dusty sunlight poured through the knothole. Grasping the rubber bulb of the syringe with both hands, she quickly placed the dispenser in the hole. She was ready. Almost immediately, a shadow darkened the beam of light and Reicie squeezed as hard as she could, sending a spray of juice spewing through the hole, inundating the unseen target.

For women, the necessary visits to any kind of toilet, much less a spider infested outhouse, was a traumatic experience to begin with, but the thoughts of being observed doing so was horrifying.

The next evening Beau and Lucian sat on the front porch talking about old times while Lila and Lacy bustled around the kitchen preparing supper.

Reicie was in her bedroom upstairs just finishing writing a letter to her father. She got up from the desk to go down and help in the kitchen. As she did, she looked from the window down into the backyard and saw Cass crawling underneath the back porch.

The Sugarbush

"What on earth is he up to now?" she thought. "Oh, he's probably trying to find a coin or something he dropped that fell through the cracks between the boards."

She waited a few minutes, but he didn't come back out.

"What is he doing under there?" she pondered. Then a thought occurred to her. Often during hot weather her dogs would lay under the porch where it was cool. When she would go out to get water she could look down through the narrow cracks and see them there. If she could see down through the cracks, Cass could see up through them. That's what he was doing underneath the porch! He was trying to look up the women's dresses!

Reicie walked out the kitchen door onto the porch and hung a pail under the water pump spout. She was standing directly over the prying eyes as she began pumping the handle to fill the bucket.

"He can't see much!" she said, to herself, "but he's going to get an eye full in more ways than one."

When the bucket was full, she lifted it off of the pump spout and promptly dumped the contents on the boards under which Cass was lying.

"Aunt Lila!" she shouted. "I'm going to scour off this dirty porch right quick. Then I'll be in to help you and Lacy."

As irritated as she was with Cass, Reicie could not help bursting into laughter when she saw him emerge from the end of the porch and disappear around the corner of the house on his hands and knees.

"Something must be mighty funny out there!" cried Lacy, as she walked to the screen door. "What are ye laughing so about?"

"When I dumped the water to scour off the porch, I chased out a critter."

"Oh, my!" cried Lacy, "I hope it weren't a skunk?"

"It was a skunk all right!" replied Reicie, "but I don't think it'll be back."

Later in the week Reicie pumped water from the well to heat for her evening bath. After filling the tub, she took the pail back to the kitchen and returned to take her bath. Before shutting the door, she intuitively looked around for Cass, who was nowhere in sight.

As she shut the door to the bath, she saw the linen closet door move ever so slightly.

"Oh, there you are!" she said, angrily.

She opened the door and found Cass crouched under the bottom shelf.

"You're welcome to use my water when I'm finished," she said in a low sharp tone, afraid of being heard. "You'll have to wait outside until I'm done. Now get out of here." Cass uncoiled from the cramped space and making no excuses, smiled shyly at her as he left the room.

Reicie caught him once more before the family left for Louisiana. It was the biggest surprise of all and showed his determination. After dark, Cass had climbed a tree by the back corner of the house, but could not see into her bedroom window from his perch. Determined, he climbed onto the tin roof and inched himself along the eaves toward the small gable and window. Reicie had just undressed and was standing nude in front of her mirror combing her hair. She thought the strange noises she was hearing from the open window were coming from the backyard or kitchen porch. Her two dogs ran to the window, standing on their hind legs with front paws on the window sill, nervously looking out into the darkness. "What is going on out there?" she asked aloud.

At that moment, Cass' face appeared right into the muzzles of two snarling dogs sending him tumbling backwards off the roof into Aunt Lila's snowball bush ten feet below. Reicie ran to the window and was about to call out for help when she saw him limping toward the back porch, apparently still in one piece.

The harvest gathered, Lucian and his family prepared to leave on the long journey south. Lila prepared them a basket of food to eat along the way.

"Beau," Lacy said tearfully. "We know ye didn't need no help gittin' in yer crops. The Lord will bless ye fer what you did fer us. Someday we pray we kin do you'uns a good turn."

"Oh, hush, Lacy Devine! Y'all have a safe trip and good luck. It was a pleasure visiting with you. Be sure to remember us to family and friends when you get back home."

That evening, Reicie joined Lila who was waiting for Beau on the front porch. Whether in warm weather on the porch or cold weather

The Sugarbush

by the fireplace, the day always ended the same way, with everyone sitting down together to discuss the events of the day, the news and endless other subjects. This special social exchange always ended on a comical or pleasant note.

During the past ten days, Lila had noticed a growing apprehensiveness and anxiety in Reicie's behavior that was unusual for her cheerful unassuming niece. Even now, with the visitors gone Reicie seemed preoccupied, tense, as though any moment she would explode.

"Something seems to be troubling you dear," Lila said softly. "Do you want to talk about it?"

In a torrent of frustration and pent up emotions, Reicie recounted the events of the past week and the fears they had ignited.

With genuine concern Lila grasped both of Reicie's hands in hers. "I had no idea you were going through such an ordeal. You should have told me about this the first time it happened."

"I thought about telling you after the third incident," she replied, "but decided not to.

Now, I'm glad I didn't. Lucian and Lacy are such delightful people and would have been crushed if they had known about it. They already felt they were imposing on our hospitality besides feeling bad about being paid wages for helping Uncle Beau when he really didn't need help.

Under normal circumstances, what Cass was doing would have been more comical than anything else and I should be grateful to him for the lessons I learned, but right now I'm not. He brought an element of fear into my life that wasn't there before."

From that remark, Lila realized that Reicie was trying to come to terms with much more than the curiosity of a juvenile's awakening. She needed to talk, to sort things out and Lila was ready to listen.

Venturing to get at the real underlying concerns, "Lila asked. "Are you embarrassed because Cass might have seen you undressed or something?"

"No, no, not so much that," Riecie answered. "Thanks to my mother, I have a wholesome attitude about the body, man or woman. It's just that all of my life I have felt safe and protected, almost invincible. My bedroom was my kingdom, my sanctuary. I thought dreadful things only happened to other people. It never crossed my mind that it could happen to me!

There's a maniac running around in our county raping and murdering women and he's killed two men. I've been saddened to tears from the accounts in the newspaper of the suffering and terror the victims must have endured before they were killed, but I had never felt personally threatened. Now I do! I'm looking over my shoulder wondering if I'm being stalked!

I was out of the room no more than two minutes to take the bucket back into the kitchen and in that short time, Cass was able to hide himself inside the linen closet by the bath tub only a few feet from where I would be bathing. When he did that, he brought the killer into a place where I felt safe. When he climbed that tree and crawled across the roof to look in my bedroom window, he brought the killer into my sanctuary, a place I thought was impenetrable. I felt so vulnerable.

From all this I've had to face the fact that no one is ever completely safe even under the best circumstances. It was a lesson I needed to learn and it could not have come at a better time or happened in a more impressive way. I was more than surprised, I was shocked! It's imprinted on my mind and I won't forget it."

"Then what Cass saw or didn't see is not really the issue, is it?" Lila asked.

"In a way that's right,"Reicie answered. "But he was there all the time, lurking somewhere. I could feel it twenty four hours a day, even dreamed about it!

He was so persistent, I'm sure I didn't catch him every time so it's possible he saw me without any clothes on which doesn't bother me because I'm not ashamed of my body, but I am modest. Someone seeing me naked would not faze me as long as it was by my own choice or happened by accident. In the situation with Cass, regardless of how innocent the motives, there is something dreadfully frightening about knowing you're being stalked by someone watching your every move from a hiding place.

For this to have happened at this time is good and bad. It's good because I'm more aware of everything around me and no longer have that false sense of security in thinking I will always be safe, beyond danger.

The Sugarbush

It's bad because if Cass could get so close to me unnoticed, so can the killer that has everybody in the county scared to death.

I've experienced it both ways. I told you about Bobby Hagan and I peeping at each other down at the swimming hole. That was exciting, but Cass peeping at me was scary.

Maybe someday Cass and I will laugh about all this because we all go through puberty. His desire to see a naked woman is no more compelling to him than my desire was to see a naked man. I think boys really like going through that stage.

Most of the girls I've talked to say puberty was a terrible experience for them, but to me it was wonderful because my mother prepared me for it in a wonderful way. I get warm feelings just talking about it. The body changes, the sensations from innocent touches that gave me feelings I had never felt before and the curiosity, oh, the curiosity! My mind was filled with all kinds of questions that had never occurred to me before. I woke every morning and examined myself in the mirror to see if I had changed overnight and sometimes I could see that I had. That was an exciting time for me and it isn't over yet."

"Do you feel insecure or intimidated because of all this?" Lila asked.

"Insecure, absolutely not, intimidated, absolutely yes!

I'm secure in who and where I am as a person. I have never felt otherwise, even when my mother died. But this past week the light finally came on. It hurled me out of my little girl playhouse into the realization that besides the rewards in life there are also the risks and either can happen to anyone. No one is excluded. Some rewards like, Mother Nature are free for all to share. Other rewards whether personal or material, you have to work for."

Struggling to come to terms with her fear, Lila noticed Reicie's voice which at the beginning had been anxious and an octave higher than usual, gradually returned to a more relaxed normal tone. Rambling from one thought to another, saying the same things over and over again in different ways had relieved her tenseness.

"You don't need any answers from me dear. You already have them," Lila said assuredly. "You've recognized that good and bad occupy the same space and you've come to terms with it very well. That sounds like a logical contradiction and maybe it is. The world's full of'em so don't be surprised when you hear one. For example, we're living in a notoriously violent community where your good neighbors are willing to die for you one minute and kill you the next. That's a logical contradiction.

I'm glad you told me about Cass for another reason too. Now I won't have to go through life wondering how my snowball bush got so mangled, but poor Lacy will forever be wondering how Cass got poke berry juice all over the front of his overalls. I thank the Lord that given time, my snowball bush will grow out of its pitiful condition and so will Cass.

I think your Uncle Beau's coming out now. He's very protective of us so maybe it's best we don't mention what went on with Cass, at least not now. I'm sure Beau did the same thing when he was growing up but please believe me when I tell you that men have mighty short memories when it comes to things they've done in the past."

The Sugarbush

XV

Emmy Waite finished washing the breakfast dishes while her mother prepared to leave for town to work her booth at the Farmer's Market. "Mom!" she said. "I'm goin' over to Junie Feather's place soon as I finish cleanin' the kitchin'. She's done with her chores by now and we only have a little stitchin' left to finish our last quilt. Do ye think it's safe to take the path through the woods? I don't mind walkin' the long way 'round, but I'd like to pick some muscadines 'fore the birds eats'em all. The vine's full this year."

"As long as yer careful I think it'll be all right!" her mother replied. "While yer a pickin', bring me and Pa a couple a bunches. If'n they's enough there, when I git home this evenin' we'll take a peck bucket over and pick some fer makin' jelly."

Emmy left the house and walked down the long path toward the road. As she crossed, she heard a car coming, but it was not yet in view. Always afraid it may be the Grimes brothers, she hurried to get out of sight.

The balmy warmth of the rising sun had not yet melted away the mornin' dew drops glistening from the weeds and foilage. Bird chatter was busy and boisterous, almost drowning out the sound of the approaching car. Walking faster, she entered the woods following the path toward her detour to the muscadine vine.

Subtly a foreboding fog enveloped her bringing with it a chill that penetrated to the bone!

The birds stopped singing, no breeze stirred, complete silence prevailed! Slowly she came to a halt. Twinges of panic began pressing from the top of her skull forcing the blood from a gradually paling face. Ahead she saw muscadine stems lying in the path. Turning her gaze to the vines, she saw they were bare.

Frozen in place, Emmy's sense of danger screamed run, but her muscles would not respond. At that moment, a crow landed in the top of the vine tree, shattering the silence with furious cawing of alarm. Jolted out of the paralytic trance that held her spellbound, Emmy whirled and ran, dropping her sewing basket scattering the contents on the pathway.

Travis and Pace had parked beside the road intending to familiarize themselves with this very pathway and follow it through the woods to the south leg of the road where they would meet up with Seth and another deputy. Stepping out of the car, they heard Emmy when she stumbled and began screaming for her dad.

Quickly retrieving their shotguns from the car, they dashed to intercept her.

"The birds stopped a singin'!" Emmy cried hysterically. "The muscadines is gone! The crow seen somethin' bad up there! I know it!"

"Listen to me Emmy," Sheriff Gant said sternly. "You're safe now. We won't let anyone hurt you! Now come with us and show us what you're talking about."

The three ran up the path. She showed them the barren vines and the stems lying in the path.

"Sheriff" said Pace, "These stems are all over the place. Look here! Somebody was standing behind this tree. He wasn't just pickin' wild grapes, he was waitin' for Emmy."

Pace picked up a stick and probed the leaves. "Tobacco juice, lots of it and it's fresh!" he exclaimed. "The leaves are packed down where somebody's been coming and going! "He's here close, Sheriff," Pace whispered, making his shotgun ready."

"He's headed for the other end of the road and he's gotta big head start on us," said Travis. "Take Emmy back to the road and send her home. You drive around and set up a road block where it hits the paved road and stay there. Maybe we can box'im in. I'll come out of the woods about a mile from you. If Seth shows up send 'im down to pick me up, if not, I'll start walkin' toward you 'til he comes my way, but you stay put."

Travis broke into a run, but slowed to a fast walk to be sure he did not lose the trail. Soon he thought he heard something and stopped to listen. It was the sound of a car but it was too far away to tell the exact direction the sound was coming from. Following the trail he came upon a logging road bearing fresh tire tracks that were still filling with water. Now able to distinguish the direction the car was going, he broke into a run following the tracks west toward the rendezvous point with Seth.

He reached the county road and stopped to catch his breath from the long run through the woods. Looking north, he saw dust still

The Sugarbush

settling off to the side of the gravel road and prayed that Pace had reached the intersection in time to block the escape.

With Seth nowhere in sight, the sinking feeling of another opportunity lost compelled Travis to needlessly trot up the road towards the settling dust. His hope was somewhat restored when he heard a car approaching from the south. It was Seth. Seeing the sheriff waving his arms, he knew something was happening. Seth sped up and as he drew along side, Travis jumped on the running board shouting "go, go, go!"

Meanwhile, Pace turned onto the paved road and sped west to set up the road block and wait for Travis. About two hundred feet from his destination, he turned left on a track that led to a tobacco barn a short distance off the highway where he knew a farmer was flu curing tobacco.

As he came to a stop, he saw the farmer on his knees stoking one of the fire boxes.

"I'm Deputy Sheriff Tanner?" he shouted. "Have you seen or heard any cars come up loop road in the last few minutes?"

Busy at his work the farmer shouted back. "No, I ain't!"

Pace sped back out and down the highway to block off the dirt road. Shotgun in hand, he got out of the car and waited. It wasn't long before a car speeding toward him rounded the last curve and came into view. It was Seth.

Travis stepped from the running board and climbed quickly into the car. "He came this way. I saw the dust settlin'. Didn't you see him?"

"No," Pace answered. "He didn't go east or I would have passed him on the way here. A farmer right up the road at that tobacco barn said he hadn't heard or seen anything. He went west toward the junction at Aiken highway. He had to!"

"I got that sinkin' feelin' again." Travis replied in disgust.

The two patrol cars reached the junction without seeing anything. Disappointed, they pulled off the road.

"Let's get out and talk a minute," said Travis. "Then we'll decide our next move if we have one. When I came out of the woods and looked north toward Pace, dust was still settling and it had to be from the car I was chasin'. Seth, you came from the south and you didn't pass anybody before you picked me up. As fast as we were drivin' to meet Pace, we could have missed signs where he turned off to hide in the woods again. If he hasn't gotten away while we've been on this damn wild goose chase, he's somewhere between where you picked me up and the paved road where Pace was."

If that farmer is curin' tobacco, he has to be there most of the time to keep the heat up. Let's go back and talk to him again.

Pace, you block off the road again while Seth and I talk to the farmer. Let's go!"

Seth pulled around the shoo-fly at the end of the tobacco barn and parked. The farmer was sitting on a bunk bed under the shed roof drinking a cup of coffee.

"Good mornin'," Travis shouted. "I'm Sheriff Gant and this is Chief Deputy Seth Stephens. We'd like to talk to you."

"Come on over and have a cup a coffee with me," the farmer replied, "I kin use some company. Wuz it you'uns that drove in here this mornin'?"

"No, that was Deputy Tanner you talked to before."

"I ain't talked to nobody 'cept my wife. I been to the house to eat breakfast and pick up some fresh coffee grounds. I weren't here when he showed up but I seen the tire tracks when I got back. Come up here and let me show ye what he tore up. What he cain't fix, he's gonna pay fer!"

Seth looked puzzled and dumbfounded. Travis caught on right away.

"Do you have anybody helping you today?" He asked.

"Nope, jist me. This here's my last barn a the harvest; little old tip leaves. I stay here of a night to keep up the heat. Of a day I come and go. How come him to park behind the barn?

"What do you mean?"

"I seen the tire tracks where he parked his car outta sight behind the barn. The onliest reason a feller hides his car is so nobody knows he's there. Who ye huntin' fer?"

"Whoever was parked behind your barn is who we're huntin' for. That wasn't Deputy Tanner's tire tracks. He never got out of his car. He pulled around the shoo-fly and talked to a man who was stokin' the firebox on the far end of the barn, then he left. If that wasn't you he talked to, it has to be the man we were chasin'."

The Sugarbush

Travis walked up under the shed roof and picked up a stem containing several muscadines. "Do you have any muscadine vines growing around here?"

"Nope, they won't grow in these pine trees. Nothin' grows in pine trees but pine trees, soil's too poor. I don't have no idea where them come from."

"I do," said Travis. "We believe the man who was hidin' behind your barn is the one that's killed two men, raped and murdered three women and a child. We were hopin' you had seen him. Now we're glad you didn't. If he had still been hidin' here when you got back he would have killed you or tried to. You're in no danger now. I doubt if he'll ever come back into this neck of the woods again. We didn't catch'im, but we got a lot to be thankful for. Well thanks for your time and help."

"I'm proud I could help ye, Sheriff Gant. If'n it weren't fer me poking' around and takin' so long to git back over here, ye'd have another murder on yer hands. Now it makes me awful proud ye don't."

Seth pulled up by Pace's car and Travis shouted. "He got away. Meet us back at the office. Set up a staff meeting for 5:00 this afternoon. We need to go over this with everybody."

Upon his arrival, Melinda followed Travis into his office. "There's a negro man waiting to see you. His name is Silas James. He will only talk to you personally."

"What about? I'm really busy right now."

"He wouldn't say and he's been waiting quite awhile. There's something about him, his manner, the way he speaks and conducts himself. I think you should talk to him."

"Okay Melinda, send him in, but tell'im I only have a few minutes."

Silas was forty-five, tall, lean and muscular, with graying hair around his temples. As he entered the office, Travis noticed he moved with a graceful ease, exuding an air of self confidence that was neither pretentious nor threatening. He liked the man immediately.

Then Silas did something unexpected and out of the ordinary for negroes addressing whites. He reached out to shake hands and with firm conviction introduced himself. "Mornin' Sheriff Gant, I'm Silas James."

Travis, still standing and caught off guard, hesitated slightly then with a chuckle and friendly smile, grasped the large black hand. "Please to meet you Silas. What can I do for you?"

"I heared 'bout the big problem ye run up on," Silas replied. "If'n ye'll put me to work I kin hep ye git shed a that problem. I spent twenty years workin' fer the State a South Carolina Prison's Warden handlin' blood hounds, trackin' down fugitives, escapees and readin' crime scenes fer evidence and clues. Many a time he had me a workin' with city police, county sheriffs' and sometimes G-men. Ye better know right off bein' as how all the lawmen wuz white, they never liked it at first, that is 'till they seen what I could do that they could take credit fer. If'n ye hire me, it ain't gonna be no different here.

I got a natural callin' fer readin' sign and trackin' down folks whether they's good, bad, men, women, children or critters. That's all I kin tell ye."

Travis' answered. "Well Silas James, if you can do what you say you can, your timin' couldn't be better. Before I put you on the payroll, are you willin' to give me a demonstration? I just came in from the scene of an attempted assault. I'd like you to read it for me while it's still fresh. We almost boxed this guy in, but he got away. You wanna give it a try?"

"I'm ready when you are!" said Silas. "I'll always be ready, twenty four hours a day. I gotta couple a young hounds if'n we ever happen to need'em. I keep 'em 'round fer somethin' to cuss at. Don't tell me nothin' more 'bout what ye want me to look at. Let's wait and see what I come up with."

When they arrived at the path in front of the Waite farm, Silas went to work. Examining the ground he began to explain what the sign told him.

"Two men and a woman come back and forth on the path from the road. Somebody dropped a spool of thread with a sewin' needle stuck in it and they's a thimble layin' under that gooseberry bush. They wuz two men been standin' behind these trees. They wuz tryin' to git the woman between'em. The leaves is thick on the ground, but the

The Sugarbush

soil's damp enough so's when you brush'em away they's a light outline of the footprints. Both of'em's got big feet and they big men, weightin' two hundred pounds or more. They's fresh prints and old prints, so they been comin' here ever'day or so. They chew a lotta 'baccer and you don't have to see it, ye kin smell it. They was eatin' muscadines off'n that vine yonder 'cause they's seeds and stems scattered 'bout. They six foot tall or better 'cause they picked all the muscadines pert near ten foot up on the vine. They never stayed more'n a couple hours 'cause they never took a leak or nothin'. Now let's foller their trail and find out where they wuz a goin'. Ye can see fresh tracks goin' down through the woods. They's three men and they a runnin'. The lighter weight man is a runnin' on his toes and the two big men is runnin' flat footed and clumsy, all over the place like if'n they wuz drunk. Hard as they wuz puttin'em down, ye ought a felt the ground a shakin'. Ye kin tell by the long strides they young and in good shape."

After following the trail for about two hundred yards, Silas stopped and plucked several strands of hair from some low overhanging limbs. Handing them to Travis, he said. "The lighter weight man has dark brown hair. One or both of the other two men is got black hair."

Soon Silas reached the logging road where a car had been turning around and parking. "They been in here more'n wunz't. "Anybody kin read this sign. Ye can see where they pissed and took a dump a day or two ago. From the looks a the turnin' radius, they drivin' a tin lizzie coupe."

"We've got one more place to show you," Travis said. "Let's get back to the car and drive around to the tobacco barn."

When they got to the barn the fire boxes were freshly stoked, but the farmer was not there. Silas quickly explained a car had come in fast causing some damage. He showed where it had been parked behind the barn and pointed out where one man had stood by the corner to conceal himself while the other man was doing something else. "These feller's got good instincts. They knowed ye'd try to head'em off and box'em in. When they drove in to hide, the farmer tendin' this 'baccer weren't here. That's all I kin see right now. How does that fit up with what y'all know that I don't know?"

"You know more than we do, Silas, and you weren't here," Travis answered exuberantly. "Let's talk about the strands of hair you found. The brown hair has got to be mine because I was chasin'em and remember runnin' into those branches. The black hair belongs to the guys I was chasin' and it's curly."

"It's black fer shore," replied Silas. "Curly, maybe so, maybe not. When hair that coarse gits jerked out of a body's head, it curls up like a pig's tail. It's hard to say one way another."

"I'll remember that," said Travis, scratching his chin. "Right now I'm tryin' to put all this into perspective. You've taken the guess work out and that means a lot. Two men workin' together is a surprise to me, but nobody else. Everything we come up with keeps pointin' back to the Grimes brothers. They have black curly hair, they're big, tall, clumsy, clever and capable."

"Silas," Seth asked with an edge of sarcasm. "The farmer could have been here when those guys drove in to hide. He could be friends of theirs. What makes you so damn sure he wasn't here?"

"I go by what the signs tells me Chief. Them fellers is dangerous and they wuz skirred, makin'em twiced agin' as dangerous. They come in fast, run over that pile a 'baccer sticks layin' yonder, bustin'em up, and then pulled behind the barn runnin' over two stringin' horses. Friends don't do shit like that to friends and I don't see no dead bodies nowheres."

"You're right, Silas," Travis intervened with a chuckle. "The farmer was at home when they came in and as a result, he's alive and well. Any more questions there Chief Deputy?"

"Just checkin'," Seth answered.

"Sheriff Gant," Silas asked, as he pulled a hair off of a splinter in a low hanging rafter. "Does that farmer have blond hair?"

"No, maybe his wife does," Travis replied. "Let's go. We have a staff meetin' at five o'clock. On the way into town we'll fill you in on everything we know."

At 5:00 PM, Travis opened the meeting by introducing his new supply room attendent, Silas James, and gave a brief history of his skill in handling blood hounds and tracking.

"As you know," Travis continued. "The warrants for the arrest of Jess and Jarred Grimes are still outstandin'. Let's keep up the

The Sugarbush

pressure until they're apprehended. You've all heard about the attempted assault today on the Waite girl south of town. The suspects outsmarted us again and we're sorry about that, but we've got a lot more to be glad about. Three people who are alive this afternoon came within a heartbeat of being murdered this mornin'.

Emmy Waite was walkin' alone through a patch of woods near her home. Suddenly sensing danger, she turned and ran, saving her own life. Her instincts were correct. She was within twenty feet of the killer's ambush.

On a hunch, we just happened to be nearby and intercepted Miss Waite. We sent her safely home and gave chase. The killers knew they had to get clear of the area fast or we would have them boxed in.

Not too far away and barely outside of the box, a farmer was curing a barn of tobacco. He unexpectedly ran out of fresh coffee grounds and went to his house to get more. Shortly after he left, the killers drove in and concealed their car behind his barn from where they watched us continue pursuing in the wrong direction. Shortly before the farmer returned, they drove back out and made good their escape. Before and after the killers came and went, the farmers timing was perfect which saved his own life.

As I pursued on foot through the woods, Deputy Tanner drove around to set up a road block. He stopped at the tobacco barn just long enough to ask the farmer if he had seen or heard a car come up the dirt road only two hundred feet to the west. The farmer answered no, which was an honest answer because he wasn't the farmer, he was one of the killers.

When I walked in this room a few minutes ago, I heard Deputy Tanner lamenting because he missed his chance. He was so close! He almost had him!

Let me elaborate on those well intended remarks for a moment. Deputy Tanner did not almost have him, the killer almost had Deputy Tanner and not because Deputy Tanner did anything wrong. He was indeed close, no more than thirty feet, but if he had been as close as he needed to be in order to apprehend the suspect, he would not be here to talk about it.

Why? Because Deputy Tanner would have approached the suspect and a hidden accomplice with no sense of danger. Like the farmer, he saved his own life.

Am I making my point? All of you are thinkin', Grimes' brothers! Remember them, but also change your focus to other possibilities because if it's not them, somebody in this room may be acquainted with the killers. Possibly many of us know them. Approach everyone with caution! Burn that thought into your minds and be sure those working for you understand it.

Here's more good news. I asked Silas to go back out to the scene and interpret the signs to see what he made of them.

He told me more than I knew and I was there. All the things we've been guessing and speculating about were clarified today. These are the things we now know for sure. I concede that two men workin' together are responsible for the killings. They are big strong men, weighing around two hundred pounds. At least one of them is over six feet tall and has black hair. They're young, in good physical condition and wear about a size ten brogan work shoe.

We all agree that when they select a victim they are determined and focus on that person. It was demonstrated today. They had been stalkin' Emmy Waite for some time. They attack during daylight hours because that is when the victims they know the habits of are available and vulnerable. It also provides the rural setting they prefer. They feel at home in the woods, but will attack from the seclusion of barns or outbuildings if the setting is isolated enough. That was the case in the murder of my Aunt Bertha.

Today was the first failed attempt they have experienced that we know of. We don't know if that will slow them down or not. We'll have to wait and see.

Keep constantly alert. Silas says it is not uncommon in a manhunt like this for the hunted to become the hunter, and he's right. That was proven today in the case of Deputy Tanner in his encounter with the killers' at the tobacco barn. Be on your toes and watch each others back. The killers' were lucky, but they also outsmarted us. Don't underestimate them!

The next morning, Pace hurried into the sheriff's office."Travis, I think we just got the break we've been lookin' for. The sheriff from Brownsville, Texas called me back. He located the mailman for the Mosley's route. On the day Annie Mosley was murdered, he delivered their mail around 12:30 PM. Like I thought, he started his route early so he wouldn't have to rush to catch the train. As he drove away from the mailbox, he saw Annie comin' down the lane after it. That makes the coroner right about the time of Annie's death. This changes everything, doesn't it?"

"It clears up the time of death, for sure! Travis said, thoughtfully. "See if Jess and Jarred's alibi's still holds up with the new time."

I've already done that. They don't!

XVI

It was the first week in October. Reicie Dupre undressed and reclined on a secluded knoll looking down on the river threading its way south between curtains of brilliant fall colors. Her thoughts went back to the Pisgah National Forest and innocent childhood days, envisioning times when she and her mother lay nude in the cool autumn breeze, gazing out over the mountains that faded into a translucent veil of purple infinity.

Her eyes moistened, revealing the tenderness of those special memories. She recalled her mother explaining the coming and going of the seasons and how the cycles were common to all creation relating to birth, life, death and rebirth. She talked of how man used his observations of the ever changing positions of the moon, stars and planets to determine the beginning and ending of the four seasons, dates on a calender that in the lives of mankind served many useful purposes, but in the reality of nature were totally meaningless. And how mother nature reigns fickled but powerful, tantalizing man with mere hints of what she will do next, sometimes fooling the fruit trees into blossoming early only to be laid barren by a late frost, and other times bending the abundant fruit laden branches to the ground. One time abundant and forgiving, the next time barren and unforgiving.

"Why didn't God make all of the seasons the same, beautiful and abundant," Reicie asked.

"He once did," her mother replied. "Remember? God planted the Garden of Eden and created Adam and Eve to live and work there. God gave them free choice and they chose to disobey Him. That one act of disobedience changed everything. God established new laws of nature to fit the new conditions. He left the new laws of nature to rule on their own and never interferes unless He finds it necessary to remind us of something we are so anxious to forget, His presence. The heavens and all creation are bound by these laws of nature, but one of those laws pertains strictly to the creatures God created in His own image, the human race. It is the law of human nature, the choice between good or evil, obedience or disobedience. It is the only law in God's universe that we can choose to obey or disobey and we are the only creatures with that prerogative. I pray that you make the right choices in your life."

The Sugarbush

Reicie rolled onto her back, playfully trying to catch the many colored leaves fluttering down to cover her naked body in nature's camouflage. She looked up through the tree branches at the fluffy wind driven clouds and contemplated her own interpretation of the seasons.

Winter began when the first silver frost blanketed the landscape with frozen air filled crystals of moisture pushing up out of the earth, forming multiple miniature ridges of soil draped in delicate filigree webs of ice that vanished at the touch of a sunbeam.

Spring began with the appearance of dainty violets held gingerly in the clasp of lush green foliage nurtured by a hidden brook, a pathway lined with bright yellow jonquils, blossoming fruit trees and birds singing profusely.

Summer began with all of Mother Nature fully clothed, early sunrise, long days, balmy evenings, moonlight strolls, wading in cool streams, hymns of praise and lively gospel sermons reverberating from the open windows and doors of churches on Sunday morning.

The beginning of autumn was the most elusive and exciting of all. It began with a sudden change in the atmosphere. Going to bed one evening and waking the next morning knowing that something in the air was distinctly different. The breeze did not feel the same. It carried a dry crispness, the sweet smell of harvest, grain stubble and corn fodder, all suggesting winter is nigh. Back to school, looking out the windows to see the lush green of summer gradually giving way to the many colored leaves soon to fade and tumble baring the hardwood trees and bushes naked to the rigors and chill of winter. What a wonderful time ahead. Halloween, Thanksgiving and Christmas.

Reicie turned back on her stomach, squealing softly as the leaves gently tickled and scratched as they slid off her skin, leaving behind an army of mites, ants and inch worms prowling over their amazing discovery looking for a choice morsel to take a bite of. Frantically brushing them off, she laughed, reminded of how Gulliver must have felt being carted away tied, bound and covered with tiny people who were equally amazed at their discovery.

Now concentrating her gaze on the river in anticipation of the initial surge of water that would come rolling down when the Lookout

Dam flood gates were opened, she heard the hiss of releasing water pressure. The hiss grew in volume to a roar.

Soon a mini-tidal wave of white capped waters tumbled down the river washing the banks of debris and uprooting small trees that quickly vanished around the bend. Then everything seemed as it was before.

As Reicie stood up and prepared to leave. A damp chilling draft created by the powerful surge of energy, swept up the hill raising chill bumps causing her to shiver.

She bent down massaging her legs, gradually working her way up to the thighs and buttocks. Eventually her hands came together between her legs moving with deliberate firmness through the pubic area up past the navel to cup and lift her breasts then ending the motion with arms stretched above her head. Gracefully rotating her lithe body in circular motions, first one direction and then the other, she stretched backward then forward, finally bending to pick up her dress and dropping it down over her head. Brushing back her moist and tangled hair, she lifted the blanket, shook it in the wind, draped it over her head and turned toward the distant yellow glow shining warmly from the window of her bedroom.

"Come!" she commanded softly to her dogs.

Not far away, Garrett Simms and Landis DeHart could have cared less about the beauty of the autumn evening that surrounded them. They had found the new location of the Grimes' brother's moonshine still. After weeks of searching without success, the surprise discovery of the day seemed too easy. Although well pleased with their luck, they were apprehensive and anxious to leave the area.

Parked near an old sawmill site, before setting off on the search they had taken the precaution of concealing the car to resemble just another pile of dead tree branches.

It was dusk when they finally reached the clearing and hurried forward to remove the camouflage of brush. Throwing the branches left and right, they stumbled backwards in surprise and fright at the sight of two grinning faces, distorted in rage.

Jess and Jarred exploded from the brush knocking the wilted cousins to the ground and quickly disarming them.

The Sugarbush

"I'll cover'em, Jarred!" Jess shouted victoriously. "Ye bring up the car. We'll hogtie them pig shit squealers and cram their rattin' mouths full of snot rags."

The hunters had become the hunted and now captives.

While Jarred was bringing up the car, Garrett and Landis tried to buy their freedom by offering money, the car or any of their possessions that might appease the wrath of their captors.

"Shut up, ye ignernt shit eatin' dogs," Jess barked.

After being securely bound and gagged with their own bandannas, they were thrown on top of one another, wedged between the front and back seat of the vehicle.

The car moved slowly up the narrow maintenance road to the crest of Lookout Dam and stopped.

"Leave the motor runnin' and the lights on," said Jess. "I'll git out and scotch the back tires so's she don't roll backards."

Jess and Jarred dragged the two helpless men over the rough concrete surface to a point directly over the funnel of raging water below. Anxious, Jarred cut the rope looped around Landis' neck.

"Hold it!" Jess cried. "Garrett's goin' first! Remember little brother, DeHart called us worthless bastards and pulled a gun to kill us. He goes last! I want'im to see what he's in fer."

Jess cut the rope looped around Garrett's neck and pressed the side of his head hard against the concrete.

"All right, Jarred! Sit on'im so's ye kin hold his legs down. Ye got the straight razor?"

"I got it!"

"All right! Go to cuttin'off'n them big ears!"

"Hold'im, Jess! He's a buckin'! Bust'im one!"

"Hell no! I want him to feel it a comin' off!"

Jarred stretched the ear away from the side of Garrett's head with one hand and with the other sliced it off.

Blood squirted from the wound, filling the ear cavity and spreading on the concrete. "Looky here!" said Jarred, staring in the dim light at the severed ear in his hand. "It don't look so big off as it did on."

"Throw it off'n the dam!" Jess chuckled, twisting Garrett's head and brutally slamming it down on the open wound. "Git the other'n! Hurry up!"

Groaning in pain and starved for air, Garrett lay still as Jarred cut off the other ear and tossed it over the wall.

Landis, watching the brutal butchery tugged in desperation, managing to slip one foot out of his boot and free of the bonds. Hands still tied behind his back and dragging the rope attached to one ankle, he struggled to his feet and ran for his life.

Jarred and Jess turned just as Landis started his desperate dash.

"Ketch'im, Jarred! Ketch'im!"

Even with both hands tied behind his back and a bandanna crammed in his mouth making breathing difficult, the flight for survival gave Landis an edge in the foot race.

Landis was about to escape. In a final effort, Jarred lunged forward stepping on the rope trailing behind the fleeing prey, sending both men crashing to the concrete.

Landis took a hard blow to the head as he fell. Struggling to breathe, he was not able to recover quickly enough to get back on his feet before Jess was upon him.

Landis kicked with all the strength he had left, striking both Jess and Jarred in the face repeatedly during the violent struggle.

The brothers, gasping for air, pounded the hapless victim into unconsciousness. Jarred fumbled in the darkness to open the straight razor. "I cain't see a damn thang, Jess. Strike a match."

Trembling from exhaustion, Jess would strike a match and the breeze would blow it out. Then another and another until both ears were severed and cast into the darkness. Jarred used the razor to cut and remove the ropes. "He's a comin' to Jess. Shew, he stinks. He done shit and pissed his pants. I got his arms ye grab his feet."

"I got'em baby brother, Jess shouted. "Groan, ye stinkin' son-of-a-bitch. We know ye kin talk, we seen ye kin run, let's see if'n ye kin fly. Swing'im Jarred. On the count a three, let'im sail."

The roaring water silenced the impact of Landis' body on the concrete spillway below.

"Somebody'll see him a layin' down there!" Jarred shouted.

"No, they won't! They openin' the gates on this side tomorrow mornin'early. That'll wash him away. Now let's git Simms down there with'im."

Garrett was a gory picture lying there on his back with his head in a steadily spreading pool of blood. Circumstances had unmercifully

The Sugarbush

prolonged his torture, providing unwanted time to regain his senses. He thought his cousin, Landis, had gotten away, but realized that for himself, there was no chance of surviving. His fear turned to anger, resolving to not lose hope and put up the best fight he could until the end.

In agonizing sadness and pain, Garrett wept. The brothers had been gone for what seemed like an eternity, lending hope that maybe the torture was over and they were not coming back. It was a cruel thought. His heart began to pound as once more he fought off terror. He heard them running toward him. They were very close. He muffled his sobs and pretended unconsciousness.

"He's out cold, but he might be playin' 'possum," Jess panted. "I'll hold'im while ye cut off'n them ropes. Then I'll git his arms, ye git his feet jist like we done with DeHart."

As they stood up, Jarred shouted. "Wake up ye no eared bastard!" The command was not necessary. The lifeless form exploded with a last vestige of energy, kicking Jarred in the face with both feet and slamming his head backwards striking Jess hard on the chin and mouth.

Garrett's last desperate effort to break free was short and futile. Still struggling when they cast him into the roaring abyss below, the last words he heard were, "since ye like them big ears so good, go find'em!"

Before good light the next morning, the dam tender drove up the maintenance road to the crest of the dam and got out of his truck to make a visual inspection of the gates before raising them to release more water.

Accustomed to the routine, he sauntered across the dam to a point above the gates and looked down to be sure there was no debris in the guides. Satisfied that everything looked okay, he turned to leave and stepped on something soft. Thinking it was a snake, he jumped back, cursing for his carelessness. Recovering, he bent down and shined his flashlight on the unusual object.

Still not sure, he picked it up and with a gasp, let it fall back to the concrete. It was an ear. A human ear!

Travis rolled over in bed and reached to answer the phone. It was Chief Deputy Stephens.

"Sorry to wake you on Saturday morning, Sheriff, but the same thing just happened to me and you know how it goes when duty calls. The office just got a call from the power house operator at Lookout Dam. His dam tender found a man's body lying in the spillway. That's all I know right now."

"Round up Pace and Silas James," Travis replied. "I'll be at the office in twenty minutes."

The caravan of sheriff's cars followed by an ambulance raced into Catfish and down Island Ford Road toward the dam. As they passed the entrance to the old Cline place, Travis turned to Silas. "That's where Sheriff Coley was killed. This is the closest I've been to the place since that day."

Silas pulled into the parking area at the crest of the dam and stopped. The dam tender, flushed and excited, began talking before Travis and his men were out of the car.

"Just settle down!" said Travis. "Start over from the beginning."

"Well, sir," he said. "I come up here this mornin' 'bout daylight to inspect the gates on the other end a the dam 'fore I opened'em. When I started to leave, I stepped on somethin' soft and jumped back 'cause I thought I done stepped on a snake. In warm weather when the sun's a shinin', this place is plumb eat up with snakes, but since it turned cold of a night, I wudden payin' no mind to watch fer'em. It skirred hell outta me! When I took and looked closer at what I stepped on, I couldn't figure it out. So's I picked it up and it was a ear, a human's ear. I dropped it damn quick, right back where it was a layin'. Then I started lookin' about and seen all this blood ever'wheres. That's when I looked down and seen that feller layin' in the spillway. If'n I hadn't a stepped on that ear, that feller would be long gone down the river by now. They's blood puddles all over the place and two of'ems got footprints in'em. They's a boot and a sock layin' over yonder too.

"Other than picking up the ear, did you disturb anything else?" Travis asked.

"No, sir! Not that I know of!"

The Sugarbush

"Good! Now you stay right here by the car until we look things over. We may want to ask you some more questions."

"Well now, Sheriff, kin ye git that dead feller off'n the spillway? The lake's a risin' and we need to open them two gates."

"Yes we can! Just give us a little time here. We'll let you know when we're done.

Seth, post a man at each end of the dam. We don't want any sightseers wandering around out here. After the dam operator called us I'm sure he called his wife or somebody else whose been spreading the word. Go ahead and bring up the body. Take plenty of pictures."

"Okay," Travis continued. "Let's see what we have. From the looks of the drag marks and blood trails we've got a road map, but I can't make heads or tails of it. "Silas, can you connect the dots?"

"It took me awhile Sheriff," Silas answered, "but I figured it out. They's two victims and two killers, that's plain to see. They captured the victims somewhere else and brought'em here. It's the dark a the moon so's they parked here with the lights on and dragged'em out on the dam. As dim as the drag marks is, ye kin still see threads and fibers from cotton ropes they wuz tied up with. They wuz drug at the same time by two men 'cause the scuff marks from the killer's shoes is different. One had rubber soles and the other'n's leather. They drug'em to the first set a spillway gates and stopped. If'n they cut off'n one man's ear, they more'n likely cut off'n the other'n's too. That accounts fer the blood on this end next to the downstream parapet wall. When they wuz done doin' that, the trail of blood shows they throwed'im off'n the dam.

Now if'n ye take notice, they ain't no drag marks from here to over yonder on the other end of the dam where the ear's a layin'. That means that while they wuz a butcherin' on the first man, the other'n managed to git his boot off. Ye kin tell that by a lookin' at the heel of the boot and the leather scraped off on the cement. The boot off allowed him to slip his foot out the ropes and make a run fer it, but they ketched him. Now come over here and I'll show ye how I know they ketched'im. Ye see right here, they's skin and blood on the cement where one a the men chasin'im fell hard and tried to break his fall with his hands. Right back here they's a short piece of cotton rope with black marks from the rubber soles on his shoes. He stepped on the rope that must a been trailin' behind the feller that got aloose and they both fell. Right up here ye kin see blood and hair where the victim's head hit the cement. They wuz a struggle 'cause they's two overall buttons layin' there and a few blue denim threads. They beat'im near to death 'cause he got quiet. They wuz so fer from the car it wuz to dark to see so's one of'em was striking' matches so's the other'n could see to cut off'n the ears. They swung'im backards and forwards so's they could heave'im far as they could over the wall. Ye kin tell that by the pattern a blood splattered on both parapet walls.

The palms a one of the killers' hands is scraped up good, but he's skinned up worser'n that. Look here! They's two trails of blood drops goin' back a different route to the car. I figure the victim wuz a kickin' 'cause his hands wuz still tied and I'd say both the killers is marked up a plenty.

Look at the footprints in the blood. They size ten and a half. I know that, 'cause that's the size I wear. They look the same, but they ain't 'cause the pattern a the soles is different. Both killers will have blood on their shoes if'n they don't wash it off. That's 'bout it. Whatta y'all think?"

"Silas!" Travis answered with a chuckle. "I was thinking exactly the same thing you were!"

"They just got back up with the body," said Seth. "The dead man is Landis DeHart. Both his ears were cut off and the damnedest thing, when the men picked up his body to put it on the gurney, they found his other ear underneath him. The other victim has got to be his cousin, Garrett Simms. I'd bet my life on it!"

"So would I!" Travis agreed. "Organize a river search. We need to find his body. The current is to strong for dragging, so don't even try it. There's a lot of fallen trees along both shorelines and if we're lucky, the body might hang up in one of'em. Search from the water using boats on each side of the river. With the flood releases, if the body didn't get hung up on something it could be a long way down river by now. Call the adjoining counties down river and ask'em for a hand. Seth, talk to the power company. Ask'em to hold off releasing any more water for as long as they can."

"I jist looked at the body," interrupted Silas. "He's still got on his left boot and they's blood on the sole. The right foot too. He left his mark on whoever killed'im, that's fer shore."

The Sugarbush

"Okay, listen up!" Travis said sternly. "Off hand, the Grimes' brothers' are the only ones I know of who had the motive and the mentality to commit a slaughter like this. Their luck just ran out, but we still have to catch'em. Wherever they're hiding, they're feelin' pretty safe believing the bodies are miles down the river by now. They're probably convinced that nobody knows or ever will know what happened to Landis DeHart and Garrett Simms. They also know there's a warrant out for their arrest and I think they're dodgin' it for no other reason than to annoy us by thumbing their noses' at the law. If I'm right about that, it may give us an edge in the hunt.

Everytime the Grimes' farm was searched there was evidence that the two boys are livin' there at least part time if not all the time. The driveway goin' into their place is long enough for them to see us in time to skedaddle, so let's see if we can cut off their escape route; maybe we'll get lucky.

Let's send four of your men to work their way up behind the barn and spread out. We'll give'em thirty minutes to get in place before we move in from the front.

Seth, when we go in, you search the house. You've done it before and if anything is that much different you'll notice it. Take Silas with you. We're looking for bloody overalls with missing buttons, bloody shoes, a knife, rope, or anything that will tie them to the murders. Pace and I will take two men and search the premises and outbuildings.

While we're waiting here we can finish gathering the physical evidence and casts of the foot prints. We're gonna need every available man and vehicle. Goin' into the Grimes' farm, I want it to look like an old fashioned calvary charge on wheels. It's our turn to put the fear of god into somebody."

XVII

Beau and Reicie finished breakfast and started toward the barn. "Reicie!" said Beau. "You curry comb the horses and saddle'em while I finish up feeding."

Reicie opened the tack room door to get a curry comb and immediately slammed it staggering back, screaming for her dogs and Beau.

Appearing out of nowhere, her dogs stood at the door barking and snarling as Beau ran to her side.

"What is it?" he shouted. "What's wrong?"

Faint from the sudden shock of the grisly image, she hung on to Beau for a moment. "There's a man in the tack room! He's hurt!"

"Wait here and hold the dogs while I take a look."

"Mud, Sand, come!" she commanded.

The dogs ran to her side and she knelt down holding them back by the collars.

Beau cautiously cracked the door and peered inside. "What in god's name!" he exclaimed.

The man was kneeling on the floor, sitting on his legs and mumbling deliriously. His hair was matted with mud, algae and bits of debris. His eyes, black and bloodshot stared out in blank confusion, his swollen face distorted in pain.

"This man is hurt, bad! Somebody cut off his ears! I'll put him on the horse. Let's get him to the house."

Lila had heard the commotion and stood on the back porch watching as they approached.

"Who is that?" she cried.

"We don't know," Reicie answered. "I found him in the tack room."

"Open the door!" shouted Beau. He carried the babbling man into the kitchen and laid him on the floor by the kitchen stove.

"He's in shock. I saw a lot of this in the war. Get me some bandages and a blanket to wrap him up in. Heat some water and fill the hot water bottles. I've got to get these wet clothes off of him and get him warm or he'll die before we get to the hospital."

"Take him to Dr. Rawlings. It'll be quicker," said Lila.

The Sugarbush

"Today's Saturday, Lila."

"Oh yes, I forgot. Dr. Rawlings is at the hospital on Saturdays."

"Lila, get dressed while I get his clothes off and bandage his wounds. Reicie, you take the horse to the barn then hurry back and get ready to go. By the time y'all are ready I'll be done here."

As they drove toward town, Reicie sat in the back seat to comfort the injured man who was now asleep. Speaking softly, she said. "As soon as he got warm he dozed off, poor man! I keep asking myself, what kind of a person would torture somebody like this?

"I don't know," Beau answered. "According to his driver's license, his name is Garrett Simms. He was carrying some cash so whoever did this to'im wasn't after money."

After leaving the hospital they stopped by the sheriff's office and explained to the desk sergeant what had happened. The sergeant asked them to check back before leaving town because Sheriff Gant would want to talk to them when he returned.

Pace wheeled into the Grimes' farm driveway and sped toward the main house followed by Seth and another patrol car.

"See that column of smoke down by the barn," cried Travis. "They must be butcherin' hogs today."

"How do you know?" Pace asked.

"It's just an educated guess, but it's that time of year. After they kill the hog they have to dip the carcass in scalding water before they can scrape off the hair, kinda like scaldin' a dead chicken to remove the feathers. The smoke you see is coming from the fire that heats the water in the scaldin' barrel. Don't stop at the house, drive straight to that smoke."

Mr. Grimes was alone, busily scraping the carcass of a large hog. Travis and Pace jumped from the car hoping to intimidate the old man, but he never even looked up from his task.

"We're looking for Jess and Jarred! Where are they?"

"If'n you ain't blind, it's damn plain to see they ain't nobody here but me. Now git to hell off'n my property. Ye ain't welcome here!"

"Why thank you, Mr. Grimes," Travis replied. "We'll just make ourselves comfortable and sit a spell. Your boys can't be too long gone, their scraping tools are laying on the bench full of hog hair.

Deputy Tanner, keep a shotgun on our host while I have a look around. If he gives you any trouble, blow his damn head off.

"You don't need to look around," Pace shouted. "Our rear guards are bringing in two prisoners, handcuffed and apparently not too happy."

"You mean to tell me we actually caught somebody for a change," Travis shouted.

"They walked right into us, Sheriff. You should a seen their faces when they looked up into the muzzles of these shotguns."

"It's a wonder you even recognized'em," said Travis, his face now darkened with controlled anger at seeing the bruised and swollen faces, evidence of the murdered cousins desperate struggle to survive.

"We done know 'bout yer chicken shit warrants," Jess yelled. "Serve'em and git off'n our place."

Now close enough to read the sheriff's expression, the blood drained from Jess' face. His belligerent glare transformed into a look of suspicion, a flash of fear and apprehension.

Seth approached, calling Travis to the side. Unable to hide his excitement he whispered, "Silas found everything. Their bloody overalls, socks, rags, pieces of rope, a bloody straight razor, everything! Both pairs of overalls are missing a button. They hid the stuff in a salt sack behind the brine box in the smokehouse. The straight razor has Mr. Grimes' initials on the handle. I asked Mrs. Grimes if she had ever seen it before and she told me it was her husband's and for me to put it right back where I found it. Silas is puttin' everything in the trunk of my car, then he's gonna drive it on down here.

The Grimes' brothers' shifted nervously as the private conference broke up and Silas drove down to join them.

"What's that nigger doin' here on my place?" bellowed Mr. Grimes. "Ye git the hell away from here nigger!"

"He's with us," Travis calmly replied. "When we leave he'll leave. If you open your big mouth one more time, you'll be joinin' us too.

Okay boys, turn around and open your hands!"

Seeing the lacerated heels of Jarred's hands, Travis was astounded at the accuracy of Silas' observations. "Jarred, you're gonna wish you never stepped on that rope to catch Landis DeHart and so is your brother."

The element of surprise could not have been more convincingly demonstrated. The brothers looked at each other in disbelief and dismay.

"Who in hell is Landis DeHart," Jess replied belligerently.

"He's only half of your problem," Travis barked. "You're both under arrest for the murders of Landis DeHart and Garrett Simms.

"We ain't murdered nobody," Jarred shouted.

"Hey, Sheriff!" called Silas. "Come over here! I wanna show you somethin'. Look how they stuck this hog to bleed it. See here! Right under the left leg into the heart and here's what they stuck it with."

Laying on the bench was a pointed blade, ten inches long, one inch wide and razor sharp on both edges.

"Bring it with us," Travis whispered. "I want the coroner to examine it to see if it matches the stab wounds of the rape-murder victims. Seth! Have your deputies put the prisoners in the car and take off their shoes. I want Silas to look at'em."

One of the deputies removed the brogans from the feet of the two brothers and handed them to Silas.

"Jist like we figered," said Silas. "They bloody."

"Ye damn right they's bloody ye dumb nigger," Jess shouted. "We been a butcherin' hogs! What in hell did you'uns expect? A damn nigger don't know the difference between our blood and a hog's blood."

"Neither do I," Travis responded. "Y'alls blood and a hog's blood is probably a perfect match. Seth, see to it those shoes get labeled so we know who they belong to and take pictures of the soles. Then send the prisoners straight to the county jail."

"Things are finally coming together, Sheriff," Seth commented as they drove toward town. "It's been a long time since I felt this good. We got'em dead to rights for all this killin'. Now Gordon Jackson can stop talkin' behind your back and our friends might quit dodgin' us."

"I'm glad you feel good Seth," Travis replied. "I feel good too, but not for the same reasons you do. I don't care about Jackson's two faces and I don't care about fair weather friends who avoid and ostracize me over an honest difference of opinions. I feel good because an hour ago we had eight unsolved murders, now we have six. Besides some good luck for a change, two of the crimes were solved through good detective work that produced rock solid physical evidence and the arrests of two suspects that will be convicted on the basis of that evidence. Maybe I've been lookin' a gift horse in the mouth all along, but I'm not ready to admit I'm wrong yet."

"Travis!' Seth replied in frustration. "The evidence, circumstantial or not, has always been strong. Their alibis don't stand up and now we have a murder weapon. What more do you want! What's it gonna take for you to own up to what everybody else already knows! We have the murderers' in custody. With them behind bars the killin's are gonna stop."

"You're jumpin' conclusions, Seth," Travis replied. "First let's see if the coroner can match that blade to the wounds of the women victims, and if it's a match, that may be good enough for you and everybody else, but I'm still the boss and only the grand jury can override me. The blade is the first piece of good physical evidence we've been able to come up with. I would like to have something more to go with it that would put the Grimes' at the scene of at least one of the rape-murders. A matching footprint or anything. It's not just circumstantial evidence that's sendin' up the red flags, it's other dissimilarities too. After what I've seen today, those dissimilarities don't look quite so dissimilar, but there's still a doubt in my mind. It's possible you'll get your way in the end anyhow because Gordon won't be content sendin' Jess and Jarred to the electric chair for murders unrelated to the rape killings. We'll have to wait and see. Anyway Silas, tell us how you found the clothes and razor. What led you to'em."

"It worked out real fine Sheriff, that's all. I done had twenty years a practice. In South Carolina most everday they had me doin' all kind a searches, misdemeanor and felony that wuzn't always bad serious. Like I done told ye, I gotta particular callin' fer this work. I know what to look fer. I don't never think 'bout ketchin' nobody. Fer somethin' like today, I think on ever combination I know of to figure the right mind set fer the criminal I'm workin'. It ain't that hard when ye git used to it. Sometimes I mess up and has to start over to git back on track.

Women criminals is lots more dangerous than men, but they thinks alike and foller jist so many mind sets. I think I knows'em all by now. Some criminals have lots a common sense and good instincts fer survival. Ye 'bout never find where they hid something, but they mess up in other ways. They all clever in different ways and I can spot one kind from another. 'Course sometimes, it's jist plain luck. That's what happened today, jist plain luck. I ain't done nothin' special. When we got outta the car, Chief Stephens and two deputies went right to the house. I went straight fer the car. They wuz traces a blood on the steerin' wheel and pedals, but the thang I took to wuz the blood trail leadin' to the smoke house. It all made sense. Them boys never meant to leave them clothes hid in the smoke house, they jist stuck'em in there 'till they could git shed of'em fer good. Since they wuz smoke curin' meat and saltin' down fatback, they knowed if their Ma went in there to tend the fire, she wouldn't be lookin' 'round hot and hard to breathe as it is. They wudden worried 'bout the law ketchin' up to'em neither. They wuz rattled 'cause they counted on everthin' goin' right. Well it didn't, and they got flustered, careless and I wouldn't doubt a little skirred. That come 'bout 'cause Landis near 'bout got away and damn near kicked their faces off. It wuz plain to see they undressed right there and walked over to the well to draw water and wash up. They wuz blood stains on the gourd dipper handle. I never looked no more after I found the salt sack holdin' the overalls and straight razor. Criminals that clever act 'bout the same way evertime. It weren't nothin' special. I jist got lucky, that's all."

Travis responded. "If you feel better not takin' any credit for yourself, that's okay. What you did today wasn't luck. Did you ever think about writing a book, say a trainin' manual," Travis asked? "With your talent and experience, you could teach law enforcement agencies and get paid for it. We sure have learned a lot from you. I'd be glad to help you put it together when you're ready."

"I've thought on it myself," Silas answered. "A book 'bout the ones we ketched and how we ketched'em, and the ones we didn't ketch and why we never ketched'em would make good readin'. Somethin' could be learned from mistakes I made 'bout what to do and what not to do that might save a tracker's life. Pointin' out what a clue is and what a clue ain't, how to find'em and what they tell ye to make'em work fer ye might be hepful. A book would git ye off to a good start if'n ye born with the feel fer investigatin', trackin' and readin' sign. It's somethin' that kin be teached fer shore. Still yit, ye gotta git out and do it if'n ye 'spect to be good at it. A book's the onliest way I kin pass on what I know 'cause 'less somebody tells'em, folks got no way a knowin' what color my skin is. As fer as trainin' goes, white folks ain't ready fer a black teacher and might never be.

While we talkin' 'bout teachin' and learnin', I kin tell ye somethin' ye ain't ketched onto yit. Some folks cain't be teached nothin'. They won't learn from teachin, books or experience.

Experience ain't experience if'n ye don't learn somethin' from it. Folks that refuses to learn is like a dead tree stump ye keep stumbling' over ever so often, but ye don't know why come ye keep gittin tripped up. One day ye fine'ly figure out the onliest reason yer stumblin' is 'cause the stump's in yer way. Bein' it's dead and never wuz worth nothin' to ye nohow, ye pull it up by the roots and git shed of it. Then ye'll be walkin' ahead without havin' to watch where ye goin' all the time."

"We'll follow up on this conversation later," Travis remarked as he turned in at the county jail. "When you're finished here, Seth, I'll see you back at the office."

Travis entered his office followed by the desk sergeant. "Sheriff," he said. "Early this morning a family from Catfish brought a badly injured man in to the hospital. They say his name is Garrett Simms."

"Garrett Simms is alive!" Travis exclaimed.

"Yes sir, just barely. The report is right there in front of you. His ears are cut off and he's beat up bad. Nobody knows what happened to'im. They got'im sedated. He's sleepin' last time I heard. As soon as he wakes up and can talk, Doc Rawlings is gonna call and let you know.

"Thank you, Sergeant. That's the best news I've had since I got this job."

Melinda, Travis yelled. "Call Seth and Pace at the county jail and tell'im to forget the river search for Garrett Simms. Tell'em to get here quick as they can."

Shortly thereafter Seth and Pace hurried into Travis' office."Did we hear right. You want the river search for Simms called off?"

The Sugarbush

"Yes. He's alive and don't ask me how he survived. That's our second miracle for today! Travis answered.

"The second!" Seth exclaimed. "What was the first one?"

"We finally caught somebody, that's what. Everything around here happens in bunches."

"Who found Garrett," Pace asked.

"Beau Fontaine's niece, Reicie Dupre. Garrett was in their tack room and nobody besides us knows how he got there. Fountaine's farm is about a half mile down stream from the dam. Right now, Simms is sedated and sleeping. As soon as he's awake and can talk, Doc Rawlings is gonna call us."

"There's our eyewitness, Sheriff," Seth shouted.

"We can't be to sure about that yet," Travis replied. "He's in bad shape. Right now it's touch and go. He could die before he wakes. If he does wake up he could have brain damage. Who knows! Let's hope for the best.

The Fontaine's are gonna stop back here before they head back out to Catfish. As soon as I talk to them, we'll go over to the hospital."

"Sheriff," said Pace. "I should take Melinda and go to the hospital right now. As serious as Garrett's condition is, somebody ought to be by his bed side just in case he wakes up and doesn't have long to say some last words."

"Good idea Pace. I sent Melinda home. Pick her up and take her with you."

After retelling what happened to Sheriff Gant, the Fontaines and Reicie left with a promise from Travis that he would keep them informed about Garrett's condition.

The phone rang and Travis answered. It was Doctor Rawlings.

"Sheriff", he said. "You better get over here right away. The bedside nurse just informed me that Simms has been stirring and should be waking up any minute now. If he wakes up before you get here, that's okay, because usually when a person hurt this bad first comes to, they're incoherent and confused. I can overcome his exposure to the elements, yet tough as he is, I'm still worried. His blood pressure keeps easin' down. I know he's bleeding internally, but he has to be awake to say 'ouch' before I can find out where he's losing the blood from. I have to examine him before you can talk to'im."

"I understand!" Travis replied. "I'll be there in a few minutes."

Travis joined the small group gathered around Garrett's bed.

"Sheriff," said the Doctor. "When he wakes up, the nurse is going to ask him some simple questions that he should know the answers to. If he answers correctly, we'll know he's coherent enough to let me know where he's hurting. Then you can talk to'im."

Soon Garrett opened his eyes, at first staring at the ceiling then shifting his eyes to dwell for a few seconds on each person in the room.

"Mr. Simms," the nurse asked softly. "Can you hear me?"

He stared at her saying nothing.

"If you can hear me, tell me your name?"

He continued to stare at her quizzically.

"Mr Simms, can you tell me what day this is?"

"This doesn't look good at all," Dr. Rawlings whispered to Travis.

"Mr. Simms," the nurse said in a loud voice. "What month is this?"

Garrett's swollen eyes surveyed the room once more then he said. "Why ye askin' me all them dumb questions fer? Jist tell me where I'm at and why I hurt so bad?

Everyone in the room breathed a sigh of relief and began to chuckle.

"You've been injured," the nurse answered. "You're safe now. You're going to be just fine."

"I'm alive in a hospital!"

"Yes. Doctor Rawlings is right here and needs to examine you and ask some questions."

"I'm "bout to perish. Kin I have a drink a water?"

"Of course," said the Doctor. "Drink through the straw and take small sips about a minute apart. Don't talk anymore right now. You're losing blood internally and I need you to help me find out where. When I press on your abdomen tell me where it hurts."

"I ain't lettin' ye press on nothin' 'til I have my drink a water and talk to the sheriff."

The Sugarbush

"I'm right here, Garrett."

"Landis got aloose and run. Did he git away?"

"No, I'm sorry! He's dead!"

"They cut off'n my ears, and throwed'em over the dam. Did they do that to Landis?"

"Yes. We found both of his ears but we didn't find yours. Who did this to you?"

"Ye found Landis' ears?"

"Yes! But tell us who did this. We've arrested two men and we need you to identify'em. We'll bring'em right here into your room. Do you feel up to it?"

Garrett wiped away his tears and tried to smile.

"I ain't sayin' who done nothin' and I ain't pointin' nobody out 'til ye promise me somethin'."

"All right," Travis replied. "What is it?"

"It's gotta be between us, nobody else. Ye gotta promise."

"You've got my word if I can do it. Tell me what you want first."

"All right! Bend down so's I can whisper in yer ear."

Travis bent down and listened intently. "Okay!" he said. "The doctor has to approve it first."

"Ye ask him and if he don't let me, I ain't tellin' nobody nothin'."

Travis and Dr. Rawlings walked out into the hall and returned after a brief conversation, chuckling and shaking their heads.

"You got it, Garrett. "Tell me what happened?"

Garrett told about the Grimes brothers' subduing him and his cousin when they returned to their car after finding the still. He described the torture and the desperate struggle he put up before being thrown off the dam.

"Do you feel up to facing the Grimes brothers now?" Travis asked.

"Do they know I ain't killed?"

"No, and are they in for a shock," Travis answered.

"That's better yit. I won't close my eyes agin' 'til I see them devils standin' at the foot a this bed. That's all I'm livin' fer."

"Good. Seth! Have the prisoners brought over. Hold'em in the waitin' room down the hall. I need somethin' from the office. I should be back by the time they get here."

Jerry S Jones

Travis soon returned and asked everyone to step out of Garrett's room for a few minutes, after which, he called them back in.

"Okay Seth, bring'em in! As soon as you have'em standing at the foot of the bed, the nurse will open the curtain."

They could hear the clinking of the shackles as the prisoners shuffled down the corridor towards the room.

"The prisoners don't know why they've been brought here," said Travis. "Play close attention to their reactions. This is gonna be good."

Tension was high as Seth pulled back the curtain.

The brothers were in shock, staring in disbelief, unable to speak.

"Howdy boys," said Garrett. "It's me alright. Ain't it nice a you'uns to stop in fer a visit with a sick friend. When you'uns leave here stop and see Landis. He's jist down the hall a eatin' dinner."

"Sheriff, I want you'un to all know that them's the two devils that cut off'n me and Landis' ears and throwed us off'n the Dam. That's who done it and I swear to it. I told you'uns we'd git you worthless bastards. When they sit you'uns down to fry yer asses, y'all think 'bout me and Landis and Chad. We done it to ye and now we even. Now! Looky here what I found while I wuz floatin' down the river!"

With this, Garrett's arms flew out from under the sheet holding one of Landis' ears in each hand. "I found'em, ye murder'in dogs, I found'em! Ye didn't think I could, did ye? Well here they is. Doc Rawlin's is fixin' to sew'em back on right now. Ye wanna watch!"

"How'd he do that Jess," Jarred shouted.

"Shet up," Jess growled. "We don't know that feller. It's a trick they pullin' on us!"

"No it ain't, Jess! That's Simms and thems his ears! How'd he do that?"

"It's a trick baby brother! Now shet yer mouth!"

"Get'em outta here!" said Sheriff Gant. "We've seen and heard enough."

After the prisoners were escorted out, Travis explained that the last thing the Grimes' said to Garrett as they threw him off the dam was, 'that if he liked his big ears so good he could go find'em'. "The two severed ears we found belonged to Landis Dehart. Garrett just wanted the last word."

The Sugarbush

Garrett was clearly exhausted, but insisted on finishing the harrowing tale of his miraculous survival.

"I remember a fallin'. A cool wet spray wuz hittin' my face and it felt so good. I don't remember hittin' the water. It wuz more like I wuz fallin' through a feather bed, a rollin' and tumblin' ever' which a way. Then all at wuntz I come a flyin' up outta the water jist like the river wuz a spittin' me out. I could breathe through my nose, but I wuz a gaggin' 'cause I still had that rag stuck in my mouth. I think that's what kept me from a drownin'. When the fall didn't kill me, that rag kept the water out. I pulled it out and what a difference. Suckin' in all that good fresh air made me fergit my pain fer awhile. The current wuz fast and a carryin' me with it, then it seemed like I wuz kinda in a quiet pond. I don't know how long I swum, I jist knowed I wuz so tired and waterlogged I couldn't pick up my arms no more. I ask my Lord Jesus how come'im to save me from gittin killed when they throwed me off'n the dam jist so's He could drown me. When I started goin' under the water fer drownin', my knees hit the bottom, then I knowed what Jesus wuz up to. It took me awhile to crawl out on the bank.

I don't know how long I laid there, but when I come to I wuz freezin' cold, shakin' and hurtin' all over. Way yonder up the hill I seen a little yeller light a shinin' and I started crawlin' on my hands and knees thatta way. Sometimes I'd git up and take a step or two then I'd fall back down, but I kept on goin' and a singin', 'This little light a mine, I'm a gonna let it shine.'

After the longest time, I couldn't see my little light no more. Then I smelt a barnyard and heared livestock a movin' 'round. I got to my feet and took a couple a steps and run agin' a wall. It knocked me back down and ye talk 'bout hurtin'! It hurt so bad I couldn't scream and I wuz tryin' to. Well I got back up on my knees and touched the wall and wuz a feelin' it. I found a door handle and pulled. I reckon I stumbled or fell inside. I ain't fer sure! All I remember is it smelt like leather and horses. I figure I wuz out fer quite awhile. I woke up and heared a man and woman a talkin' and laughin'. Her voice wuz clear as music, so's I figured it wuz maybe God a talkin' to a angel. I tried to git up, but that's the last I remember 'til now."

Jerry S Jones

"The voices you heard were Beau Fontaine and his niece, Reicie," said Travis. "You were in their tackroom. They bandaged you up, took off your wet clothes and wrapped you in a blanket with hot water bottles to warm you up. Then they loaded you in the car and brought you to the hospital. They saved your life."

"Ye thank'em fer me and tell'em I won't never fergit'em keepin' me alive long enough to face them Grimes' devils agin' and git even fer me and Landis and Chad. When ye find my old car, give it to Chad's Ma and Pa."

"You're gonna get well, Garrett! Just rest now."

"I'm hurt too bad to git well and I can't rest 'til I see a Pentecostal preacher. Will you call one fer me right now?

The preacher came and later that night, Garrett died.

Sunday morning, Travis drove to Catfish. When he arrived, the Fontaines and Reicie had just returned from church. While Lila heated the coffee, the sheriff told them Garrett had died from internal injuries and explained that the Doctor knew he was bleeding to death from a ruptured spleen, but couldn't get him stable enough for surgery.

The afternoon before when they first met at the sheriff's office, Lila noticed that Reicie and Travis seemed overly courteous, reserved, even shy in the few comments between them.

"Sheriff Gant," said Lila. "Reicie can show you the tack room where she found Mr. Simms and then walk the distance he crawled from the river."

"I would appreciate that," Travis answered. "Thank you."

During the walk, Reicie and Travis went on to more pleasant subjects, listening to each other with riveting attentiveness, exchanging comments in polite tender tones of voice, quick to make allowances for their different points of view.

XVIII

Headlines in the Sunday morning newspapers heralded the capture of the "Sugarbutchers," bringing the reign of terror to an end. Full coverage was given to the barbaric executions of DeHart and Simms, with little sympathy for the murdered men, referred to only as ex-convicts.

The public, freed from the bondage of constant fear, reacted with mixed emotions ranging from appeased rage and joyful relief, to a lynch mob mentality seeking instant justice.

Travis continued to warn the public that copycat killers were not uncommon and advised continued caution and vigilance.

His popularity restored and with a good reason to vote for him, Travis won the election by a wide majority of votes and settled into the job of county sheriff with renewed confidence.

Seth knocked on the sheriff's office door. "Come on in and have a seat, Seth," Travis shouted cheerfully. "I just got off the phone with Gordon Jackson. He called to say the dagger we found at the Grimes' farm gave him all the evidence he needs to charge Jess and Jarred in the rape related murders. He went to the Grand Jury today and got their blessin' to amend the indictments for the Dehart, Simms murders to include the rape murders and the attempted assault on Emmy Waite. That's eight counts of first degree murder, four counts of rape and one count of attempted assault. A thirteen count indictment? That's bad luck in spades, wouldn't you say?

The case goes to trial the last week in April of next year. One of his big sellin' points was the time and money it would save the county if the defendants were tried on all thirteen counts at the same time. The truth of the matter is, that a conviction for the murder of two convicts on parole is not sensational enough for Gordon. I've never ruled out the Grimes' brothers, but I've had my doubts. Now it's out of my hands.

It was February. Four months had passed since the arrests. With the Grimes brothers in jail, the assaults came to an abrupt halt. The county was safe again.

In Catfish, Sorghum Hawley brought his mule and wagon to a halt under the tobacco barn shed, dismounted and built a fire to warm by. Once warmed, he mixed a batch of mortar and began daubing cracks between the logs of the barn where the chinking had fallen out. Hearing hoof beats, he turned to see the mailman, Fentress Akers, approaching on his big red horse.

"Come on in by the fire," Sorghum shouted. "Ye picked a mighty cold day to be deliverin' mail a horseback!"

"Yes sir, and ye picked a mighty cold day to be chinkin' yer 'baccer barn. If'n it freezes tonight ye'll have it to do all over agin'."

"Yeah and if it don't freeze, I'm ready fer harvest time. Climb on down and warm up."

"Believe I will. Fireball can use a breather 'fore we head fer the barn.

"Fireball huh. If'n ye'd a been here last spring and seen Cush Hagan come by here with ole Fireball, ye'd a named'im caboose."

Chuckling, Fentress asked. "Why come ye to say that?"

'Well sir, me and the wife wuz sittin' here under the shed sortin' 'baccer plants when we heared a awful racket a comin' down the road. It wuz Cush Hagan in his buggy with yer horse in the harness. They wuz a flyin'! Cush wuz a cussin' and layin' on the buggy whip. I'd swear that buggy come ever bit a three feet off'n the ground when they hit the bridge yonder. When they got to the top a that hill the other side a the bridge, he turned 'round and come back the same way. A little while later on, here comes Bobby and Sis in the buggy. Yer horse wuz all lathered up and a prancin' along as perty as ye please."

"Cush wuz prob'ly runnin' the corn out of'im same like I been doin' today. I'm some gentler 'bout it than he wuz."

"Not accordin' to Cush, he wudden. He says that horse wuz in the last war and mustta got shell shocked or somethin'. Ye jist can't tell what might set'im off crazy."

"Tain't so Sorghum. I ain't had no trouble with'im."

"Well sir Fentress, ye look warmed up so grab a handful a that mortar. Ye kin hep me chink and dob the rest a these here cracks."

"I ain't warm enough to chink or dob no 'baccer barn but I'm warm enough to git on to the house. Thank ye, Sorghum. I'll see ye tomorrow."

The Sugarbush

"Stop by anytime, neighbor. I'll be workin' here all week."

Fentress rode out and down the road, stopping long enough to let a car pass, then proceeded on. When he reached the middle of the bridge, the car that had just passed backfired with a resounding bang.

Sorghum looked up from his work to see the big red horse rear and fall backwards across the bridge railing on top of Fentress and disappear into the creek below.

"Lord above help us!" he cried. "That horse done killed'em both."

Quickly, he dropped the traces off the wagon single tree, hung them on the harness haines and mounted his mule. When he arrived at the bridge, he looked down to see the badly injured horse thrashing in the creek with Fentress nowhere in sight.

Maneuvering down the bank into the creek, Sorghum secured the harness traces to the saddle horn and dragged the struggling horse toward the bank. Soon a stirrup with a foot in it emerged from beneath the water.

Sorghum freed the body of his fatally injured friend and laid him on the creek bank. Removing the pistol from the holster on Fentress belt, he put the moaning horse out of it's misery. The occupants of the passing car that backfired and set the tragedy in motion, never knew it happened.

Fentress was well known and liked by everyone on the mail route. At his funeral at Thyatira Lutheran Church, the preacher declared solemnly that the loss of two prominent Catfish residents in less than a year was evidence of satan's continuing presence in the community.

"We kin fight off Lucifer through prayer and repentance," he shouted. "Satan incarnate mutilated two souls and cast'em off'n Lookout Dam to certain death! Like the two thieves that hung with Jesus on Calvary, one repented and lived long enough to witness his own murder! Now he dwells in Paradise, eternal life secure, waiting fer the second coming of our Lord and savior, Jesus Christ! What a precious free gift from the Lamb of God, praise Jesus! Don't y'all think fer one second that 'cause they locked up them two Grimes' devils, we outta Satan's reach. No siree. Remember! When Jesus cast Lucifer outta heaven, one third a the angels wuz casted out with'im, so's they's still plenty a devils' left to go 'round. Our

Christian brother, Fentress Akers, is beyond the demon's grasp, but y'all ain't. Escape the devil 'fore it's too late. Times is hard, but they's ever'lastin' comfort waitin' fer ye if'n ye'll jist turn to Jesus."

Dessie Hagan was visibly shaken as she and Cal left the church for the cemetery. "Burton Coley put a curse on them warrants," she whispered. "Jist look. There's Bobby talkin' to Casey Workman and Pursey McCall and all three of'em's named on one a them warrants. Who's gonna be next! What we gonna do! Praying ain't helpin' none."

"We cain't do nothin'," Cal answered. "Me and Bobby done talked it over and we don't like it neither. Don't fergit, Burton got killed lookin' fer us and everbody in Catfish knows it. If'n folks finds out we knowed anything, they'll swear we the one's put a curse on them warrants."

It was April. Harley Dokes and his three accomplices in the death of Ross Elders were sent to prison after being found guilty of aggravated assault and voluntary manslaughter. The murder trial of Jess and Jarred Grimes was two weeks away.

Cal Hagan sat on his front porch listening with amusement to Bobby's tales and family gossip.

"What wuz y'all laughin' 'bout awhile ago? I could hear ye all the way to the chicken house," Dessie questioned, as she joined them on the porch.

"Tell it agin', Bobby," said Cal.

"Well Dessie, ye know how devilish Pop can be and I guess ye know he's been tryin to git off'n a big drunk and it always ends up the same way. He gits so sick he can't eat and starts a prayin' to die! Finally last evenin', Sis got'im to eat a couple hard boiled duck eggs and two big bowls a pinto beans and onions. This mornin' he wuz still a layin' in bed, feelin' a whole lots better. Sis looked out the kitchen winder and seen Noah Wilkes a comin' towards the house. "Pop," she says, "Uncle Noah's a comin' to visit."

"Yeah and he'll be lookin' fer a drink a liquor too. I ain't got no liquor today, jist a stinkin' breath. When Noah comes in, tell'im I done died. I'll cover up with the sheet."

The Sugarbush

"Mornin' Sis," Noah said cheerfully. "I come to check up on Cush to see if he's still a livin' since he jist got off'n a drunk."

"Lordy, lordy, Uncle Noah, ain't ye heared? Pop's a layin' in there dead. I cain't stop a cryin' and Mom's so broke up, Aunt Candace is sittin' with her."

"Ye don't mean to tell me no sech a thang!' Noah said in disbelief.

"Sis says 'bout then Noah started a bawlin' and his big ole nose started a runnin'. He don't never carry a handkerchief and wuz a tryin' to wipe off'n the snot smearin' it all over his face. Sis got'im a rag but it wuz too late. Noah would wipe his nose with his arm and then wipe his arm off on his overalls. Sis says she wuz doubled over laughin' and Noah thought she wuz a cryin'.

Pop said he got so tickled a listenin' to what wuz going on, it strained him so awful he couldn't hep but cut loose a couple a mule sized farts that stunk so bad they wuz makin'im sick agin'. 'Bout that time, Noah, a bawlin' and snot still a runnin', pulled back the sheet to look at Pop and says, "oh my Sis, don't he look natural. Ye better let me call fer the undertaker 'cause he's done gone to stinkin'."

Well sir, Pop couldn't stand it no longer. He come outta a that bed a laughin' and a runnin' fer fresh air. Noah wuz more put out than anything else, but he got over it purdy quick 'cause he wuz so happy Pop weren't dead. Ye know Pop, he wudden done yit.

Noah told Pop that he shore could stand a drink if they wuz any liquor left on the place. Pop says he happened to remember a jar a liquor he found when he wuz cruisin' timber fer Taylor Upton. He said it wuz the meanest liquor he ever tasted in his life. He tells Noah, "after I done pulled sech a dirty trick on ye, I gotta jar a liquor I'm gonna give ye."

He says Noah unscrewed the lid and never even spit out his chaw a 'baccer. He jist turned up the jar and started takin' big gulps. He let the jar down and commenced to gag' and spit. Pop says they wuz so much 'baccer juice in the liquor it wuz turnin' yeller and he wuz a laughin' so hard he couldn't talk. Finally he asked him how he liked the liquor. Noah says, "Cush, by gum it's jist right. If'n it wuz any meaner, I couldn't drink it, and if'n it wuz any better, ye wudden a give it to me!"

Jerry S Jones

"Good fer Noah," Dessie giggled. "It's time he got one on Pop. 'Fore I fergit it, did you'uns see the pictures a Jess and Jarred on the front page of yesterday's paper? They ain't shaved or had a haircut since they wuz locked up last September. They look like a couple a apes."

"Yeah! We seen'em!" Bobby replied.

"I bet their Mama don't like it," said Dessie. "She always saw to it them boys was neat and clean. She'll make'em clean up 'fore the trial. Have you'uns noticed everthang seems so much better even if'n it ain't. Ever'body I see out here in the country or in town is lots happier. I know the new President's makin' the whole country feel better, but around here the hope started when they locked up Jess and Jarred. All that rapin' and killin' they done made ever'body see that hard as we been havin' it, thangs kin be a whole lots worse."

"Ye mighty right 'bout that!" Cal and Bobby agreed.

"Well, here it is Saturday," Bobby said. "While y'all married folks is sittin' at home, I'm dressin' up and headin' fer town. The city square's gonna be crowded up with good lookin' women that's been cooped up all winter. Thanks fer lettin' me use yer car."

"Ye stay outta trouble, Bobby Hagan! Have a good time, but stay outta trouble," Dessie shouted as he drove away. "Bobby shore does git a bang outta Pop Hagan's mischief, don't he Cal?"

"Yeah, but Pop's mischief ain't always funny," Cal answered. "Ye ain't never seen'im when he comes home drunk a beatin' Mom and draggin' her through the house by the hair of her head. When we wuz kids we wuz hoein corn in the bottom and run outta drinkin' water. Bobby wuz no more'n six and he stopped to git a drink from the creek. Pop come to check on us and caught'im there playin' in the water. Bobby seen he wuz mad and tried to run, but Pop caught'im and throwed 'im in the creek. A dead limb under the water stobbed plumb through the cheek a Bobby's ass and he pert near died. Drunk or sober, Pop's gotta bad streak a meaness and so does Bobby. When they good, they ain't nobody better. When they bad, they ain't nobody worser."

In town, Bobby parked the car at his uncle's blacksmith shop. Soon he had the horse harnessed and hooked up to the buggy.

The Sugarbush

"How come ye always use the buggy?" Bobby's uncle asked. "I couldn't wait to own a car so's I could stop buyin' hay and oats and commence buyin' gas and oil."

Bobby laughed. "I like the car better too, but ridin' 'round town square I always got a gal with me. They like ridin' in a buggy."

The younger teenaged country boys came into town packed into cars with no room to spare. Much to the amusement of the city kids they would ride around the square hanging out of the car windows shouting and whistling at the girls, completely ignorant of the fact that no young lady respectable or otherwise would dare accept a ride in a car loaded with overactive adolescent hormones.

Bobby had no problem getting girls to ride with him in the buggy, but anytime the horse raised its tail to relieve abdominal stress the girls would ask to get off though never in time to avoid the embarrassing situation they were trying to escape.

Later in the evening Bobby parked his buggy and entered the City Grill to eat. When he came back out he saw Reicie Dupre sitting in it with two other young ladies.

"Hi Reicie!" he said eagerly. "Ye wanna take the girls for a ride around the square?"

"No, but thanks for the offer. We climbed up here to talk. How have you been, Bobby?"

"Jist fine and dandy. Spring plowin's all done and the crops are planted so I'm restin' til the weeds start growin' and that won't be long. Ye been a swimmin' yit this year?" Bobby asked.

"Not yet!" Reicie answered, hiding her amusement at the question. "It's still seems cold to me."

"Maybe so," Bobby replied with a look of disappointment. "The water might still be cold even if the days ain't."

Reicie had deliberately deceived Bobby. Sunday morning after church she made her way down the secluded pathway to her swimming hole and tied her dogs nearby.

After spreading a blanket atop leaves covering a bed of soft spongy moss, she slipped out of her clothes and waded into the water shivering as it crept up to her neck.

The pool was in the shade and the water was cold. She brushed back her hair and climbed out on the opposite bank to stand on top of the old maple stump in the warmth of the sun.

Jerry S Jones

Sunbeams highlighted her glistening auburn hair as the cold water dripped off the extended nipples of her breasts like crystal teardrops while rainbow hues of moisture sparkled through abundant waves of pubic hair. Stretching in the cool breeze she stepped off the stump, waded back into the pool and out on the other side. She sat down and pulled the blanket around her to absorb the water. At that moment her dogs came to their feet emitting low growls and gazing toward the opposite ridge.

"Hush now," she whispered, jumping up and grabbing their leashes. "It must be Bobby, who else could it be?" Sure that he had not been there when she first arrived, she was just as sure he was there now.

A year ago she had experienced unexpected pleasure and excitement from their innocent spying on each other's nakedness, but now the very thought of anyone watching her every move from a place of concealment was frightening. Covering herself with the blanket, Reicie rushed out of sight, dressed quickly and hurried up the path toward home. It was not until she broke out of the woods in view of the house that her anxiety subsided.

"Bobby, where ye been at so long?" Cush asked his son.
"I been down on the creek seinin' fer minnows. Why come?"
"After dark I want ye to deliver a gallon a liquor over to Will Foley's place. Ye wanna use the buggy?"
"Naw! I'll walk over! It ain't that fer."

Later that evening, Bobby cut across the pasture toward the Foley farm to deliver the gallon jug of moonshine.
Will was watching for Bobby and met him on the front porch.
"Come on in son. I'll put this liquor up and git yer money."
As Bobby stepped into the parlor he saw four men sitting at a table playing poker. He recognized Will Foley's nephew who had just been released from prison.
"Well look what the hogs' done rooted up," the nephew shouted. "Damned if it ain't one a Cush Hagan's litter. He's jist as damned ugly as his low down triflin' old man. Take a seat and we'll win back the price a that liquor."

Will came back up the hall handing over the money and standing between Bobby and the four men.

"Ye shet yer damned mouth!" he shouted to his nephew. "They're drunk Bobby. Jist go on and pay'em no mind."

"I'm leavin', I ain't fergittin'." Bobby replied.

"Where I jist come from," the nephew yelled. "When I tell a feller to sit down they by god sit! Now sit yer sorry ass down here like I told ye to."

"I said fer ye to shet yer damn mouth!" Will shouted. "Bobby's a leavin' and y'all are too if'n ye say another damn word."

"Good riddance!" came the response. "What damn prison did he jist break out of anyways. Go on home and tell yer Paw he can suck my dick ye kyard son-of-a-bitch."

Bobby whirled and charged toward the surprised tormentor, knocking him into the corner of the room. The other three men joined the fray tripping Bobby. When he hit the floor, his hand landed on a large crab orchard rock being used for a door stop. Leaping to his feet, the rock became a lethal weapon. In less than a minute all four men were on the floor as Bobby continued to bash them with crushing blows.

In a blind rage, he turned toward Will who had been trying to quell the fight. Will saw the crazed look in Bobby's eyes and ran down the hallway into his bedroom and locked the door. Bobby chased him and kicked open the door. Will was waiting with a 410 gauge double barreled shotgun pistol. When Bobby entered, Will's wife began to scream. Will fired a shot at Bobby's feet and shouted for him to get out of the bedroom.

Bobby responded by throwing the rock at Will, hitting the coal oil lamp and plunging the room into darkness. Another blast followed and all became quiet except for Bobby's dying death rattles.

Will carried the body out to his car and sat it up in the back seat. Returning to the bedroom, he asked his wife to see to the wounds of the battered men in the parlor. He picked up a jar of whiskey, drank down a dipper full and left the house.

All night long he drove from farm to farm waking the tenants, asking if they needed a worker to help with spring planting, explaining that the person in the car was drunk, but could sleep it off in the barn and be ready for work by morning.

Smelling the liquor on his breath and seeing the blood on his clothes, they quickly sent him on his way.

By daylight Will came to his senses, drove to the Hagan farm and pulled around back of the house where Lucy Hagan stood on the porch washing her hands. He got out of the car. "Lucy, I brung Bobby home."

Drying her hands, she stared at the figure in the back seat of the car. "Yes, Will Foley," she replied in a cracking voice. "And ye brought him home dead."

"I wuz defendin' myself, Lucy. I didn't mean to kill'im. We wuz all raised up together and been friends all our life. Ye know I wouldn't do sech a thang a purpose."

Sis ran out the door and down the steps screaming and began beating Will with her fists.

He grabbed and pulled her to him sobbing and begging forgiveness.

"It wuz a accident, Sis, I swear it. Bobby wuz fixin' to beat me to death with a rock. I never meant to hurt'im."

Cush was finishing up milking when he heard the commotion and walked toward the house. Lucy, tears streaming down her face walked to meet him.

"What's goin' on up here?" he asked angrily.

"Bobby's dead! Will brung'im home. He says he killed Bobby by accident and I believe'im."

"Well now by god, Will Foley's gonna die!" Cush muttered.

"No he ain't!" Lucy screamed. "Theys been enough killin' fer one day. Now ye listen to me, Cush Hagan. Bobby's dead 'cause ye sent'im over to Will's with that liquor. Do ye understand ye carry some a the fault? It could a been ye 'stead a Bobby. Now ye come help git our boy outta the car and lay'im on the porch so's I kin wash'im up decent. While me and the young'uns is a doin' that, ye go down to Mr. Huitt's Store and call the sheriff. The truth will come out and I cain't take no more ruckus."

After hugging, they returned to the car and laid the body on the porch. Will tried to talk to Cush, but was coldly ignored.

"Ye go on home now, Will!" Lucy said softly. "Tell the wife me and her'll pray together."

The Sugarbush

Later that morning, Travis turned into the Fontaine's farm lane and drove towards the house.

"Good mornin', Sheriff. What brings you out on the river so early in the morning?" Lila asked. "Come on in. I'll pour you a cup of coffee. We're just about ready to leave for the Farmers' Market. Beau, come on in here, we've got company."

"Howdy, Sheriff!" said Beau. "I'm afraid to ask what brings you out to Catfish. I hope it's a social visit."

"That's what it started out to be," Travis replied. "I got your message and was comin' by to tell you the county attorney says you won't have to testify in the murder trial next week. First I had to stop over at the Hagans' place, then at Will Foley's. There was a brawl at Foley's house last night and durin' the fight, Will shot Bobby Hagan and killed'im."

"Sheriff!" said Lila. "The Foleys and Hagans are good friends. What happened?"

"We're still sortin' through the details. Will and his wife says it was self defense. Bobby's Dad and Mom didn't agree, but they didn't disagree either. Folks out here stick together. I've never seen anything like it. When you get to know'em they're friendly, accommodating and have a good sense of humor. They work hard and help any neighbor in need, yet at the slightest provocation that most people would ignore, they start killin' each other. Some time back, Bobby's Aunt Candace told Sheriff Coley that when a Hagan got mad they could taste their own blood, and I believe it."

Just then Reicie came down the stairs looking more radiant than ever. Travis did not try to hide his approval.

"Good morning," she said happily, kissing her Aunt and Uncle on the cheek. I saw you driving in, Sheriff Gant. It's nice to see you under more pleasant circumstances."

Seeing the glances passing between them, Reicie asked. "Did I speak to soon?"

"I'm afraid so," Travis replied. "Do you know Bobby Hagan?"

"Yes. I knew him from the eighth grade at White Church School. Why?"

"Last night he got in a fight and was shot dead."

Opening the door to let her dogs out, Reicie said. "I'm so sorry to hear that though I'm not surprised. Bobby was hot tempered and couldn't seem to walk away from trouble. Most of the boys out here are that way. The girls aren't that way at all. They're sweet and kind.

Catfish doesn't have a High School because nobody ever goes past the eighth grade and most of them don't get that far. It wouldn't do them any good even if they did want to go to High School. No teacher that knows what Catfish is like and is in possession of half their senses would try to teach out here. If they can't keep teachers at White Church School because the boys are so rowdy and mean, imagine what it would be like in High School. No thank you!

Catfish is exactly like one of Aunt Lila's house plants called The Venus Fly Trap. It's ununusual and deceptively beautiful to the eye when admired from the outside. Venture inside this beautiful thing and it will absorb you, eat you alive one bite at a time. Look at what's happened here in less than a year. Sheriff Coley killed accidently by his own deputy, Junior Upton accidently drowned, two men murdered at Lookout Dam, our mailman killed by his horse and now Bobby killed in a fight. Four women and two men have been murdered by two rapist who just happen to be from Catfish. I can't think about it anymore. Are we ready to leave for town?"

"I think so," Beau answered. "On the way we should stop by the Hagan's place to express our sympathy."

"That's fine Uncle Beau, but please," Reicie complained, "I don't want to go over there. You and Aunt Lila go ahead and offer my sympathies too. Come back by and pick me up."

"I'm going straight into town," Travis interrupted. "You can ride in with me if you want to and it's all right with your folks."

"Of course it's alright and I'd love to," Reicie replied demurely.

Watching them drive away Lila put her arms around Beau. "Dear, there's something different about our niece lately and we know what it is. I've never seen her more alive and beautiful. She'll be leaving us soon. From what she just said I think she already has."

"Didn't you think she was indifferent to the news about Bobby," Beau asked.

"I guess you could call it that, but remember, we've always told her not to dwell on bad thoughts or bad happenings. Right now I don't think anything could make her or the sheriff feel bad. From their first meeting, they were smitten with each other and you know it as well as I do."

XIX

"I'm really sorry I had to be the one to bring the news about Bobby," Travis commented as he drove towards town.

"Don't be," Reicie replied. "Since my Mother died I don't take death very seriously anymore as long as it's not mine. Mother was sick a long time. I stayed by her bedside and watched the illness literally eat her alive. Never once did she complain. During that time she taught me all about life and how to accept death. What she taught me then is my strength now, but it didn't help when she first died. I had become accustomed to seeing her in that horrible condition. I thought we would go on forever talking and crying and laughing. What an awakening. After she died, I can't describe the pain and sorrow I endured for months on end. I am so thankful for that period of suffering, not only because we loved each other so dearly but more so because she deserved and was entitled to my grief. I thought I was going to die too, then one night in a dream her words came back to me. Time and time again she had told me that when tragedy strikes and you are fortunate enough to survive it, you might as well not have survived if you allow yourself to sink into self pity rendering both the experience and life meaningless. Tragedy has its burdens but so does happiness and success. They're intertwined.

"What about your dad. He was there. Wasn't he a comfort to you?"

"No, he wasn't. To this day he feels that my coming into the world came between them and worse, that I'm somehow responsible for her sickness and death. Even before mother fell ill he envied the time we spent together as I was growing up. She refused to leave me behind in order to travel with him like she did before I was born. If mother had lived we would probably have had a pretty normal family, but she didn't. After that he became a person I don't know. Six years ago he brought me and my two dogs to Aunt Lila and Uncle Beau's, dropped us off and left the same day. I haven't seen him since and he's not that far away. I've never had a father image like other kids so I don't know what it's like and get along fine without it.

Actually after mother died I was relieved to get out of those mountains because I was surrounded with ignorance and violence there too. I thought I was getting free from it all until I got to Catfish and found out I'd been thrown out of the frying pan into the fire.

When I started ninth grade in Newton, the kids avoided me because they found out I was from Catfish. That sort of attitude in its self is a cruel form of ignorance and abuse I was determined to rise above and I've done it. I'm accepted and popular for who I am as a person and admired for my academic achievements. My classmates at school came from well-to-do families that can afford the best of everything yet I, Reicie Dupre, from Catfish, was voted the 'best dressed girl' in the entire school and "the girl most likely to succeed' in my graduating class. No one could possibly know how much that means to me. I'm honored and nobody can ever take that honor away from me.

Someday I want to tell my dad about it. Uncle Beau is not like a dad to me, he's like what he is, my uncle. Even though Aunt Lila resembles my mother in many ways, she's still my aunt, not my mother. They want me and make me feel needed and I'm lucky they do. The relationship between my dad and I is more like pen pals that have no emotional attachments and no particular urgency about seeing each other. He has always sent money for my upkeep, but Aunt Lila and Uncle Beau put it in my bank account along with the money they pay me for doing chores. Besides that, dad puts extra money in my account too. So in a way he does care. The point is, when I lost my mother I lost my dad too."

"We have a lot in common Reicie, only my situation was the opposite," Travis replied. "I never knew my dad. When I was a baby he left for the wild west to homestead some land, then he was coming back to get Mom and I. Twelve years passed before we found out he was dead. Mom handled that news well, but she didn't know how to start living again. It was a frustrating time for her. Then one day she was introduced to a man from California who was back here buyin' cotton fabrics for his company and I guess the sparks flew. After a fashion, they got married and she finally got to go west. They're very happy. Off they went, half their lives over, acting like kids just starting out. That was a sight to see."

Reicie's honesty and assertiveness raised a compelling urge in Travis to validate all she had said. He fell comfortably into telling the story of his impoverished childhood and the perfectly timed

The Sugarbush

opportunity provided by a chance encounter with Sheriff Burton Coley, an opportunity that changed his life. It was only when he had finished that he felt a huge weight lifted from his shoulders and a feather light weight on his wrist, Reicie's hand. "I only wish you could have heard and seen yourself as I just did, grateful, humble and excited. That is exactly what my mother meant. Learn, count your blessings, think happy thoughts then move on. Like right now. This is exciting, Sheriff," Reicie exclaimed. "This is my first ride in a police car."

"Reicie, do you think you could call me Travis? Please."

"Of course," she answered, laughing mischievously. "Look at the stares we're getting from passing cars and pedestrians. They don't know if my riding with you is formal or informal. They must think you've arrested me. The couple who just passed were staring so hard they almost ran off the road."

Glancing behind them, Reicie burst out laughing. "Travis, we've been creeping along. Aunt Lila and Uncle Beau are right behind us and they made a stop at the Hagan's farm. Don't you know they're wondering what we've been up to! It can't be too bad. They're laughing too."

Driving through town toward the Farmers' Market, talking, laughing, and cheerfully waving at people on the street, Reicie screamed. "Travis! You just ran a stop sign! Everybody saw you!"

Laughing and embarrassed, Travis pulled to the side of the road and began writing himself a traffic ticket, waving to Lila and Beau as they drove by.

"Are you going to plead guilty and pay the fine," Reicie asked in amusement!

"Yes and no," he answered, attempting to suppress his laughter. "I'm pleading guilty, but I don't have to pay the fine because I'm in the Newton City limits and that's out of my jurisdiction."

"The license of authority," Reicie shouted, clutching her breasts in mock despair!

"We better get a move on," Travis remarked. "Your folks will be waiting."

The following Monday, Travis was waiting when Reicie arrived at the Farmers Market and ask her to have dinner with him, after which he would drive her home. She accepted laughing happily, explaining that it was the first time she had been asked out since graduating from high school.

"That was only a week ago for gosh sakes," Travis said laughing. "Give it time. I'm sure you didn't go to any dances or parties by yourself. Pretty girls are always popular."

"I was very involved in school activities," she replied. "So were a lot of other kids and they didn't have to be pretty or handsome to be popular. I dated and went to parties and dances, yet I never had a crush on any of the guys. They seemed like younger brothers, but I never let them know I felt that way. I did have a crush on one of my teachers when I was thirteen. How embarrassing. That ended when I saw his wife and children. I've never felt so foolish in all my life, and I can prove it. You're the only one I've ever told about it."

Everyone who knows me says talking to me is like talking to an adult and that's understandable. I'm an only child who has always lived in the country and my childhood playmates were adults. The only time I was around children my age was in school or when visitors stopped by, and that was seldom. I heard adult conversations, I read adult books and played adult games. I loved growing up and was very happy. If I missed something, I don't know what it is. What about you?"

"I dated a lot of different girls in high school and college, nothin' serious, just a fun time. I don't even remember much about it. All I can think about is you and the time we spend together. I really have enjoyed it."

"So have I," Reicie replied. "I'll see you here at five o'clock."

XX

It was the last week in April. Jury selection completed, the trial started on Monday morning and moved along rapidly.

County Attorney Jackson knew the law and to his peers was considered a tenacious and wily adversary in the courtroom.

A stepping stone to more lofty goals, this trial was one of those rare sensations that could catapult even the most obscure prosecutor into instant stardom. Nobody knew that better than Gordon. It was an opportunity that wouldn't be lost.

Several reporters from nationally syndicated newspapers and magazines had converged on the small town county seat to cover the trial. Charming and eloquent, Gordon's opening statement was in most part addressed to them.

"Gentlemen of the Jury," he began. "Sitting right over there at that table are four men. Two of them are the brothers, Jess and Jarred Grimes, accused in a thirteen count indictment for committing eight of the most heinous premeditated murders imaginable, four savage rapes and a thwarted attempt to commit yet another.

Now don't be confused. In case you haven't been able to figure out who's who, the two men in the blue serge suits and bright red neckties are not the accused, they're the defense attorneys. The killers are the other two yokels peeping through those brush piles of hair."

The courtroom erupted into laughter as the two lawyers, unoffended by the reference, stood up smiling broadly and bowed to the spectators, prompting the Judge to pound his gavel demanding order.

Gordon continued. "In the days leading up to this trial the defense presented two petitions for consideration by the court. One requesting a change of venue and the other requesting that the present indictment be thrown out in favor of thirteen separate indictments. Both were submitted on grounds that the constitutional rights of the accused to a fair trial could not be otherwise guaranteed.

A change of venue was denied simply because there is no corner of this state where the atrocities committed in our county over the past year have not been front page news and the predominating topic of conversation. That petition was denied. We will clean up our own mess.

The request for thirteen separate indictments was denied because after the Grand Jury reviewed the State's overwhelming evidence against the defendants in the eleven rape-murder related charges, they deemed it appropriate and economically prudent for the tax payers of this county to include those charges in two identical indictments, one for each of the defendants.

Why am I telling you all this? I'm telling you because each and every citizen is guaranteed fair and equal treatment by our judicial system and nobody holds that right in higher esteem than I do. I want to insure that when all is said and done, there will be no doubt in anyone's mind that the defendant's constitutional rights were duly protected.

The accused are well aware of the overwhelming evidence against them, yet they have plead not guilty to every count in the indictment. They're thumbing their noses at this court of law and the grieving families of the victims.

The defendant's rampage of rape and murder that held the good citizens of this county in the bondage of terror for four months, started nearly a year ago at The Sugarbush roadhouse on a Saturday night, May 21, 1932.

On that night, following a violent altercation inside the dance hall, the defendants left the premises, but returned to wait in ambush in the woods behind the dance hall from where they made good their threats to hang the manager, Kirby Suggs, to death with his own bullwhip, and to rape and sodomize a waitress, Bernice Boles, also murdered during the assault.

It ended four months later on Saturday morning the first week in October, with the arrests of the defendants for the murders of cousins, Landis DeHart and Garrett Simms, two convicts on parole from county jail. On the evening of their deaths, the victims had inadvertently stumbled onto the location of the defendants moonshine liquor distillery and were killed by the defendants to keep them from reporting the discovery to the county sheriff.

For years, DeHart and Simms were nothing more than petty thieves, public nuisances, thorns in the side of our law abiding community. In death they were redeemed by unwittingly making one noble contribution to society and that was a big one. They led us to the perverted, cold blooded killers sitting at that table and the murder weapon they used to penetrate the hearts of four women and a twelve year old child. Not one assault has occurred since the defendants were arrested and jailed six months ago. Do we have the killers in custody? I don't think there's any doubt about that.

Bernice Boles lived a life supported by vice. The sheriff's report shows she was employed at The Sugarbush roadhouse as a waitress. Everybody else, including the newspapers say she was a known prostitute. Well if she was I didn't know it! I'm sure that you didn't either until you read it in the newspapers. Whether she was or wasn't is totally irrelevant, a mute point! She is guaranteed the same constitutional protection as any other citizen of America. She's innocent until proven guilty in a court of law and for her that's never going to happen.

Lindy Blue, the young negro women falls into the same category. Folks say she was a prostitute. I didn't know that either. I need to spend more time sitting around in the barbershop.

Kirby Suggs and Shelton Brooks lived sordid lives and had numerous brushes with the law which were all related to brawling, gambling, drunkenness and things of that sort. Like Bernice Boles and Lindy Blue, they indulged in vices.

As these victims were murdered and the word hit the news stands and air waves, there was a disturbing absence in the expression and outpouring of sympathy, compassion and sorrow by the general public and our Christian community for these unfortunate souls and their families.

There was a common theme from the newspapers, the streets and the pulpits, that cried out in unison, 'good riddance, they reaped what they sowed!' That is simply not true folks. Their lot in life was in no way shape or form deserving of being beaten, hanged, raped, sodomized, or thrown under the wheels of a moving train to be literally bruised into two pieces. Consider the horror, the incomprehensible pain and emotional agony of being conscious and watching someone pull out a straight razor, open it and with great pleasure, begin cutting off your body parts and throwing them away as if they were garbage. Then as a final terror, picking you up and throwing your mutilated body off a dam into a raging river and certain death.

As strong as I possibly can, I want to stress that we must see past the stigma of foul reputations and sordid living if we are to remember that these victims were once innocent children that grew up to make bad choices. Like the thief on the cross, they are entitled to our forgiveness, our sorrow and our outrage at the way they died.

I will venture to say that in every family there is at least one black sheep hidden in the closet who has voluntarily pulled away from a loving family to follow the wrong path.

In the midst of tragedies similar to these, would families and friends deny prayers and grief of a loving and forgiving Christian heart. I don't think so.

Loving your neighbor as yourself is a virtue that is embraced by all Christians as a wonderful thing, that is until they have someone to forgive and that someone just happens to be an arch enemy or a person of questionable moral character that they can't stand the sight of. It's hard, real hard. But remember, loving your neighbor as yourself does not mean that you have to feel fondness and affection for them, because you don't.

It doesn't mean that they're not as bad as you thought they were, because they are.

It doesn't mean that they shouldn't be punished for their badness, because they should.

Hate the sin, but not the sinner even to death. It's as simple as that and includes the two sick minds on trial in this court room today.

I will show you pictures of each and every victim in graphic detail. If any one of you on this jury have ever had thoughts that the murders of the victims who lived sordid lives were less tragic than the murders of Bertha Tate and Annie Mosely, after looking at the pictures you will no longer be able to draw that distinction. We must not condemn or judge those who are no longer here to defend themselves. They will be judged in a higher court, but today in this lower court they will share equally in our sympathy and outrage.

The rape of, Bertha Tate, and little, Annie Mosely, have rightfully been the most prominent in public expressions of outrage. This emphasis is not prejudiced, but rather underscores the barbarism that every victim endured and the depths of depravity that possess the defendants.

The Sugarbush

The eyes of a nation are on us today, especially you the jury. We will dispel every remnant of prejudice and bias we have been accused of in newspaper accounts written by our out of town guest reporters.

We no doubt left that impression from our initial reaction to the first rape-murders at The Sugarbush. They were indifferently passed off as the work of an avenging angel sent to punish the wicked. With great joy and shouting from the pulpits, the second rape-murders that took the lives of a bootlegger who ran a gambling parlor and a young negro woman said to be prostituting herself to white men, confirmed that the avenging angel was still among us and on the prowl. The joy and shouting turned quickly to weeping and terror when the killers struck into the heart of our Christian community. It wasn't a discriminating angel after all! It was the non-discriminating devil and he sure wasn't selecting his victims according to their works. Now that we've confessed that our first impressions were wrong, we can redeem ourselves by seeing that justice is served fairly and equitably in the matter before us.

Speaking of the devil, there's two of them staring at us right now. I want the jury to stare back at them and stare closely. All you see is anger, hatred and defiance. I believe that describes a devil, but since we've only seen the results of his presence in the world and not his physician appearance, the word devil does not seem adequate to describe the defendants sitting there reeking of evil and the putrid stench of death.

You will see perfectly matching casts of the defendant's footprints taken on top of Lookout Dam from pools of blood that poured from the bodies of Garrett Simms and Landis DeHart while being mutilated by the defendants. Landis Dehart was killed and so was Garrett Simms, but Simms miraculously survived and lived long enough to identify the murderers. We will show you the straight razor belonging to the defendant's father that was used to cut off the victims' ears. We will show you the bloody overalls, bloody shoes and blood stained rope used to bind the victims. We will show you pictures of the defendants injuries inflicted by Simms and DeHart during a fierce struggle to survive.

You will hear testimony from victims who were assaulted and raped by the defendants prior to The Sugarbush slayings. They survived the assaults, but never pressed charges because they feared retaliation by the defendants. They're still afraid and ashamed, but through a sense of duty have come forward of their own free will, happy at last to confront their tormenters and lay down their heavy burden.

You will be sickened by the testimony you hear and evidence you see. I will show that the defendants have a history of beating and raping women and with each assault, the violence became progressively worse, reaching the very depths of depravity with the rape and murder of Sheriff Travis Gant's Aunt Bertha Tate, a seventy year old widow and retired public servant known and loved throughout the county.

There will not be a dry eye in this court room or among the crowd gathered outside when you hear testimony from the witness who discovered the pitiful torn remains of Annie Mosely, a twelve year old child who was born with Downs Syndrome. You will see her sweet innocent face in family pictures. You will see her ripped clothes matted with dried blood, her own vomit and body fluids. You will see photographs of her beaten lifeless body covered with coagulated blood and crawling with green flies invading her every body cavity.

Without exception, you will hear testimony from the coroner, that although the women died from stab wounds to the heart, in every case the internal injuries inflicted by rape were life threatening. So severe was the internal trauma, it is believed the defendants were inserting foreign objects into the vaginal and rectal orifices of the dying women.

The testimony you will hear and the evidence I will present on each and every charge will be so conclusive that your retiring to the jury room to find a guilty verdict in all thirteen counts will be nothing more than a formality. I will ask for the death penalty and will settle for nothing less. Thank you. Your jury, Counselor."

Counsel for the defense approached the jury and began his opening statement.

"Gentlemen of the Jury. My associate and I are sitting next to the defendants and if they reek of evil and the putrid stench of death, we can't smell it. My clients are clean, however personal appearance or personal hygiene are not described in the Constitution of the United States of America as prerequisites for receiving a fair trial. Any such

The Sugarbush

references by the prosecution should be ignored. I would hate to think that the guilt or innocense of my clients hinged on the prosecutors ability to smell."

Once more laughter erupted in the courtroom, but quickly subsided when the judge reached for his gavel.

Defense counsel continued. "My associate and I didn't smell evil and death, but we did smell something. A rat!

I petitioned the court to throw out the current indictments in favor of separate indictments for each charge, not only because it would deny my clients the right to a fair trial, but also because in their current form they deviate drastically from established judicial procedure. I've never heard or seen anything like it before!

If this is any indication of the judicial mistreatment I can expect during the trial and as a result my clients are found guilty, I will appeal the conviction. I can guarantee you if that happens the Appellate Court will throw out your verdict and grant my clients a new trial. I plead with you to consider the evidence and the credibility of the witnesses for the prosecution carefully. Emotions are running high. I trust you will not let them effect your good judgement.

The investigations of the rape-murder related deaths by the county sheriff were never successful in placing my clients anywhere near the scene of the fatal assaults when they occurred.

From the outset of the investigation my clients have been found guilty by public opinion only and as a result have been hounded, harassed and abused constantly for the past year by the sheriff.

My client's parent's home and farm has been searched and ransacked three times by the sheriff.

My clients have confirmed alibis for their whereabouts at the time every assault occurred.

I will prove that Landis DeHart and Garrett Simms were manufacturing illegal moonshine whiskey in the community of Catfish.

I will show that another of their cousins working with them was burned to death at the distillery when he accidently inundated himself with alcohol catching himself on fire.

I will show that Landis DeHart ran to the Grimes farm a half mile away and asked my clients for help which was denied because my clients were under surveillance by the sheriff. This infuriated DeHart and Simms who vowed revenge.

I will show that when the charred corpse of the cousin was taken to an undertaker to be prepared for burial, the undertaker reported it to the sheriff who took advantage of the tragedy and under the threat of sending DeHart and Simms back to county jail for violation of their parole, enrolled their assistance in a plan to frame my clients for making moonshine whiskey.

Before the sheriff's plan was put into action, Simms and Dehart were murdered by someone unknown. We contend that when the sheriff barged onto the Grimes farm, the mother of my clients was distracted while the evidence was planted by the sheriff's negro driver.

My clients are innocent victims of a conspiracy and I intend to prove it.

Thank you.

A wealth of evidence in the murders of DeHart and Simms set the tone for victory by the prosecution. The casts of footprints from two different patterns of shoe soles matched perfectly. Blood types matched. Blood specimens from Landis Dehart's foot and boot matched the defendants. Two pairs of blood stained overalls, both missing a button and the missing buttons found at the murder scene. The binding rope and straight razor. Pictures of the injuries sustained in the struggle by the victims and the defendants, spoke volumes in support of the prosecutions case.

Any defense based on conspiracy seldom succeeded, but in failure, frequently provided grounds for an appeal. Attorneys for the defense were depending on that. They had not come into court with any expectations of winning the first round in such an emotionally charged environment, but firmly believed in the innocense of their clients. Intense scrutiny of statements from the defendants, their parents and of pertinent files from the sheriff's office appeared sufficient to support a conspiracy strategy.

Now, defense council was having second thoughts reinforced by comments they overheard between their clients concerning things that only an eyewitness to the murders of Simms and DeHart would have known.

The Sugarbush

Sheriff Gant was the first witness for the prosecution in the rape related murders. During cross examination by the defense, the sheriff's straight forward candidness was not what they had expected from the leader of a conspiracy. Travis readily agreed that the prosecutions case was wholly circumstantial, the only piece of physical evidence being a dagger found at the defendants home and exhibited by the prosecution as the murder weapon.

Cross examination of the sheriff complete, the defense attorneys concurred that it was hard to picture him as a conspirator and ask for a brief recess to confer privately with their clients.

The guard ushered the prisoners out of the court room into a small conference room to join their angry lawyers.

"What we comin' in here fer?" Jess asked.

The lead attorney answered. "We came in here to get the truth. The State is kicking our asses off out there an—

A puzzled look on his face, Jarred interrupted. "Who in hell's the State, Jess? I ain't seen'im."

"Me neither little brother."

"The State is the prosecuting attorney, Gordon Jackson, tha—

"Well then by god call'im by his right damn name, ain't that right, Jess."

"Alright, let's start over, we don't have much time." said the lawyer hurriedly.

"We thought we had a strong case on conspiracy and a fighting chance, but it just crumbled and the trials only half over. You lied to us!

"Gordon Jackson's the damn liar," Jarred shouted.

"Oh is he? Let's talk about that. He proved that you owned the liquor still where a man was burned to death. He proved that you owned the liquor still Garrett and Simms found the day they were murdered. He proved the evidence he found at your home belonged to you. We sat right beside you out there during the sheriff's testimony on the Simms-DeHart murders and heard Jarred correcting errors in the sheriff's testimony. If Gordon Jackson is the liar here, without a shadow of a doubt he's convinced us of one certainty. You two murdered Garrett Simms and Landis DeHart. You know it, we know it and you know we know it."

"Y'all ain't 'posed to listen to me a talkin' to Jess!"

"Yep and y'all ain't 'posed to lie to yer lawyers," he answered, mimicking Jarred. "We did have a good chance of getting you off on the rape-murder charges, but that's not going to happen either. Our credibility's zilch."

"Yer what's what?" Jarred asked curiously.

"Forget it! Just tell us about rape and murder again."

"We ain't murdered no women!" Jarred shouted.

"We ain't murdered no men neither little brother," said Jess.

"We're not getting anywhere and our time is almost up. Here's what we're going to do. We want to make a plea bargain. Just hold it, Jess, and I'll tell you what that means. We want to meet with the judge and prosecutor and make a deal to keep you out of the electric chair. I want you and Jarred to plead guilty in the Simms-Dehart murder case with a sentence of life in prison in exchange for dropping the rape-murder charges.

"We ain't pleadin' guilty to nothin' and that's final," Jess growled.

"Then the only thing we can do is try to get you off with a life sentence."

Walking back to the court room, the associate defense lawyer asked. "Do you really think the prosecutor would have been receptive to a plea bargain"?

"Never! We don't have anything to offer in exchange. It was a dumb idea, but I would have tried it anyway. I don't care how dumb I look if I can avoid the death penalty. So far Gordon's done an exceptionally good job and he's not done yet, but we sure are.

Circumstantial evidence or not, we can't believe anything our clients say. We can't defend these guys because they won't let us. They aren't even concerned about the possibility they're going to be put to death. We are, but they aren't. The jury is going to decide the verdict, but they only recommend the sentence. The judge makes the final call on that. I'm going to approach the bench with Gordon, concede defeat and ask for a life sentence. If he's strongly opposed to it, at least we'll know we have to make our plea to the jury during the summation."

The Sugarbush

Defense did approach the bench. Gordon was opposed to anything less than the death sentence and the judge didn't seem receptive to the idea of life sentences either.

Late Thursday morning, the prosecution rested.

In the final analysis, the case for the defense in the rape related charges was based entirely on cross examination of witnesses for the prosecution. Even the newspapers were impressed with defense counsel's candor in discrediting questionable witnesses and prowess in reducing the prosecution's hoard of circumstantial evidence to a level of reasonable doubt. That's where it ended. That was the defense.

They put only one witness on the stand, the defendants father who confirmed his son's alibis. Gordon, in a dramatic display of disgust at the fathers quite believable testimony refused the opportunity to cross examine him.

On Thursday afternoon, the defense rested.

Early Friday morning the jailer and guard from the county jail drove down the ramp into the basement garage of the court house with the prisoners.

Dressed in black and white striped prison clothes, handcuffed and shackled, the Grimes' brothers were a frightening sight with their manes of hair and shaggy beards. The paddy wagon doors were opened and the prisoners ordered out.

"Horace," said the jailor. "The laundry man's a usin' the freight elevator. Take the prisoners up the back stairway to the holding cell. I'm goin' to the City Diner fer coffee and breakfast.

Horace Sykes was subcontracted by Catawba County to the Prohibition Enforcement Branch of the Federal Government as an escort for prisoners being sent to the Federal Penitentiary in Atlanta, Georgia. He was experienced and competent. When not on contract assignment he performed regular guard duties at the county jail.

Later that morning as court was convening, the jailor and his guard approached the holding cell to escort the prisoners into the court room.

"Whew, they shore are rotten this mornin'," the jailor exclaimed!

"Git us outta this stinking nasty mess!" Jess shouted. "It ain't our fault yer damn fancy plumbin' ain't workin'."

The guard opened the door. The cell was flooded with urine, excrement and soggy toilet tissue.

"Y'all made yer own stinkin' mess," the jailor growled. "When we break fer lunch ya'll gonna clean it up or waller in it and it don't make no difference to me which one. By now y'all oughtta learned how to use inside plumbin' without a clogging' it all to hell up. Now come on outta there and let's go! Stop when we git out in the hall. We gonna stand a few minutes to let the stink git off of you'uns. I ain't takin ye in the court room 'til ye air out. It's bad enough they have to look at ye much less smell ye!"

Summations to the jury began. Gordon had saved his most dramatic performance for this moment.

"Gentlemen of the jury. My summation will be short. The guilt of the defendants on each and every charge has been clearly established leaving no room for a reasonable doubt.

We are all fully aware that the evidence presented by the State in the rape related murders was almost entirely circumstantial. Defense counsel very skillfully pointed out the miscarriages of justice that have occurred in convictions based on circumstances. I am fully aware of those pitfalls, but on the charges facing the defendants today, they do not apply.

I ask that one thought be burned into your minds. Since the defendants have been under lock and key, not one assault nor even an attempted assault has occurred. Our county is made safe again.

The question is not about guilt. We know they're guilty as charged. The question is, what are you going to do about it?

Defense counsel will make a plea for the court's mercy and ask that the defendants not be put to death but rather be sentenced to life in prison.

Let's explore how heinous a crime must be in order to justify the death penalty.

Would severely beating and hanging a man be bad enough?

How about beating, raping, sodomizing and stabbing three women and a child to death?

The Sugarbush

Is beating a man and throwing him under the wheels of a moving train to be cut in half enough?

Consider two men being beaten and butchered alive then thrown off of a dam to be splattered on the rocks and concrete below. Is that justification?

The next example I saved until last and I want to apologize in advance to relatives and friends of the victim for the pain it may cause them.

I think everyone in the county knew Bertha Tate and how she died. Well not entirely.

For very sensitive and private reasons at the request of her family, we never mentioned that the stab wound to Bertha's heart was not the cause of death. She actually died of heart failure after which the defendants set about raping and sodomizing her corpse. When that was done, they stabbed her in the heart and were dragging her body to the pig pen with intentions of feeding it to the hogs, which was fortunately averted by the arrival of Sheriff Gant for an unexpected visit.

It was only after days and nights of agonizing reflective deliberation that I determined I should describe that event in particular in such graphic detail.

Now I ask you. Is that heinous enough to justify the death penalty?

The State of North Carolina Legislature recently reinstated the death penalty and installed a completely rebuilt and modernized electric chair. If the examples we have just explored are not sufficient justification for putting it to use, then reinstatement of the death penalty is rendered meaningless.

The decision is yours. Thank You.

Spectators in the courtroom were in tears. The defense attorney was equally impressed with the prosecutor's sincere and highly emotional presentation. On his way to the jury box, he winked at Gordon to express his approval.

Defense began his summation.

"Gentlemen of the jury. It would indeed be a travesty of justice and ludicrous of me to doubt the undeniable evidence presented by the prosecution on the charges accusing my clients with the murders of Landis DeHart and Garrett Simms. I will not do that.

It would also be a travesty of justice and ludicrous of me to abandon my clients by even considering conceding defeat based on the paltry circumstantial evidence presented by the prosecution in the rape-murder related charges. If you should find them guilty on those eleven charges, you are risking participation in a grave miscarriage of justice when it is absolutely unnecessary.

Why take such a risk in order to appease public opinion, when a fair verdict can be reached that will serve justice, protect the public while punishing the guilty.

I have a suggestion for you that provides the perfect risk free verdict that meets all your objectives.

Career criminals have and age old system of justice that includes a code of honor which they themselves police. Betrayal, one of the cardinal violations of this code usually demands execution of the perpetrator, but in the sick minds of criminals is not considered murder, but rather taking care of business. The defendants were betrayed by their partners in crime who were therefore executed for their betrayal.

Do not misunderstand me. I'm not implying that murder under certain circumstances is acceptable and under others is not. Murder in any form, for any reason, under any condition is a capital crime that must not go unpunished. I'm merely saying that underworld executions fall into a separate category whereby the benefit derived by civilized society from the elimination of, in this case, two career criminals, should be a consideration for reducing the severity of punishment imposed on the executioners. Justice among thieves is an ancient, unsolicited service to law enforcement and law abiding citizens and the charges in question provide you the jury with the perfect solution for the perfect verdict.

My partner and I are vehemently opposed to the death penalty as an encroachment on God's authority and Devine system of justice. Biblical scripture tells us in no uncertain terms. 'Vengeance is mine saith the Lord.'

Therefore I urge you to consider my suggestion in good faith and in the context of Biblical teachings. Sentences of life imprisonment without parole will meet all of your objectives.

Thank you.

"Your honor," Gordon said with a chuckle. "As is my prerogative, I request a rebuttal of defense counsel's summation."

"Proceed," said the Judge, unable to suppress his amusement.

"Gentlemen of the jury," Gordon said, still smiling. "What you just heard was a novel concept of justice that I am not familiar with.

Two weeks ago, I had the unfortunate task of sending four young men in their late teens to prison for taking the law into their own hands. In their case, an innocent husband and father of four was, for all practical purposes, scared to death.

Any unlawful behavior, practice or action, cannot be labeled justice in anyway, shape or form.

Retribution among thieves is the vilest form of vigilante undertaking, is not and never has been a service to anybody but criminals, is a detriment to society, and demands the harshest punishment permissible.

Reducing the severity of punishment for criminals murdering criminals, then declaring such acts to be an age old service to mankind, is contrary to every moral principal known to mankind.

Embracing such a concept would soon lead to sanctions for ridding society of all troublemakers which would quickly put mothers-in-law on the list of endangered species."

For the third time during the trial, the courtroom was filled with laughter instead of tears.

The courtroom silenced once again, Gordon continued.

"Suffice it to say, the defense attorney's truly sincere opposition to capital punishment and efforts to avoid it transcended all reasonable thought then descended into the realm of comical satire for which at this moment I'm sure he is reconsidering. Thank you once again."

Returning to his chair, it was Gordon's turn to wink.

Immediately following adjournment of the court, Travis collared Gordon in the Judge's chambers.

"Today you took political grandstanding to a new low at the expense of me and my family. For the world to see, you made public highly personal information contained in classified confidential police files that had been entrusted to your professional integrity. You had enough to make your case without doing that. As long as I'm Sheriff of Catawba County you'll never see another file from my office. I'll give you what you need and nothing more. Now get the hell out of my sight."

Shaken and pale, Gordon straightened his coat and tie and retaliated.

"What are you being so damn self-righteous about, Gant. We're not responsible for the tragedies of the past year. We both wished to god they never happened, but they did and each of us has to deal with them in our own way.

Whether you like it or not this case made you the high sheriff of Catawba county and it's going to make me Governor of North Carolina.

Quit acting like a punch drunk hick. Let's go. Everybody's waiting in the courtyard for our joint statement."

XXI

"Horace,"the jailer barked. "Lock'em up and come on down to the City Diner. We'll be in the banquet room. I'll send over meals fer'em. They can eat in the stinkin' mess they made or do without."

When Horace reached the holding cell and opened the door, Jess, in a pleading voice said. "Look at that stinkin" hole! They ain't even a place to stand outta the shit and it weren't our fault. How ye 'spect us to eat in all that nasty mess, Horace."

Preoccupied with joining the celebration at the City Diner and irritated that he might be delayed, Horace walked quickly between the brothers to take another look.

In an instant Jarred dropped to the floor to form a tripping hazard. Jess lunged knocking the surprised and terrified guard on his back, immediately leaping into the air and coming down on his chest full force with both shackled feet. Jarred, already back on his feet, silenced the feeble cries for help with the butt of the shotgun. Retrieving the keys, they were quickly out of the handcuffs and shackles and dragged the guard into the cell. Now free from bondage and armed, they looked at each other in disbelief.

"It worked! We done it," Jarred whispered.

"We ain't outta here yit little brother," Jess replied. "Foller me and be ready fer a fight."

They made their way down the stairs into the basement without incident. Hearing the elevator coming down they crawled into the laundry truck to hide. When the elevator stopped and the door opened, another cart was shoved onto the truck.

"I wanna go to lunch!" shouted the garage attendant. "How much longer ye gonna be?"

"About five minutes," the driver answered. "I got one more cart to brang down."

From their concealment the brothers heard the elevator door close and the garage attendant's footsteps as he walked back to his booth. In what seemed like an eternity to Jess and Jarred, the driver returned. He loaded the last cart onto the truck and drove out of the garage.

In October when Jess and Jarred were first arrested, their dad paid them a visit at the county jail.

"Now y'all boys listen to me," he said in hushed tones. "Jist shore as hell they gonna put you'uns in the 'lectric chair fer butcherin' up them fellers' and throw'in'em off'n the dam!

You'uns ain't gonna git out of it neither 'cause they gottcha dead to rights. I'd a lot druther you'uns die a fightin' than sittin' 'round waitin' fer'em to cook ye to death.

I don't care what nobody says, don't you'uns own up to nothin', never!

First chance ye git, make a run fer it. I don't know how ye gonna do it, ye'll have to think on that yeselfs'. Jist figer on it."

"It ain't right Paw,' Jarred said, his voice raising in anger. "Them double crossin' blabber mouths' needed killin', ain't that right, Jess?"

"Shet up, Jarred and keep yer voice down," the old man whispered.

"But Paw!"

"I said fer ye to shet up and keep yer voice down and I ain't tellin' ye agin'. We done been through all a that. Jist you'uns listen to me now. I'm tryin' to tell ye somethin'.

Quit cussin' and fightin' with them guards. Do ever'thang they tell ye jist like ifn' it wuz me and yer Mom a talkin'.

Let yer hair and beards keep a growin'. The worst ye look the better, 'cause that's the way folks will remember ye. If'n ye make yer gitta way, split up and make tracks fer yer Uncle Obed's place. He'll hide ye in his 'tater cellar 'till the rukus dies down, then you'uns kin git gone from here."

"I never knowed he had a 'tater cellar," Jess remarked with a surprised expression on his face.

"Me neither," Jarred chimed in. "Where's it at, Paw?"

"Obed'll show ye if'n ye git there. If'n ye don't git there ain't no need fer you'uns knowin' where it's at. Y'all jist hide in that kudzu thicket behind the hog lot. When it's safe, he'll come to ye."

"Paw," Jarred ask. "What if'n the law finds us in there?"

"They ain't likely to! Obed's been a bootleggin' all his life and gits raided ever so reg'lar. They ain't never found where he hides his liquor 'cause they ain't never found his 'tater cellar.

First thang you'uns do if'n you'uns git away is shave off'n them beards. Obed'll cut yer hair.

The Sugarbush

They'll be new overalls, brogans and ever'thang ye need. They'll be two pistols and plenty a shells all a waitin' fer ye. The railroad depot switch yard ain't but half a mile from ye. When Obed tells you'uns thangs is right, y'all hop a freight train east and work yer way to the Dismal Swamp. They's a landin' on, Alligator River, named, Gum Neck. Settle in there so's I'll know where to find ye."

"We need our money Paw," Jess whispered.

"I already stashed it with Obed. When ye git there, he'll give it to ye. Divide it up and keep it on ye all the time case ye git spotted and have to make a run fer it."

"Paw," said Jarred. "Ye talkin' like we done broke out a'ready.'

"Yeah son. They ain't nothin to say if'n ye don't! I'm a leavin' now and I'll not be back 'till the trial."

The brothers became model prisoners, remaining quiet and engaging in conversation only when necessary. They obeyed every command promptly and without complaint. Refusing to shave or cut their hair was of no concern to the judicial system. In fact this pleased the county attorney whose prosecution strategy could only be helped by their savage appearance.

The good behavior was beginning to pay off. Being shuffled back and forth from the county jail to the county court house day after day, they noticed that the head jailer began letting his guard do most of the escorting.

Horace relished the responsibility, but as a matter of routine had become lax in his attention to the ever present danger. And why should he be overly concerned? The prisoners were in handcuffs and shackles. He was armed with a double barreled shotgun and a revolver, inside a court house on the town square that was crawling with law enforcement officers.

The prisoners had become familiar with the routine and layout of the court house building. They had an idea. It was a desperate idea that would have to be played out as it developed, if it developed. They knew the possibility of success was slim to none, but they had to try, even if the slightest opportunity provided the chance. Deliberately plugging up the toilet bowl was the only diversion they could think of. It worked!

A waitress from the City Diner made her way down the court house corridor to deliver meals to the prisoners just as she had done many times before.

"Horace, where y'all at?" she called out. "It shore stinks in here."

Hearing gurgling sounds, she looked curiously at the blood on the floor around her feet, then looked into the holding cell and saw Horace laying in the sewage, bubbles of blood bursting from his gaping mouth.

Screaming in terror she dropped the meals. Turning to run, she slipped on the bloody floor and fell hard. Crawling on hands and knees toward the door, she struggled to her feet and ran down the hallway.

Travis had declined an invitation to join Gordon and the other local officials in the banquet room of the City Diner in preference to sitting at a table by a front window to eat lunch with Seth and Pace.

He looked out the window to see the jailor being questioned by several reporters.

"What's the jailor doing over here, Seth? He's supposed to be with Horace."

"Hell if I know," Seth answered. "He's talks to those reporters every chance he gets. There's no tellin' what kinda shit he's feedin'em."

"Well I'll take care of that," said Travis, getting up from the table and walking quickly towards the entrance door.

Suddenly the crowd gathered outside turned and looked toward the courthouse. Travis saw the object of their attention and ran to meet the waitress, stained with blood and screaming hysterically.

"Horace is a dyin' over there. Them convicts is gone!" she cried out.

In a state of shock, Travis shouted. "Somebody take care of her," and dashed for the court house followed by Pace and Seth.

By the time they got there, Horace was dead. Travis took charge and began barking orders.

"Pace, get an ambulance over here. Have'em come to the basement freight elevator. Seth, call the City Police and have'em seal off the area, then call Melinda! Tell her to call in every off duty deputy she can locate. When you've done that, meet me in the basement garage."

Travis ran down the stairs to the garage.

"Where's the garage attendant?" He shouted.

"I'm over here, Sheriff. I ran outta the City Diner right behind ye."

"Did you see anything?"

"I didn't see nothin', Sheriff, but I know how they got outta here. They's a laundry truck pulled outta here jist as I wuz goin' to lunch! They mustta been hid in it!"

Pace and Seth burst through the stairway door.

"Whatta you wanna do now?" Sheriff!

"Seth, you take care of things here! It looks like they got away on a laundry truck, but search the buildin' anyway. Don't do it alone, wait for your men.

Pace, you come with me. The laundry truck was the last vehicle to leave the garage. Let's get over to their plant and fast. Seth, Jess and Jarred are armed with a shotgun and pistol."

"I understand," Seth replied.

When Travis and Pace arrived at the laundry plant, the truck was parked at the loading dock.

The driver had not yet unloaded the contents.

In the process of dragging the guard into the holding cell, the fugitives had embedded the soles of their shoes with the overflowed sewage that covered the floor.

The stench was obvious as Travis and Pace climbed into the back of the truck.

From two of the carts, dirty linens smeared with blood and excrement had been thrown aside leaving the imprints of bodies that had lain hidden under them.

"They were here, all right!" Travis said. "In prison garb they won't get far before somebody spots'em. There's a phone over by the dispatcher's desk. While I'm calling the office, find the driver of that truck and bring him back here to me!"

"Sheriff Gant's office!" Melinda answered.

"Melinda!" Travis said, "Call off the search at the court house. The prisoner's got out of the building on a laundry truck. Tell Seth to set up a stakeout on the Grimes' farm, set up roadblocks on every road out of town including railroads and then meet Pace at the laundry plant on Second Avenue.

Call the radio stations and tell'em we have an emergency. Ask them to warn the public of the escape and the danger. They should secure their vehicles, lock their doors and open them only to people they recognize.

Everybody owns a gun. Stress that no one should try to be a hero by taking the law into their own hands. They might end up shooting a relative, friend or innocent stranger. That could happen! The railroad runs just behind the laundry. Besides the hobos, there's lots of vagrants passing through looking for work."

"Travis," Pace interrupted.

"Hang on a minute, Melinda," Travis said tensely turning to answer Pace. "What is it?"

"We have a new problem, Sheriff. Besides linens and guard uniforms, prisoners black and whites are part of the laundry. We don't know if they changed clothes between the court house and here or not. It only makes sense that they would have."

"Of course they changed. We've got our heads up our asses," Travis muttered. "This is the worst thing that ever happened to me!

"Melinda, the escaped killers may be dressed in city jail guard uniforms. The public must be made aware of that. I don't know how the radio stations are going to say all this, but tell'em it's gotta be said in a hurry. Find Silas James. Tell him to bring his bloodhounds and meet me at my office."

"Sheriff," Melinda replied, "Silas has three day's off. He called in yesterday and said he was going out on the river to fish a trot line. He won't be back 'til Sunday morning, but I know where he's fishin'."

"Send a deputy after'im," Travis replied. "If you don't have a deputy free, send a clerk."

"I'll take care of it, Sheriff," Melinda replied calmly. "When are you coming back to the office? There's a crowd waiting for you, not to mention the phone calls."

"Tell everyone to sit tight!" Travis responded. "I'll be there within the hour."

"Sheriff," Melinda said, her voice trembling, "Horace Sykes is dead."

The Sugarbush

"Yes, I know. I'll be there as soon as I can."

In the meantime, Pace walked through the noisy laundry plant to the front office and called the plant manager to the side.

"I need you to come with me out to the loading dock right now. I'll explain as we walk."

"If it's about the commercial license tags for my trucks, I already took care of that," the manager stated curtly.

"That's not why we're here, but since you mentioned it, we'll check that out too. First we need to talk to the driver of the truck that just came in from picking up laundry at the city jail. Where is he?"

"All the hands eat their lunch over by the steam tank. He oughtta be there!" came the nervous response. "You look mighty serious Deputy. What kinda trouble is he in?"

"Lets find him damn quick. Sheriff Gant is waiting for us by the dispatcher's desk."

Travis was just hanging up the phone when Pace returned with the manager and truck driver.

In an unexpected move, Travis whirled around to face the men. "Which one of you was driving that truck?" he demanded.

"That's my truck," answered the startled driver. "I'm the onliest one that drives it."

"I understand you're a mighty good friend of Jess and Jarred Grimes. "Is that right?"

Travis asked.

A confused look crept across the man's face.

"Ye mean them brothers bein' tried fer killin' all them folks.?"

"You know who the sheriff's talkin about," Pace shouted. "They're buddies of yours. Don't play dumb with us! Were not stupid!"

Now trembling in frustration, his face flushed red, the driver blurted out in anger.

"I ain't stupid neither. I know who I know. I know who my friends are and them two ain't amongst'em. I seen their pitchers in the papers and I heared all the talk goin' round like ever'body else in the county. That's all I know 'bout'em and that's the truth of it."

"Okay! Okay!" Sheriff Gant quickly interrupted. "Everybody calm down! We believe you! We just needed to be sure you weren't involved."

"Involved in what?" the manager yelled. "What the hell's goin' on here!"

Travis answered. "Around noon the Grimes' brothers escaped from jail and killed a guard in the process. We know they got out of the court house basement garage by hiding in the back of your driver's truck. They could have gotten off the truck somewhere between here and there. Either that or they waited until you parked at the dock. Did you make any stops after you left there?"

"In my truck," the driver cried. "Them murderers' was hid in the back of my truck?"

"Did you make any more stops?" Travis repeated.

"Not fer laundry!" he answered. "Jist traffic lights and stop signs, that's all!"

"Did you see or notice anything out of the ordinary?"

"Nothin'," he replied. "We wuz all eatin' lunch inside. The loadin' dock bay doors are shet so we couldn't see out neither. They could be hidin' in the plant. They could a got inside without nobody seein'em. It's such a racket in here we wouldn't a heared 'em movin' about."

"They're smarter than that," Pace responded. "We'll look around anyway."

"I've got to get back to Headquarters!" Travis exclaimed. "Pace, you take over 'till Seth gets here. Set up your command post at the loading dock. Do house to house searches, garages, basements, tool sheds, barns, brush piles, thickets, woods, culverts, outhouses. They've gotta be holed up nearby. You know what to do. Keep me updated by phone and let everybody know that Horace Sykes died. They stomped him to death."

Back at Headquarters, Travis confirmed to the press and the county leaders that a successful escape attempt had occurred resulting in the death of a guard. Giving no details at the time, he announced that a massive manhunt was underway urging watchfulness and caution until the prisoners were back behind bars.

The Sugarbush

With all the manhunt responsibilities delegated to his senior staff, Travis retreated to his office to think things through and wait for Silas James.

At three o'clock in the afternoon, Melinda informed him that the jury had found the brothers guilty as charged in all thirteen counts of the indictment, recommending the death penalty.

"That's just dandy!" he muttered. "We gotta find'em first. Now I know how the Mexican police felt when Will Rogers said they caught Pancho Villa in the mornin' additions of the newspapers and let him go in the evening additions."

At nine o'clock, Seth called in to report no progress in the search.

Weary and discouraged, Travis paced the floor.

Melinda walked in announcing that Silas had arrived.

Silas hurried into Travis' office.

"Howdy Sheriff. Ye shore know how to mess up a good fish fry. I done heared 'bout the jail break."

"Thanks for comin'!" Let's go! I hope the scent is not so cold your hounds can't pick it up. I'll give you the details on the way to the City Laundry plant. Every minute counts."

"Hold on, Sheriff! I come straight here from the river. My son left me off to talk to ye while he fetches the hounds. We got time a plenty to talk 'til he gits back."

Silas listened intently as Travis recounted the details of the escape.

"Where are they?" Travis moaned. "Those guys were wearin' black and white stripes when they escaped. Seth thinks they changed into guard uniforms when they were in the back of the truck. The only thing that kills that notion is that nobody could find the black and whites they changed out of, that is, stinkin' and stained with blood. Nobody and I mean nobody saw anything! Even in guard uniforms they couldn't have fooled anybody. Not with that shaggy hair and those ragged beards."

"Sheriff, I don't know why 'tis when criminals gits ketched, the law and everybody else git in their minds that they wuz caught 'cause they dumb. They's times maybe like that but ye can't think thatta way. Escaped convicts in particular holds a powerful sense of self preservation. We can save some time if'n we go over to the court house so's I can git the sheets off'n the holdin' cell bunks to scent the hounds with."

"Let's go!" replied Travis. "I had everything left just as it was. Nothing has been cleaned up yet. I wanted to see what you make of it."

When they walked into the holding cell area, Silas looked around quickly. "They plugged up them toilets a purpose so's they could call off the guards mind and git'im between'em. We'll come back after them sheets later. Let's foller them tracks."

Entering the basement, Travis began explaining how the Grimes' brothers had climbed into the laundry truck to make good their escape. He turned to see Silas walking cautiously toward the boiler room, shining his flashlight on the concrete floor. Bending down for a closer look, Silas rubbed his finger across the floor then brought the finger to his nose and smelled it. He straightened up, stepped to the side and pushed open the boiler room door.

Sensing the meaning, Travis drew his sidearm and quickly moved forward, suddenly filled with an odd sensation of relief and excitement.

"I hope you're right!" Travis whispered.

"If I is," Silas replied, "they done gone from here."

Entering the boiler room, Silas examined the room cautiously. Looking intently at a large metal cover over a valve pit, he called the sheriff to his side.

"See how much cleaner that checker plate is from the floor 'round it? See that dirt and grit heaped along the hinged edge?"

"Open it, Silas! I'll cover you."

"No need fer a gun now, Sheriff. See here where they picked up the dirt when they crawled outta the hole?"

Silas pulled up the heavy lid to expose the pipes and valves concealed below.

"They were hiding in there all right!" Travis agreed. "It still smells like a septic tank. Let's check out the locker room."

All the locker doors had been pried open and the contents rifled. The prison issue clothes, including the shoes were scattered on the floor and the sinks littered with hair.

"They were here all the time!" Travis cried in disgust. "Now we know why nobody saw anything. I couldn't understand how they had

The Sugarbush

simply vanished. The sheriff and his department are lookin' worse all the time!"

"Ye done the right thang, Sheriff Gant. No matter how it looks, all the signs pointed to the laundry truck and I'd a done the same, I 'spect."

"Silas! You knew they never left this building on that truck!"

"I suspicioned it. I weren't shore 'til ye told me Pace couldn't find no sign of'em a changin' clothes. That's when I knowed they ain't hid out on no laundry truck."

"They're smart, Silas! To have pulled this off they gotta be."

"Oh they no doubt smart, Sheriff. Their escape plan wuz plain dumb even if'n it worked. They ain't runnin' on smart, they runnin' on luck. Ever'thang's fallin' to their favor. Outside a cleanin' up our own carelessness so's we ain't heppin' make their luck, they ain't nothin' much else ye can do 'cept keep a huntin'. We jist wait fer the favor to turn on'em and it'll turn on'em fer shore."

"Yeah Silas. They're walkin' the streets clean shaven, haircuts, civilian clothes, new identities, money in their pockets. It's understandable that nobody recognized'em. Everybody's been lookin' for the Grimes' brothers they pictured in the newspapers. They won't head for Catfish, I'm sure of that. I think they'll hole up closer to town, don't you?

"The closer the better," Silas answered. "If'n thangs went their way, they done had a place lined up to go to. Fer shore they split up and come back together at their hideout. That's where they at by now."

They've got an uncle who lives close to town. Pace should be there searchin' the place right now. It's gonna be a long night, Silas. Let's get back to the office and tell your son that we won't be needin' the hounds."

Looking embarrassed, Silas replied. "No need to do that, Sheriff. He ain't brangin'em."

"You knew all along!" Travis said, laughing. "Let's get to the laundry. We need to tell Seth what's going' on."

On Monday morning with no sign of the fugitives, Travis met with his staff and asked Silas to join them.

"I want to make some changes that I believe will improve our resourcefulness," he said.

"Pace is my administrative assistant and driver. With the new developments, he will be dividing his time between Seth and I, leaving me without a driver. That's where Silas comes in. He has more experience in trackin' down criminals than all of us put together and we need his help now more than ever.

With the manhunt goin' on, we'll be able to utilize Silas' experience without raising the hackles of the politicians and white general public. Effective right now, he's my driver. When I'm on duty, wherever you see me you'll see him."

There's two more things you need to know about that must be kept confidential. In our search for the Grimes brothers, Silas will be in no less danger than we are and at times maybe more so. Jess and Jarred hate us, but they hate Silas almost as much as they hate Gordon Jackson. It's not right for Silas to share the same danger we do and not have the means and legal authority to defend himself and cover my back. The only way to do that is to deputize and arm him. His authority will be limited to defending himself and any member of the sheriff's department, especially me. His badge and weapon will be concealed under the jacket of a driver's uniform. If there are any objections, I want to hear them now."

"I have one," Seth responded. "The only thought that occurs to me is that if this gets out, where are we gonna find jobs when you get voted out next election. That is, if we don't get lynched first. Other than that I'm with you."

Laughing with the others, Travis answered. "We have four years to think about that. I know you meant it as both a joke and at the same time a legitimate concern. Silas understands and accepts the risks the same as we do. If it does come up, I believe that under the circumstances, I can justify my decision.

What about the rest of you? No objections! Okay, any questions?"

"Yeah Sheriff, I've got a question about something else." said Pace. "It's keepin' me awake when I'm supposed to be sleepin'. Horace Sykes was the best. He escorted Federal prisoners to and from Atlanta, Georgia and never lost a one. How did the best let two prisoners escape, killing him in the process? He's dead and I'm havin' trouble bein' sorry about that. I'm royally pissed off at him and I'm not the only one."

"I understand what happened," Travis answered. "I'll do my best to explain it to you.

Being a prison guard and prisoner escort is a thankless, boring job that requires a certain mentality. The people who choose that career love it and are suited for it. I can't speak for anybody else, but I know I couldn't do it. To me being a prison guard or jailor would be no different than being buried alive.

In his entire career, Horace never escorted what the Feds' considered a dangerous criminal. He was only assigned to escort good ole boys that got caught bootleggin' or makin' moonshine. Good ole boys don't put up a fight when they get run down, they don't shoot at the law, and only try to escape before they're caught, not after. They give up, go to jail, post bond and continue makin' liquor while they're out on bail waitin' to go to trial and laugh all the way to the bank.

Horace knew the prisoners were dangerous. I don't know what went wrong. Maybe it was the excitement of the moment. They got him between'em and the rest you know.

None of this would ever have happened if the head jailor had followed established procedures requiring two armed guards at all times when escorting prisoners charged with violent crimes. Horace made a mistake that would have been forgiving had his star struck boss been there to back him up. If it's any comfort to you, I'm looking for a new jailor."

XXII

Late Tuesday evening following the jail break, Linus Lamar and his wife sat with a few friends on the front porch of their home across the street from the local elementary school where he worked as janitor and boiler tender.

Lamar was sick. He had been suffering from a lingering malady his doctor had been unsuccessful in treating. For the past five months his wife Carol had been working in his place.

Getting up from her chair, she excused herself and walked across the dirt road and up through the school yard playground to stoke the furnace once more before retiring for the night.

She crept cautiously down the dark stairs to the boiler room and opened the door. It was pitch black inside. She flipped the light switch and nothing happened.

"Consorned it," she mumbled to herself. "I ain't got no spare light bulb. I'll open the furnace door; that'll give me light enough to see fer now."

She opened the furnace door dimly lighting the room in a flickering orange glow, which illuminated the darkness enough for her to see well enough to throw in a few shovels of coal. As she bent to pick up the coal shovel a savage blow intended for the side of her face brushed the top of her head. Screaming in terror, she glanced up into a man's face covered with coal dust and draped in spider webs. The second blow from behind found its mark knocking her to the floor. Grabbed by the hair, her head was jerked up and clamped between a vice of choking knees. An arm went under her waist lifting her up while groping fingers tore at her breasts. From behind powerful hands ripped off her under drawers. Choking for air she was penetrated with a violent painful thrust that lifted both her feet off the floor.

Her husband and his companions heard the scream and raced toward the boiler room followed by several neighbors. Hearing the loud yelling from the approaching men, the rapists dropped Carol to the floor and quickly crawled up and out through the coal chute, disappearing into the night.

Carol saw her torn under drawers lying on the floor in front of the furnace. Struggling to her feet, she picked them up threw them into the furnace and slammed closed the door. On her way up the cellar steps, she ran into the midst of her saviors. Her husband Linus was not among them. He had collapsed before reaching the cellar entrance.

Mid-morning the next day, Travis met with his staff. "Okay, I've read the report. What else do we have?"

"Some good stuff," Seth answered. "It's a helluva lot more than we've had before. We got good casts of the footprints they left and as soon as the duplicates of the shoes stolen from the guards come in, we'll see if we have a match. We'll let you know how it turns out. Silas used sheets from Jess and Jarred's bunks to scent the bloodhounds, but they couldn't pick a trail. We think the hounds got the scent confused because the Grimes boys are wearin' the guards shoes they stole from the locker room. The victim says she was attacked by two men and swears it was Jess and Jarred."

"Could she see that good?" Travis inquired.

"She said she could see good enough to know that the one face she saw was on a big man who didn't have a beard and she would never forget that face as long as she lives. It was Jarred Grimes."

"What do you think?" Travis asked.

"What can I say. She swears that's who attacked her."

"Your report says assault and attempted rape."

"Yes. Mrs. Lamar says they knocked her down and tore the bodice of her dress and then ran because they heard the men coming to her rescue. She got almost hysterical when I asked if she was raped. She said how dare I be spreadin' around that somebody done somethin' that nasty to her. I told her I had to ask the question and we were really glad to hear that it never happened to her. That satisfied her so I left it at that. She'd rather be dead than have anybody know she might have been raped."

"Okay," Travis replied. "Get confirmation on the foot print comparisons as soon as you can. I hope we get the results we're lookin' for."

The end of May, Violet Bell, a Negro teenager and five of her girl friends were swimming nude at a creek on her parents' farm.

Two hundred feet away, hidden in the cover of the woods, two men watched the girls frolicking in the water emitting playful screams of joy. In the past, the stalkers had seen Violet come to swim alone and that's what they had been waiting for, but his time she was not alone, foiling their plans.

They watched in frustration as the naked girls bounded in and out of the water with different shades of ebony skin glistening in the sunlight. The playful teenagers played on a sandbar, building make believe sand castles topped with pebble roofs and rock chimneys. They posed for each other, caressing their bodies, lifting up their firm breasts and shrieking in merriment at the distorted reflections peering up at them from the rippling water.

Growing tired, they all waded into the creek to rinse off the sand. While dressing, Violet proposed a race back to the house, knowing that by taking a secret shortcut, she would be sitting on the back porch steps wearing a mischievous smile of victory when they arrived. She lagged behind, veered to the left and began her dash towards home.

The two men were about to leave when they saw Violet turn and come straight towards them.

Panting and out of breath, the five girls reached the house, arguing over who was first to touch the back porch steps.

"What y'all girls been up to?" Violet's mother yelled cheerfully from the kitchen.

"We had a race back here from the creek," cried the girls. "We all outrun Violet. She loses!"

"Ain't Violet with you?" Mrs. Bell asked, as she walked out onto the porch.

"Not yet, she ain't," chorused the girls. "We wuz a runnin' really fast!"

Seeing the fear on Mrs. Bell's face, the girls fell silent, ignorant of the seriousness of their playmate's absence.

Violet's dad was by the barn getting ready to harness the mule to plow the vegetable garden.

"Abner!" Mrs. Bell screamed. "Violet's a missin'! We gotta find'er! Hurry! Hurry!"

An hour later, Abner found his daughter's body. Like all the others, she had been beaten, raped, sodomized and stabbed from the left armpit into the heart.

The Sugarbush

Travis looked up to see Seth and Pace coming towards his office. "Come on in," he said. "I could use some good news for a change. Do you have any?"

"We've got somethin," Seth replied. "The same two men who assaulted Carol Lamar, murdered the Bell girl. The casts of the footprints taken at the scenes are a perfect match right down to the heel wear and sole patterns of the shoes.

That's the good news. The bad news is we don't have a match with the guards shoes the Grimes brother stole from the locker room. We were hoping the duplicates of the guard's brogans stolen during the jail break would match the casts. They are the same size, but the sole patterns aren't even close. The sizes are no problem because we know the Grimes brothers both wear the same size shoe. They must have changed shoes again. What do you think, Sheriff?"

"The escape was planned," Travis answered. "When it succeeded, they had a place to go. If they had a place to go it makes sense there would be changes of clothes and shoes waiting there for'em. If they're responsible for the latest attacks and wearin' different shoes, the sole patterns may well be different. We're right back where we started with the footprints. Carol Lamar says it was the Grimes brothers who assaulted her. That's what everybody else thinks too.

I made up a new visual aid. Let's look at it. It shows the victims' names, age, race, day of week, date, time and the results of each assault.

At the bottom of the list I've added the same information for Carol Lamar and Violet Bell to see how they fit in."

1) Kirby Suggs(28) Bernice Boles(19)(W)Sat.-May 21, 1932- 8:00 PM—
   Murder/Rape-Murder
2) Sheldon Brooks(31)(W)Lindy Blue(22)(N) Fri.-July 02, 1932- 6:00 PM–
   Murder/Rape-Murder
3) Bertha Tate(70)(W)Thur.-July 28, 1932- 5:00 PM—
   Rape-Murder
4) Annie Mosely, (retarded)(12)(W)Fri.—Aug.19, 1932- 1:00 PM—
   Rape-Murder
5) Emmy Waite(18)(W)Sat.–Sept.24, 1932-11:00 AM—
   Failed Attempt
6) Carol Lamar(54)(W)Tue.-May 02, 1933—7:00 PM—

Jerry S Jones

                                          Assault-Attempted Rape
7) Violet Bell(16)(N)Tue.- May 30, 1933–2:00 PM—
                                                          Rape-Murder

"Look at that," said Travis. "The two anomalies are the times of day the assaults on Suggs, Boles and Carol Lamar occurred, which to me isn't significant. The recent attacks are a clear continuation of the same mode of operatin'.

"We've questioned sex offenders, dairy truck drivers that travel the roads every morning and evening picking up milk and eggs, drivers who pick up carcasses for the by-products company, drivers who pick up livestock for the slaughter houses, mailmen, delivery trucks, door to door salesmen, bill collectors and life insurance salesmen. We followed up on every lead and possibility in a structured, professional manner. Everytime it's brought us right back to the Grimes brothers. The Dehart-Simms killings led us to the murder weapon in the rape-murder cases and back to the Grimes' once again.

Some of the men we questioned are down right mean, but don't seem to have the propensity for the level of savagery we've seen. Only the Grimes' brothers have shown that capacity.

Remember what Horace Sykes looked like when they got through with him. Chest cavity caved in, lungs punctured, splintered ribs penetrating the skin, his guts forced into his scrotum and out his rectum. Think about it! They stomped him to death and left him lying in their stinkin' body wastes."

There were some holes in the evidence against'em in the rape killings and the trial was high on emotions, yet all in all, Jackson used what we gave him to its best potential and presented a convincing case. Even the press was impressed.

What's goin' on now is crazy. It doesn't make sense that two desperate criminals already facing the electric chair, another murder charge and the objects of an intense manhunt would hang around town and casually go back to business as usual four days after breakin' outta jail?

At the Bell girl's murder scene, we tracked the killers to where they had parked their car. Isn't it safe to say the Grimes' brothers would have to be a couple of genuine screwballs to be taking leisurely drives around the countryside looking up old targets they hadn't gotten to yet? They were in jail for over six months. How could they know for sure the Lamar woman or the Bell girl would be where they were? Where did they get the exact same murder weapon? What do you think? Silas.

"First off Sheriff," Silas answered. "Don't never fergit that the prisons has more repeaters locked up than anybody else, women and men alike.

Career criminals always goes back to crime. Most of'em gits turned out one week and they back in jail the next and that's a fact. While they in jail they figure out how they could a done what they done and not got ketched, then they cain't wait to git outta the lock up to give it a try. That's the way they wanna live.

Common criminals knows what they doin' is wrong. Common rapist knows they doin' wrong and kin quit anytime. Uncommon criminals, the baddest kind, acts and thinks a lots different.

In their minds eyes, they don't figure they's done nothin wrong 'cause they stuck in their own reasonin'. They tells their selfs that they don't deserve to be locked up. Squealers are murdered and the killers call'em executions. Psychopathic killers thinks they doin' the right thang 'cause voices tells'em to kill. Rapist-murderers kill fer pleasure they think they's entitled to and they cain't stop it even if'n they want to. To them, killin' their victims ain't no more than a steppin' on a black widder spider. Bank robbers thinks bankers is the biggest crooks alive and deserve to be robbed reg'lar. Embezzlers thinks they deserve the money they stealin' 'cause they doin' all the work and ain't gittin' paid enough and so on. Them kind a criminals on the run ain't likely to be flashy or apt to pick up where they left off, 'specially in the same county. Most generally, they move on a fer piece, git comfortable and lay low fer however long it takes fer thangs to cool down. Then they goes back to their old trade in new territory. It ain't crazy or complicated Sheriff, it's jist too simple fer ye. Ye done figured out the answer on yer own and we in agreement. We got another set a killers out there."

"When did you know that?" Travis asked.

"Today, same as you. I suspicioned it when my hounds couldn't pick up a fresh scent at the school house. I knowed it fer shore today when the footprints didn't match up."

Travis rubbed his forehead with both hands and ran them through his hair. "When you say another set of killers, I'm assuming you mean the Grimes' brothers killed Dehart and Simms and the unknown killers are the rape-murderers."

"That's my meanin', Sheriff," Silas replied.

"Seth," said Travis. "You're my right hand man and you haven't said a word."

"I've been listenin'," Seth replied. "This is a mess. We convicted the wrong men."

"It's not a mess," said Travis. The Grimes' brothers may be innocent of the rape-murders, yet no real harm is done because the death penalty is justified for what they did to DeHart and Simms.

For the time being, the fact that we know we still have a big problem out there is to be kept between the four of us. The element of danger is status quo so there's no point in goin' public and creatin' a worse problem. I won't fill Gordon in until we come up with some new suspects."

Two days later Sheriff Gant received word from the coroner that Linus Lamar had died of poisoning which required an autopsy and criminal investigation. The autopsy report identified the cause of death as lead poisoning which had accumulated in the internal organs of the deceased through consumption of lead laden whiskey. Carol Lamar quickly revealed the source of the deadly alcohol. The dead man himself.

For the past year, Linus had been making his own moonshine whiskey on a homemade galvanized tin submarine distillery, unaware that the chemical reaction between fermenting mash and galvanized tin would leach lead out of the alloy, contaminating the liquor. Lead ingested in any manner does not kill instantly, but over a period of time accumulates in the system until the fatal dose is reached. It's a slow agonizing death.

A few days later, Travis received word from the coroner that the janitor for a small knitting mill had been found dead. Investigation by the sheriff's office revealed that the janitor, Jodeen Keller, had been accidentally electrocuted while scouring the floor, when he stepped bare footed into a pool of water electrically charged by a defective drop cord.

In Catfish, Dessie Hagan read the obituaries in the Sunday morning newspaper and sadly crossed two more names off of the warrants and wrote the word, dead. Twelve months had passed since the accidental shooting death of Sheriff Burton Coley and since then, twelve people named on the warrants had died violently. There were only four warrants left and two of them were for close friends. Frustrated in her knowledge and helplessness, she ran to the stove and burned the newspaper.

XXIII

It was a Saturday morning in Catfish. Pursey McCall sat on the front porch watching Snort Johnson, his friend and helper coming toward the house.

Earlier, Doc Roberts, the veterinarian, had come to treat a milk cow bloated on green lespedeza hay. While he was there, he castrated Pursey's old blue tick hound. As Pursey's wife put it, her husband and the old hound 'wuz a lot alike 'cause neither one of'em wuz worth a damn chained up or aloose.'

Rather than dispose of the dog for biting one of the grandchildren, Doc Roberts recommended he be castrated to take out the meanness. The old hound was prone to bite anybody he didn't take a liking to and the one person he detested most was Snort Johnson, who to escape being bitten, would climb a leaning crab apple tree in the front yard. After the dog was securely chained up, Snort would climb down from the tree and join his friend on the porch.

The hound, still croggy, sick and sore from the morning surgery, made no effort to attack, but did manage to raise up and bark at the sight of his arch enemy. Hearing that familiar sound, Snort shinnied up the leaning crab apple tree to safety.

"Come on down, Snort," Pursey shouted. "Doc Roberts castrated ole Blue this mornin'."

"Castrated'im!" Snort shouted back. "Put that hound on a chain! I ain't a skirred of'im a fuckin' me, I'm a skirred he'll bite me!"

The laughter quickly subsided at the sound of an approaching car. "Well I'll be go to hell," said Snort. "The high sheriff hisself is payin' Catfish a visit. We won't be runnin' no liquor today good buddy!"

"Oh yes we will," replied Pursey. "That young feller's been sparkin' Lila Fountain's niece fer quite a spell and right now, she's the onliest thang on his mind. Cain't say as I blame'im. If'n I wuz young I wudden mind squeezin her myself."

"She's a perty thang fer shore," said Snort. "Y'all kin fight over the niece. I'll take her Aunt any day."

"I heared that," Pursey's wife yelled out from behind the screen door. "That's all y'all two mongrels talk about. When ye in town ye tell ever'body how many rows ye laid bye a plowin' corn and when ye git back to Catfish, ye tell everbody how many women ye laid bye in town. When it gits down to the truth of it, ye ain't doin' much a neither one and I kin testify to that. Now git busy so's we kin be in town 'fore noon."

After a long ride, Travis and Reicie unsaddled the horses, put them out to pasture and returned to the house for lunch. When they were finished eating, Travis remarked. "I could get use to this in a hurry. So much has changed since we started going out together, not that I wasn't content before, I just didn't realize how much I was missing and takin' for granted. All work and no play, I guess. Spendin' time out here in the country with you, I even notice the sounds of the birds and bees. Everything kind of blends together. I feel good, really good."

Laughing, Reicie ran over, sat on Travis' lap and kissed him. "We do have so much fun, don't we? I never get tired of the sights and sounds of Mother Nature. I spend a lot of time watching her.

My bedroom faces the river. I used to sit there looking out, that is 'til all this killing started. Then Cass came snooping around spying on me and it wasn't peaceful anymore. It all turned threatening and foreboding. I even pulled down the window shades so I couldn't see out, but more so that nobody could see in. I felt like I was trapped in a box that was pitch black dark inside. Now everything is coming back to normal a little at a time, maybe even better than before. I'm not as afraid, why should I be? My sweetheart is the county sheriff."

"I've never seen your bedroom, Reicie, but I bet I can describe what it looks like."

"You don't have to silly man. Come with me upstairs. I'll show you."

They entered a neat well arranged room decorated with bright colored curtains that waved gently in the breeze, stirring the subtle scent of powder and perfume. A soft lilac counter pin draped the bed and pillows. A full length mirror encased in a polished walnut frame stood next to the bed, reflecting a wash stand bearing a bowl and pitcher of water sitting on a hand embroidered doily.

They stood arm in arm, gazing out the window at the river disappearing around the bend. The moment they had stepped into the room, the carefree mood from just being together melted into an atmosphere of enchantment. Still arm in arm, they walked through the room looking at framed photographs of Reicie's mother and dad and some other relatives.

"These are my Grandparents on my mother's and Aunt Lila's side of the family. They live in Bayou Cane, Louisiana. I know a cute story about their wedding. When they agreed to marry, they didn't want to wait for the traveling preacher to make his rounds, so they jumped a broomstick."

"Jumped a broomstick," Travis said curiously.

"Oh, you've probably never heard of that have you? Back in those bayous, they didn't have a full time preacher. He only came three or four times a year. When a couple wanted to get married, they never knew exactly when the preacher would be making his rounds so they had this little ritual they went through where they would jump a broomstick, signifying that they were setting up housekeeping together. When the preacher finally did show up, he would make the marriage official."

"How did they do it? Travis inquired.

"A broomstick was laid down on the floor or the ground, then the bride and groom would stand together in front of it. He would ask the bride if she would be his wife and she would answer yes, then they held hands and jumped over the broomstick. That was it until the preacher made his next round."

"Show me," said Travis.

Reicie took a broom from the closet and laid it on the floor. Her face flushed and radiant, she motioned for Travis to stand beside her. Laughing nervously, she said, "this game is too real, I'm trembling inside. Now I know how Grandma must have felt."

"And I know how Grandpa must have felt," Travis replied. "Now the big question. If jumping the broomstick was good enough for your Grandparents, it's good enough for us. Reicie Dupre, will you be my wife?"

"Why Travis, you're serious. If you're in no rush for the preacher to make his rounds, my answer is yes. If this is no game, I know what's waiting for me on the other side of that broomstick and at this moment, I'm so excited my knees are weak. I'm not sure I can jump."

The Sugarbush

Travis swept Reicie into his arms and stepped over the broomstick. After a lingering kiss, he began unbuttoning her blouse.

Flushed and trembling, Reicie reached back, unfastened her brasier and dropped it off her shoulders to the floor. Travis picked her up, laid her on the bed and began undressing. Watching with mixed emotions of apprehension and desire, she spread her legs, reached out and drew him down on top of her.

"Wait, wait," she murmured. "Let me help you. There, push. It's okay, it's okay. Push, push harder."

Still reeling from the experience of first love, Reicie lay with her head on Travis' chest. "When we climbed those stairs," she murmured. "I only meant to show you the view from my room then something changed. I knew we were feeling close, but we've felt that way lots of times. It didn't cross my mind that this was about to happen. So fast, more like a fantasy, a misty dream that maybe wasn't real. I remember you taking off my clothes. I remember you laying me down and seeing you standing there naked. I remember the movement, the pressure suddenly filling me up inside and I liked it. Then it was over! Here we are laying together and it's real. Just like that, it's over! I think we were so excited because it was our first time, don't you? Let's do it again, and this time, we won't be thinking about how to do it. If we pay more attention to how it feels, maybe it'll last longer, or at least seem longer.

Come on! You're not heavy on me. Okay, okay. Easy, easy. There! Now! Now! Push!

Afterwards, as they drove toward town, Reicie, with an excited tone in her voice, turned to Travis and cried. "Let's go to the mountains and visit my dad. All at once I want to see him and I want him to meet you. We'll surprise him. We can leave next Friday and come back on Sunday. Will you take me?"

"That's a good idea," Travis answered with equal excitement. "We both could use a break away from this place. It's beautiful up there and the mountain laurel should be in full bloom, just like you are right now."

"We're both in full bloom, Sheriff, and anybody who sees us will know it. How long do you think it will take us to get up there?"

"It would be more fun to drive up, Reicie, but it's at least ninety miles. The roads are narrow, steep and really crooked. It would be better if we took the train to Asheville and that will be fun too.

From there we can drive out to your Dad's place. I'll call the sheriff in Buncombe County. He'll be glad to loan us a car. Surprising your Dad is a good idea too. We'll plan on leaving next Friday provided nothing comes up that would interfere with our plans. Even if that happens and we have to postpone the trip for a few days, we're going and that's a promise."

"I'm so excited!" Reicie shouted. "There's only thing that can interfere with our plans. The Grimes brothers, so catch them before Friday. "I remember the first time I saw those two. The first thing I noticed was Jarred's right ear. The ear lobe was split in half and the two parts kind of curled up like a pie squash. Uncle Beau says the story goes that Jarred was running from the law and dived under a barbed wire fence. A barb caught in his ear lobe and ripped it. I've never seen one brother without the other and every time I do see them, my eyes go straight to Jarred's ugly ear."

"Your mood is changing, sweetheart," Travis interrupted. "The Grimes brothers are not the only problem I'm faced with everyday, the most pressing, but not the only one. You let me take care of that. Slide over here next to me as close as you can get and we'll change the subject, okay!"

"Why thank you, Sheriff, "I almost forgot. We're in full bloom and we owe it all to my great grandparents and a broomstick wedding, cajun style. We're married! We've made love twice! I can't believe it. Like Aunt Lila said, 'things will never be the same again'. She was right, but at this moment I am only concerned about one of the things. I'm sitting on a pillow and it isn't helping much."

Travis burst out laughing. "It's not that bad is it? I followed your instructions both times!"

Laughing, while shifting around on the pillow, Reicie replied. "It's hard to explain. It's such a pleasant kind of hurt."

XXIV

Obed Grimes cautiously approached the potato celler where his nephews were holed up. "Hey boys, I'm a comin' in. I got some damn good news fer you'uns. Yer Paw sent me with a change a plans. Now listen good. At first he figured the best way fer you'uns to git away from here wuz on a freight train so's you'uns could hide amongst all them hobos. That won't do now 'cause the law is still a checkin' ever' freight comin' and goin'. I been a watchin' and one thang they ain't checkin' is passenger trains. When yer Paw tells me to do it, I'm buyin' y'all tickets on the night train that goes through Rocky Mount. Ye'll git off there and make yer way on to Gum Neck. I'm goin' down to Maiden to buy you'uns some city clothes and shoes. Yer Paw says fer y'all to keep yer hair trimmed, grow a mustache and wear them dark spectacles. Stay perty close together, but don't act like yer acquainted.

Now remember ye'll have yer tickets, so's all you'uns have to do is wait near the depot and when the train comes, jist git on. Find a seat and wait 'till the conductor comes by to take yer ticket. Don't 'cause no fuss that'll draw attention to ye."

"Uncle Obed," Jess growled. "Ye tell Paw we'll see'im when he kin git to Gum Neck. We been hunkered down in this dirty 'possum den fer six weeks and if'n they ain't a watchin' them passenger trains, what are we waitin' fer? Git them clothes and tickets fer us, we a leavin' here."

Out in Catfish, Cal Hagan was plowing out the middles of his corn field. Coming to the end of the row and turning the mule, he looked up to see Dessie walking rapidly toward him. From the drawn expression on her face, he knew the news wasn't good. Bursting into tears, she cried, "Cal, Pursey McCall done died this mornin'."

"Whoa mule," he said softly, lifting the lines from around his waist and hanging them on the plowshares. "It ain't no sech a thang. I never knowed Pursey was ailin'."

"He weren't ailin' 'till last night. He come home drunk and et a spoilt hotdog that giv'im food poisonin'. The wife figured he wuz sick from the liquor so's by the time she found out he et that hotdog it wuz to late. Doc Rawlin's couldn't save'im."

"Now ye listen to me, Dessie Hagan. I kin see right off it's them warrants a botherin' ye, ain't it? Ye stop that foolishness right now! Them warrants ain't had nary a thang to do with Pursey gittin' on a drunk er nary a thang to do with'im a eatin' a spoilt hotdog and killin' hisself! Ye jist sit yerself down on that stump yonder 'till I plow out them last couple a rows and we'll go to the house fer dinner."

"He's number thirteen, Cal. I'm a gittin' shed a Burton Coley's jacket and them warrants with it. I'm puttin' that blasted curse right back where it come from."

"If'n it'll hep ye to fergit, that's fine with me," Cal shouted. "Gee haw, mule."

Back in town, the owner of The Sugarbush, Shelly Summers, waved anxiously to Sheriff Gant as he came out of the courtroom.

"Hello Shelly," said Travis. "What brings you to the county seat?"

Looking around nervously she whispered, "We need to talk! Meet me in the parkin' lot at Setzer's Hardware store." Without another word or waiting for a response, she quickly exited through the side door.

When Travis arrived at the parking lot, he had to hunt for Shelly. He found her standing beside a car parked under a mimosa tree at the back of the store. "You look troubled Shelly. What's goin' on?"

"I ain't troubled, Sheriff, I'm mad. A long time ago one a my girls told me somethin' that's come back up agin'. I'm gonna tell ye what it is, but understand I ain't lookin' fer no favors in return. I ain't gonna tell ye which girl it is 'cause nobody needs to know that. She come to work fer me from Winston Salem six and a half years ago. When she got to my place, she was skirred shitless and I coaxed her into tellin' me what happened over there.

She told me she'd made arrangements to do a two on one house call and the men wuz to pick her up jist after dark at the town square. When their business wuz done, they wuz to brang her back to the same place.

When they picked her up one of the fellers' wuz sittin' in the back seat and asked her to git in with him. He told her they wuz a goin' to a secret place and fer her not to git upset 'cause he wuz gonna blindfold her. Then he made her lay her head in his lap and wudden

The Sugarbush

let her sit up. She laid there tryin' to figer out which a way they wuz goin'. She knowed they was headed toward Elkin when she got in the car.

She says they weren't in no hurry, jist talkin' and drivin' along normal. They weren't on the pavement more'n five minutes before they wuz off on a dirt road. On the way they crossed three short bridges and the last one wuz wood planks. After about twenty minutes, they stopped and the feller drivin' got out to open a gate and wuz talkin' to a couple a big dogs. She said she knowed they wuz big 'cause they barked big. After he shet the gate, they drove a good piece 'fore he stopped agin' to let the feller and her git out. She says she still had on the blindfold, but she knows the one a drivin' parked in a garage 'cause the sound a the motor changed and she heard'im close a double door.

To this day, she don't have no idea where she wuz 'cept out in the boondocks close to water 'cause she could hear bull frogs a croakin'. Then they led her up some steps onto a porch and into a house. They wuz holdin' on guidin' her and they opened a door to what she thinks wuz a big closet 'cause she could smell moth balls. She heard'em messin' around and openin' another door with squeakin' hinges. That's when they told her they wuz fixin' to take her down some stairs.

Up 'till then she says she wuz uneasy, but not skirred 'cause they was talkin' so nice and a jokin' 'round all the time makin' it sound like a game. Besides that, they hadn't laid a hand on her the whole time. Usually when the girls go on a house call, especially a two on one, as soon as they git in the car the customer starts gropin 'and slobberin' all over'em. These fellers didn't do that.

Thangs changed at the top of them stairs. She got skirred. She told'em she wudden goin' down in no cellar. They sweet talked her sayin' down there's where the fun starts. She counted fifteen steps to the bottom. They opened another door, took her inside and she heard'em close and lock it. When they took off the blindfold, the room was lit with red, yeller and purple lights strung around up next to the ceilin'. The room wuz littered with leather whips, straps, ropes, chains and all that kinda stuff. She knowed they had her trapped. She begged and pleaded fer 'em to take her back to town. She told'em she'd give'em all the pussy they wanted fer free if they'd promise not to hurt her. All that beggin' never helped. All night long they done some unhuman thangs to that young'un. She screamed 'til she lost her voice. Ever'time she passed out, she'd wake up and they'd be doubled up on her still a doin' thangs.

I wudden born yisterday. I know they's people that gits their pleasure thatta way, I jist didn't know how bad it could git. Payin' fer a poke is one thang, but that ain't what they done. They raped her ever' way a body kin be raped. Spittin' on her, pissin' on her, and that wuz when they wuz bein' nice."

Jist before daylight, they dressed her, put the blindfold on and headed back to town. They told her that bein' the common whore she wuz, she better keep her mouth shet or they'd be obliged to hunt her down agin' fer another surprise party.

She ended up spendin' a week in the hospital. A 'course them Doctors' knowed what happened to her, but she never told'em who done it 'cause she wuz skirred and didn't know who they wuz nohow.

She says the feller drivin' wuz a big, tall heavyset man with black curly hair and she ain't never seen'im since.

The slender blond headed feller she did see agin'! In the newspapers! It's Gordon Jackson!"

Travis hurried to his office. "Melinda, tell Seth and Pace I need to see'em in my office, pronto."

When they came in, Travis told the story he had just heard. "We must keep this quite for now! The girl is tellin' the truth, I just know it. Nobody could make up a story like that, yet after six and a half years, she could easily be mistaken in identifyin' Gordon. If she is wrong and this gets out, the damage will be irreparable."

"That must be why Gordon's never married," Seth replied. "For years I've heard rumors that he likes trashy women.

Travis interrupted. "Stop right there Seth! I'm not married and I've been attracted to some gorgeous women with trashy reputations. That doesn't make me a sadist and it sure as hell doesn't make them bad girls. They'd be glad to change places with the privileged class princesses if they had the chance. Foul reputations are only foul if they're true and we don't base any assumptions on damn rumors. Don't start jumpin' conclusions again. Stick with the facts. I'm dependin' on you.

The Sugarbush

I want you and Pace to go to Winston Salem today. You should be there before dark. After you've checked into a hotel, call Melinda and let her know where I can reach you.

We need to find the house where they took the girl. You shouldn't have any trouble findin' it if Gordon's our man and it's his own personal property. Just check in the Register of Deeds office under his name.

If it's not his, it has to belong to his partner. If that turns out to be the case, the first thing I want you to do is try locating the place by the mental description Shelly gave me. That's the hard way to go about this, but it will attract less attention. The mystery man will be easy to find because we have plenty of resources like college records, year books, classmates, teachers and so on. That'll be our last resort because when we start snoopin' around and asking questions, the word is goin' to get out in a hurry. Along with R. J. Reynolds, the Jackson family is one of the largest benefactors of Wake Forest College.

In any case, when you find the house, do whatever it takes to get inside. Since I'm orderin' you to break the law if you need to, it's better you don't let the Forsyth County Sheriff know you're workin' in his jurisdiction. Take an unmarked car and dress in civilian clothes.

Today is Wednesday. I'm leavin' town Friday evenin' and I'll be back Sunday evenin'. That gives you four days. I'll see you Monday mornin' unless you know somethin' before I leave Friday."

Friday evening, Sue Workman drove Reicie to the train station to meet Travis. Inside, Reicie checked her bag and inquired if the train was on time. Returning to the car, she and Sue walked to a small park next to the depot and sat down at a picnic table to talk.

"The train is running on time and it can't be too soon for me. I'm so excited," Reicie exclaimed.

"I wish to god I was takin' a train outta here fer a weekend in the mountains," Sue cheerfully replied. "Trouble is, I cain't git Casey outta Catawba County. When he come back from the big war he swore he weren't never leavin' home agin' and he ain't neither. Yit I cain't complain. We got a good life, me and Casey. You'uns have a

Jerry S Jones

good time and I'll see ye when ye git back. I better git on over to the Farmers' Market and see if I kin make a dollar."

Reicie sat alone, watching the freight cars being switched on the far tracks.

"Why good evening Miss Dupre."

She whirled to see Gordon Jackson, smiling broadly as he approached.

As though on cue, he quickly grasped her hand, patting it gently. "I didn't mean to startle you," he said sympathetically. "My enthusiasm came from the delightful surprise at finding you here. You must have been deep in thought."

"Not so much in thought, Mr. Jackson. With all the noise I didn't hear you coming," thinking to herself. "For a scoundrel, he can be charming."

In an instant, the theatrical display of sympathy vanished as Gordon continued. "I like trains. Most everyone likes to watch them. That's the reason I had this little observation deck built. It was a pet project of mine.

Like sea going ships, trains are thought of as great, passionate ladies. Beautiful heads, bosoms of fire, cargo compartments and cute red cabooses. I like the little red cabooses best, if you get my meaning."

Surprised at his disrespect and unsure of how to respond to the suggestive connotation, Reicie replied. "Oh yes, Mr. Jackson, I understand. Your favorite color is red. Do you come here often to watch cabooses?"

Gordon laughed at the witty response, wondering if she was being coy or was just naive. "Watching cabooses is my favorite pass time," he answered. "Today however, I'm meeting a friend on the train. We were room mates in college at Wake Forest in Winston Salem. We're going up for an alumni reunion planning session. Have you ever been there?

"No, I haven't, but I've heard that it's a nice city."

"That's understandable. Very few of our rural residents ever venture outside the county. Are you just amusing yourself watching the trains or waiting for someone?"

"Both, Mr. Jackson."

The Sugarbush

Completely disinterested in the purpose of her presence there, he quickly added, "Call me Gordon. I like that better."

"I'm not accustomed to calling my elders by their given name?"

"You'll get used to it. I'm not that much older than Travis. The difference in our ages shouldn't stand in the way of us getting to know each other better."

Taken back and at a loss for words, Reicie managed to say. "I hear your train coming in Mr. Jackson."

"We still have a few minutes to discuss a dinner date," he replied. "I think you will find what I have to offer quite appealing. We have something in common. We're ambitious."

Struggling to maintain her composure, Reicie stood up, her response cut short by the intrusion of a man dressed in ill-fitting clothes and wearing dark glasses.

Gordon glanced behind him to see the object of her attention, then returned to the conversation. Reicie sensed something familiar about the stranger who seemed to stare for a moment, then turned hurriedly, almost running into a second man who appeared dressed in identical attire.

"Why am I suddenly terrified?" she pondered. Her complexion went pale at the mental recall of the stranger's features as he turned to leave. His right ear lobe was torn!

"Jess," whispered Jarred. "Beau Fontaine's girl and that son-of-a bitch, Gordon Jackson, is right over there. They seen me!"

"I'm a watchin'em, little brother. They ain't on to ye 'cause they still a talkin'. They a startin' to walk back along the path to the depot. We'll mosey 'long behind'em. Soon as the train stops, we'll git on and do like Paw said."

"Mr. Gordon, would you walk me back to the depot? Reicie asked.

"With pleasure," he answered, attempting to put his arm around her waist. "Along the way we can continue where we left off. If you'll slow down and allow me to explain, I think we can reach an understanding of my most honorable intentions."

"Let go of me!" Reicie said in an angry, frightened whisper. "We've got to get to the depot! Jess and Jarred Grimes are right behind us! Don't look back. Just keep walking!"

Thinking it was a joke, Gordon turned and shouted. "Howdy boys! Nice of you to give up!"

"He knows us Jess," Jarred yelled, fumbling for his pistol.

Seeing the pistols clearing the fugitives coat pockets, mirth turned to panic. Gordon grabbed Reicie around the waist with both arms, using her as a human shield and dragging her backwards. "Get away from me!" he yelled!"

Travis walked out of the ticket office onto the boarding platform just in time to see Gordon grab Reicie and two men leveling guns on them.

Gordon's frantic cries for help were barely audible above the noise of the arriving passenger train. Having forgotten he was not armed, Travis instinctively reached for his service revolver, cursing at its absence. Without hesitation, he dashed forward shouting. "This is the Sheriff! Drop those guns!"

The locomotive had come to a stop. Unaware of the deadly drama going on beside the tracks, the engineer pulled the pressure relief valve lever for the drive wheel pistons which released a dense cloud of steam that filled the space between the attackers and their targets.

The Grimes brothers now completely obscured, Gordon shoved Reicie violently forward in their direction, turned and ran.

Travis, running hard was seeing everything in slow motion. In disbelief, he saw Reicie stumble and fall to the ground and Gordon running madly towards him. Like a developing photograph, as the steam faded the ghostly image of two men began to emerge, pistols leveled, pointed in his direction.

Travis dived for the ground, shouting. "Get down, Gordon!"

The shots cracked in unison. One bullet entered the base of Gordon's skull exiting through his mouth, showering Travis with teeth and blood. The other bullet entered under his left shoulder blade penetrating the heart and traveling downwards, collapsing the left lung and lodging in the ruptured intestines. The falling body seemed to float to the ground, bounce once and lay still."

Jumping to his feet, Travis saw the two men disappear around the front of the locomotive and Reicie running to meet him. "It's the Grimes brothers," she cried. "I tried to tell Mr. Jackson, but he didn't believe me."

The Sugarbush

"Get to the depot and call for help! I'm going after them!" Travis replied.

Hoping the brothers hadn't noticed he was unarmed, Travis rounded the front of the train and saw them sprinting toward a string of idle boxcars. The switch engine was pushing back with another string of cars to couple up and the gap between them was closing fast. The brothers wanted those cars between them and the sheriff. Jarred, the younger and faster of the two yelled. "Come on Jess, we kin make it," as he bolted between the cars with ten feet to spare.

Jess, not far behind stumbled and tried to regain his balance, but could not halt his forward momentum. He was in the center of the tracks when the final distance between the cars closed, latching him at the waist into the coupler. Half in and half out of the locking device, the condition of his body was beyond description.

Travis watched, relieved that the cars drifted backwards taking the ghastly sight out of view for the moment. Reaching the crushed body, he looked across the tracks into the anguished, tormented face of Jarred Grimes and the muzzel of his pistol at point blank range. The sound of a shot echoed sharply off the boxcars.

Travis saw Jarred repel backwards, his pistol flying out of his hand and discharging harmlessly into the air.

A voice from behind asked. "Ye alright, Sheriff?" Travis turned to see Silas James. "Here's my pistol. Better stick in in yer belt. When I dropped ye off, I ain't got gone yit when I heared them shots. I come a runnin'. Little advice fer ye, Sheriff. On or off'n duty, always carry yer piece."

"I'll remember that from now on and thanks," Travis answered, still feeling his body for a gunshot wound.

Suddenly the scene was flooded with deputies and city police. "Listen up," Travis shouted! "You deputies give the police what ever help they need, but only if they ask. Do not touch anything. This is their jurisdiction! Silas, come with me. I have to get back to Reicie."

In the depot Travis and Silas found a tearful Reicie surrounded by sympathetic bystanders. When she saw him coming, she ran into his arms.

"I'm Sheriff Gant folks. Thanks for your help and please excuse us."

"I'm not hurt," Reicie whispered. "Just get me away from here!"

"I can't leave yet," he replied. "Silas will take you to my place, but first I need to ask you a question. "What happened and why was Gordon here with you?"

Reicie told him all that had occurred. While they were talking the station master, concerned with the safety of the passengers, hurried the departure of the train.

After giving his statement to a city police detective, Travis left the scene.

On a hunch, he called Seth and Pace at their hotel in Winston Salem and told them the story.

"I know this is grasping at straws, but it's worth a try," he said. "The guy Gordon was meeting could be the other half that will complete the picture. You have his description and if he's as big as we've been told, he ought to stand out in a crowd when he gets off the train. Good luck."

On Monday morning Seth and Pace met with Travis to report the results of their investigation. It wasn't good news. The big man didn't get off the train as expected, however the search for the house was narrowing down. They hadn't found three small bridges, but they had found one with wood plank decking which led to several isolated home sites on a broad creek.

"If Gordon and the mystery man are the rape-murderers," said Travis, "with half the team gone, any plans they had will have to change.

They're not holdin' a wake for Gordon so we'll have to wait until after the funeral to decide our next move. If a big man attends the service that fit's the image of what we think he looks like, we can put a name to a face and save time.

The service is at 10:00 A.M. at the Baptist Church in the Oakwood section of Hickory. The three of us will attend in uniform and we want to be the first ones there. They've reserved a seat for me with the rest of the elected officials and civic leaders up front behind the immediate family.

Across the isle from the family they've reserved a section for close friends and relatives. Keep an eye on that group. Seth, you and Pace stand in the back on each side of the entrance door. Pace, you're from Hickory and a member of the social register so you take the lead if the big man shows. You know what to do. All we want is a face and a name. After we leave the cemetery we'll compare notes. If he doesn't show, we've still got the college records. Let's hope for the best."

XXV

The sheriff and his deputies were the first to arrive for Gordon's funeral and took up their respective positions. As the church began filling up, almost everyone who came in knew Pace, greeting him warmly with hugs and affectionate salutations which prompted him to realize the advantage of ushering attendants to a pew. Seth followed suit until all the pews were filled. No standing room remained in the aisles. To make a little more room for the standing crowd, Seth and Pace stepped into the entrance foyer.

"We saw every single soul that came through the doors," Seth said in dismay. "Maybe this fellow is not as big as they thought."

After the church service, the foyer doors were opened in preparation for the crowd to exit and prepare for the traditional motorcade to the cemetery. With the help of the city police, Travis led the way.

Driving slowly through the cemetery toward the grave site, Travis sighed, "Well the big man didn't show."

"Maybe he don't exist," Seth replied.

"Sure he does, Seth. There he stands."

"Well I'll be damned, I believe you're right," Seth replied.

Pace began laughing gleefully. "Look at that guy. He's huge. He'll never see two hundred and twenty pounds again, but I'll bet he can still run a good hundred yard dash. After the grave side service is finished, I'll introduce myself."

Travis and Seth waited in the car while Pace met his social obligations to Gordon's family and to his own family and friends who were there. They watched as Pace hugged Mr. and Mrs. Jackson, timing it perfectly for an unavoidable introduction to Gordon's dear friend from Statesville, North Carolina, Wilson Tully.

"We can go anytime you're ready Sheriff," Pace remarked as he returned and climbed into the back seat of the car. "That's our man and you wouldn't want to meet a more thoughtful gentleman.

Before he started to college he lived in Europe for three years, rotating from country to country following the social calendar for the wealthy. He and Gordon were room mates and graduated together with law degrees. His family are bankers and he's one of their lawyers, but he still travels a lot. Reicie thought Gordon's mystery

The Sugarbush

friend was already on the train, but he wasn't. They had planned to meet at the depot in Statesville for a weekend business meeting at Wake Forest. When Gordon didn't show, Wilson telephoned and got the bad news. The meeting was rescheduled for this coming Saturday and Sunday and he plans to drive over Friday afternoon.

"You pulled a lot of stuff out of him in a short time," Seth commented.

"Not really Chief. That's the kind of things they like to talk about."

"Here's the plan," said Travis. Y'all leave as soon as we get back to the office. You should get to Winston Salem before the Register of Deeds office closes. You can get your research done and find the place tonight, maybe even get inside for a look. If you find what we suspect is there, give me a call and I'll get there as quick as I can.

Now listen up, this is important. Accordin' to the law, willin' adult participants in the privacy of their own homes who engage in sadistic sexual acts are not breakin' any law; they are only guilty of bein' born with a perversion whereby cruelty is a source of sensual pleasure to'em. The worst thing that could happen, is for their perversion to be publicly exposed. I can't express strongly enough how sensitive this development is. Everything we're doin' now is cloak and dagger stuff and if you get caught, lie your way out of it. Don't spill the beans!

We must tread cautiously and deliberately step by step. First, let's validate the story we've been told. If that pans out, our next objective is to see if there's any evidence layin' around that could link these guys to the rape-murders. If that turns up somethin', I'll have a close look at Gordon's schedulin' records for the past year to see where he was at the time the crimes were committed. I can do that without his secretary knowin'. Does everybody understand."

Seth answered. "Clear as a picture."

"Good," Travis replied. "It's time we Got Silas involved to see if he's run up on anything like this. After we talk to him, you guys can be on your way. When you know something, call me at home, but don't say the word sheriff and don't say my name in case the hotel switchboard operator is listenin' in.

Make it brief, yes we did, or no we didn't. If it's yes, Silas and I will be on our way."

Silas listened attentively to all the events that had occurred, alternately rubbing his forehead then resting his chin on his hands until everybody had put in their two cents worth.

"They's a lot a that kinda carryin's on goes on and in twenty years I'es seen my share," he began thoughtfully. "Most reg'lar, carryin's on like that don't never see the light a day. Like ever'thang else, birds of a feather flocks together. It's a real private thang amongst'em them kind and word gits 'round 'bout who likes what. I ain't never run up on'em killin' nobody. That's as much as I know."

"Thanks Silas," said Travis. "Anything else?"

"I don't have anything," answered Seth. "We're gettin' a late start, but since we already know just about where the place is, we won't need to do any research at the Register of Deeds office. That will save us some time."

"Ye done found the house?" Silas ask.

"Not exactly, but we're close. We lost a lot of time because what Shelly's girl told her was wrong. There was only one bridge, the one decked with wooden planks."

"Beggin' yer pardon, Chief, the girl wuz right. Ye on the wrong road. Women got a built in sense 'bout them thangs."

Travis interrupted laughing. "Do your research first Seth. If Silas is wrong, I'll buy you lunch."

Seth replied sarcastically. "If Silas is right, I'll buy everybody lunch."

"I have a question," said Pace. "If he has guard dogs, what are we supposed to do, shoot'em!"

"Real smart, Pace," Travis remarked.

"I was talkin' to Silas," Pace laughed. "I have absolutely no experience at distracting vicious dogs in order to break and enter. Any suggestions?" Silas.

"Change places with the dogs," he replied. "Ye'll still have the fence between ye, only difference is the dogs'll be on the outside and you'll be on the inside. More'n likely the gate'll be bound with a chain and padlocked. Ye'll need bolt cutters, a master chain link, fifty feet a cotton clothes line rope and a sack a meat scraps from a butcher shop. Don't git no bones a'tall, jist meat scraps. I got ever'thang ye need in the supply room 'cept the meat scraps. Ye kin pick them up in Winston Salem when ye ready fer'em.

When ye drive up to the gate, the dogs will come a runnin' to challenge ye. One of you'uns walk down the fence line aways and the dogs will foller ye. Throw'em some scraps to keep'em busy while the other'n of ye slips outta the car with the bolt cutters and the rope. Cut one of the links that the padlock's through, unlatch the gate and tie the rope to it. Feed out the rope back to the car and hang on to it. Then whoever's with the dogs kin make a pile of scraps fer each dog out side the fence 'bout ten foot apart so's they don't go to fightin' over'em. Then both of ye git back in the car and back up slow openin' the gate. The dogs'll come out and head fer the meat scraps. Drive through, shet the gate behind ye and untie the rope. Hook up the chain and padlock with the master link and ye got yerselfs locked inside. Then pile some more meat scraps inside the fence close enough that the dogs kin see'em. That'll keep'em close 'till ye come out.

When ye git to the house, if'n it's two stories, yer best bet fer gittin' in without bustin' in, will be through a upstairs window 'cause they hardly ever locked. To git up to'em ye might have to climb a tree or stand on the car, but however, you'uns'll find a way. If'n' the dog's ain't there when ye head out, dump out the rest a the meat scraps inside the fence, drive through the gate and start blowin' yer horn. They'll come a runnin'. I'll go git yer supplies together."

"Why no bones?" Seth ask.

"'Cause somebody'll see'em and wonder how they come to be there."

The next afternoon, Travis got the call he'd been waiting for. It was a yes. "Silas, we got a yes! Let's go. Melinda, I should be back Friday afternoon. You know where I'll be".

Arriving at the hotel in Winston Salem at dusk, Travis went in to register then returned to the car. "Silas my friend, pull around behind the hotel and park. I rented a double room on the second floor next to the stairway. You're my bell hop. Grab both our bags and follow me up the stairs. We're sharin' a room for the night."

After settling in, Travis called for Seth and Pace to join them.

Jerry S Jones

"Silas James," Seth exclaimed as he entered the room. "You look me straight in the eye and tell me you ain't never seen that place before."

"Who's buyin' lunch?" Travis asked.

"Does close count," answered Seth. "We weren't off but two miles. It was on the same creek though. That should count for something."

"You oughtta see that setup, said Pace. "It's secure without being conspicuous. It's fenced with five foot narrow gage wire fabric with three strands of barbed wire on top. He's got two of the ugliest, meanest cur dogs you ever saw. Nobody is allowed inside, I mean nobody. The fence is posted every twenty feet all the way around."

"Somebody's allowed to get inside to feed the dogs," said Travis.

"The hell they are," Seth replied. "There's a nice spring for water and he's got a hog lot bin feeder full of dog chow that those mutts couldn't eat up in a year.

The house sits down under the hill about a hundred yards from a wide creek. You can't see it until you're right on top of it. When it was built, they didn't cut one tree unless it was absolutely necessary. When you walk in you'd think you were at Grandpa's and Grandma's place. It's not your normal two story house. The upstairs is more like an attic dormitory with gabled windows and a half a dozen single beds. Silas was right. That's the way we got in.

You would never know from the outside or inside that there's a basement. The big corner bedroom has a walk in closet and the stairway down to the cellar is concealed behind a built in unit of shelves. Next to the floor is a push-pull latch that you have to hunt to find. When you pull it up, you can swing the whole unit just like opening a regular door and the hinges still squeak. They sound just like the creaking door on that radio program."

"Jack Packard and the Intersanctum," said Travis.

"Yeah that's the one, Seth replied.

"The girl was right," said Pace. It's fifteen steps down to the cellar floor and then about ten feet to the chamber door or what ever you call it. To the right, there's a small dark room Shelly's girl didn't see because she was blindfolded. There are hundreds of graphic photographs of Gorden and Wilson Tully performing sadistic sexual acts with different women in different situations. They're not the

The Sugarbush

only ones either, they entertained guests too. There are men on men, women on women, men and women two and three on one. You name it. You can tell the regulars from the unsuspecting prey they lured in for a surprise party. The pictures say it all. We brought a good sampling out with us because we know they'll never be missed. I took my own pictures of everything and developed them right there on the spot so you could see'em right away. We've arranged them in two piles for you to look at.

Even though we knew what to expect, that torture chamber was still a shock. It was depressing, like being in a dungeon, if you can imagine that. Whips, chains, racks, steel knuckles and all kinds of gadgets to hurt people with. I took pictures of everything. Start with either pile you want to."

"All of their photos are focused on sadistic sex acts," said Travis. "They must pass'em around, exchange'em or sell'em to other individuals or groups. I've seen enough."

"Chief," said Silas. "In this pitcher Pace took, theys a set a daggers hanging' on the wall and one of'ems missin'."

"That's another lunch you owe me, Seth," Pace said, laughing. "I need to go on a diet and I will after I've used up all of my free lunches. If you don't stop making wagers with me against Silas, you're going to be broke and I'm going to be fat."

"Tell us about the daggers," asked Travis.

"There's ten in the set," Pace answered. "They're an inch wide and razor sharp on both edges. They start at six inches long and increase in two inch increments up to twenty four inches. The ten inch dagger is the one that's missing.

Here's something nobody was expectin'. Get ready for the surprise of your life. This is the Wake Forest annual for the year Gordon and Wilson graduated."

Travis stared at a picture of two men wearing blue bib overalls, floppy hats, brogans and holding shotguns. "They have beards; who are they?" Travis asked incredulously.

Pace answered. "Read the caption."

Travis read the caption out loud. "Gordon Jackson and Wilson Tully brought the house down in their portrayal of two hillbillies in the senior class comedy, 'The Mountaineers Come To Town.' They took their roles seriously, learning to dip snuff and chew tobacco which they now declare ain't so bad. R. J. Reynolds Tobacco Company will be glad to hear that. Good job guys."

"Pace," said Travis. "I can say the same thing to you and Seth. Good job guys. He won't miss the pictures, but he might miss the year book."

"We know that," Seth replied. "We left the front door unlocked. We'll take it back in the mornin'. I have another problem that maybe you can help us with Silas. The master chain link you gave us worked okay, but it's the wrong size. I brought the one I cut back with me and took it to the hardware store to be sure I was buyin' the right size. My problem now is that it's bright and shiny."

"I kin fix that," Silas said. "We need some full strength clorox bleach."

"I'll be right back," Seth replied.

He soon returned with a water glass of clorox he got from a broom closet at the end of the hall. Silas dropped the shiny new link into the solution and they watched it begin to fade.

"Let it soak fer a couple hours then rinse it off. Then ye soak it in plain water 'til mornin' to put the rust on it," said Silas. "They'll never know the difference."

"Thank's Silas. How'd you learn all these tricks?"

"If'n ye gonna ketch a thief ye gotta think like'im."

"Let's talk about our plan," said Travis. "I wanna see where Tully's place is so we'll meet in the parkin' lot at four o'clock. We'll follow you out. Pace, you pick us up some hot coffee and breakfasts' to go. While we're waitin' for daylight we can eat. After the year book is back where it belongs and the master link is changed out, Silas and I are headin' back.

Seth, Tully will probably stay there while he's in town. He might even have some company. Keep an eye on'im and you can use your own judgement as to how you're gonna do that. Stay until he heads back to Statesville and follow'im. When he gets home and turns out the lights for the night, y'all come on in. Tomorrow afternoon, I'll get into Gordon's office and have a look at his schedule and appointment book. It might be Monday before we talk again."

The next mornin' at daylight, Pace insisted on going back into the Tully cottage alone to return the year book. With great care he made certain the premises looked exactly as they had found it. Clearing the premises without incident, he returned to the rendezvous point.

"I'm glad that's over with," said Travis. "If you characters get into any trouble after I leave, at least it won't be for followin' my orders. I'll give you a call tonight. Let's go Silas."

Travis was contemplative on the return trip. "Silas, he said. Since this investigation started over a year ago, many times I've second guessed my instincts and the conclusions I've drawn that were based strictly on the little evidence we had to go on. I did that because I wanted to keep an open mind. The Grimes brothers were always the only suspects we had. Even with the strength of the circumstantial evidence, I still had serious doubts that they were guilty of the rape-murders. As it turns out, I was right. Now with this new twist, I've got the same doubts about Gordon and Wilson, but I have this gut feelin they're tied into this whole thing as observers in some bizarre sort of way. I'm trying to make sense of it and I'm almost there. It's that feelin' you have when you're on the verge of a big break through that's gonna pull everything together. I know just as sure as we're drivin' along talkin', that early on in the investigation we missed something that would have solved this case and saved some lives. We're about to find that missin' link and that's gonna be the hard part. I'll have to live with that mistake for the rest of my life. When we get to the office, I'm gonna call Seth and tell him and Pace to come on home tonight after they see if Tully shows up with any company. I'll fill'em in on my plans tomorrow mornin'.

"We gotta talk about that, Sheriff," Silas replied. "Pace seen somethin', and he asked me to tell ye 'bout it on the way back to Newton. While he was busy with his kodac, he seen the chief stick a bunch of them pitchers under his shirt. Don't worry none. When Pace gits a chance he's gonna search Seth's suitcase and take'em."

"I'm sorry to hear that," Travis said with a sigh. "I've known Seth was weak as Chief Deputy and I talked about it with Pace. We were always having to do his job for'im, but thought we should give'im more time to get settled in. He's a good deputy; I've just got'im in over his head. If he ever had any confidence in me, he lost it because I wouldn't arrest the Grimes brothers. The fact that I was right about their innocence obviously didn't change his opinion of me.

He might have decided to take matters into his own hands or maybe he took the pictures as a memento he could show off someday. I don't know. I'll get to the bottom of it tomorrow mornin'. And by the way, Silas, a while back when you were expoundin' on the the tree stump stumbling block, I got the message loud and clear."

"If'n ye kin git 'round it, Sheriff, don't fire the Chief. Git'im as fer away from the case as ye kin, but don't fire'im. If'n ye do that, ye won't have'im where ye kin keep a eye on'im. Put'im out in, Startown, workin' busy crimes that solves theirselfs, like traffic tickets and jay-walkin'.

If'n somethin' wuz missed early on that wouldda put ye on the right track and saved some lives, it come from Chief Stephens not doin' his job. When he set his mind on who he figered done it, he quit a lookin'. The last thang I wanna say 'bout this is that Deputy Tanner kin be trusted. He's got ever'thang it takes to be a jump dog detective. 'Fore long he'll be better'n both of us."

"What really has me worried, Silas, is why Seth stole those pictures and what he's planning to do with'em. The way things have gone for'im, maybe he's just resentful?

"Naw sir, he knows he cain't do no better even if he'd knowed how. He likes where he's at 'cause he ain't 'countable fer nothin'. He don't hold no grudge agin' you, me er nobody else, he jist uses us. Whether we right or wrong, he turns it to his favor. When we right, he takes credit fer it, when we wrong, he tells ever'body that if'n we'd a listened to him thangs would a turned out lots better. He's mighty happy bein' like he is and I feel sorry fer him."

"Well I don't," replied Travis. "We'll talk about it when Pace gets back.

I want you and Pace to pick me up at four o'clock Monday mornin'. We're gonna pay a visit to Wilson Tully's home in Statesville and wake'im up. I'm gonna confront'im with the photographs and he's gonna tell us everything we need to know. I can hardly wait."

Silas shook his head. "That's gonna be the hardist thang ye ever done 'cause ye gonna be standin' alone, pitted agin' the 'stablishment. Ketchin'im by surprise when he ain't woke up good yit, he might give ye what ye lookin' fer, but wuntzed he comes to his head, he'll deny ever'thang and take ye on."

The Sugarbush

"He won't be takin' me on, Silas. I'll only be involved indirectly because he's out of my jurisdiction. He'll be takin' on the sheriff of Iredell County who just happens to be his brother-in-law. I'll be glad to let him have all the glory.

Right now there's another thing I'd like your point of view on. Reicie brought up a disturbin' statistic that I wasn't aware of. Since the day Sheriff Coley was killed last May, seven residents of Catfish have died violent deaths. Oddly enough, in the same period of time seven people have died in the rape related murders, none of'em anywhere near Catfish. I understand that it's probably coincidental, yet I wonder why I think there should be some significance to it, but I do."

"They ain't nothin' to it," Silas answered. "People gits murdered or dies ever'day fer one reason another. Sometimes death comes in bunches like it's been a doin' fer the past year and only the Lord knows why. Could be the killer lives in Catfish and ain't struck there 'cause it's too close to home. Stick to ketchin the killer. Other'n that, people dyin' other ways is God's business and ye need to stay outta that."

Joining Silas in laughter, Travis replied. "I've never thought of it that way, but it sounds alright to me. I'll pass it on to Reicie and see if it makes her feel any better. When you get to Claremont, take a detour to Catfish and drop me off at Reicie' house."

XXVI

"Aunt Lila," Reicie shouted from the backyard. "I'm going to take a walk with my dogs down to my swimming hole. We won't be gone long."

"Okay, Dear!" Lila replied. "Didn't you tell me that you and Travis are going horseback riding today?"

"Yes I did. I'll be back before he gets here. I'm not going swimming."

The grass, laden with moisture from the rain quickly soaked her feet. The sweet smell of summer was in the air as she and her dogs moved silently down the path toward the creek. Reicie had not been back here since the day Bobby Hagan was killed. She chuckled at the thought of their encounter there. It had been a great hideaway where Reicie could act out her fantasies uninhibited in the freedom of Mother Nature. That's what she was remembering, but now the fantasies were just happy memories. Things had changed. Like Aunt Lila had said, "things will never be the same again."

"Come!" she said, and her dogs bounded up the path and along the ridge. "Mud! Sand! Go home! Tell Aunt Lila I'm coming."

Reicie laughed as she watched the dogs dash away. Ahead and off to one side of the path, she saw a brilliant colored toad stool.

"That's beautiful!" she said aloud. "How did I miss seeing it before?"

She veered off the path and bent down to look closer at the delicate fungi. Out of the corner of her eye, she detected a slight movement. Without moving her head or looking up, she glanced sideways, saw feet, and dove head first down the steep embankment just in time to avoid being struck by another man moving in behind her. Half way down the slope, screaming for her dogs, she grabbed a sapling and used her momentum to sling-shot herself around and scramble back up the hill, barely escaping the grasps of two men tumbling passed her. Reaching the crest and still screaming for her dogs, she ran. Terrified, she took her eyes off the path for a second to glance back causing her to stumble and fall. Hearing them coming, Reicie crawled off the path into a large hollow log hoping they would run past her. Soon everything got quiet. Reicie breathed a cautious sigh of relief. They were gone. Suddenly, two powerful hands

The Sugarbush

grasped her ankles and yanked her out of the log, dragging her skirt up over her head, blinding her.

At that moment, each of the two men was each hit squarely in the chest by a hundred pound snarling ball of fury, knocking them to the ground. Reicie jumped to her feet, pulling the skirt from over her eyes, she ran toward the house. She had heard the same snarling fury before on bear hunts with her Dad. It was the ominous sound of a life or death struggle.

Lila and Beau were sitting on the back porch and had seen the two dogs break out of the woods only to stop, listen for a second, then run back the way they had come. It was only when they saw Reicie running out of the woods that they realized she was in danger.

"Get the shotgun, Beau, something's wrong!"

Reicie ran into the arms of her Uncle.

"Two men attacked me, Uncle Beau. My dogs are fighting'im. Please help my dogs!"

"I've got Reicie. You go on, Beau!" Lila cried.

Beau heard the sound of the battle, but as he got nearer, all became quiet except for the sound of someone running away through the woods. Catching only glimpses of the two men, he nevertheless fired two shotgun blasts in their direction.

Mud and Sand were dead from stab wounds too numerous to count. Beau rushed back to the house and Reicie ran to meet him.

"My dogs!" she cried. "Where are my dogs?"

Beau took her into his arms. "I'm sorry," he said softly. "They're dead. I'm goin' for the sheriff. I'll bury'em when I get back."

While the attack on Reicie was underway, a typical Catfish comedy was unfolding not too far away. Casey Workman's wife had dropped him off at Cush Hagan's farm for a visit while she made a trip to Huitt's store.

All the Hagan's were gathered by a barbed wire fence looking across the pasture toward Bud and Candace Shuman's house.

"You got here jist in time to see the show!' Cush shouted.

"What show's that?" Casey asked.

"Bud's been on a drunk and he's walkin' down the lane a singin'. Soon as Candace git's a holt of'im he'll be a singin' a different tune. Watch what happens when he goes inside the house. He'll not be in there long 'fore he comes a flyin' out the door with Candace right on his ass."

Cush was right. Bud came tearing out the door with Candace hot on his tail, and right behind her, followed their six year old son, Bud Junior.

Bud jumped the barbed wire fence and ran across the pasture toward the laughing audience of spectators. Candace hiked up her dress, jumped the fence and was gaining on her inebriated husband. Reaching the middle of the pasture and out of breath, Bud climbed to safety in a lone persimmon tree.

"Pop's climbin' the 'simmon tree, Mama!" shouted Bud Junior. "Tho' a rock and knock'im outta there."

"Naw son! We won't rock'im. Go to the house and fetch me that double bitted ax. We'll chop the son-of-a-bitch down."

Candace ignored the pleas of her trapped husband and began to chop down the persimmon tree. As the tree began to fall, Bud tried to jump to the ground and run, but instead, landed off balance and broke his leg.

"Whup'im, Mama, whup'im!" shouted Bud Junior.

Candace calmly cut a branch off the tree and proceeded to do just that.

"Cush!" Lucy said. "You better git out there 'fore she beats him to death. Bud ain't a lyin' 'bout breakin' his leg. I heared it pop when he hit the ground."

"Yeah I guess I better," Cush answered, still laughing. "Casey, ye wanna ride down to Doc Rawlins' office with me? I already got the team hitched up to the wagon. Bud needs to git that leg set 'fore it swells on'im."

"Yeah, Cush! I'll ride along with ye."

Crossing Foggy Bottom Creek bridge where the mailman was killed by his horse, Casey remarked. "Looky up yonder, Cush. Somebody done slid off'n the road into the ditch and got stuck."

"Bud!" Cush yelled. "They's a car slid off'n the road atop the hill. We gonna stop and pull'em outten the ditch. I'll ask'em if'n they kin take ye on to the Doc's. It'll be faster fer ye thatta way."

The men were so intent on getting their car back on the road, they didn't notice the wagon approaching.

The Sugarbush

Comin' to a halt, Cush and Casey climbed down from the wagon to help. "Hey fellers," Cush shouted good naturedly. "If'n you'uns slowed down a tad, ye could stay outta them borrow pits."

The men whirled around wide eyed in fear, their faces, arms and hands lacerated and bleeding.

Walking forward, Casey shouted in concern. "What in hell got a holt a you'uns, a wildcat? You'uns need doctorin' worser'n Bud!"

Without warning the men drew knives and charged.

"Look out Casey they gone crazy," Cush yelled.

In the slippery mud, Casey and Cush managed to knock their assailants to the ground, but not before suffering severe knife wounds.

"Git to the wagon Casey," Cush shouted. "They to much fer us to handle!"

Seeing the men struggling in the slippery mud to regain their feet, Cush jerked the oak handle for the wagon brakes from the iron bracket and knocked them both back to the ground, opening severe wounds to their scalps.

"We cut bad Cush, let's git outta here," Casey yelled, taking up the reins.

Approaching the hill above Foggy Bottom, Silas looked ahead and saw Beau Fontaine with a shot gun in his hands, standing in front of his car and another car off to the side of the road.

"Look yonder, Sheriff," said Silas. I smells trouble!"

"Stop in the middle of the road Silas. If we get out of these ruts we'll get stuck!"

Travis jumped out of the car. "What's wrong Beau!"

"Two men attacked Reicie," he cried. "I was chasin'em. They ran into the woods towards the river."

Stunned, Travis asked "How bad is Reicie hurt!"

"Not that bad, thank God, but they killed her dogs."

"Who are they?"

"We don't know. Reicie didn't see their faces and when I got here they were just goin' into the woods."

"Loan me your shotgun, we only have one," said Travis. "Get my car outta the road. Go to Doc Rawlin's place and call Melinda. Tell her what's happened and asked her to send help. Have'em meet you at the river trussel. They were headed that way. They have to cross

Lyle's Creek and the railroad tracks if they're runnin' down river. Leave some of the men there and bring the rest back here. Thanks Beau.

"Let's go, Silas. We'll talk on the way. There's a few isolated farms scattered up and down the river and I'm worried about that. They may be headed for one of'em.

"Look at these strides and footprints," said Silas. "It's yer killers alright. They runnin' like they's drunk."

The woods were dense with steep hills and gullies thick with undergrowth. As wet as the ground was, it was still going be hard to move quietly.

Travis and Silas followed the trail into the woods and stopped momentarily to allow their eyes to adjust to the shadows. Damp and humid from three days of rain, ground fog hovering over the undergrowth created a foreboding sense of impending doom and obscured their vision for any substantial distance ahead. Scattered storm clouds blowing across the sky in and out of the sun's rays, kept their straining eyes constantly readjusting to changes in brightness.

Silas led the way quickly along the trail which at first cut a wide swath that was easy to follow, then gradually became less obvious.

"Do you think they know we're behind them?" Travis ask.

"Not yit Sheriff."

"Do you think they're headed for the Statesville highway?"

"Maybe, but they cain't make it that fer! Look at yer clothes!"

"Yeah, they're soaking' wet."

"Wipe yer face with yer hands."

"I'm bleedin', Silas. Did I scratch myself?"

"Ain't yer blood, Sheriff. Belongs to them two fellers ahead of us. They bleedin' bad.

"I don't see any blood on your face."

"It's there. Blood don't show near as plain on black leather as it does white."

"If they're bleedin' that bad, whatta you think they'll do next?"

"They'll stop to regain some strength and give the blood a chance to clot."

"The deeper we get in the woods, the darker and foggier it gets."

"The sun never shines in Catfish woods. I doubt if it would wanna come in even if it could."

"Silas, look! There's a steep drop off just ahead."

"I see it, Sheriff; it's leadin' down a gully 'tween two ridges 'bout a hundred foot break to break. See right here at the top where they wuz standin', millin' 'round and a lookin' ever which a way tryin' to decide what to do next. They done made up their minds. Now they's huntin' us!"

"How do you know that, Silas? Maybe they've decided it's every man for himself."

"That did come to mind, but the sign says dif'ernt. Come on down to the bottom and I'll show ye. Pay close 'tention to what ye see and learn it good. Even at that, we both might end up dyin' tryin'! See yonder where they went on down the gully a hundred foot er so and then back tracked so's to trick us into fallin' into their trap. If ye look yonder close, ye kin see where they's split up; one goin' up on the left ridge and the other'n goin' up on the right."

"They're tryin' to get us between'em, Silas."

"And git behind us too, Sheriff!"

"Surely they won't take us on," Travis replied nervously. "They're carryin' knives. We're armed with pistols and doubled barreled shotguns. They don't stand a chance!

"That's what, Horace Sykes, thought jist 'fore he got stomped to death by Jess and Jarred Grimes when they escaped from the courthouse jail last April.

"Thanks for remindin' me. Now I'm scared! Do you think they're scared?

"Like any men they's a skirred to die, but they's hurt to bad to run. They's gotta fight!"

"Silas! The only shells we have are in the shotguns!"

"That's a plenty, Sheriff. If'n we have to shoot and need more'n four shells to brang'em down, these fellers is gonna bleed all over us."

"Maybe they'll give up! It's important for us to take'em in alive if we can."

"They jist might if'n ye git the chance to offer, yit I'm a'feared we in a life er death contest."

"Alright Silas, let's flush'em out. You take the left ridge and I'll take the right!"

"We best stay together, Sheriff. We cain't cover each other if'n we don't. See that little clearin' yonder 'bout fifty foot. When we gits there, we'll stand back to back and wait. When it gits quiet to where they cain't hear us movin'' on, they'll try sneakin' up on us. When they comes, ye challenge'em to give it up and hope they does."

Reaching the clearing and taking their defensive positions, Travis continued talking quietly.

"I don't know why you think they'll come lookin' for us, Silas, and I don't know why we're standin' here! They've always kept runnin' before and they've always gotten away. Why should they change what's worked for'em in the past. I think they know there's only two of us after'em, so by dividing us up, it'll be one on one. Horace was killed because he let his guard down; we won't! If somethin' doesn't happen in the next few minutes, we're goin' after'em one at a time, but we'll stay together."

"Ye might be right, Sheriff, but let's do give it a couple minutes. Them fellers done lost a bucket a blood apiece and that's what's behind my thinkin' they'll stop a runnin' and lay in fer us. I'll be ready to move out anytime you say the word."

Just then, subtle noises, getting louder by the moment, were detected coming from the ridge Silas was facing.

"Somethin's comin' Silas! Move wherever you need to be to get off a clean shot, but don't shoot to kill!"
"Let's stick with the plan, Sheriff, back to back."

The sound of breaking twigs, damp rustling, and clothes scraping on underbrush grew louder.

"Okay Silas, now I've got somethin' comin' too and it's not bein' to sneaky about it. I can see brush movin', nothin' more. I'm gonna give it a try. Alright you men, we know you're there!" Travis bellowed. "This is, Sheriff Gant! Throw down your weapons and come out with your hands up."

The Sugarbush

"They's 'bout on top of us now, Sheriff; a little down hill maybe! Brace yerself fer a charge."

Suddenly, as though on cue, two gruesome figures rose in slow motion out of the thick brush and from Travis' and Silas' position looking up from the bottom of the ravine over shotgun barrels, the illusions were enormous and terrifying. The men stood, wild eyed, unsteady and wavering, their matted hair, skin, and soggy clothes caked with mud and blood still trickling from gastly gaping wounds inflicted by Reicie's dogs and the wooden brake handle wielded by Cush Hagan.

"Drop the knives and raise your hands," Travis shouted, as he and Silas moved backwards up the gully to a safer position. "Who are they Silas?"

Before Silas could answer, the man on the left stumbled forward and came crashing into a heap at the foot of the steep slope. Groaning in pain, he straightened himself enough to lay back against the bank and gasping for air, cried out, "Dooly! I'm cold."

"I'm a comin', Dorsy. Mama's callin' us to supper. We'll git warm first."

Travis lowered his shotgun and watched in disbelief. "The Hensley twins, Silas! It's the Hensely twins!"

Dooly slid down the embankment, crawled on hands and knees across the gully, and cuddled next to his brother. Clutching each other in a last child-like embrace, they went limp.

Silas approached the bodies cautiously. "They both dead, Sheriff. They done bled to death. Them knives they wuz carryin' is 'zactly like the one we took from old man Grimes.

"I'm in a state of shock, Silas. I'm sad, confused, regretful and angry. I'm in shock because the Hensley's are the last people in the world I would have thought we were chasin'.

I'm sad because they would have lived out simple lives in a simple little world, mindin' their own business, if it hadn't been for two bullies, Kirby Suggs and Bernice Boles. They caused it all, and it killed them along with seven others.

Nine horrifying deaths later, here I stand, confused and regretful because the Hensley's were the first to be questioned and were never thereafter considered as suspects.

Jerry S Jones

I'm angry because I know that on day one, a simple clue or something which would have led us to the Hensley's was missed and because of that, five more lives were lost, losses which I feel personally responsible for. I've gotta talk to Seth and Pace. Only ten hours after The Sugarbush murders, they questioned the twins, their parents, neighbors and the mechanic who was workin' on the boys' car. What Seth and Pace found out eliminated them as suspects and I trusted that conclusion."

"Sheriff," said Silas. "Ye gotta be able to trust the people ye got workin' fer ye and it jist might not be the fault of yer men that them boys got passed by. I've worked with the best and they makes mistakes, but they learns from'em and moves on. You'uns wuz bound to make mistakes 'cause you'uns never had no experience a'tall workin' a murder case, much less one right after another'n. No doubt 'bout a lead gittin missed, but ye did lot's more right than wrong. Ye wuz right all along 'bout them Grimes brothers not bein' the rape killers. Ever'thang ye said not only made sense, it come out to be so. Fer the rape-killin's, ye all but drawed us a pitcher of what kinda fellers we wuz lookin' fer and it fit the Hensley boys right down to the shoes they wear, yit ever'time their names come up, we never give'em a second look 'cause ye wuz told fer shore they wuz to home when Suggs and Boles wuz murdered. 'Fore this is over, ye'll know ever'thang that wuz done wrong and ye'll be the wiser fer it. Then ye kin thank God fer the knowledge and pray ye never agin' have 'cause to call on it.

I done seen here yer feelin' sorry fer them twins 'cause they wuz off some in the head, but let me tell ye somethin'; they knowed right from wrong. The Grimes brothers wuz a mite off in the head too, but I ain't heared 'bout nobody feelin' sorry fer them. It's a fact that there rukus out at The Sugarbush set the Hensley's off a rapin' and killin', but ye wrong to think they'd a never done no harm to nobody if'n that ain't happened. Them boys wuz monsters all along, a sittin' on a slow burnin' fuse and bull-whippin' er not, they wuz fixin' to go off any minute. It ain't revenge er satisfyin' grudges they wuz 'bout; not them devils! They wuz after satisfyin' lust fer blood and pure hatred fer women and the worser they could hurt'em, the better they liked it. Sooner'n not, ye'd a had'em to hunt down and kill; better now'n later and there they lay, where they cain't hurt nobody ever

The Sugarbush

agin'. Ye cain't never waste pity on any criminal, 'specially cold blooded killers that's got no respect fer human dignity, and what's more, their victims don't want no pity ner sympathy neither, they wants justice. Now they's got it.

This is a good day and tonight's gonna be better. I won't be hearin' them victim's voices wailin' in a damp, cold darkness, cryin' fer help and beggin' fer mercy they knows they ain't gonna git. It's safe agin'. Thank the Lord, it's over.

I know what ye goin' through, Sheriff, so's ye don't have to say nothin' to nobody 'till ye've had time to think it over."

"I've already thought it through, Silas, and things don't look any better. Bring those knives. Let's go!"

When Travis and Silas reached the road, Beau and the reinforcements were just arriving.

"Travis," Beau shouted as he jumped from his car. "It was the Hensley twins that attacked Reicie. They jumped Cush Hagan and Casey Workman and cut'em up real bad. While Doc Rawlin's was workin' on Cush, Casey sat out in the buggy and bled to death."

"So did the Hensley's, both of'em," Travis replied. "Reicie's dogs killed'em. Here's your shotgun and thanks for your help. I have something I want you to look at, Beau. Have you ever seen any knives like these?"

"Sure have, Travis. They're special made for slaughter houses. Hickory Meat Packing Company used to sell'em. There's still a few of'em around. I've got one myself."

"Thanks, Beau. Another thing; are you sure that Reicie is okay?"

"She's shaken up, Travis, that's all. You go on. I'll tell her what happened."

"Good! Tell her I'll be out tomorrow. Sergeant!" Travis barked. "Take your men and follow our trail into the woods. You'll come to a gully and there you'll find two dead men. Bring'em out and take'em to the morgue. I'll be there in a couple hours. Let's go, Silas."

As they were leaving, Travis said, "Silas, I just found out where the murder weapon came from; Hickory Meat Packing Company. Beau told me and he has one just like it. The murder weapon was such a big mystery. After all is said and done, out here in the middle of nowhere, I ask my sweetheart's uncle if he's ever seen a knife like that, and he's not only seen one, he own's one. They're all over the place. Why couldn't we find that out 'till now?"

Silas burst out laughing. "We give up tryin', Sheriff. We knowed the murder weapon wuz a pertikler kinda knife and thinkin' it wuz one of a kind, we let it git lost in the mystery, figerin' when it finally did turn up, the case would be solved, and it wuz. I'm a laughin' 'cause if'n we'd a knowed from the start them knives wuz all over the place, we'd be winterin' with the geese in Canada 'bout now."

"Or the insane asylum in, Morganton," Travis shouted through his own laughter."

The next stop was the mechanic's garage near the Hensley farm. There, the mechanic told, Travis, that on the Saturday afternoon before The Sugarbush murders, he noticed the Hensley twin's car was miss-firing when they pulled in to have a flat tire fixed. When they got out of the car, he saw they were cut up, bruised and bleedin' and when he asked them what happened, they wouldn't say, but the intensity of the rage smoldering in their eyes made his blood run cold.

Although the car was unreliable because the coil was getting hot and shorting out, it was still usable. Afraid the brothers might get stranded, the mechanic talked them into leaving it at the garage until he could go into, Newton, to pick up a replacement. Because he had other shopping to do, it was after 10:00 that night before he got back home. It was then he noticed that the twin's car had been moved from where it had been parked and the motor was still hot. He asked his wife, who told him that around 5:00, after he left for town, she heard a car start and looked out the window to see the twins driving off. Then about 10:00, she heard a car come in, and thinking it was him returning from town, peered out to see the twins getting out of their car and walking toward home.

When asked if on Sunday morning following the murders, he had been questioned by a deputy sheriff about how long the car had been parked there, the mechanic answered that he was never questioned by anybody.

While Silas looked on as a silent observer, Travis took statements from the excited couple, then drove on to the Hensley's farm to personally give the parents the bad news.

Driving away from the Hensley's farm toward town, Travis began talking. "Silas, from what I've learned in the last several hours, I've pretty well come to terms with the realities of this whole investigation from start to finish. Progress, growth or whatever you want to call it, means learning from the mistakes that were made and I've done that. The one, huge, case breaking omission wasn't a mistake, it was an intentional act. Seth thought questioning the mechanic was a waste of time because in his minds eye, he already knew who murdered Suggs and Boles.

In our defense, being unaware that a crucial lead was missed from the very beginning, I can say this was a very complicated murder investigation that would have tested the metal of even the most seasoned homicide detectives.

We started out with what we thought was an isolated case of double murder committed by two suspects seeking revenge at a notorious back woods roadhouse where that kind of violence, in that type of an environment, does not really come as a surprise. Open, shut case? That's what almost everybody thought and for what it's worth, I'm not sure that the events of today are going to change that opinion very much.

Then, a bedlam of unimaginable savagery, a raft of misleading circumstantial evidence made even more convincing by coincidence and timing, began evolving in such rapid succession that combined, it took precedence over my common sense and gut instincts. All along I had that gnawing feeling that something wasn't right. We talked about it on the way back from Winston Salem today. Things got so crazy after the Grimes' brothers escaped from jail, I lost what focus I had left. It took the murder of, Violet Bell, and the footprints that matched those found at the Carol Lamar crime scene to bring me back to my senses and recognize what the evidence was telling me all along: That we had two pairs of killers at work, with altogether different motives for committing murder.

We were finally on the right track following a hot lead that took us from the fringes of society to the realm of the elite and that was scary. I can't tell you how glad I am that it turned out to be another wild goose chase.

In all of this, I made some mistakes, but they're defensible.

When I promoted Seth to Chief Deputy, we were in a crisis management situation. I did so knowing he was not the best choice, but I had to act quickly and thought he was entitled to the opportunity and could learn. In his case, I'm only guilty of being proven wrong. Having tolerated his narrow mind and obstinance on several occassions, I should have monitored his work more closely, but I didn't because he and Pace were working together and I had confidence in them as a team. It wasn't Pace' job to be checking up on Seth and it probably never occurred to him to do so.

Knowing what I know now, it all makes sense. When Jess and Jarred were arrested and locked up, the attacks stopped cold. The timing was coincidently perfect. The killer's hunting season was over. The weather turned cold and wet and with the harvest in, the women's work habits changed keepin'em busy inside the house, thereby limiting the availability of vunerable targets. Also, the killer's cover was gone. They preferred rural wooded areas that provided concealment where they could lay in wait to ambush their victims, an advantage that was lost when the trees and bushes shed their follage. Remember too, the Hensley twins prowling the roads looking for work from early spring until late autumn was such a common sight, they went virtually unnoticed. Not so in the winter. They would have been noticed and folks would have been wondering what they were up to.

The coincidence didn't stop there. When Jess and Jarred broke out of jail, the Hensleys' hunting season had just begun anew. And you're right, Silas. It wasn't all coincidence. They were clever, calculating, and knew exactly what they were doing. They must have known their mental handicap was an advantage in disquising their sadistic nature the same as Gordon Jackson and Wilson Tully knew their intelligence and wealth was an advantage in disquising their's. My knowledge of mental retardation or family taints resulting from incestuous relationships is limited, but this case proves that there are instances where, regardless of the mental illness, some areas of the brain can be normal or even especially bright. We never would have even imagined that the twins were capable of such careful, thoughtful planning or such clever use of their wits.

I'm proud of the exceptionally good detective work we did that solved the Simms-DeHart murders before the bodies were cold and

The Sugarbush

that wouldn't have happened without your help, Silas. Now that this is over, I'd like you to stay on. I'm not asking you to do this because you saved my life down at the depot shootout, I'm doing it because you're needed here."

"I thank ye and accept the offer, Sheriff," Silas replied. "This kinda work is my life and I thought I'd lost it fer ever. I come to yer office that day never thinkin' you'd hire me. Ye see, Sheriff, ye saved my life too. Now we kin leave it at that."

"That's a good deal, Silas," Travis said with a laugh. "When you get to the office, park in the back. After I'm done with the press conference, come up to my office and help me finish the paperwork. I want to be sure no details are left out. Then we can call it a day."

"If it's alright with ye, Sheriff, I'd like to stay on at the office 'till Pace and Seth gits in from, Winston Salem. Pace asked me to wait up fer'im. I won't be talkin' to'im 'bout nothin' that ain't none a my bizness."

"That's fine. I have to deal with Seth first thing in the morning. I'll see you and Pace at 11:00."

Past midnight, Travis was awakened by a knock on the door. It was Pace and Silas.

"The Hensley's! I can't believe it, Travis. How did they do it? Their car was broken down! What did they use for transportation? Did they borrow a car? I know you know and Silas isn't talking."

"One thing at a time, Pace. First, tell me what you've got."

"If you're not awake now, you soon will be," said Pace. "I found the pictures in Seth's briefcase. I picked the lock to get to'em. He doesn't even know they're gone, and that's not all I found. Look at this! The missing dagger!

"The picture of the daggers hanging on the wall of the torture chamber, one's missing. Is that it?" Travis asked.

"That's it, Boss."

"Leave the pictures and the daggar with me," said Travis. "You tell me why the Hensley's alibi wasn't checked out, then I'll answer your questions."

"It was." Pace answered. "Seth told you about it. I heard him!"

"He didn't question the mechanic about how long their car had been parked at his garage."

"Sure he did, Travis. It's all in his report. I read it."

"I know what's in the report, but it's all a lie. Seth never questioned the man. Tell me what happened."

"Okay. When we went to question them early Sunday morning, Seth dropped me off at the store just across the road from their farm and asked me to see what I could find out while he talked to the twins and their parents. The owner and his wife told me they saw the twins walking up the lane to their home at around 2:30 Saturday afternoon and that if they left again, they never saw them leave. I asked them if they knew why the twins were walking and they said they didn't know. It wasn't long before Seth picked me up. We compared statements and they checked out. I asked Seth why the twins were afoot and he said their car was being repaired at a mechanic's garage down the road and had been there since 2:00 Saturday afternoon. He said that he had talked to the mechanic and that the alibi checked out. It never crossed my mind to doubt his word."

"It never crossed my mind either," Travis replied.

"No wonder you weren't talking, Silas," Pace replied. "All the lives that could have been saved. If this gets out, Seth just might get lynched.

There's something else. When we got to the office and heard about what happened with the Hensley's, Seth turned pale as a ghost and now I know why. He knows that you're on to him. He started ranting that we had it all wrong. He said that Reicie mistook the Hensley's awkward way of being friendly in a threatening way and turned her dogs loose on'em. Then, when Cush and Casey stopped to help'em, the boys thought they were being assaulted again and put up a fight. He's crazy, Travis. First it was the Grimes brothers, now it's Gordon Jackson and Wilson Tully and he says he can prove it. I thought you should know what he's thinking."

"And you're right," said Travis. "Thanks men. I'll see you later this morning. Go on home and get some sleep."

Travis was up early. Just before leaving for the the office to meet with Seth, he received a telephone call from, Bret Steelman, the Iredell County sheriff. After a long conversation, he hung up the

The Sugarbush

phone, breathed a deep sigh of relief, and left, driving east toward, Statesville.

When he reached the county line at the bridge over the Catawba River, Sheriff Steelman, was already there waiting for him. They shook hands and Travis handed him an envelope containing the pictures and the dagger Seth had conviscated from Wilson Tully's hide-away in Winston Salem. After a few words and a farewell handshake, they departed company.

Back at the office, Seth had come in early, cleaned out his desk and left a handwritten letter of resignation. Travis was pleased. So far, the scheme seemed to be working.

Pace and Silas walked into Travis' office just as he was hanging up the phone. "Here's a package for you, Sheriff, said Pace. "The desk sergeant says he doesn't know who left it, but it wasn't there when he came to work this morning."

"Lay it on the table," Travis replied. "Right now we need to talk. Seth is no longer with us; he resigned."

"Resigned," Pace mumbled. "You didn't fire'im."

"No! I didn't have to, and it's better this way. This morning I got an unexpected call from Sheriff Bret Steelman, in Iredell County. He told me he had received a disturbing call from my Chief Deputy, Seth Stephens, which he would like to discuss with me. Seth told him about the pictures of Jackson and Tulley in action, the dagger, the house in Winston Salem, everything, and offered to turn all of the evidence over to Sheriff Steelman if he would give him a job so that they could work together to break the big case. He put Seth off long enough to call me. I told him that, as far as Catawba County was concerned, the case was closed and that Wilson Tulley's sexual orientation was no longer any of our business. I advised him that every shred of evidence that Seth thought he had locked in his briefcase was now in my possession and would soon be in his if he would like to assume the responsibility of derailing Seth's madness. He was only to eagar to oblige. He called Seth back, suggesting that he avoid any contact with me, clean out his desk and leave a letter of resignation on my desk, after which he was to bring his evidence and meet Sheriff Steelman at a roadside park near Statesville. It was a good plan. They did meet and Seth apparently made a complete fool of himself. Sheriff Steelman says he has the situation under control and that's all I want to know. Now I'm in need of a Chief Deputy, Pace. The job's yours if you want it."

"I want it," said Pace. "Thanks Travis."

"You're welcome," he replied. "The pleasure's mine because I know I'm making the right choice this time. Hand me that package; let's see what's in it."

Tearing away the wrapping, Travis pulled out Sheriff Burton Coley's jacket containing the original copies of sixteen warrants with a note attached. "Look at this," he whispered. "Burton's jacket that he was going after the day he was killed out in Catfish! I've never seen these warrants before. The note says all these people are dead."

"If I was superstitious," said Pace, "I'd say this whole nightmare started with Burton' losing his jacket!"

"If I was superstitious," Travis replied, I'd say this whole nightmare ended with us finding Burton's jacket."

ABOUT THE AUTHOR

The author, Jerry S Jones, was born in Hickory, North Carolina. His wife of over thirty three years, and all her relatives from both sides of the family, were originally from the Catfish community. Through the years the author took notes and listened intently to relatives from both sides of his wife's family tell stories of their adventures and experiences growing up. These stories were all spellbinding and covered the whole range of human emotions, however, the stories that fascinated and amazed the author most, were those recalling bitter grudges, revenge, vendettas, anger, and rage out of control.

Many of the tales revealed a spirit of accommodation, helpfulness and generosity towards neighbors and those in need. Yet for the slightest provocation, real or imagined, the retribution extracted by the injured party was savage and barbaric.

More disturbing and frightful than anything else, was the conviction that their violent behavior was completely normal, rational and justified.

These true stories have been combined in fiction form to make up *The Sugarbush*.

The author's wife (deceased) and their four children to whom *The Sugarbush* is dedicated, are closely related to five of the characters who died violent deaths during that time.

The author invites the readers to visit his website at www.thesugarbush.net and welcomes questions which will be answered promptly.

CPSIA information can be obtained at www.ICGtesting.com
Printed in the USA
LVOW13s2023171213

365625LV00001B/54/A

9 781403 355218